WIZARDROUS
A RIGHT PROPER JOURNEY!

J. A. HINSVARK

Cover artwork by Mousam Banerjee (www.illus-station.com)

ISBN: 978-1-7349218-1-6

For Shaun, who never stopped encouraging me to write.

He is the real hero of this story.

Table of Contents

Chapter One
Scrying Eyes

The Wizard was an unusual man, a very lazy and unhappy man, and about as far as possible from what one might expect upon hearing his name. "Wise" was the last word that would come to mind. Scratching by as one of the least prolific researchers for the Circle of Mages, he would whittle most of his days away at local pubs. Very few called him a friend, and even fewer knew his real name.

He lived in the city of Theiyre, the capital of the kingdom of Koric. A poor man, the best he could afford was a secondhand tower deep in the city's slums. Over the years, his antisocial attitude and dangerous, magical experiments had earned The Wizard a nasty reputation with his neighbors. For every explosion, there were at least a dozen prayers that he finally blew himself to bits.

A tall and thin man, The Wizard had an unnaturally youthful appearance for someone at the age of forty-seven. His wavy, fiery orange hair grew halfway down his back, and he had a beard that could practically dwarf that of a dwarf. Contrasting wildly, he had eyes of vibrant magenta, like spring orchids.

At the moment, he was wearing nothing but a pair of boxer shorts and a white tank top. Lying on the tattered, old couch that he called his bed, he was nursing a rather severe hangover he had acquired after the previous night's festivities. Holding a large bong in the shape of a green dragon, he would

Chapter One

occasionally put his lips to the dragon's mouth, lighting its rear end and taking a puff.

The Wizard's quarters were dank and musty, and smelled more or less like his tent had at *Wandstock*. The room was relatively empty, aside from his sleeping couch, an end table with a shadeless lamp, a mostly empty bookshelf, and innumerable empty liquor bottles.

In the corner, there was a cobwebby old fireplace, on the mantle of which sat a row of various liquors. On the very end, there was a single, dusty photograph of The Wizard standing with an older man with a well-kempt grayish-red beard; this was Ziro Xuntasi, previous Archmage of Koric and The Wizard's father. He had gone missing over a decade ago, and no one ever found out what happened to the body.

If you are wondering why The Wizard does not have his father's surname, or seemingly any surname at all, let me just say that it is complicated.

Suddenly, his relative relaxation was shattered by an earsplitting shout.

"Hey asshole, get up!"

Groaning, The Wizard sat up and tried to rub the pain out of his eyes. Looking up, he saw the familiar glare of his apprentice, Samantha. She was a petite young woman, with short brunette hair tied in a ponytail; her eyes were as clear blue as an arctic spring, although they currently burned with the fire of a woman scorned.

She was standing over him, with a packed suitcase in one hand and a bundle of electronics in the other.

"Care to explain why I just found this camera in my chambers with a direct line to your crystal ball?" Samantha chucked the bundle of electronics at The Wizard. It struck him on the forehead before he could answer. "I almost quit before, when you blew up the bathroom! And after that, when I found out you were practicing voodoo on me in my sleep! But this is it, I can't put up with your bullshit anymore!"

"Woah, woah, woah," said The Wizard, "stop dropping those truth bombs, or you're gonna blow my mind!" Taking a massive toke off his bong, he held it out to her. "Want some?"

"You are fucking unbelievable!" Samantha threw her arms up in exasperation. "When I took this job, I thought all the rumors about you were exaggerated; if anything, they are an understatement! I've only stuck around

2

this long because your dad used to be the Archmage; I thought that maybe, under your seemingly infinite layers of shit, you had some actual potential to be a great wizard. Apparently, I was wrong about a lot, because you're a fucking loser."

"So I take it this means you *can't* watch my cat this weekend?"

Gaping incredulously, Samantha scoffed. "No, it means I don't want to, and I never did. Fuck your cat, it's the only creature I know that might actually be more infuriating than you."

"What do you mean?" The Wizard grinned sheepishly. "Kit Mingers is a good kitty!"

"Are you serious?" Pursing her lips, Samantha gestured to a large tuxedo cat on a heap of laundry in the corner. "Look! He's having sex with your robes right now! I've had to kick him out of my office almost every day because of that shit. Why won't you get him neutered?"

"I did, but I'm pretty sure they grew back."

"Oh, whatever." Rolling her eyes, Samantha turned her nose up in a huff. "I just don't care anymore. I'm out of here."

Grabbing her suitcase, Samantha started to leave. Turning around at the door, she smiled contemptuously. "By the way, the Circle is sending an inspector to grade your lab tomorrow at ten. Good luck getting that shithole up to code without my help!"

She laughed loudly as she walked out, slamming the door behind her.

"Well, shit…" muttered The Wizard, "looks like we've got some work to do, right, Kit Mingers?" He glanced at his cat, who was making direct, piercing eye contact with him while continuing to hump his robes.

Kit Mingers let out a booming, baritone meow that reverberated throughout the room. A glass of water shook on The Wizard's end table, and a book fell off the shelf.

"We've *really* got to do something about that curse of yours…"

The following morning, light rain spattered the dilapidated wooden tower that The Wizard called home. The address was five-nine-three Wheeler Street. With two lofty stories, the tower loomed over the nearby houses. It had almost no paint left on its siding, although there was evidence in small patches that it was once dark blue, with yellow trim. Several of its windows were broken, and several more boarded up, and there was a charred hole blown out of the middle. Essentially, it was one stabbing short of condemned.

Normally, the view inside the windows was even worse. This particular morning, however, it had been empty since the crack of dawn. In fact, upon seeing the absence of moldy furniture and clutter through the windows, a few of his neighbors assumed that he was either moving out or dead; in either case, they were already planning a celebration at the nearest pub.

Imagine their disappointment when they eventually discovered the truth.

In the foyer of his tower, The Wizard was speaking to a scowling, silver-haired man in a crisp, pinstriped suit. This man introduced himself as Inspector Perkins; he was, as he had described himself, "the man unfortunate enough to draw the short straw in the deliberation of this assignment."

The Wizard's foyer was in the shape of a semicircle, with a wall running directly down the middle of the tower. Although it was presently devoid of furniture, the room was by no means clean. Dust coated the floor, and marks could be seen where furniture had been. The only thing in the room, aside from the two men, was a wooden spiral staircase; the creaky, old steps ascended to a landing about twenty feet above.

A doorway in the wall opposite the front led to a dingy and equally empty kitchen. Behind the staircase, another door hung open, leading to a cramped cleaning closet. It appeared to have been doubling as an office, and the back wall had tally marks carved into it; whomever's office it was, it was as though they had been counting the days until freedom.

A small balcony protruded from the landing, from which hung a magnificent, crystal globe chandelier: one of the few of his father's valuables The Wizard had not yet pawned off for drugs. Hanging from the ceiling above the landing, there was an identical chandelier, as well as an empty space where another had been. Beautiful as the chandeliers were, their bulbs had burned out ages ago.

As The Wizard was finishing his explanation as to why none of his lab equipment was present for the inspection, Inspector Perkins' expression seemed far from satisfied.

"So…" said Perkins, tapping his foot impatiently, "you're telling me that you *forgot* about this inspection when you scheduled these 'renovations'?"

"Yeah, things just piled up…" Tugging his collar nervously, The Wizard averted his eyes. "It was supposed to be done three days ago, but the painters rescheduled… I've gotta wait 'til they're done to get my stuff… everything's in storage…." He trailed off, scratching his head nervously.

Conjuring a clipboard, Perkins quickly jotted down some notes. "Right… and I suppose you thought this all to be more important than the inspection that was appointed *six weeks ago*."

"Was it that long ago?" asked The Wizard, feigning surprise. "I guess I've just been too immersed in my research lately to keep track of my schedule."

"Interesting…" His scowl intensifying, Perkins quickly scribbled a few more notes. "Very interesting… considering you just told me your equipment has been in storage for the last two weeks."

"Well…" Pausing for a moment, The Wizard wracked his brain for a cover story. "That's because I've been working out of the storage unit lately. In fact, I had my assistant send a memo to humanoid resources last Monday, moving the inspection out there; so, if you never got that, it's really more her fault than mine."

"It seems wasted on you to explain everything that's wrong with that excuse." Crossing his arms, Inspector Perkins sneered with cold spite. "You're on thin ice, Wizard. Your assistant requested a transfer this morning, and considering her reports and your history, the Circle has decided that we will not be assigning you a replacement. Any more screw-ups and you won't be receiving any further grants towards your… *research*. Do I make myself clear?"

"Crystal…" muttered The Wizard, thinly veiling his contempt. "So, is that all?"

"For now." Jotting a few more notes on his clipboard, Perkins walked to the front door. Turning around, he glared at The Wizard. "You know, if I had my way, you would be out of a job already! Get your shit together, your daddy isn't the Archmage anymore. You'll soon receive a letter with the date of the makeup inspection; don't miss it, or it will be your last." He left before The Wizard could reply, slamming the door behind him.

What I wouldn't give for this to be my last inspection, thought The Wizard. He peered out his front window, until he was sure the Inspector was

5

out of sight. Once he knew he was in the clear, he turned around and snapped his fingers.

Instantly, the furniture around his foyer reappeared, although there was not much of it. A long table sat to the right of the door, covered in arbitrary scraps of paper and the occasional liquor bottle. In the corner to the left of the kitchen door, there was a dusty grand piano, missing five or six keys. A row of dead, shriveled cannabis plants sat under a busted grow light in the opposite corner.

In the center of the room, there was a Mersian rug weaved of coral silk and sargassum velvet. Although that sounds like it could be fancy in a fantasy setting, let me emphasize that it is not; it is crusty, brittle, and smells just as bad as one would think. The floor was littered wall to wall with scraps of paper, liquor bottles, and petrified food scraps, with a path cleared from the door to the staircase.

Heaving a sigh of relief, The Wizard slumped against the front door. "I can't believe that worked... I wasn't sure if one night was enough to master the vacancy charm!"

Even if he had time to prepare for the next inspection, he was still daunted by the thought of cleaning his lab. He ascended the spiral staircase, and then haphazardly climbed up the spiral ladder that led to his lab. As he climbed the absurd spiral ladder, he thought to himself, as he had many times before, that it was a terrible idea to snort fairy dust with the architect during the design of his tower.

When The Wizard finally reached his lab, his heart sank. Every surface was coated in a variety of strange, colorful substances, which were in turn coated in dust; each table was littered with vials, dials, files, and an absurd amount of spiderwebs; and the floor had broken glass scattered all over it. In the corner, there was a cage full of rabid, emaciated lab squirrels. The only thing in the room that was clean was the filing cabinet that held his father's research notes, although only by virtue of the enchantments it held.

Sighing in despair, The Wizard dreaded the thought of cleaning this mess. He rifled through a nearby pile of parchment until he found a relatively blank piece. Grabbing a quill from the table, he scribbled a simple flier reading *"Help Wanted - Wizarding Assistant - Requires Two Arms, Two Legs, Two Eyes, Magic - Pays Minimum Wage"*. He neglected to include any contact information. After he finished writing, he waved his hand above the flier and duplicated an entire stack.

Now that The Wizard had some time to think, the urgency of his situation began to sink in. He felt like he needed a drink, so he grabbed the stack of fliers and started back down the spiral ladder. The last thing he saw was the floor rushing towards him.

Late that afternoon, The Wizard awoke with a splitting headache. He was lying in a pile of papers on his second floor landing. It took him a moment to remember what happened; however, when he looked up at the spiral ladder, he quickly recalled that he had once again fallen from it. As he stood up, he figuratively cursed the architect of his tower.

As he walked out of his front door, he was met with a blaze of fiery colors, as the gold and pink of the sunset met the blazing orange of the autumn trees. Atop a hill in the center of town, the white marble tower of the Circle of Mages was awash in a sea of trees, gleaming with vibrant hues.

It was a traditional celebration of the autumn equinox in Theiyre to enchant the leaves to become magical fire, dancing off the trees as the autumn progressed. The city glowed with an intensity that could be seen across the land. Even the slums in which he lived were adorned with wonderful enchantments.

Without giving a second glance to this vibrant vista, The Wizard quickly made his way down the block. He headed straight into his favorite bar: a quaint little dive known as *The Wizarding Hole*, which was named for its best customer. A sign rested to the right of the door, reading "This establishment is both gluten-free and vegan-free".

Quite a few more people than usual were in the bar that day: there were four, in fact, and they seemed to be celebrating something. Hanging above the bar, there was a hastily-made banner bearing the words "he's gone"; however, when The Wizard walked through the door, the celebration quickly died down. The next few moments were tense for the revelers, as they came to terms with the disappointing reality. As The Wizard walked up to the bar, he was too entrenched in his own issues to notice the situation at hand.

"Hey, what's the lack of commotion about?" The bartender had just emerged from a room behind the bar, carrying a bottle of champagne. He

Chapter One

was a tall, thin man, with ragged blonde hair and light stubble. Normally, he had cool eyes and a sly smile; at the moment, however, he looked depressed. "I thought y'all were celebrating." Suddenly, his eyes fell on The Wizard, and his face lit up. "Well, butter my ass and call me a biscuit! My best customer isn't going anywhere!"

"Hey, Chris," said The Wizard, leaning against the bar, "how's it going?"

"Pretty good now, bro!" Chris grinned ecstatically. He had a gruff, slow voice and a rural accent. "I was worried I'd be losing your business, and that'd be more than half my revenue. It ain't always this busy... for some reason no one else is a regular here...."

At this point, the neighbors were clearing out, grumbling discontentedly as they tore down their slightly ironic banner.

The Wizard cocked his head curiously. "Why would you lose my business? The next closest bar is like four blocks away, I don't want to walk that far five or six times a day!"

Chris shrugged. "Well, all these people said they heard you died or something, and I thought you were gone..."

"Huh, weird..." After pausing to think for a moment, The Wizard's eyes narrowed thoughtfully. "Oh, I think I see what's happening here." He started laughing. "They got me mixed up with that guy from across the street, who got hit with shrapnel from my bathroom explosion last month. He's *definitely* dead!"

"I don't know, they seemed pretty happy that it was you."

"Well, whatever, those idiots make a big deal about it no matter who dies. Can I post this on the quest board?" The Wizard held up one of his fliers.

"Sure, that's fine," said Chris. "It's pretty full now though.... These two dwarves have been marauding the countryside, butchering elves, so there's a bounty on the dwarves, and a whole bunch of bounties on elves. It's a mess..."

Approaching the quest board in the corner, The Wizard posted his flier in the middle, directly over the only bounty on the aforementioned dwarves. He did a double take when he noticed an advertisement for penis enlargement potions; checking to make sure no one was looking, he grabbed the ad and slipped it into the pocket of his robes. Walking back to the bar, he took a seat in the least rickety stool.

Scrying Eyes

"Can I get a neat glass of absinthe?"

Chris nodded. "Sure, I'll see what I've got."

As Chris walked behind the tattered curtain to the back room, The Wizard drew his wand and flicked it at the crystal ball hanging from the wall. A young, attractive elven woman appeared within the orb, wearing a dark grey pants suit and sitting behind a tidy desk.

"In political news," began the woman.

The Wizard changed the channel. A man appeared in the crystal, sitting in an overstuffed leather armchair. He was slightly chubby, wearing a silver suit, with neat blonde hair and a magnificently curled handlebar mustache. He was sipping a glass of iced tea and smiling amicably. Behind him, two walls met in an obtuse corner.

"Welcome back to *The Triangle Room*," said the man, "where there are no fourth walls! I'm your host, Chestierre MacRoyalle. Tonight, we will be interviewing fashion designer Shesamanda Hasapeen, who will be telling us about a hot new fashion trend; I'll give you a hint: it's where waterbeds meet parachute pants!"

The camera panned outward to show a woman, sitting in another leather armchair. She was wearing a pair of extremely baggy, jiggly canvas pants, and had pink hair spiked up in a faux-hawk. It appeared that she had light blonde stubble on her chin.

"Thank you, Chestierre," said Shesamanda, patting the host on the forearm. "You know, I've gotta say: it's good to be on a talk show for once where I'm actually invited on stage."

"Yes, quite!" As the camera panned back to his face, Chestierre boomed with jovial laughter. "And after we interview Ms. Hasapeen, we'll meet with the toast of the Koricean stage, Andre LeBron Webster. We will be discussing his hit play, *The Phantom of the Natural History Museum*, as well as his upcoming vow of silence. Stay tuned, and I'll talk to you after the break!"

An announcer's voice spoke as the camera panned outward and the show's theme began to play on accordion. "*The Triangle Room* is filmed in front of a live studio."

The camera cut to an empty set of bleachers, with a pair of massive googly eyes duct taped to the front. A short loop of pre-recorded applause

9

played repeatedly. It then cut to a commercial for some sort of pointless novelty by the name of *Bottle in a Can*.

A moment later, Chris emerged from the back room, holding a translucent, bright green drink. He slid it down the bar. "Here you are, my friend!"

Taking the drink, The Wizard took a sip. Immediately, a sickly sweet taste met his tongue, and he spat the drink all over the bar. "What the hell kind of absinthe is this?"

"Well, I was out of absinthe," said Chris, shrugging, "so I just mixed vodka and antifreeze. I figured it'd be about the same."

The Wizard shook his head in disbelief. "Okay, first of all, it absolutely is *not* the same; and secondly, what the fuck?!"

"Sorry, bro… You want me to try again?"

"Forget it…" said The Wizard, heaving a weary sigh. He was used to Chris's mediocre mixology, but this was a new low. "Just bring me a cider."

Pouring a mug of cider, Chris passed it to The Wizard. Grinning, he pointed his thumb at the crystal ball behind him. *The Triangle Room* was back on. "You know, that Shesamanda Hasapeen lady is quite the hot meal!"

"She's a man... duh…. She definitely has a penis."

Smiling coyly, Chris shrugged. "Well, what can I say? There's more meat on the menu when you order every dish!"

"Fair enough," said The Wizard. He was more than familiar with Chris's pansexual proclivities. "There ain't nothing wrong with having a good time." His eyes suddenly narrowed. "As long as I don't ever catch you masturbating in my closet again…"

"Don't worry, that was just a five time thing." Leaning forward onto the bar, Chris squinted knowingly at The Wizard. "So... I heard Samantha finally quit on you."

"What? Where'd you hear that?"

"She came here last night. She said some shit about finding some hidden cameras, and that she was leaving town to find a '*real* wizard' to study under."

"I am a real wizard!" The Wizard's face scrunched in anger. It really irked him that Samantha was spreading such accurate rumors about him. "And those cameras were part of a sociological experiment, by the way!"

"Yeah," said Chris, his eyes twinkling cheerfully, "she told me about the experiments too."

"Damn it... just get me another cider..." muttered The Wizard. He was eager to change the subject. "So, what have you got going on tonight?"

"I'm gonna go to the casino!" Pounding his fist on the bar, Chris beamed with enthusiasm. "I've made a lot of deposits lately, and it's time to make a *biiig* withdrawal!"

"Right..." The Wizard rolled his eyes. "I hope that goes well for you this time."

After The Wizard finished his cider, he had four or seven more. Who remembers? Bidding Chris farewell, he left to put up his fliers. Walking down the street, he magically affixed them to trees and light poles. He spent several hours wandering around town and putting up fliers, and only stopped at two other bars; he was proud of himself when he passed out that night on what he believed to be his couch.

Chapter Two
The Wizard and the Wise Guy

nock, Knock, Knock. Several days later, a man knocked on the front door of The Wizard's tower in the early afternoon. The man wore a pair of denim jeans and a houndstooth jacket. He had brown eyes and short black hair with streaks of gray. He waited at the door for a few minutes, but no one answered. Shrugging, he decided to try the door; it was unlocked, but the foyer was deserted. He apprehensively started up the rickety spiral staircase.

Most would consider the course of action this man was taking to be folly, and would likely advise him against any association with The Wizard; however, this man was bound to The Wizard by a force that overwhelmed his desire to avoid such scorn: familial obligation.

You see, this was The Wizard's younger brother, Justin Greene. This was not something that would be obvious to the uninformed observer; they only shared a mother, and each looked more like their father. In recent years, Justin had grown to appear older than his brother, as The Wizard and his paternal ancestors possessed an unnatural longevity.

As he ascended the spiral staircase, Justin heard a voice rambling on upstairs. When he reached the landing, he could hear The Wizard ranting about his work from behind the door of his quarters. The door was open just a crack, and he could see the flicker of candlelight coming from the room. When he opened the door, the scene revealed was most disconcerting.

The Wizard and the Wise Guy

The Wizard sat behind a desk, scrawling madly on a pad of paper, and wearing nothing but his underwear. Various spellbooks and candles littered the desk, as well as the floor around it. As Justin approached, The Wizard did not look up from his papers or even seem to notice. He simply continued to rave feverishly as he wrote.

"Hey, buddy..." said Justin, stepping tentatively towards his brother, "you okay?"

"I'm working, man," said The Wizard, waving his hand impatiently. "I think I'm on to a new spell!"

"Wow!" Justin seemed genuinely surprised by this. "I haven't seen you invent a new spell in forever!"

Without warning, The Wizard looked up at Justin and made piercing eye contact. His pupils were dilated to the edge. "That's because I haven't done cocaine in forever."

This was a lie; he did cocaine almost every day.

"Well..." Looking around the room, Justin nodded slowly. "That explains a lot..."

"So," said The Wizard, tapping his fingers on the desk, "what brings you here?"

"I found a bunch of these posted outside the high school by my house." Justin held up one of The Wizard's fliers. "They said someone was hiring a wizarding assistant, but didn't provide any name or contact info, so I just assumed they were yours."

The Wizard squinted at the flier. "Yeah, those are mine... I need an assistant to help me prepare for my inspection on Monday afternoon."

"Do you mean the day after tomorrow, or the next Monday?"

"Today's Saturday?!" The Wizard was very shocked to hear this. "That means I've been awake for three days straight and still haven't had any applicants for the job!"

"Hold on," said Justin, furrowing his brow, "which part of that are you concerned about?

"It doesn't matter!" In a panic, The Wizard slammed his fist on the desk. "I'm in big trouble here!"

"From what?" asked Justin, flopping down on The Wizard's couch. "Is the Circle going to test your piss?"

13

Chapter Two

"Don't be silly, motherfucker; I seriously need someone to help me with this shit!"

"Well, what exactly does this job entail?"

"I'd prefer an assistant skilled in magic, but at this point, I'd be fine with anyone," said The Wizard. "I just need someone for whom busywork does not occupy just enough of their brain to suppress the part that holds back their self loathing, throwing them into a state of existential crisis, —"

As Justin opened his mouth to speak, The Wizard simply plowed forward.

"— causing them to question whether their very existence is worthwhile or futile, invariably making them feel invalidated as a sentient being, and thus completely demotivating them and rendering them psychologically incapable of finishing said busywork."

"Right…" said Justin. He looked very concerned about his brother's well-being. "I think I can help you. Have you considered hiring Jeff?"

"Your stoner son?!" Laughing hysterically, The Wizard leaned back in his chair. "He's a fucking idiot with no magical talent at all."

Frowning, Justin scoffed. "First of all, you're a bigger stoner than he is. Besides, you don't seem to have a better option, and he'll probably be willing to start work tonight if I threaten to throw him out of the house again."

"You sure you want him in this line of work? You always seemed to go out of the way to avoid it."

"Yeah, but Jeff looks up to you," said Justin. "Besides, he really needs something to do; all he's done since high school is play video games on his crystal ball, watch *Dick and Shorty*, and jack off all the time!"

Scrunching his face, The Wizard chuckled. "That's quite a resume! Sounds a lot like my friend Keith." His eyes narrowed as he tried to determine which course of action would screw him over the least. "Alright, fine… send the boy over tomorrow. We'll see how long he lasts in this job."

"That's the spirit! I remember it was me saying that about your last assistant."

The Wizard raised his index finger. "I think that was the one before, actually. I don't think you met Samantha. Anyway, I need to finish this research real quick." He leaned forward and did a line of cocaine off his desk.

14

The Wizard and the Wise Guy

"Okay, that's all I need to hear!" Justin quickly got to his feet. "I'm out of here. I'll send Jeff over in a few hours, after you've had time to put on some pants."

He headed for the door.

"Sounds good, bro. Pleasure doing business with you!" said The Wizard, about five minutes after his brother had left.

Several hours later, there was a knock on the door of The Wizard's quarters. The Wizard did not answer, as he was passed out on his desk. The door creaked open, and a young man stepped over the threshold. He had curly, jet-black hair and a short, neat goatee; horn-rimmed glasses, with hazel eyes beneath; and he wore tweed topcoat, with a light blue, wool scarf around his neck. This was The Wizard's nephew, Jeff.

Slowly, Jeff approached The Wizard's desk. As he looked around the room, he began to have second thoughts about taking this job. Suddenly, a floorboard creaked beneath his feet; before he knew it, The Wizard had leapt out of his chair, tackled him to the ground, and was pointing a wand directly at his face. This was as awkward for Jeff as it was frightening, for his uncle was still pantsless.

"Oh, it's you," said The Wizard. Getting to his feet, he offered Jeff a hand. "Sorry about that."

Slapping away The Wizard's hand, Jeff pulled himself to his feet. "What the hell, dude?!"

The Wizard shrugged nonchalantly. "You shouldn't have snuck up on me."

"I was in front of you!" shouted Jeff, sweeping the dust off his clothes. "And didn't you know I was coming?"

"Just give me a sec." Walking over to his desk, The Wizard snorted a line of cocaine. "Oh yeah, I remember that. You're interested in being my assistant, right?

"Well..." said Jeff, pausing apprehensively. He was not so sure how interested in this job he was at this point. "I'm interested in having a place to live, and my dad says I need to start paying rent."

Approaching Jeff, The Wizard hugged him tightly. Stepping back, he held Jeff by the shoulders, making intense eye contact. "Don't worry, Jeff, you

15

don't have to hide your excitement. Your dad told me how you've always looked up to me and aspired to be —"

Jeff snorted derisively. "He said what?!" Pushing The Wizard's hands off of him, he took a step back. "I have literally *never* said *any* of that. I think you're okay, dude, but every time we've met, you're either drunk or high! I still don't even know your real name!"

"Hey, that first part isn't my fault." Taking a seat at his desk, The Wizard railed another line of cocaine. "You weren't born yet when I was sober. And how many times do I have to tell you? My real name *is* The Wizard!"

Jeff smirked facetiously. "Right, and my real name is Arthur Pwndragon, and I really am a level thirty-three paladin who wields the mighty sword Sexcalibur in the endless war against the demonic armies of the writhing dark."

"What...?" Wearing a perplexed expression, The Wizard scratched his beard. "I have no idea what you're talking about... The writhing dark was sealed off by the Circle centuries ago, and there have only been four reported demon raids since then."

"I was talking about a video game... Obviously I'm not a demon-slaying paladin...." Pausing for a moment, Jeff squinted at The Wizard. "Hold on, did you say four demon raids? I learned in history class that there hasn't been any demonic activity since the *Seal of Sequestering,* four centuries ago!"

"First of all," said The Wizard, smirking superciliously, "nerd much? And secondly, all records of demon attacks are privileged information, the Circle thinks the public might panic if they knew how often it happens."

"Wow, that's messed up." Jeff was shocked; he had no idea that any demons still roamed free. "It's pretty upsetting. Still, I don't think four times is enough to incite a public uproar."

"Oh, that's just the raids, meaning attacks carried out by a party of six or more demons. Not a very organized species, demons... the vast majority of demonic activity is isolated reports of possessions by single demons."

"What do you mean, 'the *vast* majority'?" Jeff's eyes widened in horror. "How often does this happen?"

"I can't tell you that, it's top secret," said The Wizard. "I wasn't even supposed to mention demon raids."

"So why did you?!"

The Wizard and the Wise Guy

"Calm down, Jeff." Grabbing his green dragon bong off the couchside table, The Wizard took a massive puff of cannabis. He held it out to Jeff. "This should help, it's good stuff."

"Sure…" said Jeff, feeling uneasy as he digested this news. "Just please don't disclose any more top secret information, I really don't want to know."

"Okay, but if you're curious, I have a good one about what's been causing all those disappearances in the industrial district."

Jeff shook his head firmly. "I'm good, bro."

They sat and passed the bong back and forth for quite a while. Eventually, Jeff convinced The Wizard to put on some pants. After smoking several bowls, they found themselves in the kitchen. As Jeff was grilling a couple beef patties, The Wizard sat at the kitchen table, eating a cheeseburger.

"I 'ave to say," said The Wizard, through a mouthful of meat and bread, "you make one 'ell of a cheeseburger."

"Thanks," said Jeff, as he carefully flipped the patties. "I spent a couple weeks at culinary school."

Patting his stomach contentedly, The Wizard leaned back. "You know, I don't know if it's the fact that this burger is the first food I've had in two days talking, but I like you, Jeff. I think you're going to be a good fit for this job."

"Gee, aren't I the lucky one?" Jeff grimaced sardonically.

The Wizard continued to wolf down his burger. Suddenly, the sound of the refrigerator door slamming resounded through the kitchen, grabbing the attention of both men. They momentarily fell silent as a strange man stood before them, holding a freshly opened bottle of ale. He was an older man with a mangy mane of matted gray hair and a tangled beard, who wore a tattered, old trench coat over a stained tank top and ripped jeans. A strong odor of booze and tobacco wafted from him.

The man took a long pull from his bottle, before walking over to Jeff. Grabbing a burger patty from the pan with his bare hands, he ate it in one bite. Seeming to notice that The Wizard was glaring at him, he burped loudly. "What are you looking at?"

"Damn it, Gary!" The Wizard gritted his teeth angrily. "I thought I told you to stop taking all my beer."

Chapter Two

"I thought I told you to go fuck yourself..." Lighting a cigarette, Gary pushed past Jeff and left through a door in the rear of the room.

"Is that your roommate or something?" asked Jeff. He walked over to the door through which Gary had exited.

"Or something..." Heaving an exasperated sigh, The Wizard slid his palm down his face.

Opening the door, Jeff was surprised to find that it led outside, to the rear of the tower. Lined up against the wall, there was a row of overstuffed trash bins. The ground was overgrown with crabgrass and weeds, and twisting vines grew over the bins and up the side of the tower. There was a path trodden through the grass, leading to a thicket of brambles in the corner of the yard.

Deciding he did not want to see what those bushes concealed, Jeff locked the door behind him. "Does that guy *live* in your back yard?"

Peering around cautiously, The Wizard stepped close to Jeff and spoke in an undertone. "I'm pretty sure he's a spy."

"What...?" Raising an eyebrow, Jeff took a step away from The Wizard.

Pulling Jeff back towards him, The Wizard continued whispering. "I'm serious. He showed up shortly after my father passed away, when the new Archmage was voted in. I think she's using Gary to gather information on my activities to make sure I don't try to usurp her position."

"Was that ever really a risk for her?" Scoffing scornfully, Jeff narrowed his eyes at The Wizard. "Not only are you... you... but, she's the first female Archmage, as well as the first giant, and the first who isn't a direct descendant of Merlin himself. I don't think she's going anywhere."

"Wow, and here I thought *Perkins* was an ass kisser..." The Wizard's expression failed to mask his obvious jealousy. "Maybe you should work for her!"

Jeff hung his head. "I wish..."

"*Anyway*," said The Wizard, "he's been snooping around here regularly since she was appointed. I can't get rid of him, because those bushes he lives in aren't technically part of my back yard, they're considered a 'municipal alleyway'." He held up air quotes for this. "I've sent in four requests to the Circle to have him forcibly removed, but haven't seen any results. What does that tell you?"

18

The Wizard and the Wise Guy

"Umm... it tells me that you're a paranoid idiot with terrible breath." Once again pulling away, Jeff could not believe how demented his uncle truly was. "Get real! Even I know that the Circle doesn't care what goes on in this part of town. Why not just pay off a couple town guards to kick his ass?"

"Yeah... the guards don't... um... like me very much...." Absentmindedly, The Wizard twirled part of his beard. Without warning, he grabbed Jeff's arm and steered him into the foyer. "It doesn't matter, I just remembered why you're here: you've got work to do!"

"Wait..." Jeff was taken aback by this sudden demand. "What do you mean, *I've* got work to do? You're not going to help me?"

"No, idiot, that's why I hired you. Now come upstairs, I'll show you to the lab."

As they crested the final stairs, The Wizard sprinted ahead into his room. Jeff peered through the doorway to see him snorting a small pile of cocaine off of his desk. Hooting gleefully, The Wizard jumped for joy; he then leaned over and began chopping another line of cocaine. Jeff cleared his throat loudly.

"Oh, yes... Jeffery!" The Wizard leapt out of his seat. "I wasn't expecting you yet!"

"Maybe you should get some sleep..." said Jeff, biting his lower lip. "I could come back tomorrow." He was not entirely sure he meant that.

"No can do, Jeffery; we've got work to do!" With a wide grin, The Wizard pumped his fist exuberantly.

"Stop calling me that... And now it's '*we*'?"

"Indeed it is, Jeffery, for I still have to tell you what to do!"

"Of course..." Jeff did not know why he expected anything different.

"Come with me, Jeffery!" Once again grabbing Jeff by the arm, The Wizard steered him out onto the landing. He gestured to the spiral ladder. "Your venture awaits!"

"You *can't* expect me to climb that thing!" Jeff gaped at the ridiculous feat of architecture. "It's the stupidest thing I've ever seen!"

"It's all part of the job, Jeffery," said The Wizard, patting Jeff firmly on the back. "Now, I must attend to some errands, so I shall be leaving the rest

19

to you! Do not disappoint me, Jeffery." He turned and started quickly down the stairs, ignoring Jeff's protests as he did so.

Trotting jauntily down the street, The Wizard made his way to *The Wizarding Hole*. In the light of the flaming trees, The Wizard's fiery orange beard flickered like a blaze unto itself.

As he approached the bar, he heard some commotion coming from inside. Peering in the doorway, he saw Chris and a patron of the bar attempting to force out a burly, hairy man in rusty chainmail.

The man was struggling belligerently and hurling obscenities at everyone around him; he appeared to have pissed himself, or perhaps spilled a large amount of beer on his lap, for he smelled overwhelmingly of both.

"Y-you know..." the man stammered, "I wa-as the main c-character of *Final—*"

"Shut up, Siegbert," said Chris, as he and the other man forced Siegbert firmly out the doorway. "We've already heard your dumb fantasy."

As they came through the doorway, The Wizard stepped aside. Catching a whiff of Siegbert's breath, he nearly barfed. He grimaced at Chris. "That guy again, huh?"

"Yup," said Chris, scowling as they entered the bar. "Every damn new moon, them Werewolves get cocky and think they can slip into society without anyone getting the wiser."

The other man suddenly gasped and turned towards them. He was a short, portly man with neat, curly red hair and a plump handlebar mustache. "That guy was a werewolf?" he asked, wringing his hands nervously. "He bit me!" He pulled down the collar of his shirt and revealed a set of deep bite marks on his collarbone. "Can you get infected if they aren't transformed?"

"Nah, man, you'll be fine." Waving his hand dismissively, The Wizard subtly turned to Chris and mouthed *he's fucked.*

"You sure? The bite feels really gross..."

"Well, I'm no doctor," said The Wizard, turning back to the man and leaning onto the bar, "so I can't comment on what else you might be infected with; I can, however, assure you as an official representative of the Circle of Mages that you have nothing to worry about!"

The Wizard and the Wise Guy

Pulling his wallet from his pants pocket, he showed the man his official Circle of Mages identification card, placing his thumb strategically over the expiration date; the man looked reassured.

Meanwhile, Jeff had given up on ascending the spiral ladder, and had elected to clean the kitchen instead. Since The Wizard had not given him any details about his job besides showing him the ladder, and his father had simply described it to him as a "cleaning gig", Jeff assumed The Wizard would still pay him for a clean kitchen; unfortunately for him, he would soon learn that one should never make such assumptions.

The first task Jeff endeavored to complete was to clean The Wizard's refrigerator of any expired food; it turned out, however, that most of the food appeared to have been gathering mold for eons. He decided to bring the bin over to the refrigerator and begin tossing in all manners of putrid foodstuffs, one after another.

Perhaps drawn by the pungent smell of rotten condiments, the sound of glass shattering in the bin, or merely by the marked absence of The Wizard, Gary entered through the rear door. He walked over to Jeff, who backed away apprehensively. Paying no mind to the presence of Jeff or the aforementioned shattered glass, Gary began rooting around in the bin.

Eventually, he pulled out a hunk of rancid cheese. He grabbed a piece of stale bread off the countertop, drew some sliced meat from his pocket, and began to fix himself a sandwich. The bread was not quite-weapons grade, but it was definitely tool-grade. You do not want me to even describe the meat.

"Can I ask you something?" said Jeff, as he observed this disconcerting spectacle.

Gary grunted as he began to quickly devour his sandwich with inhuman intensity. Jeff took this as a "yes".

"If you're homeless, other than for the free beer and moldy food, why do you stay *here*, of all places?"

Pulling a pack of cigarettes from his pocket, Gary lit one with a mithril lighter inscribed with a pentagram. "I ain't homeless; this is just my home away from home."

"What...?" Bemused, Jeff raised an eyebrow. "What does that even mean?"

Chapter Two

"Wouldn't you like to know!" Snickering to himself, Gary made his way to the door. He slammed it behind him, and Jeff could still hear his laughter fading into the distance.

"What a freak..." Intending to lock the door again, Jeff approached it; he was rightfully unsurprised, however, to find that the lock was broken this time.

Sighing wearily, he continued to clean out the refrigerator. Once he finished, the only things remaining were a potato, a jar of pickles, a tin of sardines, and a wide variety of ales. He then dumped the contents of the bin onto The Wizard's rear lawn, having had no intent of bothering to unfasten the outside bins from the grip of the vines entangling them.

Moments later, as he was mopping the kitchen floor, Jeff heard the distinct sounds of someone rummaging through broken glass. Peering out the window, he saw Gary digging through the pile of rotten food he had poured outside, picking out hunks of this and that.

Rolling his eyes, Jeff did a mock impression of The Wizard. "'I'm pretty sure he's a spy'."

Back at the bar, The Wizard was having a jolly time, drinking and carrying on. The incident with Siegbert had sparked a lively debate between the two present patrons of the bar and its tender.

"The worst part, to me, about being a Werewolf," said the Wizard, burping loudly, "is the slow and grueling transformation."

"I agree," said Chris.

The other man stroked his bright red mustache thoughtfully. "Yeah, but would that really be worse than the risk of tearing your loved ones apart?"

"Listen," said The Wizard, putting his hand on the man's shoulder, "once someone becomes a werewolf, they can kiss their loved ones goodbye; figuratively, of course, because doing so literally would transmit the curse."

"The transformation just sounds horrible," said Chris, shuddering.

"Oh, it is," said The Wizard, nodding fervently. Leaning back, he took a sip of his drink before continuing. "It's nothing like in the childrens' stories where it happens instantaneously at the break of the full moon." He chortled to himself. "It's a long harrowing progression from human to beast over the course of the entire lunar cycle." He paused, muddling his drink casually and taking another sip. "They're only really human on the new moon, and even then they're usually nuts."

"Wow..." The mustachioed man's eyes widened. "I really dodged a bullet, getting bit on the new moon." He paused momentarily before downing the remainder of his drink and giving a rowdy cheer. "Next round's on me! Here's to good fortune!"

The Wizard almost felt bad for what awaited this unfortunate man in the days to come.

Chris poured three neat glasses of whiskey, passing one to each of the other men. He held up his drink to the ironic toast. "Here's to good fortune!"

"Yeah," said The Wizard, patting the mustachioed man on the back as he raised his glass. "Real lucky guy here!"

Chris snickered as he sipped his liquor. "So, I don't recall meeting you before tonight. What brings a handsome gentleman like you around these parts?"

"A very important mission, actually," said the mustachioed man. He hiccupped loudly, grabbing the bar to steady himself as he nearly toppled backwards.

Chris and The Wizard made furtive eye contact, barely suppressing their giggling.

"Excuse me..." His cheeks flushing bright red, the man swayed unsteadily in his seat. "I believe I may have had a bit too much..." He hiccupped again. "Anyway, I've been appointed by the house of MacRoyalle to escort Sir Timothaue from the kingdom of Royalle to the north to the mountain hall of Thrordmor, to negotiate marriage with Lady Dornice. She's the half-sister of a Dwarven princess." He added the last part like it was something to brag about.

The Wizard snorted into his drink, coughing as he tried not to laugh out loud.

The mustachioed man did not seem to notice. "I am Sir Mathiaue MacRoyalle. I am the older brother, first and second cousin, and appointed guardian of Sir Timothaue MacRoyalle!" He beamed with pride, swaying in his seat and taking a deep swig off of his drink. "Long live the MacRoyalles!"

Laughing bumptiously, he raised his glass in another toast.

Chapter Two

Did he just say he was his brother's first and second cousin? thought The Wizard. He did not want to think about how that worked. He and Chris exchanged disturbed looks, before humoring Mathiaue by raising their glasses to his weird toast. Plopping back down onto his stool, Mathiaue heaved a contented sigh.

"MacRoyalle, huh?" said Chris, scratching his blonde stubble. "I know I've heard that somewhere before..."

"I should hope so!" Mathiaue leapt out of his seat with the vigor of a much leaner man and began to rave passionately. *"MacRoyalle Meat Cubes are the very paramount of gourmet culinary bliss!"*

"Oh, shit, now I remember..." muttered The Wizard.

"They are the most sumptuous and exquisite of all delicacies!"

"Yeah, me too..." Chris nodded grimly. "From the commercial, right?"

"Only the finest of cuisines are graced with the MacRoyalle label!"

"Yeah..." The Wizard downed the rest of his drink.

"Are you ready to experience delectable delights of which you've only dreamed?"

"Umm..." Chris scratched his head uncomfortably. "I guess so...."

"Prepare to have your taste buds enveloped in the sensual embrace of flavor!"

Upon completion of his presentation, Mathiaue bowed; with a flourish, he held out a box of assorted *MacRoyalle Meat Cubes*. "Here, help yourself." He winked, his eyes twinkling with passion. "They're on the house."

Smirking at each other, Chris and The Wizard shrugged and each grabbed a meat cube. The three men continued to drink and carry on late into the night. They went through two entire fifths of whiskey, and twice as many boxes of meat cubes. At the end of the night, The Wizard convinced Mathiaue to pay not only for the night's drinks, but also to settle his tab for the last two weeks.

The Wizard was smiling as he passed out on his couch that night.

Wizardrous

Chapter Three
He Who Shall Not Be Blamed

Sunlight was cascading into The Wizard's office when he awoke. The iron bars over his windows cast long shadows, running perpendicular to the floorboards. Tiny motes of dust drifted softly through luminous beams.

Slowly rolling off of his couch, The Wizard pulled on a nearby pair of pants, and took a large puff off of his bong; coughing, he stumbled to the fireplace, clutching the fullest bottle on his mantle of drinks. Taking a deep swig of rum, he looked at the clock on the wall.

The time was five past two.

Rubbing the sleep out of his eyes, he ambled into the hall. He wondered, as his stomach growled, whether or not he had eaten dinner the previous night.

As he descended the spiral staircase, something caught his eye through the front windows. Standing at the front doorstep, tapping his feet impatiently and periodically checking his watch, was Inspector Perkins.

This alarmed The Wizard, as he had not expected the Inspector until the following morning. He began to wonder if he may have overslept.

The Inspector banged his fist on the door.

Perplexed, The Wizard hurried down the stairs and swung open the front door.

"You're late," said Inspector Perkins, holding up his watch.

"I, uh… wasn't expecting you until tomorrow."

Chapter Three

Sighing, Perkins rubbed his forehead impatiently. "The letter we sent could not have been more clear." He held up a sheet of paper covered in fine print. "The inspection was to occur on Monday, Mr. Wizard."

The Wizard suddenly understood the reason for his lethargy and powerful appetite; he had slept through an entire day!

Panicking, he struggled to think of an excuse to stall the Inspector. He stood speechless for a moment, wondering whether or not Jeff organized his lab to a respectable degree.

Perkins cleared his throat.

"Oh, yes..." Stepping aside, The Wizard reluctantly beckoned Perkins inside. "Do come in."

Looking around the room, Perkins' eyes narrowed. He walked past The Wizard and approached one of the walls. Moving his hand over the surface, he peeled off a long, thin strip of paint.

"When last I was here, the excuse you gave for postponing the inspecting was that you had painters coming." He held up the strip of paint. "Care to explain this?"

As he realized his mistake, The Wizard's heart sank. "Uh, well... they must have used cheap goblin paint or something..."

This response did not appear to satisfy Inspector Perkins. He silently conjured a clipboard and took some notes. The Wizard was troubled by this.

"Anyway, if you would, please direct me to your laboratory."

Gulping tremulously, The Wizard nodded and gestured towards the stairway. He followed as Inspector Perkins ascended to the second floor landing.

"I trust the lab is behind one of these doors," said the Inspector. "Hopefully not the burnt up one." He gestured to The Wizard's bathroom door.

"Um, no, it's..." Trailing off, The Wizard gestured apprehensively to the small balcony overhanging the foyer, on which sat the base of the spiral ladder.

"You have *got* to be kidding me." Shaking his head in disbelief, Perkins turned and walked towards the stairs. "I think I've seen enough."

He Who Shall Not Be Blamed

"Hold on!" Beads of sweat began to form on The Wizard's brow. "Just wait here a moment, I have a ten-foot extension ladder in my broom closet. I'll go get it." He rushed past the Inspector and down the stairs.

A moment later, he dragged the ladder up the stairs, repeatedly getting it wedged on the bannisters. After several minutes of labor, he heaved it up the final steps. Inspector Perkins tapped his foot impatiently as The Wizard attempted to situate the ladder into the trapdoor above; it didn't quite reach, so he resolved to merely wedge the feet under one of the top rungs of the spiral ladder.

That ought to be good enough... thought The Wizard, as he motioned for the Inspector to climb the ladder.

Perkins shook his head and laughed. Holding his hands at his side with his palms facing down, he muttered an incantation. He began to rise as though weightless.

"Hold on..." said The Wizard, through gritted teeth. "If you knew levitation, why the hell did you make me drag this extra ladder up the stairs?!"

"For the same reason we do these inspections." Pausing in midair, Perkins sneered down at The Wizard. "To make sure everything's up to code. I'm nonetheless going to have to dock you a few points until you install a permanent replacement for that... *'ladder'*." He rose up through the trapdoor.

The Wizard gave Perkins the finger behind his back. "How about I find you a permanent replacement for your dick..."

"What was that?"

"Nothing..." The Wizard crossed his arms bitterly.

"Really?"

"I just said 'I'll try to find a permanent replacement pretty quick'." The Wizard shifted uncomfortably. He knew his employment was already on thin ice; the last thing he needed was Perkins tearing him apart with this inspection.

"Oh, okay, good." Floating back down, Perkins feigned a sugary simper. "Because, for a second, I thought you might have fabricated another flimsy pretext for why your lab is in shambles."

"What?!" Dismay pooled in The Wizard's chest. "Are you serious?!"

27

Chapter Three

Perkins clicked his tongue impatiently. "Nice try, Mr. Wizard, but you won't be able to weasel out so easily this time."

Sweat ran down The Wizard's neck as he stood speechless and dumbfounded.

Taking a few final notes on his clipboard, Perkins cleared his throat. "Well, Mr. Wizard it is my great pleasure to inform you that you have *not* passed your inspection. Archmage Quan has instructed me that should you fail, I am to send you to speak with her directly. You are to report to her tomorrow, no later than noon."

The Wizard's stomach tightened. He had not spoken with Archmage Quan one-on-one since before she was elected to lead the Circle. He was sure that the only reason she would request to speak with him was to lay him off personally.

Archmage Quan had never liked The Wizard, ever since they served together as apprentices to The Wizard's father; although she always worked harder and would turn in superior research, The Wizard always received favoritism. She grew to resent him for this, and had always looked on him with disdain.

"Okay... I'll be sure to do that...." It was difficult for The Wizard to suppress his urge to punch Perkins. "Is that all?"

"I believe so." Straightening his tie, Perkins folded his clipboard neatly into his satchel. "I bid you good day."

Smiling with grim satisfaction, he turned and sauntered down the stairway.

Standing silently, The Wizard stared down the stairwell in disbelief. Eventually, he decided to check what Perkins was talking about. He ascended the precariously wedged extension ladder. Poking his head through the trapdoor, he looked around the lab; it was in the exact state in which he had left it.

His chest swelled with rage as he climbed down the ladder. He began to contemplate various ways he could violently assault Jeff as revenge for the injustice he believed himself to have suffered. Incensed, he pulled on his robes; they were deep blue, with gold trim, and had a hole worn out in the seat.

He Who Shall Not Be Blamed

Grabbing his staff from the rack in his office, The Wizard stormed down the stairs. He did not normally use his staff, except when he wanted to deliver a particularly vicious beating. It did not possess any actual magical powers, it was simply the most knobbled one he could find.

Several hours later, The Wizard arrived at Justin's house; it would not have taken so long, if he were not so preoccupied with rage that he "got lost" at several pubs along the way. He approached the front garden of the baby blue cottage. A gentle breeze blew with the scent of morning dew and lavender.

The Wizard seethed as he tore through the gate.

Approaching the front door, he raised his staff in both hands. Slamming the end into the door like a battering ram, The Wizard began to knock on the door. He knocked three times. With each knock, the door quaked uncontrollably. Cracks began to form at the point of impact. After the third and final knock, the door flew off of its hinges.

The inside of the house was quaint and cozy, with rough hewn cedar furniture and jade damask wallpaper. There was a fireplace to the left of The Wizard, in which crackled a merry fire. Two corduroy armchairs sat before the fire, and there was a leather couch against the far wall. There was a dining hutch against the right wall, full of decorative plates bearing the likenesses of wolves.

Justin had raced frantically to his parlor to see what on Notearth was causing such violent trembling of the entire house. He was wearing nothing but a houndstooth bathrobe and gray wolf slippers. As he entered the room, he was narrowly missed by his front door as it spun through the air.

He looked positively murderous. "WHAT THE FUCK?!"

"Oh, my bad," said The Wizard, as he stepped through the fractured doorway, "I thought that would hit Jeff."

The door had struck the couch at the far end of the room, snapping the frame and splintering to pieces.

"What?!" Justin's right eye twitched with rage. "Are you insane?!"

"Damn near!" The Wizard cackled furiously, his eyes alight in a manic frenzy. He pushed past Justin and started up the stairs. "Where the hell is Jeff?"

Chapter Three

There was a sound of hurried footsteps upstairs; a moment later, Jeff appeared, leaning over the balustrade. He watched The Wizard climb the stairs, wearing a bemused expression.

"What's going on?"

The Wizard did not answer as he continued up the stairs. As soon as he reached the landing, he whirled his staff vigorously, walloping Jeff forcefully on the buttocks.

Staggering, Jeff swayed back, grabbing the bannister for support. He wallowed in agony as The Wizard struck him again, this time over the head. Jeff fell to his knees, clutching his battered scalp.

"You're fired!" yelled The Wizard, thwacking Jeff once more over the head. He then calmly turned around and strolled down the stairs, whistling a jaunty tune.

Justin, who had overheard what had transpired above, was standing at the foot of the stairs. He held out his hand firmly, stopping The Wizard as he attempted to step past. He trembled in fury, glowering at The Wizard.

"How dare you?! Do you have any idea how much it will cost to get that door replaced? It was teak!"

"Huh… no wonder it took three knocks…"

"That's your takeaway?!" Justin punched the wall. "That door was an antique, it came with the house!"

Stumbling down the stairs, Jeff paused on the midway landing. He glared down at the two of them silently for a moment, clutching the handrail for support. His voice shook unsteadily as he spoke.

"What the hell is wrong with you?!"

"Seriously…" muttered Justin.

"You too!" Meandering erratically down the remaining stairs, Jeff approached his father. "I can't believe he just beat me over the head with a staff, and all you care about is that creaky, old door!"

Justin shifted awkwardly. "I was getting to that…"

"And you!" Thundering up to The Wizard, Jeff poked him in the chest. "I spent my entire Saturday cleaning your shit, and this is how you repay me?! I should kick your ass!"

"I think you're forgetting who holds the bigger stick!" Smiling nastily, The Wizard held up the knobbled end of his staff.

He Who Shall Not Be Blamed

Shrieking with exasperation, Jeff glanced around. He spotted a particularly large, jagged shard of the door; grabbing it, he charged recklessly, thrusting the point at The Wizard's crotch.

With a whirl of his staff, The Wizard parried the attack, attempting to deliver a riposte directly to Jeff's crotch. He was unsuccessful, instead striking an ornate, porcelain urn resting on a nearby table. Shards of patterned pottery and human ashes rained down on the two men as they wrestled each other to the floor.

Eventually, Justin managed to pull the two of them apart. The Wizard's pants were soaked in a stream of blood issuing from a stab wound Jeff had left on his thigh. Jeff had vomited a small pool of blood on his shirt when The Wizard had punched his diaphragm. Luckily for both men, and despite each other's best efforts, they managed to evade any blows to their testicles.

The three of them stood completely still, glaring at each other. After a few moments of uncomfortable silence, The Wizard began to chuckle softly. Slowly, Justin joined in, and they both began laughing boisterously.

Jeff looked completely flabbergasted. "What is wrong with you two?"

"This just reminds me of childhood," said Justin, "except that I'm the one watching and laughing instead of mom."

"If only she were still here to egg us on..." The Wizard stared wistfully into the distance.

The two brothers hugged. Approaching Jeff, The Wizard attempted to hug him as well; Jeff recoiled, and The Wizard instead patted him on the back.

"Sorry about that, perhaps I overreacted a smidgen."

"You think?!" said Jeff, gaping incredulously.

The Wizard crossed his arms. "Yes, Jeff, I do."

Jeff heaved a sigh of exasperation.

"What got into you, anyway?" Putting a hand on The Wizard's shoulder, Justin cocked his head inquisitively. "I haven't seen you flip out like that since we were kids and mom smoked your stash."

"Oh, yeah..." Scratching his beard, The Wizard nodded pensively. "That was just before I went to live with my dad. As for this one, —" he gestured to Jeff "—the idiot failed to clean my lab even a little. I got fired because of him."

"What?" Jeff raised his eyebrows in surprise. "How did that happen?"

31

Chapter Three

"I failed the inspection because of you!" yelled The Wizard, balling his fists. "And now the Archmage wants to see me in her office!"

"Really?" Jeff grinned enthusiastically. "Can I come and meet her?"

"You son of a bitch!" This time, it was The Wizard's turn to lunge at Jeff. Justin quickly leapt between the two of them and held off his assault.

"Hold on," he said to The Wizard, "you haven't actually spoken with her yet? Maybe she won't actually fire you... she may just want to berate you for incompetence!"

"That's a good point..." Ceasing his advances, The Wizard nodded slowly. He looked at Jeff considerately for a moment. "Maybe you *should* come with, Jeff... I think Quan should see who's fault this *really* is!"

"If you say so." Shrugging, Jeff rolled his eyes. "Any excuse works! Just let me get my stuff!" He hurried up the stairs.

Justin cleared his throat. "So, what exactly do you intend to do about my shattered door and mother's urn?"

"Oh, that's no problem," said The Wizard, waving his hand. He flourished his staff and muttered an arcane verse under his breath.

The splinters of teak floated together, arranging themselves one by one; slowly, they reformed into the original shape of the door. Pointing his staff to the doorway, The Wizard guided the door back into place. It fastened itself to the doorframe, closing gently. The Wizard repeated this process on the urn, placing it back on the table. He was even able to get most of their mother's ashes back inside of it.

At first, Justin looked impressed; however, as he inspected the urn, he noticed something peculiar: the shards had not actually been rejoined, but instead were merely held in place by some form of adhesive. Frowning, he walked over to the door and examined it as well; it, too, was simply glued back together.

"You couldn't actually fix them?" he asked, massaging his forehead in frustration.

"They are fixed!" Rushing to the door, The Wizard firmly opened and shut it. A small piece fell off of the corner. "Ignore that!" Quickly shoving the piece back into place, he then proceeded to fling the door open and closed several times. "See!"

Justin sighed wearily. "That's not what I had in mind."

He Who Shall Not Be Blamed

"Sorry…" Shrugging, The Wizard scratched his head sheepishly. "That's all I can do. It's hard enough to get all the pieces set properly, but binding the molecules back together takes a lot of energy! Conjuring glue is much easier."

"Well, I suppose it works for now… You're still paying for that, though." Justin hung his head defeatedly. It was clear he did not expect to see a coin from The Wizard.

At that moment, Jeff ran down the stairs. He was wearing a long set of shiny, black robes; on his head sat a curved, pointed hat; he wore a black leather belt fastened with a silver buckle around his waist, a smaller, matching band on his hat. It did not go well with his jet black hair and goatee.

"What are you wearing?!" Leaning forward, The Wizard slapped his hands on his knees, cackling hilariously. "Do you have a flying broomstick to go with that outfit?"

"What?" Turning slightly red, Jeff averted his eyes. "It was on sale at the Sorcery Shack. It's unisex!"

"But *why* are you wearing it?!" The Wizard continued to laugh ridiculously.

"I wanted to look professional!"

"Well, go change! You look like an idiot."

Jeff narrowed his eyes at The Wizard and shook his head. "No."

"I think it looks good on him," said Justin, nodding earnestly.

"Fine, whatever." The Wizard shrugged, with a smirk on his face. "Let's just go then."

He turned and left through the newly remodeled door. As Jeff followed, Justin leaned in, gesturing to The Wizard. "He's just jealous because moths ate holes in the seat of his best robes."

Chuckling, Jeff followed The Wizard out through the garden.

Chapter Four
The Circle of Mages

ot much was said as Jeff and The Wizard trekked across town. They walked down the main avenue of the commercial district. Circle Tower loomed atop a great hill in the distance, silhouetted against the afternoon sun. Enchanted trees lined every street, wreathing the hill in a blaze of autumn fire. Sparse waves of cirrus clouds rippled across the sky, awash in the amber glow of the flames.

Along the avenue, a fiery canopy danced merrily beside imposing brick buildings, delicately caressing the masonry. Colorful signs and posters hung on the walls, advertising all manner of unusual wares, from fermented mermaid milk to quantum xylophones. Passersby gawked longingly at extravagant displays in the windows.

All manner of people wandered the street, about half of which were human. Beings from all around the land would come to Theiyre for its festivals, and beings of all shapes and sizes were all equally disliked by most of the locals. Theiyricans were some of the most racist people in all of Koric, much more so than the rural areas. The local shopkeepers, however, were in full support of the seasonal tourism.

Without warning, The Wizard turned and headed down a deserted sidestreet. "I have to make a quick stop out of the way."

They continued for several blocks, before The Wizard abruptly turned into a shady alleyway between two dingy buildings.

34

"Wait here." The Wizard held out his hand. "This is where I do business with an associate of mine." He winked at Jeff, as though he were being clandestine. "He doesn't like strange faces."

Shrugging, Jeff approached one of the buildings and leaned against the sill of the window. It belonged to a discount clothing store; there was a display in the window for clip-on pockets. Jeff watched as The Wizard strolled past an odious pair of dumpsters, leapt over a mysterious, steaming puddle of sanguine liquid, and approached a rusty, iron aperture in the side of one building. The Wizard began to rap on the surface repeatedly with his staff.

Taaap, tap, tap. Tap, taaap, tap. Tap, tap, taaap. Taaap, taaap, tap. Tap, tap, tap.

At the behest of the morse code for "drugs", the hatch slid open.

"I thought I told ya to stop usin' that code," said a gruff, male voice.

A head emerged from the aperture, wearing a dark, woolen hood. Most of the man's face was covered by a grimy indigo bandana. His eyes narrowed as they wandered down the alleyway.

"Who's 'e?" The man gestured to Jeff, who was skulking around the dumpsters.

"My errand boy," said The Wizard.

"Very well, just keep 'im over there." Leaning forward, the man held open his cloak to reveal a variety of pouches, potions, and poultices. "What are ya buyin'?"

"I'm looking for some of that dwarven divination dust." The Wizard sniffled as he gestured to his nose.

"A wise choice, mate..." Nodding slowly, the man drew a cylindrical vial of ivory powder from within his cloak; it bore the label *Wizard Propellant*. "How much ya need?"

"How about a quarter ounce?" asked The Wizard.

Pulling a metallic scale from beneath the counter, the man weighed out a sizable pile of powder. Squinting, he swept it into a small leather pouch. "Is that all, stranger?"

"Yeah. How much?"

"That'll be twenty sol."

"What? For a quarter?" The Wizard's heart began to race frantically. "It was two sol a gram last week!"

35

Chapter Four

"Tough. It'd be cheap at twice the price."

Grumbling, The Wizard pulled out a squat coin purse. Turning it over, he dumped the contents onto the counter. "Let's see..." Frowning, he quickly sorted the gold, silver, and bronze coins into separate piles. He had always been remarkably fast when it came to calculating narcotic transactions. "I have eighteen sol, twelve lun, and fifty-two gai; could you just forget the other twenty-eight gai and call it even?"

Nodding, the man slid the pouch of powder forward. He swept the coins into an engraved silver urn he kept beneath the counter. It jingled resoundingly as he put it away.

"Pleasure doin' business with ya." He grabbed the handle of the metal hatch, slamming it shut.

Glancing up and down the alleyway, The Wizard quickly slid the pouch into the chest pocket of his robes. Humming cheerfully, he strolled out of the alleyway. As he walked past, Jeff shot him an inquisitive look.

"Did you just buy cocaine from an alleyway window?"

"Of course I did, Jeff." The Wizard walked up the street with an extremely hurried pace. "I've had a shitty day; it helps."

"But why not just buy it from an apothecary?" Jeff was jogging to match The Wizard's stride. He gestured across the street to a store by the name of *Weed, Meth, and Beyond.* "It's not illegal like Fairy dust. Why take the risk?"

"Let's just say that this cocaine isn't exactly legally obtained." Tilting his head at Jeff, The Wizard wiggled his eyebrows implicitly.

Jeff shook his head in disbelief. "Yeah, no fucking shit... That's kind of my point."

"Listen…" Stopping suddenly in his tracks, The Wizard placed his hand firmly on Jeff's shoulder and looked him intently in the eyes. "I don't like to stoop to buy the 'premium drugs' from these price gouging pigs." He made an obscene gesture at the nearby storefront. "I'm not a mindless sheep like you, Jeff; I see no reason to blow twice the money for some blowhard's label on my blow."

Jeff slapped away The Wizard's hand. "Blow me."

They continued up the street. When they reached the main drive, they turned towards the center of town. Eyes narrowed with ardent focus, The

The Circle of Mages

Wizard strode hastily towards Circle Tower. Passerby shot disgruntled looks at them as he jostled hastily by. Following behind, Jeff struggled to keep pace.

"This place will have to do." Stopping abruptly, The Wizard pointed to the facade of a lively tavern.

The sign read *The Drunken Dragon,* and on either side of the heavy mahogany door stood a statue of a plump dragon passed out on a hoard of liquor bottles. Several patrons sat outside at iron mesh tables, chatting vibrantly.

As The Wizard pushed open the door, he and Jeff were met with the pleasant scent of grilled meat and spices and the tranquil sound of a mandolin. The room encircled an island bar, in the center of which sat a sizzling griddle. Paper lanterns hung on strings across the room. Several waiters zigzagged around the room, attending to the bustling patronage. A plump man in a gleaming dragon scale apron stood over the cooktop, scrupulously seasoning a series of simmering cutlets.

The chef waved merrily as they entered the restaurant. "Welcome, friends! Make yourselves comfortable, and one of our waiters will be with you shortly. The special today is kung pao pudding!"

After halfheartedly waving back, The Wizard meandered to the far corner of the room. He sat down in the corner booth, stretching his feet luxuriously down the bench. Jeff sat down shortly afterwards, wearing a puzzled expression.

"Why are we here?" he asked, looking around the restaurant. "There's no way you can afford this place."

"No shit." The Wizard drew the small leather pouch from the pocket of his robes. As he peered inside it, his eyes gleamed with greedy enthusiasm. "I spent all of my money on this sweet, savory snow!"

"Oh, don't tell me you're gonna —"

Before Jeff could finish, The Wizard had already poured a small pile of cocaine onto the table. He chopped it with the flat end of a butterknife. Leaning forward, he rolled up a shred torn from the dinner menu and loudly snorted several lines. Jeff buried his face in his hands as patrons of the restaurant began to crane their necks inquisitively.

Chapter Four

After he snorted the last line of cocaine, The Wizard looked up, his face alight with ecstacy. There was a sprinkling of cocaine on his blaze orange beard. He pounded his fist on the table, thrashing his head and whooping vigorously. "You can't tell me that's not magic!"

The entire restaurant fell silent, staring in disbelief.

"What? It's windy outside." Scouring the table with his index finger, The Wizard rubbed the remainder of the powder onto his gums. He stood up, held out his arms, and waved to the crowd. "Carry on, my friends!" He began to slowly sidle across the room.

Shielding his face in embarrassment, Jeff followed.

The crowd followed him with their gaze for a few moments, before one by one returning to their meals and conversations. As they walked past, the chef glared at The Wizard with disdain.

"What the hell was that?" asked Jeff, punching The Wizard in the arm.

The Wizard shrugged. "Like I said, I needed a place out of the wind."

"So you chose a crowded restaurant?! We passed two libraries on the way here!"

"Does it really matter? Technically, nothing I just did was illegal. If they don't want people doing that, they should put up a sign."

Sighing in exasperation, Jeff shook his head and fell silent.

Circle Tower loomed overhead. The two men entered the Regal Roundabout, a series of circular avenues that surrounded the tower. As they approached the base of the tower, The Wizard's eyes were drawn to an ornate manor standing just outside its shadow.

The manor was two stories tall; two bay windows on the second floor overhung a shady arcade; vines rose out of a verdant garden, twisting up the pillars and onto the olive facade; ripples of terracotta blew across the roof; a stout stucco chimney sat against the nearest wall. It was in this manor that The Wizard once lived with his father.

Perhaps if he were not distracted by this nostalgic vista, he would have seen who they were walking towards.

A large man sat on a bench at the base of the tower, wearing hot pink robes with scarlet trim. He was extremely muscular, with rippling abs and a barrel chest, his toned physique exaggerated by the flickering of the treelight. His dark, flowing hair was gleaming under the fires of autumn. He wore spectacles and held a book; next to his tan, bulging muscles, they looked as though he pulled them from a dollhouse.

He glanced up as they approached, and his face lit up with excitement.

"Do my eyes deceive me?" Leaping up, the man stowed away his book and spectacles. Charging towards The Wizard, he held open his arms.

"Ugh..." muttered The Wizard, with a look of dismay. "This guy..."

"Wiz, my buddy!" The large man squeezed The Wizard in a spine crushing embrace. "How are you, old friend?!"

As the man hugged him, The Wizard struggled to breathe. "Hey, Fabulon... can you... let me go...?"

"Oh, sorry." Fabulon hastily released The Wizard. "Didn't mean to crush you!"

"It's fine..." muttered The Wizard. His voice was raspy and thin.

"And who's this?" Approaching Jeff, Fabulon put his arm around his shoulders.

"Hey," said Jeff, holding out his hand to shake, "I'm Jeff. Nice to meet —"

"He's my new assistant," said The Wizard. "And if you don't mind, I've gotta take him to meet Quan before the day is out; otherwise, we'll have to come back tomorrow."

"Good old Wiz!" Laughing jovially, Fabulon patted The Wizard on the back, causing him to stagger. "Always in such a hurry! I often wonder how you get so much energy!"

Jeff snickered to himself.

"Yeah, it's a mystery..." The Wizard hastily stepped away from Fabulon. "Now, if you don't mind, we've got to go."

Fabulon waved as they sauntered off.

"He seemed nice," said Jeff.

The Wizard rolled his eyes. "Oh yeah, he's an absolute pleasure!"

The tall white marble doors of Circle Tower loomed before them. They were at least twenty feet wide, and nearly twice as tall. Hanging above was the crest of the Circle: six chromatic dragons twisting in a ring around a golden pentagram.

As they approached, the doors began grinding open. A vast, marble hall slowly came into view; an arcade of grandiose pillars encircled the hall, each

Chapter Four

surrounded by glowing wisps of flame; a hundred-foot-long indigo rug, hemmed with gold leaf, stretched from the entrance to a lavish pair of staircases in the center; the stairs spiraled up and around each other, connecting to dozens of platforms and balconies. The hall was bustling with men and women of all races, wearing robes of various hues.

"Wow…" muttered Jeff, gazing in awe from the base of the stairs to the vaulted ceilings. His eyes were so wide, they practically fell out of their sockets!

As they walked through the hall, Jeff looked around in wonder. Each of the pillars around the room was at least ten feet in diameter. Arcane runes and geometric patterns swirled up the sides. Behind them, the marble walls were inlaid with bookshelves, rising all the way to the ceiling. At least a hundred feet above, the walls vaulted inward around a vast octagonal skylight.

Dozens of platforms were held magically aloft throughout the room, connecting to the staircase by thin, intertwining pathways. Made of prismatic crystal, they refracted the sunlight streaming from above. Tiny rainbows danced spectacularly around the room, casting a rippling sea of color onto the walls. On each platform, there sat a desk and sets of strange, magical devices. They bustled with activity, with hundreds of sorcerers at work upon them and walking between.

Nearly everyone in the room wore robes of grey or dark colors. Some, like Fabulon, wore robes with vibrant hues. However, almost no one was wearing black robes. Solid black robes were typically regarded as formalwear. Jeff looked very out of place, wearing what The Wizard kept referring to as a "witch costume"; however, he seemed too fascinated by the tower to notice.

All manner of beings could be seen around the room. Although not exclusively, each race tended to exemplify a different branch of magic.

There were elves, with slender forms and sleek hair; they typically became alchemists or healers, as they usually practiced druidic magic, harnessing the flow of the natural world.

Several dwarves could be seen around the room, squat and burly, with massive, bristly beards that covered most of their front; they gravitated towards magic that affected material, blasting it apart or reshaping it, and thus favored the magicks of invocation and alteration.

The Circle of Mages

Gnomes and halflings were very lively and often mischievous beings, and practiced magic primarily for enjoyment. They mostly leaned towards the magicks of illusion and conjuration. Halflings historically feared the field of necromancy, but some gnomes were inclined towards it.

There were a few goblins frenetically tinkering away on strange magelectronic devices. Prolific engineers, goblins favored practical magicks; their bailiwick was predisposed to be alteration magic, as it allowed them delicate control of their work.

It was rare for other races to practice organized magic.

Trolls, orcs, and ogres were all generally regarded as lacking the obligatory intelligence, in addition to not being allowed in most cities. There had only been four adept troll sorcerers in recorded history, only one ogre, and no orcs. The trolls practiced the obscure magic of voodoo; while voodoo had some aspects of arcane magic, it relied heavily on intimidation, narcotics, and mental trickery. The only known ogre magi simply used gas magic to scare intruders out of his swamp.

While the giants could generally understand magic, they usually felt it superfluous, given their immense physical stature; nonetheless, certain tribes practiced it to augment their prowess in battle. Archmage Quan was the only giant sorcerer currently enrolled in the Circle of Magic. She came from a tribe of giant stone benders, magi practiced in mass-scale alteration magic that can slowly reshape entire mountainsides. Her family, along with the Mings and the Tiezhus, worked alongside Merlin on construction of Circle Tower, four hundred years prior.

The fairies were once avid practitioners of magic; however, since being labeled a controlled substance by Archmage Quan, they have been banished from the city. Rumors have been floating around that Fabulon is a fairy in disguise, but they are mostly just scornful allusions to the homophobic ramblings of The Wizard.

As he and The Wizard approached the staircase, Jeff gawked at a series of massive statues encircling it. They each bore the face of a previous Archmage; in the eye of the two spiral staircases, sat a statue twice as tall as the rest, bearing the visage of Merlin himself. It seemed to watch them as they approached. This statue had always made The Wizard uncomfortable.

The Wizard averted his gaze from the statue of his father.

Chapter Four

"Damn," said Jeff, looking up at the staircase towering above. "Imagine climbing that thing to work every day."

"I used to have to, at least when I came to work." Chortling, The Wizard shook his head. "Now we don't have to anymore; the new Archmage couldn't get up the stairs, so she had a team design this. Check it out." He started up the staircase; instantly, he appeared at the very top of the staircase. He stepped out onto a thick, transparent floor.

The top floor of the tower was very strange. It was at this point that the walls vaulted inward, so the room had a domed shape. The floor was a single, vast pane of foot-thick glass, with a large hole in the middle for the stairwell. The architecture was not all that was strange about this room, however: all of the furniture was of enormous size.

All manner of strange magical devices stood around the room, each at least twice the size of those below. A desk sat against the wall, standing almost twice as tall as The Wizard; although he was a tall man, The Wizard looked like a child's toy next to the woman sitting behind it.

Standing at least twenty feet tall, Archmage Quan dwarfed even the tallest of men. Lean and toned, she had olive skin and sumptuous curves beneath elegant robes of the purest golden thread. Her long, wavy black hair was held back in a loose ponytail. She didn't seem to notice him as he entered the room, as she was entrenched in a colossal tome.

The Wizard hesitated before announcing his presence. "Uh, hey... you wanted to see me?"

Archmage Quan raised a finger as thick as his neck. She continued to read her book, not saying anything. After a few moments, she sighed, placing a hefty greatsword in it as a bookmark; it may have been a letter opener by her standards, it was hard for him to tell. She set the book on her desk, next to a man-sized fidget spinner.

She glared down at him with her cold, black eyes. "I wasn't expecting you until tomorrow."

The Wizard anxiously loosened his collar. "Well, I thought I'd come in as soon as possible to contest the results of the inspection."

Quan snorted derisively. "So, you don't think you deserve what you got?"

"I just think it was hastily performed." Shifting awkwardly, The Wizard looked around. Jeff was nowhere to be seen. "I don't feel I was prepared."

The Circle of Mages

"You can't be serious! We gave you almost an entire extra week to prepare."

"Um, well..." Pausing, The Wizard looked down; through the floor, he could see Jeff hurrying up the stairs. He sighed, unable to think of a response. "Hang on..." He sprinted down the stairs.

Quan sighed and returned to her book as he disappeared from view.

Jeff jumped as The Wizard materialized at his side. He managed to catch himself on the banister as he stumbled down a few steps.

"What's taking so long?" asked The Wizard.

Jeff's look of surprise was quickly replaced by one of indignation. He leaned over, catching his breath for a moment. "You just disappeared at the base of the stairs, asshole." He threw his arms up in exasperation. "I don't know how to do that!"

"Oh yeah..." The Wizard scratched his beard thoughtfully. "I suppose I forgot to mention: you need to close your eyes and think about where you'd like to go, then the stairs will teleport you there."

"Seriously? It's that easy? I've been walking for like five minutes!"

"It hasn't been that long." The Wizard rolled his eyes. "Besides, now you know. Come on, let's go." He stepped forward and appeared once more in Archmage Quan's office.

Jeff appeared a moment later. "Wow, that was weird." He looked down through the floor. "Why not just install an elevator?"

"They tried," said The Wizard, chuckling. "Too many collisions." He pointed to the myriad of floating platforms below.

"Who's this?" Tapping her fingers impatiently on the table, Archmage Quan gestured to Jeff with her off hand. "I don't have all day, and my office isn't a shelter for vagrants."

"He's not a vagrant. This is my new assistant; his name is Jeff."

"I wasn't talking about him." With a nasty sneer, Archmage Quan raised her eyebrows suggestively. "Last time I checked, you're not employed, and you don't have a home."

"What?" Although The Wizard did not know exactly what she was talking about, it made him quite nervous. "Look, fire me or not, I have a home. I paid off the mortgage on my tower years ago!"

"True, but you owe the Circle twice its value in fines."

43

Chapter Four

"What?!" As The Wizard contemplated the harsh reality of homelessness, his heart began to race frantically. He was perplexed; he could not recall ever being served with any fines. "Since when?"

"Since the report your previous assistant turned in last week." Smiling wickedly, Quan slid open the top drawer of her desk and pulled out an official-looking piece of paper. "According to her, you skimmed hundreds of sol from your research grants in order to procure various drugs, primarily cocaine."

"But I don't do that anymuch!" The Wizard grinned sheepishly.

Pursing her lips, Quan glared at him for a moment before clearing her throat. "Apparently, you also used a polymorph potion to dodge the draft during the war with Dardren."

"I told her that in confidence!" A betrayed look crossed The Wizard's face.

"Furthermore, you spent a great deal of circle resources on..." Pausing, Quan held up the paper, squinting facetiously. "*Traps...*" She shook her head slowly. "Traps for a homeless man you believed to be a spy sent by me."

"Well..." The Wizard could not think of an acceptable excuse.

Behind his back, Jeff smirked at him.

"Traps," Quan continued, "that didn't work. Traps that damaged your house beyond repair. Considering the state of it, and the extent of your fines, I'd say it's more than generous of us to accept it as collateral."

The Wizard's heart froze. He knew that Quan hated him, but he never expected her to come down on him so harshly. Without his tower, he would have nowhere to grow cannabis; without that, he would not even be able to afford drinks from *The Wizarding Hole*. Moreover, he would not have a place to sleep!

Although The Wizard did not like being subject to Quan's will, he knew he had no choice but to come to a compromise.

"Isn't there anything I could do?"

"Well..." Quan sat forward, acting like she was considering something on which her mind was clearly already made up. "There is one thing that could redeem you..."

"I'm listening..." The Wizard narrowed his eyes cautiously, wary that Quan was liable to lead him on.

The Circle of Mages

"If you could bring me one of the lost *Arcane Tomes*, I might consider leniency."

The Wizard's mouth fell open. He was completely stunned by this outlandish request.

"But seeing as the *Arcane Almanac* has only appeared in legends for the past four centuries, and the *Arcane Dictionary* is only a legend itself, I doubt you'll have any luck." Quan leaned back in her chair, smiling superciliously down at them.

The Wizard stood silently, gaping in disbelief. He could not fathom how he could possibly complete such a task. Jeff looked extremely uncomfortable.

"Well?" Cocking her head, Quan feigned a sweet smile. "Do you think you can do this small favor for me?"

Perturbed, The Wizard's mind wandered to the cocaine in his chest pocket. He wished he could sneak away and snort a line right away, as he was at a loss for how to deal with the situation at hand.

Frowning in uncertainty, Jeff stepped forward. "Hang on, don't you think you're asking a lot of the guy?"

"I'll ask what I need of any of my subjects." Smiling imperiously, Archmage Quan intertwined her fingers. "I care very little about the opinion of rubes such as yourself."

The Wizard raised his eyebrows furtively at Jeff. "Just drop it..." He looked up at Quan, smiling with exaggerated obsequiousness. His knuckles whitened. "Of course, I'll do my best. I only hope to satisfy this task!"

"I'm sure you do..." Quan rolled her eyes. "Now, if that's all, you are dismissed."

"Sure thing!" Bowing with exaggerated veneration, The Wizard double-crossed his fingers behind his back. "I'm on it!"

They turned to leave. As they walked to the stairs, Jeff looked at The Wizard. The expression The Wizard wore was one of both determination and despair. Stepping onto the staircase, they both appeared suddenly on the ground floor below. They traipsed slowly down the long, deep blue carpet, each lost in thought about the situation at hand.

Chapter Four

As they trudged dejectedly out through the grand doors of Circle Tower, an exuberant voice called out from nearby.

"How'd it go in there?" Fabulon was leaning against a nearby tree. "I heard from Perkins that the Archmage had it out for you." He looked concerned, but seemed rather oblivious to The Wizard's dismay. "I hope she didn't give it to you too hard."

"I don't want to talk about it…" Crossing his arms, The Wizard hung his head despondently.

"That bad, huh?" Banging his arm around The Wizard's shoulders, Fabulon knocked the breath out of him. "Sorry to hear that, buddy. I get it, the Archmage can be pretty harsh."

"Yeah…" The Wizard shrunk away from Fabulon. "It sucks." He ducked behind Jeff, slinking off.

As they slouched away, Fabulon waved cheerfully after them. "It sure does!"

"What's your problem with that guy anyway?" asked Jeff, a moment later.

"None of your business, that's what."

"Okay, well —"

Suddenly, The Wizard threw his arms up in exasperation. "It's just that he thinks he's such a great guy! He's always nosing into everyone's business, always trying to 'help', and everyone thinks he's *sooo* great for it! I mean, how would *you* feel if some arrogant bastard nosed into *your* life and tried to change everything?!"

"Umm…" Jeff shifted awkwardly. He could not have put it better himself.

As he plowed forward with his rant, it seemed The Wizard was completely oblivious to the irony of his previous statement. "Plus, he wears those hot pink robes everywhere, like they make him look cool. What is that? Why would anyone think that's okay?"

"I just really don't see what the big deal is," said Jeff. "He seems like a nice guy who genuinely cares about people, which is more than I can say about *some people*."

"Oh, that's just a facade." Scoffing, The Wizard waved his hand dismissively. "He acts all warm and fuzzy so everyone loves him, but inside he thinks he's better than all of them. He doesn't actually care how anyone else feels, so long as he looks good."

The Circle of Mages

"Jealousy is more powerful than the most potent of magicks," said Jeff. "That's what my dad says, anyway."

The Wizard glared at him.

As they neared The Wizard's street, it occurred to Jeff to discuss the circumstances of his employment, or potentially the lack thereof.

"So..." He looked down for a moment, before locking eyes with The Wizard's glare. "Since you didn't actually get fired, do I get paid for cleaning your house?"

Shaking his head, The Wizard laughed with exaggerated fervor. "Short answer: no. You won't be receiving any payment for *that*."

"Of course..."

"You will, however," continued The Wizard, with no regard for Jeff's disappointed expression, "receive the opportunity to assist me on my upcoming venture!"

Jeff was apprehensive. "What? You want me to help you find the *Arcane Dictionary*?"

"No, idiot, I have another plan. I'll talk you through it tomorrow; I have to work out the details first."

Shortly after sundown, they arrived back at The Wizard's tower. It seemed The Wizard was not entirely distraught by the day's events when he bid farewell to Jeff at the door. Jeff had tried to ask if he could come in for a drink of water, but The Wizard had already slammed the door in his face.

Chapter Five
Quan's Council

Late that night, the towering, shadowy figure of Archmage Quan was slinking silently down an alleyway near Circle Tower. She wore a plain set of brown robes, and a hood hung over her face, casting it in shadow. Although she was magically reduced to less than half her size, she still stood over eight feet tall. A canopy of lightly flaming branches arched overhead, illuminating the overgrown bramble below. At the far end of the alley, there stood a much shorter but similarly cloaked figure.

"Greetings, Archmage," said the shadowy figure, in a smarmy male voice. There was a faint touch of impatience to his tone. "I was expecting you almost three and a half minutes ago."

"I'm aware, Mr. Perkins." Quan's words pierced the air with the biting sting of fiery ire; after the day of deliberation she had dealt with, the last thing she had patience for was the impatience of an inferior officer. "I was late because the work *I* do is sometimes important enough to excuse lateness."

"Of course..." Perkins bowed submissively.

The two of them covertly made their way onto the main road. They cautiously sidled down the edge of the walk, glancing subtly around as they entered the yard of an eerie, ivy-covered cobblestone manor. There were no lights on in the house, aside from a single barred window to the basement. As they approached the front door, they each looked back to make sure they were not being followed.

Quan's Council

Raising her eyebrows implicitly at Perkins, Quan gestured to an inconspicuous fern in a terracotta pot beside the door. "You first."

After a moment's hesitation, Perkins plunged his hand into the foliage. The blades of the fern quickly tensed up, biting down on his wrist as though they were the teeth of a vicious predator. Chomping ferociously, the plant stretched into a straw and slurped down Perkins' entire body as though he were solid soup.

There was a muffled thud below.

Reluctantly, Quan followed suit. As the foliage of the plant ruthlessly devoured her wrist, she was wrenched into a vortex of vegetation.

She found herself on the floor of a dank, musty cellar. Torchlight illuminated the crackling patterns of grout between the rough hewn cobblestones at her feet. A series of splintery wooden panels lined the walls; dusty cobwebs mantled the borders and spaces in between.

Although her size was reduced, Quan still had to hunch over to keep her head from hitting the ceiling.

The room's decor could only be described as *"Dominatrix Depot"*. There was a rack on one wall holding all manner of whips, chains, hooks, and shackles, many of which seemed to have been used recently; a leather-upholstered torture rack sat in the corner, with scratch marks up the sides; several mannequins were lined up in the opposite corner, wearing all manner of gimp suits, harnesses, gags, cuffs, blindfolds, and even a hot pink adult diaper; there was even a set of impressively sized genital stocks by the door.

There were cloaked hooded figures standing in a circle around her. They each wore the same dark brown robes that she wore. Their faces were all hidden by drooping hoods. One of them was extremely big and burly; one was petite and feminine; one was tall and gangling; finally, one was slumped over with a severe hunch. Everyone was eyeing the paraphilia paraphernalia uncomfortably, although there seemed to be an unspoken agreement not to say anything about it.

Quan stood up slowly, shaken up and mildly bruised. She may have been hurt worse, if not for Perkins happening to cushion her impact. He lay on the ground, battered and unconscious, with blood quickly draining from his compacted nose.

Chapter Five

"Damn it, can someone do something with that idiot?" Quan waved her hand impatiently towards Perkins' limp body. As she dusted herself off, a sparse haze of spores dispersed throughout the cellar, sprinkling the onlookers with debris. "I thought I ordered that infernal fern to be replaced with a trap door! Gnomish enchantments are so ludicrous… Plus, it looks very drab on my front porch. I mean, who pots a fern?"

"It's on the list, I'll mark it as urgent!" said a cheerful male voice, coming from the hulking, hooded figure. He effortlessly dragged Perkins into the only empty corner. Pulling a disproportionately diminutive notepad and pen from his chest pocket, he delicately jotted down a reminder.

"Thank you, my dear Fabulon." Smiling coyly, Quan twirled her ponytail in her fingers. "How could I *ever* be upset at *you?*"

There was a collective groan of disgust from the circle of unfortunate onlookers.

Shifting awkwardly, Fabulon scratched the back of his hood. His gaze wandered to the buffet of bondage, and he shuddered uneasily. He resumed his place in the circle as Quan found hers. Shunting the hunchbacked sorcerer aside, she sat cross-legged directly next to her delicious man-candy. As she gingerly positioned her ample buttocks beside him, she not-so-subtly thumped spankingly upon his bottom.

Archmage Quan's conduct had always made Fabulon feel embarrassed and objectified; however, he was far too timid to say anything about it, so he merely averted his gaze bashfully and tried to pretend it was not happening.

Everyone in the room was extremely uncomfortable. You could practically palpate the tension.

One of the hooded figures coughed conspicuously after a few moments. "So…" said a soft female voice, "why am I here…?"

"Ah, of course." Quan ceased gawking at Fabulon and addressed the room. "I trust you've all had time to become acquainted with our newest member: Samantha."

"Hi!" Waving shyly at the others, Samantha lowered her hood to reveal her face. Her brilliant blue eyes were widened apprehensively as she attempted to avert her gaze from the macabre myriad of masochist delights.

The cloaked figures all nodded. The hunchbacked one grunted disapprovingly.

Quan's Council

"Yes, we have," said the hunchbacked figure in a wet, raspy male voice. He sounded markedly annoyed. "And I still don't see why she's here. She's a novice magi with no prospects! Isn't that why we sent her to work for that idiot in the first place? Look, she doesn't even know the rules." He gestured angrily towards her face. "She removed her hood! We agreed originally that all of these meetings would be anonymous."

"Yes, Horner, you already made your concerns clear at our *last* meeting, when you met *him*." Quan gestured to the lanky hooded figure.

"Besides," said a gruff male voice from beneath the lanky figure's hood, "when I joined up, ya all introduced yerselves by name!" The man laughed, shaking his head. "And Fabulon told me that ya only came up with that anonymity clause so no one 'as to look at your 'ideously disfigured face, *Horner*." He enunciated the name with a spiteful emphasis.

Horner waved his index finger in protest. "Now, listen here, Dealah, —"

"Enough!" Quan stomped her foot down as hard as she could; cracks formed in the cobblestones beneath her feet, shaking the chains on the wall. "We have business to attend to. Now, to answer your question..." She turned to Samantha, smiling deviously. "We have been monitoring your ex-instructor carefully, but have been unsuccessful in the acquisition of certain information; this is where you come in: we would like you to tell us everything you know about The Wizard. Leave nothing out."

"Really...? *Why?*" Raising an eyebrow, Samantha narrowed her eyes incredulously. "I can assure you that none of the information that moron has is of value to anyone!"

"That's pretty much what I said!" Chuckling to himself, Dealah shook his head. "All I eva did was sell the guy coke! Then *these* goons show up..." He gestured to the others. "They accuse me of *allegedly* 'illegally' sellin' 'stolen' drugs, and tell me I'd go to jail 'less I help 'em put this Wizard guy away. Shame, too... 'e's my best customer! But what can ya do...?"

He shrugged and looked up, rolling his beady, bloodshot eyes. His hood fell back, revealing a head of tangled dreadlocks; his face was covered by the same indigo bandana as when The Wizard had stopped by his window.

"Right..." Raising an eyebrow skeptically, Samantha looked up at Archmage Quan. "What's this *really* about? Is this some kind of practical joke?"

51

Chapter Five

"I'm afraid not," said Quan. "Though he may not seem it, The Wizard is a powerful sorcerer who may hold many valuable secrets."

"You *can't* be serious!" Samantha rolled her eyes. "The man's a joke!"

"Hey, watch it!" Fabulon crossed his arms defensively. A scowl could be made out under the shadow of his hood. "That's my *best friend* you're talking about..."

Quan's stomach tightened. When she spoke, there was a quiver of envy to her voice. "*Anyway,* We believe that The Wizard knows the location of a cache of priceless magical artifacts left to him by his father; the most valuable of these artifacts is an essentially limitless reservoir of arcane knowledge: the *Arcane Dictionary.*"

"Are you serious?" Samantha's eyes widened.

Gritting his teeth, Horner scoffed spitefully. "You've *got* to stop asking that... We've got better things to do than playing stupid tricks on simpletons."

Samantha did not respond, and simply shot him a vicious look of revulsion.

"That's astounding!" she said to Archmage Quan. "I never would have thought his dad would trust him with something like that." Smirking, she snickered irreverently. "Although surely he doesn't know what they are worth. In all those months I worked for him, I saw him sell hundreds of sol worth of his father's old equipment to *that guy* —" she pointed harshly to Dealah "— in exchange for *stolen cocaine!*"

"*Allegedly* stolen!" Glowering at her, Dealah huffed proudly and crossed his arms. "I run a perfectly legitimate cocaine dealership; I'm licensed by the Bureau of Alcohol, Tobacco, and Cocaine!"

"That's not even a real place." Fabulon cocked his head bemusedly. He leaned towards Archmage Quan, whispering, "is it?"

Quan shook her head.

Samantha cleared her throat loudly. "*My point is* that he is a drug addicted moron. If he knew he had anything that valuable in his possession, he would have sold it by now and retired to live on Cocaine Mountain!"

"Okay, no way *that* is a real place..." muttered Fabulon.

Groaning, Horner threw his arms up impatiently. "See? I told you she'd be useless! Just like the best *this one* can tell us —" he gestured angrily to

Dealah "— is that The Wizard's favorite book is *A Thousand Ways to Get High!*"

"You know..." Smirking, Dealah pointed between Samantha and Horner. "You two actually 'ave a lot in common!"

It was hard to tell which of them groaned in deeper disgust.

"I see what you are saying, Samantha," said Archmage Quan, "but I think it's rash to rush to such judgement. I've known The Wizard since we were apprentices together." She cringed in disgust as she recalled the unpleasant memory of her apprenticeship. "His status back then was not only due to nepotism; he is actually capable of harnessing greater magical power than I, although his ability to control it is questionable."

Horner snorted. "Questionable at best. I'd say nonexistent."

Quan ignored him. "When his dad was alive, he was very different from The Wizard you knew. He actually tried back then." Scoffing, she shook her head. "Although, I think he only did it to impress his dad; soon as *he* disappeared, *everything* changed."

"Ugh..." muttered a shaky voice. Perkins arose from his corner and staggered towards the group. He looked perplexed and probably concussed. "What happened...?"

She ignored him as well. "We believe that The Wizard knows the location of his family's hidden artifacts, but that he does not know what they are. We've already searched his tower on several occasions when he was blacked out, and at this point we're sure they're hidden in a secret secondary location."

"I wouldn't know anything about that," said Samantha. "He would sometimes disappear for days and I'd no idea where he'd go."

"Did you land on me?" Perkins was gingerly rubbing his head. His left eye seemed to keep winking of its own accord.

"As far as we know," said Quan, "The Wizard's only correspondents outside the Circle are his brother, his drug dealer, and his bartender. Do you know if he ever associated with anyone else?"

"She doesn't know anything!" Horner waved his hand dismissively at Samantha.

"I'm going to go lie down again..." Shuffling back to the corner, Perkins collapsed to the ground.

Chapter Five

"I know his brother has a teenage son," said Samantha, "but I suppose you already knew that."

"Obviously…" muttered Horner.

Quan sighed. "Very well, Now, there is still one other way you could be helpful to us, Samantha."

"I'm listening…"

"Horner, Perkins, and I have been working on a certain project for a very long time. For reasons that don't bear going into, we can't discuss the details with you; however, what we can tell you is that for our work to continue, we need to discover the location of these artifacts."

Samantha nodded. "Okay, makes sense."

"We couldn't get any information out of him, so we brought on Fabulon to gather intel; unfortunately, it turned out that The Wizard hates Fabulon almost as much as the three of us."

"Hey, that's not true!" said Fabulon, holding up his hands defensively. "You just don't get our friendship. When he teases me, it means he likes me!"

Everyone ignored him.

"And *this* idiot is nearly as useless as his bartender!" Quan motioned vaguely to Dealah, who simply shrugged and grinned stupidly. "And I didn't even bother to blackmail the bartender into coming to these meetings, so what does that tell you? But, I digress... Anyway, you've already worked for him before, he trusts you. If you could reinstate yourself as his assistant, and —"

"Hold up, let me just stop you there." Pausing, Samantha clutched her stomach with laughter. "I'm sorry, Archmage Quan, but I wouldn't spend another minute with that man if the fate of the world hung in the balance."

Quan raised her eyebrows. "You're sure? If you do this, I can assure you that you'll be rewarded with tenure in the Circle."

"Not a chance in hell."

"Very well." Turning to Fabulon, Quan batted her eyelashes with a flirtatious simper. "Darling, would you mind please walking young Samantha home?"

Quan's Council

"Uh, sure..." said Fabulon. He had asked her to stop calling him that many times, and it clearly made him feel uncomfortable. "Let's go, Samantha."

Samantha furrowed her brow. "Wait... that's it?"

Archmage Quan did not answer. In a huff, Samantha turned to follow Fabulon up the stairs.

"Can I go too?" asked Dealah, shifting his feet uncomfortably.

"Oh, you're still here?" Quan was staring distractedly at Fabulon's butt as he walked up the stairs. She waved offhandedly at Dealah. "Go on, get out."

Dealah sauntered off after Fabulon and Samantha. Horner followed him, eyeing him suspiciously. A few moments later, Horner came back down the stairs, wearing a disgruntled expression.

"I really don't think we should invite riffraff like that to these meetings," he said. "It's bad enough you still have Fabulon around; he's a liability, we can't even talk about our full plans when he's around."

"Relax, Horner. Fabulon may be a glorious adonis with a heart of gold, but he's not smart enough to figure out what we're really planning. As far as he knows, all we're after are the artifacts."

"As long as it stays that way... You know that if he finds out what our plans are for The Wizard, he'd betray us all. He thinks they're friends!"

"Don't worry, I'll make sure he never finds out what really happened to his 'best friend'." Quan smiled sinisterly. "What we really have to worry about is making sure that coke addicted dipshit doesn't catch on to our plans. If all goes well, he'll lead us straight to the cache, and we won't need any more help."

Horner nodded. "What should we do with *him*?"

He gestured to Perkins, who was still passed out in the corner.

"Just leave him here overnight, I don't have time to carry him home again."

Meanwhile, Fabulon was walking Samantha down the front steps of Horner's manor. The light from the enchanted trees cast their faces in a flickering glow. As they left, it was clear that they were dubious about the situation.

"Do you get the feeling they're not telling us everything?" asked Samantha, as they stepped onto the street.

Fabulon nodded. "Only every time they invite me to one of these meetings."

"How long has this been going on?"

"Well, I've only been there for the last few meetings, but apparently this has been going on for months."

Samantha cocked her head inquisitively. "Do they always discuss The Wizard?"

"As far as I know, yeah." Fabulon nibbled on his bottom lip. "I just really hope they're not planning anything sinister with him. Life would not be the same without him."

Samantha laughed. "You've got that right! It'd be a lot better! Honestly, I don't give a flying fuck about that idiot, I'm just worried about what their motivations may be. I mean, if this is so important, why wouldn't they bring it before the Circle Council?"

"I've often wondered the same thing," said Fabulon. "She goes out of her way to avoid them knowing of her plans, it's very suspicious."

"Tell me about it… I have a bad feeling about all this."

"I'll tell you what," said Fabulon. "I'll do some poking around. Archmage Quan trusts me, so she might let her guard down. I've gotta make sure I've got my best friend's back!"

"About that…" Cocking her head at him, Samantha raised an eyebrow. "I've been meaning to ask: why do you even like him? He's just about the most insufferable person I've ever met, aside from maybe Horner."

Frowning, Fabulon waved his hand dismissively. "You just don't get him. He's a complicated man; he acts outwardly tough, but once he lets you inside, there is a deep sea of sorrow."

"And has he *ever* let you in?"

"Well, no… not yet…." Scratching his head, Fabulon grinned sheepishly. "But I can just see it in him, you know what I mean?"

"Can't say that I do." Samantha rolled her eyes. "By the way, what the hell is with all that BDSM equipment in the Archmage's basement?"

"I don't wanna talk about it…"

Fabulon walked Samantha to her house. She lived near the edge of town, so it took awhile for him to get home after he dropped her off. As he entered the foyer of his house, he noticed a heart shaped note on the table by the door. Without even having to open it, he knew it was yet another note from Quan saying her back door was unlocked if he wanted to come over. Heaving a tired sigh, he crumpled it up and threw it in the bin with the others.

Chapter Six
The Master Plan

The following afternoon, Jeff was awoken by a sudden and violent onslaught of shaking. Blinking lethargically, he slowly realized what he was seeing.

The Wizard stood over his bed, panting uncontrollably, eyes alight with the cocainated fervor of a man without sleep. He was wearing the same clothes and deep blue robes as when Jeff had last seen him. It appeared he had climbed in through the window, as it had been severely melted and was slowly dripping down the wall.

Jeff's room was relatively small, with light blue walls and white carpet. Everything was neatly organized, from the shelf of comic books to the curio cabinet full of plushies. Jeff lay on his stomach in a twin sized bed, under a comforter patterned with the orgasm faces of various female anime characters.

"What's going on?" Rolling over, Jeff cocked his head at The Wizard.

The Wizard grinned exuberantly. "Good news, Jeffery!"

"Oh no, not this again…" As Jeff sat up, he was already weary of this day.

"I'm about to score big, Jeffery!"

Jeff raised an eyebrow. "How much cocaine are you on?"

"I have a plan, Jeffery." Sitting next to Jeff, The Wizard placed an arm around his shoulder; with a flourish, he gestured out the window, towards Circle Tower on the horizon. "Pretty soon, we're gonna be rich!"

"Care to elaborate?"

The Master Plan

"I present to you an opportunity, Jeffery," said The Wizard, rubbing his hands together deviously. "An opportunity to participate in the ultimate heist to end all heists. After *this* heist, we're never gonna need to pull another heist again."

"Stop saying heist. What on Notearth are you talking about?"

"*The heist*, Jeffery!" With an emphatic flourish, The Wizard stood up, pumping both fists excitedly. "We're gonna be rich!"

Jeff stood up and walked to the door. "Dad! The homeless guy's back!"

"No!" Running to the door and slamming it, The Wizard frantically shushed Jeff. "Your dad can't know about this. He'll want a cut, and I'm not about to pony up the repayment he wants for that stupid hunk of wood."

"You mean our antique front door? Which, by the way, we had to take off its hinges and throw in a dumpster. What kind of adhesive did you use, anyway? It burns skin whenever it gets wet!"

"So don't get it wet!"

"It's the *front door!*" Jeff waved his hands angrily. "It rained last night, and now the mailman is threatening to sue us for 'poisoning the mail slot'!"

"Don't even trip; I know a great lawyer for that."

"What's going on?" Justin had appeared at the door, looking puzzled. His confusion quickly flared into anger when he saw the melted window. "Oh, you have got to be kidding me!" He turned to The Wizard, scowling. "You're paying for this, damn it."

"I'll pay for it after the big heist," said The Wizard. "I just need to borrow your son for an important project."

"You've got to be..." Justin's eyes narrowed. "You're back on the rocks, aren't you?"

"He's what?" asked Jeff.

Justin threw his arms in the air. "He's smoking crack!"

"I don't have time for this!" Before either of them could reply, The Wizard grabbed them both by the neck.

Both men collapsed to the ground. Their eyes were open, but glassy and unresponsive.

When Jeff awoke, it took him a moment to realize where he was. Looking around the room, he saw that he was in a dim, dingy bar. He was sitting

59

Chapter Six

alone at a table in the corner. Although the windows were caked in grime, he could tell it was now nighttime.

The Wizard sat at the bar, deep in conversation with a scruffy, blonde bartender. They each had an oversized glass of dark alcohol. As Jeff sat up, the bartender pointed in his direction, whispering something to The Wizard, who laughed derisively while staring at Jeff.

"Oh, good, you're awake!" said The Wizard. "Now I don't have to keep such a close eye on Chris…"

The one other patron in the bar looked up from a vividly multicolored newspaper he was reading, entitled *Le Illustreaux Quackette*, before resuming his covert public masturbation; Chris was aware of this activity, but did not care.

The Wizard motioned for Jeff to come join him at the bar. Annoyed and perplexed, Jeff sat up slowly and ambled to the bar. He squinted suspiciously at The Wizard as he sat down, trying to figure out what events had transpired while he was unconscious.

"Hey there, handsome!" Leaning forward enthusiastically, Chris began to rap. "The name's Chris, and I don't miss; would I be remiss if I gave you a kiss? Jeffery, can't you see, I want thee. Fill me with glee, this is my plea, I'm on my knee, set my pants free, and get jiggy with me!"

Jeff did not know what to say to this.

"Daaaaamn!" The Wizard nodded in approval. "That's almost twice the rhymes you used when we first met!"

"Well, what can I say?" Blushing, Chris giggled playfully. "I can see why you picked him. He's quite the little treasure."

"He's my nephew, you pervert; I picked him for no such reason!"

"Whatever you say!" Chris subtly winked at Jeff. "But I know what I like."

The Wizard snorted. "Yeah, we all do. You made it abundantly clear that day we were waiting by the high school for that coke dealer to get out of class."

"Which time?" Grinning, Chris downed his drink.

"What's going on, anyway?" shouted Jeff. "Forget this weirdo; why am I here to begin with?!"

The Master Plan

"Right, I almost forgot. You should do a line." The Wizard gestured to a pile of unambiguous cocaine on the bar.

"No thanks." Scowling, Jeff crossed his arms. "I just want to know why the hell you drugged me and dragged me to this bar!"

"Okay, first of all, I didn't drug you; I hexxed you."

Chris nodded in agreement. "Quite the distinction."

"Are you serious?!" Jeff banged his fist harshly on the bar. "What does it matter how you did it? Just answer the question! Why the hell did you knock me unconscious and drag me to this bar?!"

"You know, I didn't *knock* anything —"

"Damn it!" yelled Jeff. "Why did you bring me here?!"

"Okay, geez..." The Wizard grimaced. "The reason you're here is to plan for the heist. Your dad was distracting me, so I had to rectify the situation."

"So you chose to curse me?!"

"Hex!" The Wizard spoke with misplaced indignation.

"They're the same thing!"

"Look, it doesn't matter —"

"Doesn't it?"

The Wizard rolled his eyes. "No, it does not. It's all semantics. Who hexxed who isn't important. What matters is why you're here."

"Yeah, of course," said Jeff with vehement, venomous sarcasm, "to '*plan for the heist*', right?"

"Yes, so stop wasting time."

"Okay, fine." Giving in, Jeff decided to humor his uncle's insanity, and listen to his presumably half-baked and doubtlessly fully-stoned scheme. He figured it at least might be somewhat entertaining. "Tell me, what exactly are we 'heisting'?"

"I thought you'd never ask!" The Wizard grinned enthusiastically. "We're gonna break into the artifact vault underneath Circle Tower, and steal the most powerful magical staff in existence: the *Chronomancer's Continuum*."

"Wow... now *that* is what can only be described as a heist..." Shaking his head, Jeff laughed with blatant derision.

"Right?" Clearly oblivious to Jeff's ridicule, The Wizard hastily chopped a hefty line of cocaine. He leaned forward and snorted it all up one nostril; he repeated this for the other nostril.

Chapter Six

With renewed vigor, The Wizard leapt up and hooted gleefully. He began pacing back and forth, wringing his hands greedily. "If I got my hands on that scepter, could you imagine what I could go back and invent?! The magic wand! The crystal ball! The internet! The possibilities are limitless! I could get even richer than those snobby MacRoyalles!"

Jeff gaped in utter disbelief of his uncle's derangement. "Those are all already real inventions, dude... You can't just steal other people's ideas!"

"Do you not understand how time travel works?" The Wizard scoffed. "I'm going back before anyone had those ideas!" He paused, taking a long sip of his drink. "Last time I checked, something has to *exist* for it to be 'stolen', *Jeff*!"

"Sure, whatever..." It was difficult for Jeff to fathom where The Wizard got these ideas; the only conceivable answer was cocaine, and lots of it. "So how exactly do you plan to perpetrate this... 'heist'?"

"A magician never reveals his secret, Jeffery." The Wizard wagged a finger at Jeff. After a moment of glassy-eyed contemplation, he suddenly began to laugh maniacally. "However, *I* am a wizard, so I'll just tell you..."

Reaching into his pocket, he pulled out a large key with a complex array of twisted teeth. "This is a copy I made of my dad's master key. It will open any door, technically in existence, but most importantly in the tower."

"Okay..." Furrowing his brow, Jeff scratched his goatee thoughtfully. "So... if you already had this key, why not pull this 'heist' before?"

"Honestly? I made good money working for the Circle up until my dad's old research ran dry a few months ago. I've been thinking about this for a while now, and Quan pushed me to it when she threatened to take away my tower. Now I have no choice." He absentmindedly ran his fingers through his hair.

While he said this, The Wizard made a series of furtive and unusual gestures with his hand. Jeff assumed this meant nothing, and was simply a peripheral effect of the cocaine.

"Can I get you a drink?" asked Chris suddenly, with autistic overintensity.
Jeff was taken aback by the jarring request. "Yeah, sure..."
Chris began to mix a complex cocktail of colorful alcohols.

The Master Plan

"Listen…" Grabbing Jeff's shoulder, The Wizard turned his head so they were eye to eye. "This is the opportunity of a lifetime; you're lucky to be included in this!"

While Jeff was distracted, Chris covertly pulled out a small pouch from his pocket; he reached in and pulled out a small pinch of opalescent powder, snorting it before pouring the rest of the pouch into Jeff's drink.

"Oh yeah, I sure feel lucky." Jeff rolled his eyes. "Magically knocked out and dragged to a shady bar to plan for a felony; *aren't I just happy*?!"

Chris passed Jeff a most unusual drink. It had a wild tie-dye pattern swirling throughout it, and put off a strong, sickly-sweet odor; paying no heed to any of this, Jeff immediately downed it in frustration.

"Look, I don't want anything to do with your 'heist', okay?!" As Jeff said this, his head had already begun to swirl. He paused, beginning to fade in and out of focus as he struggled to remember what he was angry about. "Or do I…? What were we talking about again?"

"Thanks, Chris, I think that'll do quite nicely." The Wizard smiled insidiously. After snorting the remainder of cocaine from the bar, he grabbed Jeff by the wrist and began to lead him to the door. He cackled nefariously. "Come on, my friend, we've got a heist to commit."

The Wizard dragged his freshly drugged nephew out of *The Wizarding Hole*. One of them mentally ill and the other high on fairy dust, they headed towards Circle Tower with big plans cooking in each of their heads.

Chapter Seven
Shenanitwins

As they neared Circle Tower, it was shortly after sundown, and the pubs and restaurants of the Sorcerous District were bustling with magi fresh off the job.

A few blocks away from the Regal Roundabout, The Wizard pulled Jeff aside. They crouched in the bushes between a nearby tavern and an ornate building bearing a sign entitled *First Church of Astrolotology.* As Jeff began to giggle and ask what was about to happen, The Wizard placed a finger on his lips.

"This is the most popular bar around for wizards and whatnot," said The Wizard, gesturing to the bustling bar next to them. The sign read *Luncheons and Flagons.* "This is where we're gonna find the dumbest, drunkest wizards."

"I already found the dumbest, drunkest Wizard." Laughing raucously, Jeff pounded his fists on The Wizard's chest.

"Just shut up and follow my lead." Grabbing Jeff's wrist, The Wizard dragged him into the bar.

The inside of the bar was quite a bit larger than *The Wizarding Hole,* although it was not much cleaner. There were rows of tables, packed with patrons. On the shelves behind the bar, there was every liquor The Wizard could imagine, from scotch to creme de coca. Overhead, there was a magnificent, crystal globe chandelier. Despite the bustling patronage, the

64

only employee seemed to be an exceptionally tall gnome, standing behind the bar in a trench coat.

The room was indeed full of the dumbest, drunkest wizards around. No one noticed either Jeff or The Wizard as they entered. A man was currently tap dancing on a table in the center of the room, being cheered on by a crowd of robed beings of all breeds and creeds. There was a disproportionately high amount of dwarves, the most raucous and also most bearded of which was the aforementioned center of attention.

Pulling Jeff over to the bar, The Wizard sat him down on a stool. Staring vacantly and grinning eagerly, Jeff raised his hands and began to absentmindedly squeeze some presumably erotic hallucination; he bit his bottom lip tightly, blushing bashfully.

The Wizard groaned in disgust; he had not expected Jeff to react this way to such a mild overdose of fairy dust.

"Hey bartender, can I get a drink!" The Wizard waved to the exceptionally tall gnome behind the bar.

The gnome grinned. "The name's Knorpe!"

"And the name's Knippe!" squeaked an identical voice from below.

The gnome removed his trench coat. It quickly became clear why he appeared so tall: it was two gnomes, one standing atop the other. They were identical, from their silver hair to their red and white striped vests and corduroy trousers; the only difference was that the top gnome, Knorpe, had mutton chops, and the bottom gnome, Knippe, had a handlebar mustache.

Knippe leapt abruptly onto the bar, tossing Knorpe onto his ass. As Knippe bowed suavely, Knorpe reached onto the bar and attempted to grab his ankles.

Expecting this, Knippe leapt gracefully, spinning through the air; he grabbed a bottle each of the most high end rum, whiskey, and vodka, balancing the median of which on his head as he sailed smoothly down. His feet landed where Knorpe's testicles had been only moments before.

"May I get you a drink?" asked Knippe in a silky voice, balancing the bottles he held on the tips of his index fingers. He winked cheerfully, kicking back at his twin.

Chapter Seven

Knorpe took advantage of the uncoordinated back kicks of his twin to throw him off his balance. Grabbing one of Knippe's ankles, he pulled vigorously.

Temporarily losing his balance, Knippe lost his grip on the bottles, especially the one on his head. As they sailed through the air, Knorpe ran frantically beneath them, balancing each bottle upon his head in a precarious stack. He swayed and sweated as Knippe stood up, cocking his eyebrows mischievously.

Knippe grabbed the bottommost of the three bottles of liquor, namely rum, causing the other two to topple treacherously onto Knorpe's head. He swung the bottle of rum savagely at Knorpe's crotch.

Knorpe narrowly dodged a blow to his balls. Catching the other two perilously plummeting potations, Knorpe nastily knocked Knippe over the noggin.

Knippe's eyes glazed over with the vacancy of a gnome concussed.

"Sorry for the wait," bellowed Knorpe boisterously, bowing bombastically. It was almost as though he only said it so loud to keep up with this stupid alliteration scheme.

Knippe boorishly bumbled onto his boots, bashing his brother over the brain.

"Okay, this is getting ridiculous!" yelled The Wizard, pounding his fist on the bar. He did not have any patience for such shenanigans, lest he be involved in the act. This was getting stupid, even by his standards. This was not even good writing. "Can I just get a drink? Literally anything works, as long as it's not wacky, daft, or cockamamie!"

"Fine!" Both gnomes simultaneously crossed their arms and pouted their lips.

"Nobody gets us…" said Knorpe, grabbing a couple of argyle grails from beneath the bar; he filled each goblet with a not-so-generous amount of ice.

"You're telling me," said Knippe. He spoke unusually quickly, almost as though the two of them had rehearsed this bit ahead of time, and he was impatient to get through it. He filled each goblet with an even-less-generous amount of rum.

The Wizard nudged Jeff in the arm. "This is why I don't come here."

Shenanitwins

Knippe and Knorpe stuck their tongues out at him. After passing the two men their drinks, an ambiguous one of the diminutive doppelgangers perched precariously upon the other's shoulders, ambling unsteadily away.

Sighing, The Wizard grabbed his drink. He had had quite enough antics for one evening, and far less than enough alcohol. He downed the disappointingly diluted drink.

"Despite how often the drinks are free due to employee incompetence," said The Wizard, shaking his head in frustration, "it's not worth the employee annoyance."

He gestured to the two gnomes, who were now deeply engrossed in an attention contest; one of them banged wildly on a pair of bongo drums while the other yodeled clamorously. They were overshadowed, however, by the tap dancing dwarf in the center of the room, who was now juggling as well.

Looking over at Jeff, The Wizard saw that he was seemingly not aware of anything transpiring before him. Glassy-eyed and grinning foolishly, Jeff continued to grope enthusiastically at imaginary but presumably sumptuous breasts.

The Wizard rolled his eyes disdainfully. Making sure Jeff was adequately unaware, he slipped a small flask of sputtering red liquid into Jeff's drink.

"Here." He passed Jeff the steaming, bubbling, and occasionally sparking drink. "Drink this, quick. Make sure to make a big deal out of it, okay?"

Without paying heed to The Wizard's devious tone and expression, Jeff quickly downed the dubious brew before him. Steam began rising out of Jeff's mouth as his tongue began to boil.

Quickly snapping out of his blissful drug fantasies and into the harsh reality of being poisoned, Jeff began to scream in agony. Everyone in the bar turned and stared at him in shock; a few of them looked sober enough to be concerned.

As Jeff continued to screech and writhe in agonizing pain, The Wizard slipped into the crowd. Secretly scoping out the quality of the bargoers' apparel, he attempted to determine which would be the ideal victim of larcenous legerdemain.

He noticed a proportionately fat coin purse on the belt of a nearby obese dwarf; he subtly swiped it, subduing the dwarf's potential suspicions by

Chapter Seven

cursing away his consciousness. No one even noticed as the chubby chump collapsed to the floor; everyone was too distracted by Jeff's ongoing anguish.

"Damn, I'll have what he's *not* having!" Slapping Jeff firmly on the back, The Wizard grinned at the twin bartenders. "How about a round to cleanse all our pallets of any sympathy for this loser! It's on me!"

He reached into the stolen wallet and threw an impressive pile of gold coins onto the bar. The two gnomes poured several dozen shots of various liquors, passing them to everyone in the room. Knippe even passed Jeff a double shot, patting him on the back sympathetically.

The Wizard held up his shot glass. "A toast, to my unfortunate associate here!" As he said this, he subtly reached into the front pocket of his robe, pulling out a sack of the same opalescent powder with which he had drugged Jeff.

There were still four drinks on the bar: there was one for Jeff; one for the unconscious dwarf that so many had carelessly stepped upon; the other two drinks belonged to a pair of sorcerers, a male and a female, that had snuck away into the same bathroom a few minutes earlier. The Wizard slipped a sizable pinch of the fairy dust into the remaining drinks, before downing one of them.

About a minute later, the two magi emerged from the bathroom; the woman was scowling, and the man's face was bright red. Whatever had happened in there had not gone well. They both clearly needed a drink, which was just what The Wizard needed for his plan to work. He pointed them to the spiked shots awaiting them on the bar, which they immediately drank.

A moment later, Jeff finally worked up the strength to speak. "Why the hell did you make me drink that?"

"I needed a distraction." The Wizard raised his eyebrows meaningfully at Jeff. "Now calm down, you've made a big enough deal already."

Knippe threw aside his bongo drums. "You know, if you wanted a distraction, you could have always asked us!"

"Besides," said Knorpe, gesturing to the tap dancing dwarf, "I think they were already distracted by that attention hog."

The Wizard cocked his head. "You two saw what I was doing?"

They both leaned in close to The Wizard. "Of course!"

68

Shenanitwins

"We always monitor the shenanigan levels in our fine establishment," said Knippe, grinning proudly.

Snapping his fingers, Knorpe pointed at The Wizard. "And we've gotta say, as fellow tomfooliers, we admire your misconduct!"

"Stop changing the subject!" Jeff banged his fist on the table. "Don't expect me to let that shit slide!"

"Look, bro, you've got to chill out. Here." The Wizard slid the final drugged drink towards Jeff. "Why don't you drink this?"

"For any infinite number of reasons! Why would I?!" It seemed Jeff was a lot more aware of his surroundings than he had been previously.

Glancing at each other, the gnomes grinned. "Perhaps *we* can be of service!"

Knorpe leapt over Knippe, spinning in midair and landing on Jeff's head. Before Jeff could react, Knorpe wrapped his legs around his neck from behind. The gnome bent backwards, holding Jeff's mouth open. Knippe then grabbed the drink and threw it in Jeff's face.

"What the hell?!" Blinking liquor from his eyes, Jeff attempted to shake off the gnome. "Fuck off!"

Once again flipping gracefully over Jeff's head, Knorpe landed on the bar with a bow and a flourish. Knippe stuck his tongue out at Jeff and flipped him off.

At this point, Jeff was quickly succumbing to the second wind of fairy dust. He wondered why the two cats he saw in front of him were on two legs, and why they had clothes and beards. He turned to The Wizard and mumbled, "I'm ready for the green."

"Damn, he's shitfaced…" The Wizard raised his eyebrows in surprise. "I must have given him mine."

"No problem, we've got more!" Winking, Knorpe reached under the bar and pulled out a bundle of angry looking fairies tied up with a thick rubber band. "Want to go in the back with us and get proper?"

"Our indentured boy will take care of business here while we attend to business back there!" Knippe gestured to a young Kobold passed out under the sink.

Chapter Seven

"I'd love to get proper," said The Wizard, "but I've got a big heist tonight. Although, I do like that phrase: 'getting proper' is a great term for getting fucked up. I'm definitely gonna start using that."

"Ooooooh!" Both gnomes' eyes lit up with gleeful exuberance.

"We *looove* heists!" Knorpe grinned so wide that his wisdom teeth showed.

"Can we come? Can we?" Pouting his lips, Knippe batted his eyelashes kittenishly. They seemed to magically grow four or five times their usual length.

"Uh, sorry… I don't think there is enough treasure to go around." The Wizard was lying; he did not like to share.

"Oh, we don't care about the treasure," said Knorpe.

"Yeah, we're just in it for the feist of the heist!" Knippe beamed with gleeful anticipation.

They were also lying.

"I don't think so…" said The Wizard, averting his eyes.

"Oh, come on!" Holding up the bundle of fairies, Knorpe wiggled his eyebrows. He flicked one of them in the face, causing a large cloud of dust to poof up; this showed that they were good shit. "You know you want to!"

The gnome had made The Wizard an offer he could not refuse. "Okay, fine… But don't touch any of my treasure! You can steal the shit I don't care about. Got it?"

Both gnomes squirked with triumphant glee. With looks of zealous resolve, they vigorously high fived each other on their faces.

"Okay…" The Wizard furtively motioned to the man and woman he had drugged; the man was building a fort out of unused tables, and the woman was engaged in a contentious staring contest with the mirror. "Help me get those two out of here. My human shield and I need them for a disguise."

Jeff was too busy attempting to stand on his head to notice this remark. Although he was failing at this spectacularly, he had become the center of the bargoers' attention when he got naked. The Wizard purposefully avoided looking at Jeff's genitals, worrying that he may not be on the better end of the size differential.

"I like you!" Knippe punched The Wizard playfully on the knee. "You call them like you see them; that's a rare trait."

Shenanitwins

"So, what do we call you?" asked Knippe.

After thinking about this for a moment, The Wizard grinned fiendishly. "You can call me Ragnarok, Slayer of Kings!"

"Nah." Knippe waved his hand dismissively. "I don't think that works for you. What do you think, Knorpe?"

"I agree." Nodding fervently, Knorpe squinted at The Wizard. "You look more like a magic type. Now that I think of it, you're very similar to the old Archmage... You're more entertaining though, and you're good at pulling tricks..."

Suddenly, Knippe held up his index finger excitedly. "I've got it! We'll call you *The Magician!*"

"Perfect!" said Knorpe.

Both gnomes beamed with delight. The Wizard simply rolled his eyes and glowered at them. They seemed far too pleased with themselves to notice his discontent.

"Okay, almost ready!" said Knorpe. "We've just got to check that our heist kit is in order, and then we can do this."

The two gnomes each checked the contents of their pockets.

"Yep, it's all there!" Knippe clapped his hands together enthusiastically.

"So you guys do this a lot, huh?" The Wizard had begun to chop three large lines of cocaine.

Knorpe nodded casually. "Oh, yeah, we do this all the time."

"Of course we do!" Laughing, Knippe motioned around the room. "How do you think this terrible bar stays in business?"

The Wizard looked around the bar, half of which was now a giant table fort. "That's a fair point."

"Now, I believe something was said about kidnapping!" said Knippe loudly.

The Wizard slid his palm down his face. "Well, *I* didn't actually use the word, but yes."

Luckily, this was far from the first kidnapping to occur at *Luncheons and Flagons*; the patrons were used to it, and no one even batted an eye.

"Don't even worry about it," said Knippe, "we'll take care of those two chumps. You just wait on the roof with your chump and we'll join you shortly."

Chapter Seven

The Wizard furrowed his brow. "Why the roof?"

"You'll see!" Knorpe yanked vigorously on a velvet rope, causing a spiral ladder to corkscrew down.

"Oh wow..." Snickering, The Wizard shook his head in amusement. "You guys have one of those too?"

"Have one?" said Knippe. "We only *invented* them!"

"Of course you did..."

The two gnomes each drew matching blow dart guns from their pockets and ran off into the crowd. Looking up at the spiral ladder, The Wizard wondered how he was going to get Jeff up the thing. It was much taller than the one in his tower. He sighed, regretting having always put off learning to levitate large objects.

The Wizard conjured a length of rope and tied it around Jeff's waist. He climbed the ladder cautiously, as it was not only much taller than his, but a much tighter spiral. Once he was at the top, he hoisted Jeff up; the rungs of the ladder repeatedly bashed Jeff's head as his naked butt loomed over the crowd. By the time they reached the top, Jeff had been knocked unconscious. The Wizard pulled him onto the roof, tossing him to the side in disgust.

After a few short minutes of waiting, The Wizard was startled by the jubilant voice of Knippe suddenly piping up behind his back.

"It wasn't easy, but we caught them!"

Standing behind him were Knippe and Knorpe, each dragging a bulky burlap sack.

"Damn, that was fast," said The Wizard. "How did you get them up here so easily?"

"Oh, we just took the stairs," said Knorpe.

The Wizard scowled. "What?! Why wasn't I informed of the stairs?!"

Chuckling heartily, Knippe gestured to the spiral ladder. "What kind of businessmen would we be if we didn't push our product on consumers?"

"Okay, whatever. Why are we up here?"

The gnomes simultaneously gestured to a strange machine in the middle of the roof; it appeared to be a bastardized version of a gyrocopter, without a proper chassis, and with no rudder or stabilizers. The mast was made of a bunch of plastic pipes duct-taped together, with a seat nailed on both sides.

Shenanitwins

Strange gears and pistons stuck out at awkward angles. It had countless harnesses and ropes hanging off various places, none of which seemed conducive to safety. On the top, there was a set of wooden blades above a tattered, rainbow umbrella. The entire thing was covered in graffiti of Knippe and Knorpe that seemed to be drawn in crayon.

"Our glorious flying machine!" They beamed with pride.

The Wizard gaped at the machine in disbelief. He was already having misgivings about inviting these idiots. "You don't expect me to ride that thing, do you?"

Both gnomes shrugged simultaneously.

"Wait a minute..." The Wizard narrowed his eyes suspiciously. "I think this was the machine that flew by my house a few months ago and shot a grappling hook through my bedroom window..."

Again, both gnomes shrugged. They were grinning guiltily.

"You fuckers!" yelled The Wizard. "You're the ones who stole my bed!"

"Probably." Chuckling, Knorpe nodded fervently. "Like I said, we do this all the time."

"That bed was Hemper Pedic, damn it! One hundred percent organic hemp fiber mattresses are expensive, you little dicks! Plus I had to pay to get bars installed on my windows..."

"Sure, they are," said Knippe, "but does anyone *really* need a bed?"

"I've had to sleep on my couch for months!"

"Well, yeah," said Knorpe, "but I bet the feng shui of your room is a lot more natural without that bulky thing."

"Damn it, we don't have time for this! Forget it..." The Wizard heaved an exhausted sigh. "I'm *not* getting on that piece of crap machine; let's just walk, the tower is right over there." He gestured to the dark silhouette looming overhead.

"Wait a minute..." Knippes eyes widened. "You didn't tell us we were heisting Circle Tower!

"Yeah," said Knorpe, "you could have mentioned that."

"And you could have mentioned the stairs. What's wrong, too tough for you?"

Chapter Seven

"Not at all!" Huffing indignantly, Knorpe crossed his arms. "We hide from the town guards in there all the time! They don't get along with the mages."

"Yeah, I know." The Wizard was more than familiar with the contempt the town guards held for Circle magi. "So, what's the problem?"

"Well," said Knippe, "it's just that everything in there is stamped with their seal; it's impossible to fence."

Knorpe nodded in agreement. "I mean, we'll still come, but —"

"I knew it!" The Wizard narrowed his eyes. "You *are* after my treasure!"

"So what?" said Knorpe. "You only let us come along because we brought drugs. Who brings drugs on a heist anyway?"

Scoffing, The Wizard held his hands up incredulously. "You do, apparently!"

"Also, yes," said Knippe. "This is your heist, though; you should set a better example!"

"Fairy dust just helps to take the edge off," said The Wizard.

"Look," said Knorpe, forcefully kicking one of the burlap sacks, "we got you these two dwarves, didn't we?"

"*Dwarves?!*" Groaning in frustration, The Wizard shook his head. "I wanted you to grab those two human mages I drugged!"

"How are two tiny gnomes supposed to lug a couple of humans up those stairs?" Knippe kicked the other burlap sack, even more forcefully than his brother had. "These fat pieces of shit were already hard enough."

The Wizard glared at the gnomes. "I'm still upset at you two about the stairs... but whatever, these two will have to do..." He slid down the brim of Knorpe's sack, revealing the bushy beard and squat face of a dwarf. The dwarf's face was covered in acne. "Why'd you have to pick such an ugly bastard?"

Knippe shrugged.

"Whatever, this one can be Jeff's disguise," said The Wizard.

"You still haven't seen mine!" Pulling down the brim of his sack, Knorpe revealed the ugliest, fattest dwarf that had been in the bar. This dwarf's eyes were unnaturally close together, and he had a harelip.

Shenanitwins

Raising an eyebrow, The Wizard shook his head slowly. "Why on Notearth would you go to the trouble of hauling this fat bastard up your damn stairs?"

Knorpe winked at The Wizard. "Just for you!"

"Fine, whatever," said The Wizard, "but if you two want a share of the treasure, you have to strip these fat bastards."

"If you're planning to have your way with them, why don't you do it?" Making a kissy face at The Wizard, Knorpe wiggled his eyebrows suggestively.

"No, you idiot, I need their clothes for our disguises."

"Right, I've been meaning to ask you about that," said Knippe, pouting his lips. He gestured to Jeff's limp, nude body. "How come only you and this schmuck get to wear disguises? We have the best disguises!"

The Wizard rolled his eyes. "No one said you can't wear disguises! But the Circle know me, and they'll probably know Jeff too."

"Why is he even coming?" Knorpe was using a magic marker to draw penises on Jeff's face. "He's totally passed out, he'll be no good."

"In case I need a distraction," said The Wizard. "I toss him in the way and run, simple as that."

"You're my kind of scumbag." Knippe patted The Wizard on the back of the knee.

Leaning over, The Wizard plucked a hair from the beard of each dwarf, placing them into two separate vials of thick, red liquid. The potions bubbled and smoked, slowly changing into a black, tarry substance. He then pulled out the bag containing the remainder of his cocaine; after doing a bump, he caused the rest to shoot magically up Jeff's nose. Jeff's eyes snapped open and he grinned ecstatically.

"Here, Jeff, drink this." The Wizard held out one of the potions.

Blinking dreamily, Jeff looked up at The Wizard. "You've got my warm milk, mummy?"

"Uh, yeah, sure, whatever." The Wizard poured the steaming black liquid into Jeff's stupidly gaping mouth.

"This milk tastes like shit," said Jeff, as he gulped it down nonetheless.

"Is that any way to talk to your mummy?" Smirking, Knorpe fluttered his brow impishly at Jeff.

Chapter Seven

The Wizard scowled before downing his polymorph potion.

Knippe and Knorpe stripped the dwarves of all their clothing, stealing their wallets and jewelry in the process. They passed the clothes to The Wizard, who dressed himself before reluctantly dressing Jeff. The Wizard cringed in disgust; Jeff was now the fattest, grossest dwarf he had ever seen, with a tiny, inverted penis.

"Alright, let's go," said The Wizard, attempting to pull Jeff to his feet.

It took the help of both gnomes to do it, but eventually The Wizard managed to get Jeff to his feet. The Wizard insisted that Knippe and Knorpe show him where the stairs were. They exited through the back office into the alleyway behind the bar and the adjacent church.

On his way through their office, The Wizard could not help but notice what he was pretty positive was his mattress; it appeared the gnomes had been using it as a foundation for their blanket forts. Irritated, he slammed the back door behind him.

As they walked past the church, The Wizard looked at it and chortled. "What's with this *'First Church of Astrolotology'*?"

"What's so funny about it?" Knippe put his hands on his hips defensively.

Gritting his teeth, Knorpe crossed his arms. "Yeah, I'll have you know we own that church!"

"Really?" said The Wizard. He guffawed derisively. "You two actually worship a God? I'd have thought you'd be too self-obsessed to put anything above yourselves!"

Knippe narrowed his eyes contemptuously. "Clearly you know nothing about Astrolotology if you think we worship anything you could call a 'God'! We are simply slaves to the supreme being, Aliexnu."

The Wizard scoffed. "Yeah, whatever, sounds like a load of crap. I don't need to hear any more."

Not much else was said as they made the short walk to Circle Tower, aside from Knippe and Knorpe's muffled whispering about The Wizard angering Aliexnu. A few tense minutes later, they came upon the entrance to the tower.

The Wizard walked up and tapped his master key on the door, causing it to slowly and loudly grind open. Hoping that nobody heard, they entered the vast, darkened atrium of Circle Tower.

Chapter Eight
The Feist of the Heist

As the party of four entered the vast hall of Circle Tower, the room suddenly lit up with the glow of hundreds of multicolored wisps orbiting the pillars. The floating platforms above scintillated in the ethereal light. There was not a single living being to be seen in the room.

"So…" said Knorpe, looking around bemusedly. "I don't want to be 'that guy', but remind me why exactly you needed disguises?"

"Well, apparently we didn't," said The Wizard. "But when I planned this, I had stayed up all night and binge watched heist movies! *The Goblin Job... The Usual Kobolds... Lock, Stock, and Two Smoking Towers...* I guess they all just got to my head; I thought there would be a lot more security, and we'd need to use trickery. I guess Quan hasn't changed much around here after all..."

Knorpe crinkled his mutton chops in a snide smirk. "Amateur much? I wouldn't even call your lousy polymorph potion 'trickery'! Besides, that last one is more of a terrorist movie…."

"Ah, come on, go easy on the guy," said Knippe. "Not everyone has the guile and the gumption to convince their *doctor* that he has cancer. That took real dedication to sneak into his house *every morning* and poison his cereal!"

"Words fail me…" Sighing, The Wizard pulled a vial of clear liquid from his robes and drank it; he slowly and grotesquely transformed back into himself, before forcefully administering the same potion to Jeff. "I'm glad I don't have to look like that any more…"

Chapter Eight

The fat dwarves' clothing was somehow both baggy and tight on their bodies; The Wizard summoned a set of clothes from his house and quickly changed, not bothering to do the same for Jeff.

They crept cautiously towards the center of the room. As they neared the twin spiral staircase, an abrupt noise literally scared the shart out of The Wizard.

Suddenly, Knorpe squirked loudly. "Holy fuck!"

"What?" The Wizard frantically glanced around the room.

"Someone dropped a silver coin! Score!"

The Wizard opened his mouth to speak, but then thought better of it. Gritting his teeth and shaking slightly, he made his way towards the towering statue of Merlin in the center of the spiral staircase. As usual, it gave him the unnerving impression that he was being watched. He approached it and tapped the teeth of his master key on the base. The statue began to grind slowly backwards.

"Woah..." Knorpe's eyes widened in amazement. "These things move?"

"Not normally, but —" said The Wizard.

"We're heisting statues?" asked Knippe. "That's a first for me!"

"No, we're —"

"How are you planning to get these things out of here?" Knorpe gestured to the statue of Merlin. "Look! It's moving in the wrong direction!"

"No, it's —"

"Oh, I think I get it..." Nodding thoughtfully, Knippe pointed at the skylight, several hundred feet above. Starlight glistened in the clear sky. "We're gonna hoist it up and bust out that window, right!"

"No, we... wait, what? No... that's asinine..." Sighing wearily, The Wizard gestured forcefully at the entrance that was opening beneath the statue. "Just look, we're going —"

Knorpe furrowed his brow doubtfully. "Who's gonna buy these statues anyway?"

"*Merlin's Bush*! *Shut the fuck up*! If you just *listen* for a second, you'll see —"

"Hey, check it out!" said Jeff. He was surprisingly coherent for someone so fucked up. He pointed below the statue. "There's a secret door!"

The Feist of the Heist

Knorpe clapped his hands together enthusiastically. "Oh, shit! I never noticed that thing…"

"Me neither," said Knippe. "Good looking out, kid!"

"What's your name, anyway?" asked Knorpe. "Now I actually care..."

"I name is me… Eff?" Grinning stupidly, Jeff once again began to grope at the air.

"Meff, eh?" Knorpe nodded in approval. "It suits you!"

"Meff and The Magician!" Knippe patted Jeff and The Wizard jovially on the back of the knee; this took a fair amount of sprinting between them. "A winning combination!"

"Can we *please* just get this over with?!" Glaring in disbelief at his three accomplices, The Wizard vehemently regretted bringing any of them. "I'm getting a *really* bad feeling about this…."

"Maybe *this* will help!" Reaching into the pocket of his striped vest, Knorpe pulled out the bundle of fairies. He pulled out the largest fairy and rolled it under his nose like a tiny cob of corn, snorting vigorously. Gruffly yanking a few others out of the rubber bands, he held them out to the others; Knippe took his immediately and mimicked Knorpe's method of administration.

"It actually probably will…" The Wizard took one of the fairies. "At this point, I think I need it."

He tried to snort it like they did, but ended up dropping it; fortunately for him, it was unable to fly due to atrophy, so he was easily able to pick it up. Shrugging, he swallowed it whole. His annoyance quickly melted into acceptance; he was no longer capable of comprehending why he would possibly be unhappy.

Knorpe threw the last fairy at Jeff, who was too busy trying to lick his elbow to see it coming. It hit him square in the face, sending a cloud of fairy Dust cascading around him. The look of vacant joy on his face was quickly replaced by a look of ecstatic vim; simply put, he was right proper as fuck.

The Wizard, who had already started down the stairs, was quickly shoved down by a rampaging Jeff. As he began to dazedly lift himself off of the cold, stone floor, Jeff's foot came down, after a seven stair leap, directly on his lower spine.

Chapter Eight

A moment later, he felt the footsteps of Knippe and Knorpe fall sharply and repetitively on his skull; if he was in any fit state to count, he would have tallied seventeen footstomps.

The Wizard would have been annoyed about the massive headache the impacts would have induced, if not for his concurrent concussions coinciding with the combination of narcotics he had consumed to cause a condition of confused contentedness. After a moment of what nine out of ten medical doctors do not consider sleep, he slowly stood up.

"It's about time..." muttered Knippe.

Knorpe crossed his arms. "Yeah! To think, *you* actually accused *us* of wasting time!"

"Such a fucking hippogriff..." Although Jeff squinted sharply at The Wizard as he said this, it was hard to tell whether it pertained to the situation.

After standing dazed for a moment, The Wizard processed what had just happened. "What the hell? Did you two do a tapdance on my head?"

Knippe held up his finger matter-of-factly. "Well, technically it was a jig."

"Speak for yourself," said Knorpe.

Suddenly, The Wizard remembered why he was there. "Damn it, we have to move." He conjured a hovering, luminous sphere above his palm. Looking at the wall of darkness ahead, The Wizard was beginning to feel nervous, even through his concussed intoxication. "I'm gonna be honest, I have no idea where anything is down here.... I *do* know that there are about twenty total miles of tunnels.... As far as I know, we could be here all night..."

"Wow..." said Knorpe. "A real sleepover underneath Circle Tower!"

Knippe danced with glee. "It's like an idea come true!"

"We can't afford to have a sleepover, damn it! If we get caught, we're gonna be having a good, *looong* 'sleepover' in Detroit Prison!"

"Oh, no..." Shuddering in horror, Knorpe firmly shook his head. "I've been to Detroit before... it's a living hell... basically the worst place on Notearth... and I've been to North Koric!" He grimaced, before beginning to suck his thumb.

"I remember that!" Eyes widening, Knippe gulped fearfully. "If it weren't for the whole prison going temporarily bankrupt, you'd still be there!"

The Feist of the Heist

"Please don't remind me..." Knorpe's disturbed eyes became glassy and round, and he curled up in the fetal position. He began to stare off catatonically, mumbling gibberish to himself.

The latter behavior was typical of Knorpe, but Knippe quickly became concerned by his brother's lack of twitching. He ran over to him and began petting his silver hair; purring like a kitty cat, Knorpe quickly retired from his flashback and took up residence in reality.

"Aliexnu help me!" said Knorpe, trembling furiously. "Thinking about Detroit... stuck in this dank, musty tunnel... devoid of sunlight or clean drinking water... it was just all too much!" He grabbed Knippe's shoulders, shaking him vigorously, crying, "I felt like I was back there! I can't go back to Detroit!" He hugged his brother tightly, sobbing hysterically.

Knippe patted him on the back, muttering "it's going to be okay" into his ear repeatedly. When Knorpe finally stopped crying, Knippe added, "by the way, I know it's a bad time, but you shouldn't use Aliexnu's name in vain... I mean, he created us to come up with him! He's basically the circle of life, so show some respect, okay?"

"You're right..." Staring up at the heavens, Knorpe wrung his hands apologetically. "Please, Aliexnu, forgive my transgression. I beg of you to spare me from the wrath of your snide remarks!"

"What the fuck are you two talking about?!" The Wizard walked over to the wall and started banging his head on it in frustration. He simply could not believe how much hassle these couple of daft, little wackadoodles were becoming. At the start of the night, he had regarded them simply as walking, talking toys. Now, however, they seemed more like walking, talking tools; not the useful kind, though. At this point, unfortunately, he was positive that they would get him caught if he left them behind.

Suddenly, Jeff darted down the tunnel. "This way!"

"Wait, hold on, we —" As The Wizard held out his hand desperately, Jeff was already swallowed up by the seemingly fathomless darkness ahead.

Hooting gleefully, Knippe followed. "Onward and wayward!"

"To insanity and beyond!" yelled Knorpe, running after the others.

Both gnomes were quickly enveloped by the cavernous darkness as well. Their echoing footsteps quickly began to fade into the distance.

Chapter Eight

The Wizard stared dumbfounded into the darkness for a moment. For a moment, he wondered if he should have just left Jeff in the form of that obese dwarf. After going over the situation in his head, however, he figured that the three of them would make a good distraction. Since he could frame the gnomes in Jeff's place, he resolved to rescue Jeff if he happened upon him en route to the artifact vault. Either way, he reckoned the authorities would capture the others first, giving him time to escape.

He continued down the corridor alone, holding aloft his globe of light. It was so dark, he wondered how the others had not yet rammed headfirst into one of the walls without a light. As he continued, he passed over a dozen passages on either side; he counted, knowing that he must take the eighth right turn.

It was fortunate, The Wizard thought, that he had memorized his map of the Circle Tower basement meticulously whilst on cocaine; unfortunately for him, the map he owned was outdated by several decades, and Quan's geomancy made it very easy for the Circle to rearrange its tunnels. The Wizard was heading in the wrong direction.

Reaching the eighth passage to the right, he turned and headed excitedly towards what he believed was the score of the century. He had no idea what truly awaited him ahead; although, in a way, he was right about how significant of an impact it would have on his life.

The Wizard sprinted down the corridor with the kind of vigor only achievable with the combination of Fairy Dust and cocaine. The cobblestone walls zoomed by, the spellight glistening on their damp surface.

After several hundred feet of tunnel, he came into a large hall that funneled outward from around him. The walls spread to be at least thirty feet apart, and the ceiling quickly rose too high to be seen. In the far distance, a great wall of darkness loomed before him.

As he approached the dark expanse, a vast, metallic surface came into view. Stretching from one wall to the other, and as far above as The Wizard could see, the surface was made of a shining, silvery metal. Nothing could be seen across the surface: no protrusions; no keyholes; not even a welcome mat below; it was simply smooth metal spanning the entire wall.

"To think... the great mithril vault of the Circle, repository of the most potent magic of all time, allegedly impenetrable and all but unknown to the masses, would have such an obvious weakness!" He pulled out the Master Key, and tapped it to the surface.

Inside the door, the grinding of hundreds of gears could be heard. A gap appeared in the middle, and the door slowly began to grind open, a pale green light shining from within; impatiently, The Wizard squeezed through the gap as soon as its width allowed.

The Wizard would never forget what he saw behind that door.

The room itself was just as he remembered it: it had smooth walls on all sides, made of the same mithril as the vault door; however, The Wizard was not prepared for what it contained...

Three large glass cylinders towered before him, stretching to the ceiling, where dozens of twisting pipes fed into them. They were filled to the top with a luminescent liquid, casting an eerie green glow throughout the room. Within each container, there was a body suspended in the liquid, with a twisting array of tubes connecting to its torso.

The first tank held a withered, skeletal body, so devoid of life that it looked pickled. A smaller amount of light radiated from this tube relative to the other two.

Within the second cylinder, there floated the gaunt, wrinkled form of an old man with a long mane of greyish red hair. Despite his withered appearance, this man looked strangely familiar to The Wizard, as though they had met before. The water within this tube glowed with moderate brightness.

Finally, what The Wizard saw within the final, brightest tube made his stomach clench up. He could not believe his eyes. His heart beat frantically and sweat trickled down his cheeks, as he gazed in horror at the body within; Ziro Xuntasi, the previous Archmage of Koric and The Wizard's father, was suspended in this tube.

He did not know what to think. He had expected to find fantastic treasure behind this door, but instead had found an assisted-living nightmare. Up until now, he thought his father was dead, and never expected to see him again; now, however, he was at a loss for what to think.

Before The Wizard was able to process what he was seeing, a voice suddenly hissed from the darkness to his left.

"I see you, too, have found our operation."

Chapter Eight

Panicking, The Wizard turned and squinted to see who was talking; he held up his spellight and focused intently, casting it all around the room. A hunched form deep within the darkness suddenly became clear, and the face of a hideously disfigured man was grinning wickedly at him. The man had burns and boils all over his face and neck, long patches of greasy black hair growing between scars on his scalp, and less teeth than fingers.

"Horner!" The Wizard raised his eyebrows in surprise. "I thought you died in that fire!"

"That's what I wanted everyone to think..." said Horner, wringing his hands deviously. He gestured to the horrible scars all over his face. "And what almost happened, to be fair...."

"Well, what are you doing down here?" The Wizard gestured to the tanks to his right, containing his father and his presumed ancestors. "What have you done to my father?"

"Oh, it was not I who did this." Chuckling with dastardly pleasure, Horner stepped towards him. "This has been going on for longer than you know."

"What...?" Pausing, The Wizard squinted confusedly at the tubes standing beside them. It had never occurred to him that such a horror would even exist. It was really bringing down his high. "What do you mean?"

"I think *I* can explain!" said a high pitched voice from the doorway.

For a moment, The Wizard thought one of the gnomish twins had found them. Looking towards the source of the voice, however, he saw that it originated from an extraordinarily miniscule Archmage Quan. Standing about two feet tall, the woman who normally towered over him was glaring up at him from below, pointing a twisted wand at his crotch.

"You see —"

"Why are you so tiny?" Clutching his knees in laughter, The Wizard nearly lost his balance. For a moment, he forgot what he was perturbed about, and was consumed by comedy.

"The reduction spell isn't always perfect!" Scowling, Quan placed her hands on her hips. She closed her eyes and slowly grew in height until she was at eye level with him. Regaining her composure, she smiled maliciously. "Now, I believe you wanted to know what we did to your father, before we do it to you as well."

The Feist of the Heist

"I would, but…" Pausing for a moment, The Wizard pondered how he could escape from this situation. He decided to stall them; knowing Archmage Quan, he knew she was liable to prattle on about how she outsmarted him as usual. "First, I want to know how the hell you discovered my plan! I only thought of it yesterday, surely that's not enough time to find me out."

"Your level of forethought never ceases to amaze me." Quan grinned superciliously. "I remember you used to strut around this entire tower like you owned the place when your dad was Archmage; no one ever stopped you back then, so I suppose it never occurred to you that the place is monitored at all times."

"Well, I, uh… I thought you'd be asleep by now…."

"I was," said Quan, through gritted teeth. "But when I heard there was an intruder, I knew it had to be you; so instead of calling Circle security, I thought I'd attend to this matter personally. Now, if you'd kindly hand over that key of yours."

The Wizard drew the key from the pocket of his robes. As he whipped it out, Quan's hands tensed around her wand. He reluctantly tossed it to her.

Furrowing his brow, The Wizard gestured gruffly to Horner. "So, why's *he* here then?"

"I live here," said Horner, pointing at a pillow-bearing pile of straw in the corner.

"Horner is an invaluable asset to the Circle. He oversees our biomagical conduits." Quan gestured to the glowing tubes towering beside them. "Without his specialized knowledge, our research would have never come this far. It is these apparatuses that provide the Circle with its seemingly endless supply of arcane power."

"But… how…?" Even through the heavy dose of drugs affecting The Wizard's mind, the severity of his situation was quickly becoming clear. "Why does my dad have to be involved?" He thought back to what she had said before about doing the same to him. "What part do *I* play in this scheme of yours?"

"This 'scheme' is far from mine," Quan began to laugh, but her expression remained venomous and vindictive. "This operation has been

Chapter Eight

going on since barely a century after the Circle's inception. Did you *really* think your insane ancestors have been running the Circle all this time?"

"I mean…" Shrugging uncertainly, The Wizard scrunched his nose and narrowed his eyes skeptically. "It seemed like my dad always had it together…."

"That he did, relative to the others." With a smug smile, Quan nodded. "I would dare say he almost exposed our plans. We had to execute his 'disappearance' sooner than we had planned; long before either of these ones burnt out." She gestured to the other two tanks. "We had to build a third conduit just for him, and those things aren't cheap. It's proven to be a blessing, however, because the additional magical power we harness from him has allowed the Circle to make many advancements in my time as Archmage."

"What…?" His mouth falling open in shock, The Wizard thought about the implications of what she was saying. He stared for a moment at the bodies suspended in the tubes, contemplating horrifically what it must be like to face such an existence. "You built these devices to steal their power?"

"Steal?" said Archmage Quan. "When each of your ancestors became Archmage, they swore an oath that they would pledge their eternal servitude to the Circle, regardless of what was required of them for the prosperity of the kingdom. Wouldn't you say they are simply doing their duty?" She laughed malevolently, twisting her face and cocking her head to the side.

"Hell no!" The Wizard was shaking with a fury he could not have even comprehended earlier that night. He was not used to being on the side of morality, and the part did not come natural to him. "I always knew you totally sucked, but this is evil by… well… even *my* standards, honestly!"

"I must admit, I had my misgivings at first. I had worked to become Archmage because I wanted to help all of the people of Koric, and sacrificing even a few for the good of the many was against my nature. However, after learning of how many advancements have been possible because of this arcane power, I came to realize that some evils are necessary."

"Look, no one understands necessary evils like me," said The Wizard, "but why did this have to be my family? Sure, they're strong, but wouldn't it be much better to drain magical energy from a dragon or something?"

86

The Feist of the Heist

"It seems he doesn't know..." Chortling nefariously, Horner walked over to stand beside Quan. His disfigured face was more twisted than usual by his sneer.

With a sinister smile, Quan gave Horner a small nod. "Indeed, he does not."

"Know *what*?" The Wizard was starting to feel rather sick of the arrogant, withholding way in which they were speaking to him. Perhaps it was due to the heavy dose of drugs, but his mood rapidly shifted from fearful to angry. "Damn it, just answer the fucking question!"

"Well, haven't you ever wondered," said Quan, "how it is that you can cast powerful spells when you have such a sub par understanding of the arcane language?! How it is that *you* were ever able to outperform *me* when we were apprentices?! How it is that you don't die when you snort ten grams of cocaine in one day?!"

"Hey, that was my birthday!"

"I thought that was hyperbole, but apparently I was mistaken." Shaking her head, Quan slowly facepalmed. "Well, anyway, the bottom line is that your family has some highly magical blood. No one really knows where it originated, but your bloodline is extraordinary all the way back to Merlin."

"That is, until it comes to *you*," said Horner, laughing derisively.

The Wizard was too lost in semi-sober thought to react. "I can't believe this..."

Horner chortled disdainfully. "Neither could I."

Trembling with rage, The Wizard's knuckles turned white. "So, you think that just because we're a bit more powerful, it's worth our *lives* to be your... *batteries?!*"

"Not simply mere batteries," said Archmage Quan. "Your ancestors have proven to be a seemingly inexhaustible supply of arcane power!"

"Yes, indeed," said Horner. "Although, the power has been becoming... *diluted* over time." He subtly motioned between The Wizard and his father while he said this. "I've had to work tirelessly my entire life to improve our methods of extraction."

"Nonetheless," said Quan, "the magiscientific developments made possible by the work of Horner and his predecessors have proven to be well worth the effort."

87

Chapter Eight

The Wizard was lost for words. Moments before, in the hall, he had been consumed by the intoxicating expectation of affluence; now, however, as he looked between the snide faces of his foes, he was filled with unspeakable dread and disgust.

"So, *I'm* next on your list?"

He frantically tried to think of a way out of this situation. He knew that even if he knew how to teleport, this room was among the most heavily warded in the kingdom; Quan doubtlessly had backup guarding the way out, so running was not an appealing option. As far as he knew, he needed a miracle to get out of this situation; fortunately, it seemed that such a miracle had arrived.

"Hey, Archmage Quan!" shouted a voice from the passage behind Quan. The strapping silhouette of Fabulon emerged from the darkness. He was carrying the limp bodies of Knippe and Knorpe. His hot pink robes clashed spectacularly with the black background. "I found these two sniffing around the alchemy lab, *literally*... They were huffing potions."

Each of the gnomes' faces were alight with a look of vacant ecstasy.

"The right potions, apparently," muttered The Wizard.

"Oh my, it can't be true!" Fabulon looked sorrowfully to the ceiling and waved his hands at The Wizard. "I dared not believe it when they told me; my most trusted friend and brother in arms has fallen to the pitiful path of thievery!" He fell to his knees and held his arms pleadingly in the air. "How could this be?!"

Suddenly, the au naturel form of Jeff barreled out of the darkness. "Help, my shadow's chasing me!" He charged directly into the back of Fabulon. Scrambling to his feet, he looked behind him in terror. "*You* can't catch *me*, motherfucker! Not *this* time!"

"What the hell...?" muttered Quan.

Fabulon had been knocked face-first into the floor, causing the gnomes to skitter across the floor like butter on a hot skillet.

After a moment of stunned silence, Archmage Quan lowered her wand and rushed to Fabulon's side. She looked concerned as she lifted him up and checked to see if his handsomeness was still intact.

The Wizard took advantage of her lowered guard to pull from his pocket a fifth of high proof rum he had stolen from the twins' bar. He chugged almost a third of it, and smashed the rest on the ground near his foes. With a snap of his fingers, he caused a shower of sparks to rain down on the liquid. A blazing fire suddenly erupted before him, engulfing Jeff as well as his targets.

Fabulon leapt to his feet and valiantly threw Jeff to safety. Embracing Fabulon, Quan leapt out of the flames as well, extinguishing their smouldering robes with a wave of her wand. They landed exactly where Jeff had been a few seconds before. Jeff was now on his feet, snuffing out his smouldering pubic hair.

"*Not again!*" yelled Horner, running frantically across the room in a blaze of fire. He leapt headfirst into the tank that held the most withered body, smashing through the glass.

Archmage Quan seemed to notice this only moments before it happened. She held out her hand in desperation. "*No! Horner, stop!* That one still has a lot of power in it!"

It was too late, however, and the luminous liquid was cascading from its container. It flooded across the room, instantly extinguishing the fire. The gnomes were carried down the hall by its current. As drunk as The Wizard was, the current would have normally knocked him on his buttocks; however, this water caused a most peculiar sensation as it flowed over his knees.

It was as though his legs had been asleep his entire life and were finally waking up. The Wizard was overcome by a monumental wind of energy. It flowed up his legs, through his spine, and into all of his limbs. He felt like it was his birthday all over again. He charged with newfound vigor towards the exit.

Quan attempted to leap to her feet and stop him, but was thrown off of her feet by the current; although she weighed the same, she was not accustomed to being this short, and paid the price when she plunged face-first into the water.

The Wizard grabbed Jeff's wrist as he rushed past. He willed his spellight to hover in front of them, illuminating the path ahead where the water's light dwindled. The gnomish twins were kneeling over on the ground ahead, feverishly slurping the water off the ground.

Chapter Eight

"Come on, you idiots," shouted The Wizard as he sprinted past. "Run if you value your lives!"

"Meh..." Shrugging offhandedly, Knorpe stood up and dashed after The Wizard. Knippe followed after only a moment's hesitation.

Back in the vault, Quan had gotten to her feet and was glaring after them.

"Damn it!" She threw her arms up in anger. "I can't run as fast at this size, it's got me all thrown off!" She sighed, muttering, "it's like switching to a whole new size of heels..."

"Can't you teleport after him?" asked Fabulon.

"No, this place is too heavily warded." Reaching into the pocket of her golden robes, Quan pulled out a small remote control. "However, I can do this." Smiling deviously, she clicked one of the buttons, and the room suddenly began flashing with a violent red light; from the distance, the clanking of heavy metal echoed through the halls. "He's not going anywhere through six inches of reinforced mithril."

"Fuck, this is bad," said The Wizard, as they came upon the closed exit. "If only they didn't seal all the secret tunnels after that angry mob of Frankensteins escaped!"

The red glow of the alarm illuminated The Wizard's look of panic. It also revealed a bit more of Jeff than he would have liked to see; quite a bit more, in fact. It made The Wizard feel... *diminutive.* Averting his eyes, he attempted to blink this disconcerting image out of his mind.

Knippe narrowed his eyes. "Wait, we're not *leaving,* are we?"

"Yeah," said Knorpe, "we haven't even found any treasure yet!"

"Well, besides this..." Frowning, Knorpe jingled a small coin purse. "But it's not very full."

"Hey, that's mine!" yelled The Wizard, attempting to snatch it from the gnome.

"Ha ha!" Sneering impishly, Knippe swallowed the bag of coins whole. "What now?"

"Ugh..." The Wizard groaned in exasperation. "We don't have time for this, we need to find a new way out."

The Feist of the Heist

"Hey, you're *The Magician*," said Knippe, patting The Wizard firmly on the back of the knee. "If those dicks catch us, just curse them into food!"

"Yeah," said Knorpe, nodding encouragingly. "If anyone can voodoo something about them, it sure ain't either of us little dolls!"

"Okay, first of all, I love the idea of cursing them into food," said The Wizard to Knippe, ignoring Knorpe's terrible pun. "I'm super hungry. However, knowing them, they're probably locked and loaded with overpowered magitech. The best option is just to escape."

Leaning against the wall, Knorpe started whistling nonchalantly. He waited until The Wizard was glaring at him before speaking. "Well, I don't know if this helps, but I spotted an enormous vault door, quite a bit like the one back there, on the way to the drug depot."

"Wait, you found another vault?" His brilliant magenta eyes twinkling, The Wizard beamed with hope.

"Yeah, plus we found this fucking awesome room full of potions," said Knippe. "When you mix them, the fumes —"

"Damn it! I don't care about your drug trip! That other vault must be where they keep the artifacts."

At this moment, The Wizard began to hear the sound of hurried footsteps echoing down the corridors from whence they came. He knew they only had moments to get out of sight before their assailants were upon them.

"This way, quick!" Dashing down the hall, The Wizard ducked into the first passage to the left. The others followed shortly behind, with Knippe struggling to pull a vacant Jeff behind him. He turned to them and asked, "so, where did you find this vault?"

"I'm not sure…" muttered Knorpe.

Twirling his mustache, Knippe shrugged. "I think it was somewhere else. It definitely wasn't right here."

Sighing in exhaustion, The Wizard clutched his forehead in pain. He was probably going to get brain damage if this migraine got any worse.

"We took the third passage off of the main hall," said Jeff suddenly. His eyes were wide and his pupils dilated, but his expression was otherwise blank. "From there, we took the second passage to the right. We continued down it until we reached a hexagonal intersection. Taking the second

Chapter Eight

passage to our left, we headed straight down the corridor until we reached a wide hall, containing our destination."

After he finished frantically prattling this off, Jeff smiled vacantly again, gazing at the cobblestone wall. The others all stared in stunned silence for a few moments, until The Wizard was jarred by the sound of oncoming footsteps.

"Shit, let's go!" The Wizard sprinted down the corridor, away from the main hall. *I hope I can remember what Jeff said, because I doubt he'll be able to do that again...* he thought.

The tunnel they were traversing did not have any other passages coming off it. Eventually, they reached a sharp bend, and dashed around the corner. They came into a vast, musty hall; there were towering bookshelves, coated with dust, lining the walls and forming several aisles spanning the room.

"This is the Circle's secret library," said The Wizard. "This is where they keep all their 'forbidden knowledge', like anyone wants to read these dusty, old tomes anyway. My dad used to make me study here... Unless Quan changed this too, I'm pretty sure that when we get to the end of this room, there will be a small passage to the right that leads to the hexagonal room Jeff mentioned. If we reach the artifact vault, we may be able to fight them off using powerful magic weapons."

"This coming from the guy who thought we should heist statues," said Knippe, smirking at The Wizard.

"That was *your* idea, asshole. You guys are idiots." As The Wizard rolled his eyes, he once again heard the footsteps of their assailants echoing from the corridor behind them. "Whatever, there's no time for facts; let's just go."

They set out down one of the aisles of books. The red glow illuminated the far end of the aisle, but it seemed to creep closer ever slower. Eventually, after several minutes of running, they reached the end. There were two exits at this end of the room: one was a large wooden door directly before them; the other, as The Wizard expected, headed off to the right.

"Hang on." As they headed towards the passage, Knorpe turned around. Smiling mischievously, he pulled out a book of matches, a robust cigar, and a small tank of kerosene. "This oughta hold them off!"

"Why on Notearth do you have all that on you?" asked The Wizard.

The Feist of the Heist

"Same reason you had that rum," said Knorpe, striking a match and lighting his cigar. He opened the tank of kerosene and sprinkled it across the base of the bookshelves. Grinning between puffs of his cigar, he sauntered away from the pool of fuel. "You never know when you'll need to light up."

He flicked the cigar over his shoulder. It rolled across the floor and came to a rest a few feet away from the kerosene. Nothing happened.

"Oh, shit, hang on…" Heaving a disappointed sigh, Knorpe grabbed the cigar and took another puff. "That was supposed to be really badass, damn it…"

"Okay, that was *not* why I took that rum, by the way, but will you hurry up?" said The Wizard. "This isn't even buying us time at this point!"

"Okay, fine! Get off your drunk horse!" Knorpe's voice squirked with misplaced indignation, and his face turned slightly pink. He threw the cigar on the pool of kerosene, and the bookshelves were quickly engulfed in a great plume of flames. A muffled shout of distress could be heard from the other end of the room.

As they rushed into the side passage, The Wizard chuckled to himself. "Wow, she sounds pissed… I always forget that she actually cares about books and shit."

They continued down this passage for several minutes, until they came to a hexagonal room with a passageway on each side. The smell of burning paper wafted from the corridor behind them.

"Shit, this is where it gets confusing…" Grimacing with uncertainty, The Wizard looked around at the five identical passages before them. In all the commotion, he had forgotten in which direction Jeff had said the vault lied. He looked at Jeff. "Any ideas, Mr. Mastermind?"

Jeff began to speak in the same flat and hurried voice as before.

"Actually, yes, I have a great idea!" He pointed to the passage from whence they came. "I think we should head that way. If we do, it should be about five miles before we reach the Sea of Green; from there, we can take a boat to Treasure Island. We're gonna be rich!"

"Fuck, I think he's just tripping this time." Despairing, The Wizard ran his fingers through his beard. "I'm actually not sure what to do…"

Chapter Eight

"I don't know..." Looking behind him, Knorpe's beady brown eyes gleamed with greed. "The kid might be onto something. I think I've heard of Treasure Island before!"

A look of excitement flashed across Knippe's face. "Yeah, me too!"

"There's no such thing as 'Treasure Island', you morons!" Regret flooded The Wizard's mind as he wondered why he had ever recruited these doppelgangrenous dipshits. "And there never will be if we don't find that vault!"

"Wait, look!" Squealing in delight, Knorpe pointed down the second passage to their left. The walls of the corridor were graffitied in several places with obscene racial slurs against elves. "This is *definitely* the way we went!"

"Okay, good, let's go." The Wizard hastily darted down the passage. The others followed.

As they ran past the words "pansy-ass ent fuckers", "leaf munching centaur shit", "gluten-free douchebags", et cetera, Quan's voice echoed down the corridor.

"This way!"

Several sets of footsteps followed.

They came to the end of the corridor, where it opened abruptly into a large, rectangular room. To their right, a massive vault door loomed over them. It was much like the one before, but much bigger, and made of a dark metal with a green sheen. The rest of the room was empty, aside from a large pile of crates in the far corner.

The Wizard recognized this room; it was where his dad used to keep his cars. This was fortunate, for he knew there was a freight elevator hidden behind the crates; if it still worked, he figured it would make an excellent escape route. Unfortunately, this also meant the vault was made of reinforced adamantine, a material much harder than mithril.

"Shit..." Nervous tension welled up in The Wizard's chest as he stared up at the imposing door. Now that he was here, he realized that without his key, he had no way to enter the vault. "I think we're fucked... this vault is even more impenetrable than the last."

"What happened to your 'magic key'?" asked Knippe. "Did it run out of charges?"

The Feist of the Heist

"No, you idiot, that giant bitch took it!"

"You're gonna have to be more specific," said Knippe.

Knorpe nodded in agreement. "Yeah, to us, you're all giants."

"The Archmage!" shouted The Wizard. "The only *actual* giant who works at the Circle." He clutched his forehead in exasperation, as the footsteps drew nearer. "We're fucked, there's no way in!"

"Not so fast!" Fabulon barrelled into the room. He was cradling the unconscious body of Horner in his arms. "We may be friends, but I can't let you steal from the Circle!"

Archmage Quan followed just behind.

"Fuck!" yelled The Wizard. As he locked eyes with Fabulon, his heart sank. "Why are you helping them, Fabulon?"

"Because I am a battlemage of the Circle!" he said, although his voice lacked conviction. "I am sworn to uphold justice, and you attempted to steal from the Circle!"

"Justice?! They were holding my father in a test tube! Forget my petty thievery. How is that justice to you?!"

"Uh, well..." Fabulon averted his gaze, looking down at his feet and shifting uneasily. His expression looked to be one of extreme internal conflict.

Archmage Quan stomped her foot in anger, shaking the room. "Enough! You will do as you're told, Fabulon, no questions asked. He is a danger to the Circle. Now, stop him!"

"Please," said The Wizard, who hesitated reluctantly before saying, "my friend..." He threw up a little in his mouth. "We've always been like brothers, you know I wouldn't lie to you... about this...."

Fabulon looked up at him, biting his lower lip, his eyes full of uncertainty.

"Don't just stand there!" Quan slapped Fabulon on the buttocks. "He's unarmed, just hex him already!"

"Dude, look into my eyes!" His eyes wide, The Wizard wrung his hands imploringly. "She's only using you! She respects you less than I do... which is saying something.... Please, just do what's right! Bros before giant cunts, right? Especially when that giant cunt murdered your bro's dad!"

Chapter Eight

"Your dad's not even dead yet," said Quan, rolling her cold, black eyes. "He's just unconscious, so watch your mouth, you filthy ingrate! Fabulon, if you don't subdue him, I will."

"That's it, I can't take this anymore!" Fabulon reached into his pockets and withdrew a small crystal flask, containing a writhing thunderstorm. Without hesitation, he threw it at Quan's feet.

A tempest of lightning surged forth as the bottle shattered. Crackling bolts of electricity arced up into Quan's body, causing her to convulse in pain. Her wavy black hair began to smoke. It was enough energy to kill a normal humanoid; however, even in her reduced size, a giant like Quan would simply be rendered paralyzed. She fell forward, her wand clattering to the ground.

Rushing towards her, Fabulon rifled around in her pockets until he found The Wizard's master key. He turned and tossed it to The Wizard, who almost caught it, before bending over to pick it up.

"Sorry, my dear friend, I had no idea what she was doing to your dad." Tears pooled in the corners of Fabulon's eyes. "Do what you can to save him, I've got your back!"

"Fabulon, you idiot..." Wincing, Quan struggled to pull herself to her feet. "How could you betray me after all I've done for you?"

The Wizard and his companions rushed to the vault door, and he tapped the surface with the key. Slowly, it began to grind open. Tapping his foot impatiently, The Wizard waited for the door to open wide enough for him to enter the vault.

Giving up on standing, Quan fell back to the floor. Cracks formed around where she struck. She raised her head and glared furiously at Fabulon. "I should never have promoted you just because you're hot... I'd kill you if I didn't like you so much... You're fired, Fabulon!"

"Good, because I'm sick of your advances," said Fabulon. "Besides, I'd rather be a good friend than have a good job any day."

While Fabulon and Quan argued, The Wizard and his companions ran to the end of the door that was sliding open. The gnomes squeezed through first. A moment later, The Wizard shoved Jeff through the gap, before sidling through himself.

The Feist of the Heist

The Wizard looked around the room at the various marble pedestals bearing fantastical artifacts. His eyes immediately locked on the staff he remembered dreaming about as an apprentice: the *Chronomancer's Continuum*. It was named so because it had no traceable origin, and according to even the most accurate divination magic, it had existed forever. It had only ever been used for research; the time magic it held was potent enough to crumble entire civilizations, if it fell into the wrong hands.

The shaft was made of fine mahogany, polished sparklingly clean. At one end, there was an orb of foggy, pinkish crystal. In the center, there was a sheet of runed gold leaf sheathing the handle. The other end had five golden rings, each slightly larger than the last. The air around it seemed to swirl as though it were baking in the sun.

As he approached the staff, his mouth watered with greed. The twins seemed enticed by other artifacts, and Jeff seemed enticed by himself (you don't want to know). As The Wizard reached for the staff, he could feel the tingle of intense magic power crackle between it and his fingers.

As he grasped the handle, he could have never imagined what was about to transpire. If he could have, he likely would have prepared by snorting a bunch of fairy dust. The smooth surface of the crystal orb shimmered with pinkish light as a wave of energy sent The Wizard flying back. He felt his feet tear off the ground and out of their corporeal form.

Suddenly, he was jolted out of the physical reality around him and into a twisting vortex of magic. He began to feel the threads of information peeling back his reality, bending his mind as though it were his body and his body as though it were his mind. Trust me, you do not want to know what that is like, but suffice it to say that it sucked, in more than just his opinion.

It was poorly written in my opinion as well.

Without warning, the fourth wall was broken, and The Wizard found himself floating in my brain. You see, I was on acid when I wrote this. This part of the story is happening in my brain, okay? I know I am probably an asshole for saying this and actually holding you to it, but bear with me.

I am The Wizard.

Do you understand how close that means he came to existing?

That means that when he floated through this stream of consciousness, he was as much a part of me as the song to which I am listening; as much a part of you as the book you are reading; as much a part of this paragraph as the sentence I am typing.

Do you understand how meta this joke is becoming?

I was gonna say, "steadily becoming" until I realized how unsteadily this was devolving into an extremely shit mechanism for the illustration of the fact that The Wizard's form was not substantial at the moment.

To be completely clear, other than the fact that his form was incorporeal, it was also, at best, theoretical; I, however, would not even go so far as to say it was hypothetical. He was basically just a bad idea.

To even say The Wizard existed in my mind may have been an exaggeration at this point. I would not know. I am not the one with the time portal, okay? I am not the one existing beyond the fourth dimension right now; The Wizard, however, was subject to such a reality. Worry about him instead.

I am the one who exists, just like you; although, maybe not... it depends on when and how you are reading this. It is possible that you exist in any one of a literally infinite number of potential tangential timelines surrounding this book in an informational maelstrom composed of fictional and nonfictional realities.

Anything is possible when you eschew the laws of physics for fantastical nonsense. Am I right? For all I know, you are the one in the book, and The Wizard is reading it!

The Wizard was deconstructed and reconstructed in the singularity of millennial stupidity that is my mind. Regardless of when you are reading this, know that The Wizard only truly existed in my mind right at this exact moment. Before I wrote this, and at any point thereafter, The Wizard was just an idea, in the hearts and minds of troubled myselfs everywhere.

Suddenly, The Wizard found that he was reduced to a number. So was my value as a human being, but that is not important; focus on The Wizard.

Something from the future found that it was incapable of reconciling with The Wizard's existence, so it died. It is not important to the story, so do not worry about it; however, know that it was extremely worried about you its entire life.

This is getting weird, right?

The Feist of the Heist

That is exactly what The Wizard thought as he finally reconstituted in the form of something that made sense. He was not himself yet, because that would be ridiculous, but he was...

Does it even matter anymore? I am surprised you are still reading.

Suddenly, The Wizard forgot that he was a fictional character, and "reality" materialized around him. The book prepared to once again make sense.

Chapter Nine
Merlin's Beard

When The Wizard's feet struck the ground, it took him several seconds to regain his balance; his mind was spinning with the afterimages of the twisted void through which he had passed. It did not help that the ground around him was covered in snow. Looking around, he saw that the others had been displaced alongside him. Lying in the snow, with his naked butt in the air, was Jeff. Knorpe had landed on top of Knippe, knocking him to the ground.

Perplexed, The Wizard scanned the area around them. They were standing in a vast, open circle, bordered by uneven marble walls. Moonlight poured down from overhead, illuminating the area around them. The entire expanse was barren of anything and anyone, aside from some scaffolding on the encircling walls. The air was extremely cold, and the snow made the marble floors slick to the touch.

"What the hell happened?!" yelled Knorpe. He was standing atop his brother, looking around in a panic. "I was about to grab what I'm pretty sure was the *Holy Grail!*"

"I don't know…" muttered The Wizard, rubbing the dizziness out of his eyes. Slowly, he regained his focus and remembered what had happened. "Wait… the *Holy Grail* is just a myth, anyway… I assume you mean the *Goblet of Fire*, but that's a whole other thing…."

"Well, whatever…" Knorpe stepped off of his brother. "Where's the treasure we were gonna take?"

Merlin's Beard

"Yeah!" Standing up, Knippe crossed his arms and nodded. His silver hair was flecked with snow. "What takes?"

"Will you two just shut up? I'm still trying to figure out where the hell we are!" Frowning, The Wizard turned his back to the gnomes and scrutinized the ring of marble surrounding him. "Hmm... This looks about the size of Circle Tower, but with its walls standing only twenty or so feet... What could have happened to it?"

"Maybe we blew it up!" said Knorpe, beaming with glee.

"No, we didn't blow it up..." said The Wizard, clutching his forehead in exasperation. "There's no rubble, and the walls are covered in scaffolding." His mind began to piece together the details of what had happened. "I'm starting to worry about what just happened..."

"Yeah, no shit!" Hunching over, Knippe kicked at the snow dejectedly. "Not a single treasure! What a bust..."

"No, you idiot." The Wizard gestured to the area around them. "Look at where we are! It looks just like Circle Tower, but unfinished." He held up the *Chronomancer's Continuum*. "This staff is an artifact that can tap into the flow of time itself! Do you realize what that means?"

"We made it to Treasure Island?" asked Jeff. He was sitting with his legs crossed and a vacant grin on his face.

"No, Jeff, that's... Oh, why bother...?" The Wizard ran his fingers through his hair in frustration. He looked between the gnomes, expecting even those idiots to figure it out. He was absolutely incredulous in the face of their oblivious expressions. "Damn it, it means we got sent back in time!"

"Woah..." muttered Knorpe, his eyes widening in awe. "Like in my wildest dreams?"

"Umm... I guess so...." As The Wizard contemplated the chronologically relative scarcity of cocaine, his heart began to beat frantically. He had wanted to go back, but not this far. He pulled his beard restlessly. "It seems we've been wrenched back to the early days of The Circle, before the tower was even constructed."

The amazed look on Knippe's face once again melted into disappointment. "Does that mean there's no treasure in the vault?"

Chapter Nine

"It means the vault hasn't been built yet!" said The Wizard. He was freaking out; the last thing he wanted was to be stuck back in time with these assholes. "You know, kind of like the fucking tower itself!"

"Hey, there's no need for the attitude," said Knorpe. "We would have taken all the treasure if not for you! If anyone should be complaining, it's us."

"Are you insane?" Tilting his head towards the sky, The Wizard heaved an exasperated sigh. "You wouldn't have even gotten in without me!"

"And that was the *only* thing stopping us," said Knippe.

"Everybody just calm down." Jeff was lying on his back, gazing up at the stars. Although he looked relaxed, his entire body was violently shivering. Despite how cold it was, his manhood was still more substantial than The Wizard's. He yawned loudly, swaying in his spot. "We must all just lie back and let the icy will of the night take us to another dimension."

"Right…" As The Wizard observed his nephew's condition, he decided it would be best to find someplace warm. He was feeling the chill of the night air as well. He presumed the staff had taken them back to a winter long since past. "We should make a fire, and figure this out in the morning. I'm crashing pretty hard, myself; and I, at the very least, would like to stay thawed through the night!"

"Who should we cook?" Licking his lips ravenously, Knorpe leered at Jeff.

"*What?!*" The Wizard skewed his face, mouth agape, unable to believe what he had heard.

"He's asking who we'll sacrifice for our survival." As Knippe hungrily ogled Jeff's nude body, his stomach growled unnaturally loud for one so small. "I vote for the boy. He looks like he has tasty thighs!"

"I second the motion!" said Knorpe.

They began to advance upon Jeff, each drawing a small knife from the pocket of their corduroy trousers. Saliva dripped from the corners of their mouths.

"Stop it, idiots!" Growling angrily, The Wizard ran up to the gnomes and grabbed them by the scruff of their necks, causing them to drop their knives in surprise. "We're not stuck on a deserted island, okay?" He gestured aggressively at the marble ring around them, swinging Knippe as he did so.

102

Merlin's Beard

"Behind those walls lies the ancient city of Camelot. There's definitely gonna be food…"

He tossed the twins to the ground.

They lurched towards their knives as soon as they regained footing. The Wizard flicked his wrist, causing the knives to shoot out of their hands and land in the snow. He lunged toward the gnomes, grabbing their throats and mumbling an incantation. They both collapsed to the ground; he threw them in a pile atop Jeff, who had passed out in the snow.

As he began to walk towards the walls with the intent of tearing down the scaffolding for firewood and shelter, The Wizard heard hurried footsteps and loud voices on the other side. Torchlight ran across the top of the wall.

Suddenly, three knights ran through an opening that was presumably to eventually become the front door of Circle Tower. They surrounded The Wizard, pointing swords at his chest and torches overhead.

"What reason do you have for trespassing on the future grounds of Merlin's tower?" said one of the knights. He was thin and dark-skinned, with short hair and a goatee. "I am Sir Cumcisio, of the Knights of the Triangular Table!"

"We're a small order," muttered another knight. He was tall, bald, and muscular, with a thick, wiry brown beard. "We're hoping to one day be cleared of cowardice and earn our place at the Round Table… I am Sir Bearus!"

"And I am Sir Vivesalot, the leader of our order," said the third knight, glaring in suspicion. He had locks of wavy brown hair cascading down the back of his chainmail, and his face was coated in a light stubble. "Give us one reason why we shouldn't strike you down where you stand!"

The Wizard chuckled to himself. "Well, I've got a cat to feed in a few hundred years… Also, this." He held up his arms, narrowing his eyes in focus. A shimmering field of energy surrounded him, pulsing outward and knocking the knights back. Their swords clattered to the ground. The Wizard walked over to Sir Vivesalot, looking down and grinning wickedly. "*You're* gonna strike *me* down, you say?"

"You know magic?" Slipping in the snow, Sir Vivesalot scrambled away from The Wizard. Looking up, he trembled as his eyes widened in terror. "I thought it was only Sir Merlin and his apprentices that could control the arcane arts!"

"Look, I've had an extremely long day, and I have no patience for more goonery." The Wizard was crashing heavily from his multitude of highs, and did not have the energy to think of a particularly creative excuse. "I'm Merlin's little brother... my name is Earlin. Could you please take me to meet him?"

"Why should we believe you?" asked Sir Bearus, sitting up in a daze and rubbing his head.

"Do I need to give another example?" The Wizard held up his hand, this time conjuring a ball of white flames above his palm. It was not actual fire, merely an illusion, but the knights did not need to know that.

"Wait!" Sir Vivesalot fearfully shielded his eyes from the fire. "Fine, we'll take you to Merlin. Now that I look closely at you, you do look quite like him. Just please take the heat when he gets furious that we woke him up..."

"Please, we beg you!" His expression grim, Sir Cumcisio held up his hands in desperation. "I don't think I can take another flogging..."

"Fine. But you goons have to carry my associates."

"There's more like you?" asked Sir Vivesalot, looking around nervously.

"Oh, they're not like me," said The Wizard, chuckling to himself. "They're more like... well, you... but luckier." He began to walk back towards his party, motioning for the knights to follow. "Chop, chop. Let's get moving, I wanna get a warm bed to pass out in."

The three knights trailed tentatively behind. The Wizard held the ball of white flames about his head, illuminating the heap of unconscious bodies. Sir Vivesalot and Sir Cumcisio each grabbed one of the gnomes, and Sir Bearus grabbed Jeff. They headed towards the main entrance to the future tower.

"What the hell is with the dwarf midgets?" asked Sir Cumcisio. He held Knorpe at arm's length and squinted at him scrutinously.

"They're gnomes," said The Wizard.

"What the hell is a gnome?" Sir Bearus furrowed his brow at his fellow knights' loads. "And why do I have to carry the naked guy?"

"He's the heaviest," said Sir Cumcisio. "You drew the short straw on carrying loads when you were born with those huge muscles."

Merlin's Beard

"I wasn't *born* with them."

It took The Wizard a moment to realize why they did not know about gnomes. "Oh, that's right... gnomes didn't evolve until after magic was ubiquitous in society! It's remarkable how different the world was just a few hundred years ago..."

"What was that?" asked Sir Vivesalot. "I couldn't quite hear you."

The Wizard reconsidered mentioning time travel to these clowns. "I was just saying 'I hope there aren't any hard feelings about that spell I cast on you a minute ago.'"

Sir Vivesalot shrugged. "It's fine, I don't hold it against you."

"I mean, we *were* about to kill you," said Sir Cumcisio.

"Yeah, so I guess we're even, right?" Sir Bearus grinned sheepishly.

"Wow..." The Wizard shook his head in condescending incredulity. "How did the three of you get to be knights?"

"Well, technically, we're not knights anymore..." Sir Cumcisio hung his head dejectedly. "We were branded as cowards, and forcibly assigned to be night guards."

"Damn, that's harsh! I guess you could call yourselves the night-shift knights. Except you're not knights, so... nevermind...."

"Yeah," said Sir Vivesalot. "If people ever write books about the story of Camelot, we're definitely not gonna be in any of the good ones..."

They headed through the gap in the wall, and onto the streets of Camelot. It was a lot more quaint than modern Koric; instead of the stately manors that surrounded Circle Tower in his day, all The Wizard saw were tiny cottages.

Yawning widely, he stretched his arms. "Say, Merlin doesn't live in a little box like these, does he? I mean, he's got a guest bedroom, or at least a couch, right?"

Sir Bearus gestured to the foundation of Circle Tower. "What do you think?"

Rolling his eyes, Sir Vivesalot chortled disdainfully. "Yeah, that megalomaniacal mage has the knights building this colossal tower just to be his office. Do you really think he'd live in a place like these?"

"Which are really nice, by the way, compared to where the knights have to stay!" Sir Cumcisio crossed his arms and scrunched his face resentfully. "Our barracks are basically a straw shack!"

Chapter Nine

"I thought you said you weren't knights," said The Wizard.

"We aren't," said Sir Vivesalot, "but that just means we don't get paid. We still have a place to live; Merlin's not a *monster*."

"I'm just glad he stopped making us work on construction when everything's iced over," said Sir Cumcisio. "I've seen too many friends fall to their deaths for one month…"

"I heard that the giants were responsible for the construction of Circle Tower."

Rolling his eyes, Sir Vivesalot scoffed. "Oh, yeah, they're a *real* help, overcharging us for their magic to shape the stones, and then sitting on their giant asses while *we* have to hoist that shit up the wall with pulleys." He gestured to a pile of colossal marble bricks beside the base of the wall. They were significantly larger than any human, even Sir Bearus. "Apparently, they're 'afraid of heights'."

"Well, it makes sense," said Sir Bearus. "They say the bigger you are, the harder you fall."

"You'd know…" muttered Sir Cumcisio.

Sir Bearus smirked amusedly. "Because I'm tall? Is that even an insult?"

"Guys, be quiet," said Sir Vivesalot. He gestured to a manor they were standing before. "We're here, we need to think of what we're gonna say to Merlin when he answers the door."

The Wizard squinted through the darkness towards the manor. The moonlight illuminated it enough for him to recognize its facade. The second floor overhung an arcade of wooden pillars, and the terracotta roof had a stucco chimney on one side. Although it did not yet bear the olive green paint job, he knew it was his childhood home. It had been in his family for generations before him, and now he knew why.

The front garden was full of all sorts of strange and colorful flowers. Looming in the darkness in the left corner of the garden, there was the largest apple tree The Wizard had ever seen. To the right, nestled amongst the flowers, was a marble fountain, with a nude statue of Merlin jizzing out water.

The whole garden had been enchanted so that the snow simply melted away. The Wizard definitely did not remember any of this being there in the future. As he stepped onto the front walkway, he met a wall of warm, spring air.

"Shit, this is terrifying!" His massive muscles quivering, Sir Bearus' eyes widened in terror. "Can't we just wait until the morning? You can stay with us tonight! Our barracks are just down the hill." He gestured towards the slums that would one day become The Wizard's stomping grounds.

"I don't want to stay with *you*!" The Wizard wrinkled his nose at the thought of smelling Sir Bearus in close quarters for an entire night. "Let's just knock on the door, I'll do the talking."

"Well, can't we just leave it to you?" asked Sir Vivesalot, his eyes widening imploringly. "I mean, there's no real need for us to stick around, right?"

"No, you can't leave..." Although The Wizard had heard many myths of Merlin's legendary temper many times, the horrified way the knights spoke of Merlin was making even him nervous. With a flourish, he held his faux-fireball towards them. "In fact, knock on the door for me, and I'll stand in the back. Do it *now*."

The knights looked at each other apprehensively. They huddled up and whispered vehemently for a few moments. Sir Vivesalot and Sir Cumcisio pushed Sir Bearus forward after some muffled deliberation. Flipping them off behind his back, he sulked towards the front steps of the manor.

The others followed behind him. The Wizard extinguished his illusory fireball.

Throwing Jeff down on Merlin's front porch, Sir Bearus approached the door slowly. He tentatively raised his fist, and tapped on the door ever so slightly. Immediately, lights flared from the windows of the master bedroom. The hurried pounding of angry footsteps could be heard stomping down the stairs moments later. As the door flung open, Sir Bearus cowered in terror, shielding his face.

Standing in the doorway was a man nearly identical to The Wizard. He had a long mane of grayish-auburn hair, and an even longer beard. He wore a blue silk nightgown and a long, tasseled nightcap. Fluffy, pink squirrel slippers adorned his feet, contrasting wildly with his surly expression and flaming longsword.

Chapter Nine

"How dare you disrupt my beauty sleep?!" he yelled, waving the blazing blade in Sir Bearus's face. His eyes moved shrewdly to the nude, unconscious body on the porch, and then to the rest of the group. His scowl intensified. "What mess have you awoken me to?"

Too terrified to speak, Sir Bearus simply stared up at Merlin.

Stepping forward timidly, Sir Vivesalot gestured to The Wizard. "We found your brother lurking around the construction site. Apparently he was looking for you..."

"I haven't got a damn brother!" Merlin narrowed his eyes suspiciously at The Wizard. "So, who the fuck are you?"

"Umm..." Grimacing nervously, The Wizard tried to remember his assumed identity. "Hey, *bro*... it's me, Earlin...."

"Do I look like an idiot to you?" Merlin was holding the flaming sword directly at The Wizard's heart, its light glinting off his violent violet eyes.

The Wizard felt the heat of the sword singe the fibers of his robes. He stumbled backward, falling on his bottom. He stared up fearfully at the wrathful glare of his ancestor. He could feel the power emanating from him.

As Merlin met The Wizard's gaze, his eyes widened. He furrowed his brow and slowly lowered the sword. He looked down on him with a look of mixed disbelief and amazement.

"Incredible..." he muttered, extinguishing the flame of his sword as he slid it into his sheath. He held out his hand. After helping The Wizard to his feet, Merlin rubbed his eyes and squinted at him. "I couldn't believe it when I saw you, but you simply must be the boy from my prophecy!"

"Who are you calling a 'boy'?!" The Wizard pursed his lips indignantly. He was well into his forties, and he did cocaine like a man.

"*Don't interrupt, boy!*" Stepping back Merlin thwacked The Wizard fiercely over the head with the sheath of his sword. "As I was saying, I recently had a vivid dream about a descendant of mine being ripped out of time, and bringing me great power and knowledge." He beckoned The Wizard inside. "Please, do come in. You can even bring your... followers...?"

"They aren't all my followers," said The Wizard, grabbing Jeff by the ankle. He wrenched him roughly through the doorway and slid him under the robe rack. "Just the unconscious ones, otherwise *these* stooges," he gestured between the three knights, "can sleep on the streets for all I care."

The knights resentfully handed the gnomes to The Wizard, who tossed them in Jeff's direction. They each landed face first on the hardwood floor.

Sir Bearus glowered at The Wizard. "You know, we see ourselves more as musketeers than stooges…"

"Does this mean we can be reinstated to the knights?" Sir Vivesalot wrung his hands pleadingly. "Since we helped your brother?"

After considering this for a moment, Merlin nodded. "He's not my brother, but sure. I will restore your knighthood on the morrow."

"They tried to kill me," said The Wizard.

Holding up his hand, Merlin blasted the knights back with at least twice the force that The Wizard could muster. It did not even look like he was trying. Without even bothering to watch them land, he slammed the door. As he turned around, his eyes fell on Jeff's puckered, frostbitten anus; gagging in disgust, he conjured a pair of red flannel pajamas over Jeff's body.

The inside of Merlin's house was more quaint than The Wizard expected. The foyer was small, with a robe rack next to the door, and an abnormal amount of shoes for a man. There was a wall of tapestries to their right, bearing arcane symbols. Across from the front door, parallel to this wall, was a wooden staircase. In the wall to the right, a door hung open, revealing a grimy bathroom.

Against the side of the stairwell was a couch, facing into a living room to the left of the foyer. Across from the couch was a fireplace, in which crackled a merry fire. The coffee table in the middle was covered in papers and food scraps, with a scarlet and aubergine damask area rug beneath it. Right of the fireplace, there was an enormous pile of scrolls, potions, and other junk. To the left, there was a standing globe of Notearth. Hanging over it all was an ornate caged chandelier that The Wizard remembered was still there during his childhood, centuries later.

"So who are you, anyway?" asked Merlin, cocking his head inquisitively at The Wizard. "The prophecy was vague; it merely made it clear that you needed my help, and that the fate of the kingdom hung in the balance."

"I am your great, great, great… I am one of your descendants. My name is The Wizard." The Wizard held out his hand.

Chapter Nine

Merlin did not shake it. "What the hell kind of name is that? I don't like the idea of one of my descendants going by such a stupid name."

"Well, that's my name," said The Wizard. "Sorry it offends you so much."

"Well, whatever. Anyway, now that we've dispensed with that riffraff outside, care to explain these ones?" Merlin gestured to the unconscious bodies bleeding on his floor. He closed his eyes with a look of focus for a moment. He then gave The Wizard a look of solemn disapproval. "Their arcane auras are highly unusual. I would surmise that they have been displaced in time."

"Uh, yeah, that's right..." The Wizard was impressed and a little intimidated that Merlin could discern so much with a simple aura reading. "That's actually why I need your help... I didn't want to travel back this far, and I don't actually know how to operate this thing..." He pulled out the *Chronomancer's Continuum*, holding it out to Merlin. "So... if you could send us back to our own time, that'd be just swell!"

"This thing does indeed emanate powerful magic." Merlin appraised the staff scrutinously. "However, I sense something is wrong..."

As Merlin grasped the staff from The Wizard's hands, the pink crystal orb fell off the end, clinking resonantly on the ground. The shaft splintered in several places, causing the golden rings that jangled on the end of it to spill to the ground. All that was left in Merlin's hands was the runed gold sheathing that covered the center of the shaft.

"Well, that can't be good." Grimacing nervously, The Wizard gawked at the ruined remains of the staff.

"I don't understand..." said Merlin, staring at the handle in astonishment. He gathered up the rest of the staff, placing the pieces in sequence on his coffee table. "I still sense great magical potential within these fragments, but the flow of energy has been completely disrupted..."

"Maybe it got overloaded..." After a massive yawn, The Wizard shrugged. "The thing was always a piece of junk; no one could ever get it to work."

"Foolish boy, you broke it!" Swiftly grasping the crystal orb, Merlin swung it at The Wizard's head.

Expecting this, The Wizard attempted to duck out of the way; unfortunately, Merlin attacked with blinding haste, and struck him before he moved so much as an inch. Head spinning, The Wizard felt as though he had been bashed by twenty men.

"Interesting..." Nodding considerately, Merlin carefully assessed the head of the staff. He grinned at The Wizard, who was still seeing triple. "It seems that this crystal has powerful temporal properties. Even without a proper channeling rod, I was able to harness its power to hit you on the head fourteen times over the span of two seconds. This is an incredible discovery!"

"Yeah, so fucking incredible," muttered The Wizard. He laid back on Merlin's couch, rubbing his head gingerly. "It was worth every concussion..."

"You only have yourself to blame for that, boy!" Merlin waved the crystal in The Wizard's face. "You overloaded it, like an idiot. Be more careful and maybe next time that won't happen."

"What won't happen, getting beaten over the head?"

"Yes." Snickering, Merlin took a seat next to The Wizard. "Besides, it's not like *you* have to worry about concussions."

"What the fuck is that supposed to mean?!"

"Woah, woah, relax." Merlin placed his hand on The Wizard's shoulder. "I meant no insult that time; although, I can see how it was construed that way. Anyway, surely you know that beings like us can't be injured the same way a human can, right?"

"What do you mean, 'beings like us'?" Bemused, The Wizard groaned. He was too tired to take in much more information. "Is this about my 'magical blood'? Because I've only just learned of that myself, and I'm starting to wish I hadn't."

Merlin gasped. "What?! How could you have 'only just learned' of your innate abilities? You were born with them!"

"Well, my dad certainly never told me..." As he said this, The Wizard wondered why his dad had kept him in the dark. He had not had time to think about that much, but it raised a lot of questions. "I mean, I always knew we were powerful, that's why our family has always led the circle; I just had no idea that our blood was magical..."

"More than our blood, our very essence; our souls, if you will," said Merlin. "We are the chosen bloodline of magic, destined to both bring magic

111

to the world, and save the world from it. We are the disciples of the Arcanes, born to tear apart the ancient order of things and reform the world's design. We are each born with a purpose."

"That sounds like a lot of work," said The Wizard, "and I already have shit to deal with; I don't have time to find out whatever 'my purpose' is in the world."

"Ah, but you don't find your purpose..." Merlin stared into the distance, nodding pensively. "It finds you. Don't you get it? Any 'shit you have to deal with' is part of your destiny!"

"Well, isn't that just *delicious*?!" Scoffing, The Wizard threw his arms up in frustration. "It is already such a treat that I get to give up on my plans to save my dad from that test tube, all the while babysitting *these* idiots..." He jerked his hand towards the pile of gnomes and Jeff. "Why *not* put a cherry on top of this shit sundae?!"

"Wait, wait, hold on a second," said Merlin. "What was that you said about your father and a test tube?"

"Oh, right..." The Wizard hung his head in melancholy. Horrific visions of his dad in that tank flashed through his mind. He shuddered. "I forgot to mention that the Archmage from my time had him imprisoned. They have —"

"Hold on," said Merlin, raising his index finger, "you're not the Archmage? When did it get out of the family?!"

"Well, technically I'm the first..." muttered The Wizard, averting his eyes.

"What?! And just whose fault is that, exactly?!" Eyes narrowed, Merlin brandished the crystal orb at The Wizard.

"Look, that's not the point," said The Wizard. He could not wait to move on to a different subject. "They're keeping him and my grandfather in these huge glass tubes; apparently, the Circle has been draining them of their magical power for generations. They're being used as batteries..."

"This is troubling indeed..." Pulling a long wooden pipe from within his robes, Merlin began packing the bowl full of particularly premium cannabis.

The Wizard could smell the dank bud as soon as Merlin opened what appeared to be a dimebag of holding, a variation of a bag of holding. A bag of holding is a magic item enchanted to contain a small pocket dimension,

Merlin's Beard

allowing the user to hold massive quantities of items without being burdened by weight.

With a snap of his fingers, Merlin lit the bowl and took a massive toke. "I've often worried that magic could eventually corrupt humanity, and to have my fears confirmed is no welcome news… however, I'm glad you brought this issue to my attention, because we can take preventative measures."

"Like what?" Taking the pipe, The Wizard took an enormous toke as well, effectively clearing what remained of a half-gram bowl. It was the greatest tasting cannabis he had ever smoked, and it hit his brain harder than Merlin had. "I'm not sure we can stop this… As far as I know, paradox theory states that no event can be changed that will prevent the one who changed it from doing so. We may have bit off more than we can chew…"

"Yes, yes, I know all that." Merlin waved his hand impatiently. "I'm not suggesting we alter the course of events, but that we take measures to prevent them from going further. If we can send you back to your time, we should send you properly equipped."

"Okay, I like that plan," said The Wizard, scratching his beard. "But what do you mean by 'if' you can send me back?"

"Don't worry about it." Waving his off hand dismissively, Merlin began packing another bowl. "I like a challenge, and I'm sure I can figure this staff out eventually; just be patient. Here, take greens. This shit's enchanted as fuck." He winked, passing the pipe to The Wizard.

"Thanks." The Wizard took a puff and passed it back to Merlin. He lounged back on the couch, stretching luxuriously. His head no longer hurt, and he was wrapped in the warm embrace of the strongest weed he had ever smoked; however, one thought still burned in his mind. "I'm willing to do whatever it takes to help. I'll admit, I haven't always been a hero, or even a good person; now, though, I'm hungry for vengeance: starved, one might say. I can't stand the image of my dad suspended in that machine."

"Don't get ahead of yourself, 'big hero'." Laughing amiably, Merlin patted The Wizard on the back. He finished the bowl with one colossal toke. "We've got a lot of work to do first. Now, you keep using these food metaphors, so I'm pretty sure you're just hungry."

113

Chapter Nine

"Yeah, that too. I haven't eaten all night!" The Wizard felt much better now, as Merlin's magical marijuana had taken much of the edge off of his narcotic crash; however, he was so hungry he could suck a horse's dick, as long as he got to eat it afterwards. "What have you got to eat?"

They got up and meandered through Merlin's mess into the kitchen. There were papers, bubbling vials, strange crystals, and whirring gadgets everywhere; however, there was no sign of anything that could possibly be described as "food".

"Shit," said Merlin, as he rifled through the cupboards. "I've been meaning to go shopping. I've been spending too much time lately dealing with problems arising with the holiday celebrations…"

Merlin looked in the refrigerator. The Wizard noticed that it was much nicer than his refrigerator, despite being four hundred years older; in fact, most of Merlin's stuff was much nicer than The Wizard's. He felt decidedly self-conscious about this.

When Merlin stepped aside, The Wizard saw that the fridge was practically empty. His heart sank as he looked inside and saw nothing but a lumpy ball of sticky, brown chunks; a pitcher full of some creamy, pungent yellow liquid; and a large jar full of some strange black, thorny root clusters.

"Yeah, sorry," said Merlin, scratching his head. "All I have to eat is nutcake and cheesenog…"

"Seriously?" Wrinkling his nose in disgust, The Wizard reached for the jar of thorny root clusters. "What about these?"

"No, don't eat *those*!" Merlin slapped The Wizard's hand away from the jar. "Don't even touch those; don't even sniff the inside of the jar! Trust me, it's a *really* bad idea…"

This intrigued The Wizard. He figured it would be best to wait until Merlin was not around, but he was dead set on finding out what on Notearth those were.

Merlin set the nutcake and cheesenog on the counter. "Anyway, feel free to help yourself to these… I know *I'm* not gonna eat any more of that garbage!" He yawned loudly, stretching his arms above his head. "I'm gonna go back to bed. After you finish eating, feel free to crash on the couch."

He started towards the door to the living room.

114

Merlin's Beard

"Hold on," said The Wizard, "I wanted to ask a few more questions about all this destiny crap!"

"And *I* wanted to be undisturbed until morning, but we can't have every wish come true!" In a huff, Merlin turned and stormed out, grumbling to himself. "Nowhere in my prophecy was I ever warned that I wouldn't get any beauty sleep…"

The Wizard stood before the dubious food that had been placed before him. Opening the fridge, he considered trying one of the thorny root clusters. They looked disgusting and painful, but the way Merlin forbade him from touching them simply made him want them more. He assumed they would get him high as fuck. After a moment, however, he decided that he needed sleep, so he figured he had best not risk it.

Ambling into the living room, The Wizard threw himself on the couch. His mind was racing with all the information that had been piled upon it. When he fled from his assailants below Circle Tower, he had not had time to sit and process what he now knew. Now that he had time to think without a distraction, the weight of it all had begun to sink in. This was a bad time to be crashing from fairy dust; he was exhausted and dispirited, but still too wired to get any sleep.

So many questions raced through The Wizard's mind. How was he going to save his dad? What would happen if he gets stuck in the past? Who else is part of Archmage Quan's evil cabal? It seemed like he had none of the answers. The previous day — no, rather, four hundred years in the future — he had been nestled under a blissful blanket of ignorance. Now, however, his mind was riddled with anxiety.

Although he had never been close to his father, The Wizard still loved him with all his heart. The years since his father's passing had been particularly hard on him, and he missed him dearly. If he had the chance to get him back, he knew he would stop at nothing to get that done. His heart soared as he thought of getting to spend even a single day with his father.

There were so many things that had been left unsaid; so many stories had been left untold; so many drugs had been left unsmoked; and so many days together had been stolen from them. The Wizard could not stand it, thinking of how a man that had meant so much to him had been ripped away. Worse

115

Chapter Nine

yet, it had not been the cruel hands of fate that had taken him, but the calculated plans of a trusted ally.

The Wizard was far too exhausted at the moment to plot his revenge against Quan. Although he was desensitized by years of bitterness and regrets, The Wizard felt a deep sadness well up in his chest. He sniffled as tears began to well in his eyes. Relieved that no one was around to see him weeping, The Wizard sobbed into a throw pillow.

Even with Merlin's magical marijuana, it took a long time for his mind to relax enough to allow sleep. His dreams that night were plagued with grotesque images of Horner performing horrific medical experiments on his father. He awoke in a cold sweat no less than eight times, panting uncontrollably. Although the cannabis allowed him to get back to sleep, it did very little to help him with these vivid nightmares.

Chapter Ten

The Arcane Origin

he first thing The Wizard noticed when he awoke the following morning was the black and white cat having aggressive coitus with his mouth. Its ballsack was dangling directly before his nostrils, and it was rubbing its anus on the tip on his nose.

Grimacing in disgust, The Wizard smacked the cat off of him.

It hissed at him as it hit the floor, and ran off up the stairs. As it retreated, The Wizard noticed that it looked identical to his cat, Kit Mingers; this was exceptionally strange to him, as he had caught Kit Mingers engaging in that very behavior. Deciding not to worry about it, he hurried into the kitchen to rinse off his face.

After he finished thoroughly scrubbing his face in the sink, The Wizard decided to take a look around. He glanced into the living room, and saw that Jeff and the twins were still sleeping in the corner; it seemed that at some point in the night, Knippe and Knorpe had adjusted themselves so they were using Jeff as a pillow. There was no sign of Merlin, so The Wizard started rifling through his mess.

Most of the papers on the countertop were blueprints for magitech that The Wizard could not begin to understand. Some of them were recipes for potions with unspecified effects, and others were recipes for meals with unspecified flavors. The Wizard found it unusual that none of the papers bore any arcane formulas.

Chapter Ten

The Wizard's eyes fell on the nutcake and cheesenog. It had been about a day since he had eaten, and he figured he would at least try them.

The nutcake was as hard as a rock, and its surface was like superglue. When he attempted to bite into it, his teeth got stuck for a moment. Despite the stickiness, it was extremely dry; when he finally gnawed off a piece, it hurt his teeth to chew; he had to spit half of it out to be able to gag down the rest.

The Wizard opened a window and angrily threw the rest of the nutcake into the garden. He also poured the cheesenog out the window; he was not even going to try that foul concoction.

As he looked out the window, The Wizard admired Merlin's enchanted backyard garden. In the far back, there was a row of the largest cannabis plants he had ever seen. A pathway of yellow bricks led from a door in the corner of the kitchen, weaving through a sea of multicolored flowers.

The entire garden was overshadowed by an encircling hedge of cypress, dotted with tiny red flowers. There was a rainbow of roses lining the path, some of which had rainbow petals themselves. There were a motley of multicolored magnolia blossoms mantling a myriad of bushes against the house. In each of the far corners by the cannabis sat a sakura tree, with peculiar purple petals.

A sea of tulips filled the left side of the garden, forming what appeared to be Merlin's visage. The right half of the garden had a series of concentric terraces, upon which sat a spectrum of iridescent orchids. Sitting atop the highest terrace was the strangest orchid The Wizard had ever seen: its flower was the spitting image of Merlin's face.

It was strange to see such a beautiful, thriving garden when The Wizard knew there were several inches of snow just beyond the hedges. He could not help but think that, at one point over the centuries, his ancestors had really let this place go; it did not have any of these fantastic enchantments when he lived there as a child.

Suddenly, Merlin's voice piped up from behind The Wizard. "Pretty cool, huh? I made some of those myself."

The Wizard was startled by this, as Merlin had magically popped up behind him without a sound. He nearly leapt out of his skin, dropping the cheesy pitcher. It shattered into hundreds of pieces, which left trails of residual cheesenog as they scattered across the floor.

"Shit, sorry about that," said The Wizard, catching his breath. He waved his hand, causing the shards of glass to skate into a pile. Grabbing a washcloth from the countertop, he kneeled down and began to wipe up the cheesenog. "I'll clean this up for you."

Merlin shot him a scrutinous look. "Why are you scrubbing like a common servant? You've got magic, boy; use it!"

"Janitorial spells aren't really in my repertoire."

"Part of me just died inside." Scowling, Merlin put his hands on his hips. "Those are some of the easiest spells in the world, and you can't be bothered to learn them? Where is this family going...?"

Ignoring him, The Wizard wiped up the last of the cheesenog. With a wave of his hand, he caused the shards of glass to float in the air, and dropped them in the trash can.

"Hold on, boy..." Without warning, Merlin levitated The Wizard by the collar of his shirt and made piercing eye contact with him. "Are you telling me you don't even know how to use magic to properly fix that?"

"Matter reconstruction is hard, asshole! Put me down!" Gasping for air, The Wizard frantically pulled on his collar. He kicked angrily at Merlin for a moment, before suddenly falling to the floor as the spell was released.

As The Wizard stood up, he lunged at Merlin.

Flicking his wrist, Merlin caused The Wizard's robes to fly up over his head.

His robes tangled over his head, The Wizard stumbled around for a moment. He was wearing nothing but light pink silk underwear underneath. He had removed his pants when he had drenched them in sweat the night before.

Merlin burst out laughing. "What the hell are those?!"

The Wizard quickly stopped in his tracks, frantically untangling his robes. A few seconds later, he pulled them down where they belong. His face was redder than his beard.

"They only had them in this color... They're comfortable!"

"Yeah, whatever." Merlin turned around and walked into the living room, motioning for The Wizard to follow him.

Chapter Ten

As The Wizard walked into the living room, he saw Merlin bent over his companions, violently shaking them awake.

"How do you like it, huh?" shouted Merlin directly into their ears. He knocked each of them over the head with his fist. "Not so nice to be woken up by bullshit, is it?"

"Get the fuck off," muttered Jeff, pushing the gnomes off of him and looking blearily up at Merlin.

"What the hell?" Knippe got to his feet and stretched.

Knorpe didn't say anything. He simply stood up, glared at Merlin, and headbutted him in the shin.

"Ow, that hurt a little bit." Looking down irately, Merlin kicked Knorpe in the chest, sending him flying.

"Who the fuck are you?" asked Knippe, as he helped Knorpe up.

"My name is Merlin... and before you say anything, I don't give a fuck who you are."

Jeff's sleepy eyes lit up with awe as he looked up at Merlin. He just sat there, his mouth gaping stupidly.

Wincing in pain, Knorpe tenderly massaged his ribcage. "Well, how the hell did we get here? Last I remember, we were sailing for Treasure Island."

"Ask him." Merlin jerked his arm gruffly at The Wizard, who was laughing hilariously.

The twins ran over to The Wizard as Jeff stood up.

"Are you *really* Merlin?" asked Jeff.

"Indeed I am. Step aside, boy." Pushing past Jeff, Merlin threw himself on the couch. Chuckling, he watched as the gnomes berated The Wizard.

Jeff narrowed his eyes skeptically.

"You son of a bitch!" yelled Knorpe, glaring venomously at The Wizard. "You knocked us out!"

"Where the fuck is my knife?" Knippe was frantically searching each of his many pockets.

"Oh, shut the fuck up; I've got your knives right here." Reaching into his pocket, The Wizard pulled out a pair of knives and threw them at the gnomes; the blades stuck in the floor directly between each of their feet.

The Arcane Origin

Knippe and Knorpe slowly bent down and picked up their knives, never taking their eyes off The Wizard as they did so. They glared up at him, fists clenched on the handles of their blades.

Rolling his eyes, The Wizard conjured an illusory fireball above his hand and brandished it towards the gnomes. "Put those things away, idiots. I did what I had to do, you guys were acting like idiots. It was just a mild coma charm; you'll just be groggy for a few hours, and then you'll be fine."

With resentful huffs, the twins slowly stowed their knives in their knife pockets. They walked over and sat on the couch, pouting and loading a bowl of Merlin's weed. The Wizard dispelled his fake fireball.

"Hey, I never said you could smoke that!" Merlin ran over and snatched the pipe out of Knorpe's hand.

"What, you mean *this*?" Grabbing the dimebag of holding, Knippe poured a steady stream of nugs onto the rug. "Woah, there is way more weed in there than I thought...."

Over an ounce of weed fell out before Merlin snatched it away from him. "Don't do that! Do you have any idea how long it took to fill that thing up one nug at a time?!"

"Could someone please explain to me what the fuck is going on?" Jeff walked up to The Wizard, his face red with rage. "The last thing I remember is *you* climbing in through my window and waking me up. After that, it's all just patches."

"Really?" said The Wizard. "Damn, dude, you can't handle your drugs!"

"What the fuck did you do to me, asshole?! Where are we? Who the fuck is this guy who say's he's Merlin? Why don't I remember a damn thing? *Explain.*"

"Look, dude, you were never going to go along with the plan if you were sober... I slipped you a little fairy dust; so what?"

"Go along with what plan?" After a moment's pause, Jeff's eyes widened in horror. He groaned, burying his face in his hands. "Oh yeah, I remember... the *heist*... I swear, if you actually got me to do that, I'll —"

"You'll what? Tell your dad? Report me to the authorities? We broke into the vault under Circle Tower and stole a valuable artifact; we're already in deep shit."

Chapter Ten

His eye twitching madly, Jeff tensed up. "What do you mean '*we*'? I never wanted to do this shit. I never cared about your stupid time machine —"

"*Cronomancer's Continuum!*" said The Wizard. "It's a staff, not a machine…"

"Shut the fuck up!" Jeff shoved The Wizard as hard as he could.

The Wizard caught himself on the kitchen door frame. Steadying himself, he advanced upon Jeff. As the Wizard raised his hand, Jeff flinched; however, The Wizard simply smiled and placed his hand on Jeff's shoulder.

"Listen, bud," he said. "I know you're upset, and probably with good reason. But our plan worked. We got the staff, and we actually travelled back in time." He gestured to Merlin. "This is *actually* Merlin; we traveled all the way back to Camelot!"

"Seriously?" Pivoting on his heels, Jeff shot Merlin a distrustful look. "You're not having a laugh, are you?"

"No, he's telling the truth," said Merlin, who actually was laughing at this. "I really am Merlin, and this really is… well, not Camelot anymore… I've been trying to think of a new name for the Kingdom. I feel that people need to be distanced from Camelot to remind them who's boss after the fall of the Pendragon dynasty."

The Wizard raised his index finger pointedly. "How about you call it Koric? That's what it's called in our time."

"Well then, I suppose I have to call it that, to prevent a paradox," said Merlin. "I like it; Koric is a strong name for a kingdom."

"Right on," said The Wizard. "The kingdom is Koric, and this city is Theiyre."

"Good to know this city is still there."

"Oh, I see, it's name is already Theiyre!"

"Its name is already where?"

"No, Wheiyre is a city to the south. This city is Theiyre."

As this exchange was taking place, Jeff's mouth slowly fell open in incredulity. Listening from the corner, Knippe and Knorpe looked steadily more impressed.

"That makes no sense, damn it. What is this city's name?"

"No, it's not. Whutt isn't a city anymore."

"Most of the world isn't a city, you idiot. What are you talking about?"

The Arcane Origin

"Theiyre, stupid!"

"Who's stupid?! Other than you, obviously."

"Shut up, you assholes, don't change the subject!" His hands perched on his hips in annoyance, Jeff squinted scrutinously at Merlin. "Prove that we're back in time and that you're Merlin."

"Just take a look outside," said Merlin.

Jeff ran up to the front window and looked out. His mouth fell open in awe once again as he laid eyes on the incomplete foundation of Circle Tower, coated in winter snow. He stared outside for a moment, speechless and completely still. He turned around, his face frozen in shock.

"If this is a prank, it's a *really* good one…"

Smiling considerately, Merlin walked up and patted Jeff on the back. "It's okay, I understand; it's a lot to take in. Now, *sit down, boy!*" Grabbing Jeff by the throat, he threw him onto the couch. He then motioned for The Wizard to do the same. "You too!"

Merlin raised his hands at a large pile of books in the corner of the room. They all blew aside, revealing an overstuffed leather armchair underneath. He pulled the chair magically across the room to the other side of the coffee table and sat down.

"Now, I know you have a lot of questions," he said, "but I'm only going to do this once. You have one hour; start asking."

Jeff was massaging his bruised throat. "You could have just asked me to sit."

"I don't have time for that," said Merlin. "I have to oversee the suppression of the holiday celebrations in just over an hour."

"Where's the treasure he stole?" Arms crossed, Knorpe jerked his head towards The Wizard.

"You mean this?" Raising an eyebrow, Merlin motioned to the shattered staff sitting on the table between them.

"Oh… I thought that was just part of your mess..." His face falling, Knippe grabbed the crystal and held it up. "How much is it worth like this?"

"It's worth nothing, because it's not for sale!" Merlin swiftly lunged forward and grabbed the crystal from Knorpe. "I'm going to fix this staff, and then I'm going to keep it safe."

123

Chapter Ten

Leaning forward, The Wizard furrowed his brow. "Hold on, you're not giving it back?"

"Of course not. I need to make sure it's where it's supposed to be in four hundred years. Otherwise, you'll never have found it."

"Wait..." A look of wonder slowly dawned on The Wizard's face. "You mean this *is* the staff I found in the vault?"

Merlin smirked facetiously. "Of course it is! Don't you remember finding it?"

"No, I mean —"

"I know what you mean, I was just messing with you." Raising his pipe to his lips, Merlin cleared the entire bowl in one hit. Knippe and Knorpe looked extremely impressed. "I know it sounds crazy, but this staff exists in an infinite temporal loop. When I attempt to divine its history, its timeline is an endless circle; apparently, this was always predestined." He chuckled, scratching his beard. "My prophecy is turning out to be a little more complex than I expected!"

"So," muttered Jeff, scratching his head, "you're *really* Merlin?"

"Yes, idiot, we've been over that!" Scoffing, Merlin raised an eyebrow at The Wizard. "Who is this kid anyway?"

"He's my nephew, Jeff. No relation to you though. I only brought him along in case I needed a human shield or someone to pin the blame on."

"What the fuck, dude?" Glowering at The Wizard, Jeff threw his arms up in exasperation. "I can't believe you; you're a complete sociopath! When this is over, I am never talking to you again."

"Yeah, whatever. That statement presupposes the notion that I give a shit."

Jeff let out a scream of rage and lunged at his uncle. The Wizard threw a punch directly at Jeff's throat. However, both of them were stopped suddenly, just before impact. Merlin was holding his hands up, his face scrunched in frustration.

"Calm down, now!" With a flick of his wrist, Merlin forced them both back into their seats. "I have had just about enough bullshit for today, and I haven't even gone to work. I am in no mood for this."

"Okay, fuck..." Jeff adjusted himself into a less stiff position.

Pursing his lips, The Wizard jerked his thumb at Jeff. "He started it."

The Arcane Origin

"I don't give a damn!" Raising his fingers, Merlin force flicked The Wizard between the eyes. "Now shut up unless you have important questions."

"Do you have any food?" Drooling, Knippe peered ravenously into the kitchen.

"Do you like nutcake or cheesenog?"

"Go fuck yourself!"

Merlin shook his head impatiently. "Anyway, if you have any important questions *about your situation*, hurry up and ask. Chop, chop."

"Are we going to be able to get back to our time?" Biting his lip anxiously, Jeff eyed the ruined staff.

"Probably," said Merlin, stroking his beard thoughtfully. "I was laying awake for a while last night, thanks to being rudely awoken by a matter that could have waited until morning, and I had some time to think about the situation. Now, these pieces are the source of the staff's power." He levitated before their eyes the crystal head of the staff, the runed gold sheathing of the handle, and the rings that spanned the shaft. "They each serve an important purpose...

"The crystal is built with an unfathomably intricate lattice structure, directing the flow of energy in patterns almost as complex as a human mind. It is truly the most advanced piece of magitech I have ever seen." Merlin slowly rotated the crystal, staring at it almost lovingly. "It's built of near perfect material; I think this crystal could last until the end of the universe.

"These runes on the handle spell out an incredibly advanced arcane formula." He magnified the runes onto a large, illusory double of the handle; even The Wizard could not understand the arcane formula. "It appears to take raw energy from the user, and send it to the crystal in extremely specific patterns and frequencies. It would seem that the crystal has to be activated by this key, and a sufficient quantity of magical energy, to fully activate.

"Finally, these rings are augmentation rings." He levitated the five rings into a concentric circle, causing them to spin like a gyroscope. "You see, they have runes on the inside." Conjuring an illusory double of one of the rings, he flipped it inside out to reveal the inscription. "They are designed to interface with the channeling rod itself, rather than the user. Essentially, they

125

allow a sufficiently refined channeling rod to complete this massive energy transfer without instantly exploding."

"Wow… And I thought these guys were nerds!" Laughing boisterously, Knorpe gestured to The Wizard and Jeff.

Knippe gave his brother a high five.

"Be silent!" Scowling, Merlin force flicked both gnomes on the foreskins.

The Wizard laughed, and he too got force flicked on the foreskin.

Nodding knowingly, Jeff adjusted his glasses. "So, what you're saying is… if we can get a good enough rod made of the same material, the staff will work again?"

"Very good!" Relaxing his arms, Merlin lowered the pieces of the staff onto the table. "You're a bit smarter than you look, kid."

"That's what I said when I met him, too; word for word! Well, except the 'very good' part… I don't think I've ever said anything like that to Jeff." Grinning, The Wizard raised his hand for Merlin to high five him.

Merlin left him hanging until he awkwardly lowered his hand.

"Do we get paid for any of this?" asked Knippe, looking around greedily at all of Merlin's stuff.

"Okay, since no one's gonna say it, I'll just ask," said Merlin. "Who are they and why the fuck are they here?"

Grinning sheepishly, The Wizard scratched his mane of fiery orange hair. "Honestly, I'm not one hundred percent sure about either of those questions. I, uh… got pretty fucked up last night."

"Ugh…" Merlin groaned in disgust, burying his face in his hands. "So, this is where the family is going… It's one thing to get wasted, but not when you have important responsibilities! If my son ever associated with rubes like them, I'd flog him with my staff."

Crossing his arms, The Wizard snarled furiously at Merlin. "Hey, fuck you, don't talk to me like I'm a loser. I don't remember hearing about any of the Archmages before me getting sent back to meet you and fulfill a prophecy to save the world!"

"Who said anything about 'saving the world'? Besides, you're not even Archmage. You're a disgrace to the chosen bloodline of magic!"

The Arcane Origin

Throwing his head back, The Wizard groaned. "What do you even mean?! I keep hearing stuff about my 'magical bloodline', but what does that even mean? What are we?"

"Like I said, we are the chosen bloodline of magic."

"That is the most bullshit response I've ever heard." The Wizard ran his fingers through his hair in frustration. "Please just tell me what the hell you mean..."

"If the answer is not clear to you now, it is clear to me that you are not ready." At this point, Merlin was smirking. It was obvious he took amusement from The Wizard's confusion.

"You're a fucking asshole."

"So *this* is where you get it from," said Jeff, sneering at The Wizard. "I always thought it might be, because my dad always told me what an asshole your dad was... I just didn't really believe it, I always thought he was just making excuses for you!"

Merlin waved his hand dismissively at the two of them. "Yeah, yeah, we're all assholes here. Now, this isn't about feelings, it's not about *you*, it's about the damn situation. So far, the only one of you who's asked anything useful is the boy."

"Fine," said The Wizard, heaving a weary sigh. "What time period are we in, exactly?"

"Finally, a worthwhile question!" Nodding thoughtfully, Merlin scratched his grayish-auburn beard. "Well, as you can see outside, my tower is still under construction. It has been enough time since the fall of 'King' Arthur that the people have forgotten him and accepted my changes to the kingdom.

"Although magic and reason have reigned for many years, we have yet to extinguish the people's belief in the old religions. They still celebrate these ridiculous holidays, sacrificing animals to demons they call 'gods' and getting completely hammered. There are hundreds of these shitty cults, always fighting even years after the *Seal of Sequestering* was created to seal away their 'gods'... Sorry, I digress, I just get irritated around this time of year.

"Anyway, my point is, knowing all that, could you perhaps deduce what period this is?" Merlin raised his eyebrows patronizingly at The Wizard.

Chapter Ten

"Uh…" The Wizard looked around uncomfortably, searching for something else to talk about.

"If I had to guess," said Jeff, nodding thoughtfully, "I'd say somewhere between twenty-three and twenty-seven years after you brought magic to the world."

Merlin gave Jeff a rare kindly smile. "Very good! It's December of the year twenty-six, to be exact. I'm actually impressed. Tell me, how did you know?"

"Because," said Jeff, "after the great holiday slaughter of the year twenty-seven, you were finally able to convince the people that these holidays were barbaric. Anyone who disagreed was either incarcerated or already dead. You passed a law at the start of the next year banning organized religion from Camelot."

"Great, now that's information I can use," said Merlin. "I'm glad it's going to happen so soon!"

"Yeah, but thousands of people are going to die…" muttered Jeff. "It's going to be a massacre…"

"I like this boy!" Nodding approvingly, Merlin left his leather armchair and approached Jeff. "You're actually clever, kid, unlike the rest of them." He held out his hand. "What was your name again?"

Beaming with pride, Jeff shook Merlin's hand. "Thanks, it means a lot to hear that from such a remarkable sorcerer. My name is Jeff; it is an honor to meet you, Archmage Merlin."

"Don't use your mouth to make him *too* happy, suckup," muttered The Wizard.

Ignoring this comment, Merlin patted Jeff on the head. "No need to be so formal, my boy!" He returned to his armchair, lounging back and resting his feet on the table. "Look, forget what this asshole says, you're part of the family. Now, when I get back from work, we should have a long talk about history; I have a lot of questions. This stupid thing can only tell me about stuff that's already happened…"

Merlin reached into the pocket of his robes and pulled out a book that was altogether too large to fit in there without magic. It was a thick, leather bound tome. Gold leaf bordered the cover, forming a series of arcane runes;

in the center of the cover, it bore the symbol of the Arcane of Wisdom. When Merlin threw it on the table, Jeff and The Wizard both gasped in amazement.

"Is that what I think it is?" asked The Wizard.

"Yes. I mean, maybe..." Merlin squinted dubiously at The Wizard. "What exactly *do* you think it is?"

"Seriously?" Sighing, The Wizard gave Merlin an incredulous stare. "The fucking *Arcane Almanac*, obviously."

"I guess you're not *completely* clueless, then."

Jeff raised his hand to high five Merlin, who did not leave him hanging.

"So, that's really what it is?" asked Jeff, staring at the tome in wonder.

"Most indeed, my boy, most indeed!"

The Wizard scoffed. It was beginning to vex him how quickly Merlin was getting chummy with Jeff. "Oh, so now he's 'your boy'?"

"Yes, he's 'my boy', and you're just 'boy'! Now shut up, *boy!*"

"Wow..." Gaping in awe, Jeff ran his fingers across the embossed cover of the tome. "You know, this has been missing for almost four hundred years! I never thought that anyone would lay eyes on it again!"

"Really?" said Merlin, scratching his beard. "That's very curious... I have an idea, but I'll have to give it some thought..."

Suddenly, Knorpe pounded his tiny fist on the coffee table. "Okay, this is bullshit! We nosed into this situation to get treasure, but instead *this idiot*—" he motioned angrily to The Wizard "—breaks the only treasure. Now we have to listen to this stupid nerd lecture too?!"

Knippe was rocking back and forth in the corner. "When will it end?"

"Do they matter?" asked Merlin, cocking his head at The Wizard.

"What was that?" said Knorpe.

Both The Wizard and Jeff shook their heads fervently. With a snap of his finger, Merlin caused both gnomes to fall unconscious to the floor.

"Okay," he said, "any more questions before I go?"

"Do you also have the other two *Arcane Tomes*?" asked Jeff.

"Yes, I do. They were given to me on the day of my creation."

The Wizard raised an eyebrow. "You mean your birthday?"

"Simply put: no. I was not born as you were, but was created by the universe itself to restore the balance between order and chaos."

"What a bunch of crap..." muttered The Wizard.

Chapter Ten

"I think I get it," said Jeff. "I've heard legends that you were created by the Arcanes themselves to bring magic to the world. Is that true?"

"You've got it, my boy! I'm glad one of you knows what they're talking about. I hate answering questions."

"Wait, so you're like, half-Arcane?" asked The Wizard.

"That's one way of putting it. A very stupid way of putting it."

"Well, how would you put it? Will you just tell me what the fuck we are?" It was driving The Wizard cuckoo that Merlin was being so cryptic and withholding.

"Fine, I shall," said Merlin. "I was just having fun watching you try to figure it out. You remind me of my son, he still hasn't really figured out how to be clever either."

"Where is your son, anyway?" asked Jeff. "His name was Svendalf, right?"

Merlin narrowed his eyes at Jeff. "Please don't speak in the past tense while you're in my time."

"Oh shit, I'm sorry!"

"No worries, my boy. I was just messing with you. But seriously, stop doing that. Anyway, Svendalf is off hunting demons; we sealed most of them away, definitely all the big threats, but there are still a lot of stragglers."

He turned to The Wizard, who was tapping his foot loudly. "As for what we are, we are beings of magic itself. Within our mortal vessel, our true form is that of pure magical energy. We are similar to the Arcanes themselves, but on a much lesser scale.

"When the Arcanes created me, they felt... if you can call what they do 'feeling'... that the world was sick; that the balance between order and chaos was flawed; that powerful beings like demons held too much sway over mortals. That is why I was created, to bring magic to the mortal races.

"Some of the Arcanes imbued a portion of their power into potent magic artifacts to help bring about their devices. From the Arcane of Power came the *Arcane Dictionary*, the sacred tome that holds all the formulas for the precise control over magic; from Knowledge came the *Arcane Encyclopedia*, containing every piece of information in existence about our natural world; from Wisdom came the *Arcane Almanac*, containing the recorded history of everything that has ever happened.

The Arcane Origin

"The three *Arcane Tomes* were the only artifacts bequeathed to me, but I know there are others. The Arcane of Order was the force responsible for creating the *Seal of Sequestering*. Without that, we could have never opened the gateway to the Writhing Dark and sealed away the demon race. Other than that, I am unclear on the others, but perhaps the *Chronomancer's Continuum* is a creation of the Arcane of Time..."

"Damn..." His eyes wide, Jeff gaped at Merlin in amazement. Chortling, he gestured to The Wizard. "It's hard to believe *this guy* is descended from such powerful beings!"

"Yeah, well..." said Merlin, smiling snidely, "I get a sense that our bloodline has gotten... *watered down* over the years."

Disregarding this insult, The Wizard cocked his head inquisitively at Merlin. "So, I'm like... what? One-sixty-fourth 'Magic'?"

"Something like that..." Merlin rolled his eyes. "Anyway, I've got to go to work. You had your hour, that's enough questions."

"I still have questions!" The Wizard pointed to the clock. "And it hasn't even been a half hour, by the way!"

"And yet, inexplicably, I already prefer the idea of doing my job over staying here." Merlin pulled a fur cloak from the rack and put it on over his robes. Pulling an ornate staff out from behind the robes, he started out the door.

"Wait a damn minute!" Leaping out of his seat, The Wizard ran over and grabbed Merlin's shoulder. "Could you at least tell us where the hell to get food around here?"

Merlin sighed in exasperation. He waved his hands back at the table, conjuring a large, steaming roasted turkey, a plate of rolls and butter, and a pitcher of lemonade. "There. Are you happy?"

Annoyance gripped The Wizard's mind like a vice. "If you could do that the entire time, why didn't you last night? I'm fucking starving!"

"If you never learned basic conjuration magic, that's on you, *boy*." Merlin turned and left, slamming the door behind him.

With a sneer, Jeff slapped his hand on The Wizard's back. "How's it feel?"

"How's *what* feel?"

131

Chapter Ten

"How's it feel to have someone talk down to you and treat you like an idiot?"

"Gee, I don't know, Jeff," said The Wizard, glowering at Jeff. "Wanna find out how it feels to be pinned down and force fed a block of stale nutcake?"

"Is there any other kind of nutcake?" Laughing, Jeff kicked back on the couch and loaded a bowl of Merlin's weed. The hit he took was only able to blacken the corner of the massive bowl, and he coughed intensely as he blew it out. "Damn... that's good stuff."

The Wizard continued to give Jeff the stink eye.

Coughing, Jeff held out the pipe. "Want some?"

The Wizard sighed, and sat down next to Jeff on the couch. Taking the pipe, he figured he would feel better after hitting it. The two of them smoked several bowls of Merlin's weed. Jeff did not even mind that The Wizard bogarted most of the weed, as it was the most powerful weed he could possibly imagine.

It was not long before they were laughing, eating turkey, and swapping stories of the parts of the preceding night that they could actually remember.

"So you guys burnt down the Circle's secret library?" Laughing hysterically, Jeff leaned forward and slapped his knees.

"We burned a bunch of books, bro," said The Wizard, nodding and grinning proudly. "It was awesome. I bet Quan is pissed!"

"Serves them right. They shouldn't hide knowledge from the public, it's holding back the progression of society! It does kind of suck that the books got destroyed, but I was never gonna get to read them, so whatever."

The Wizard punched Jeff in the arm. "Those gnomish morons were right; you're a total nerd!"

"Whatever, I just think we all have the right to know the truth."

"The truth is that you're a nerd!"

Beaming with pride, Jeff held his head high. "Yes, I am! I think if everyone were a bit more of a nerd, the world would be a better place."

"Honestly," said The Wizard, patting him on the back, "I agree. I like nerds; they do all the work while I fuck off and party!"

"You don't say! And here I thought you worked!"

The Arcane Origin

"Hey, I work!" The Wizard crossed his arms indignantly.

Jeff furrowed his brow. "Oh, yeah? Name one time."

"Well... I worked pretty hard on that heist, didn't I?"

"You got high as fuck on Fairy Dust and improvised it, and you brought along three unnecessary accomplices just so you'd have to do less work!"

"It's not like you idiots actually saved me any work," said The Wizard. "Anyway, can we talk about something else?"

Smiling smugly, Jeff shrugged. "Sure. What do you have in mind?"

The corners of The Wizard's lips curled in a nefarious smile. "How about we drown the twins in warm water while they sleep?"

"You mean put their hands in warm water?"

"I guess so." The Wizard shrugged. "That could be fun too."

They went into the kitchen and rooted through Merlin's stuff until they found a few grimy bowls. After filling them with tap water, The Wizard caused the water to heat well past its boiling point. He handed one to Jeff, who shot him a bemused look. Approaching the gnomes, he poured the water directly on Knorpe's crotch.

Jerking violently awake, Knorpe scrambled away. "What the fuck are you doing?"

"Yeah, what the hell?" asked Jeff. "I thought we were pulling a piss prank."

"I thought this would be funnier." Chortling, The Wizard tossed the bowl at Knorpe. It narrowly missed his head.

"Sure, why not?" With a shrug, Jeff poured the contents of his bowl all over Knippe's face. "I'm still pissed that these dicks helped you drug me."

Plumes of steam rose from Knippe's blistering cheeks. "Ow! You son of a bitch! What was that for?"

Leering down at the gnomes, The Wizard palmed his fist menacingly. "That's what you get for being born!"

As he gingerly rubbed his steamed peas and carrot, Knorpe stared daggers at The Wizard. "You may laugh now, but soon you will feel the rash of Aliexnu! It will burn your genitals with the fury of a thousand bottles of aftershave!"

"Alright, so far I haven't said much about this ridiculous religion of yours," said The Wizard, "but what the fuck are you talking about?"

Chapter Ten

"You dare besmirch the glory of Aliexnu with your questions?!" Eyes flashing madly, Knorpe drew his pocket knife. "You will regret this blasphemy when the time of the Great Abduction comes! Having the audacity to question the sacred truth of Aliexnu will be the last thing you regret!"

The Wizard groaned. "Oh, why did I ask…? Please, someone kill me…."

"Oh, that's a bad idea," said Knippe. "The holy books say that if you die by anyone's hand but your own, you will burn in Aliexnu's mouth for eternity."

Snickering derisively, Jeff rolled his eyes. "This kind of insanity is why I don't believe in the gods. Well, besides the Arcanes, but they don't count."

"Say that again!" Brandishing his blade, Knorpe got in what would have been Jeff's face if he were three feet taller; instead, his face was right in front of Jeff's balls, and he failed to look very threatening. "Say that to my face, bitch."

"Look, let's all just calm down," said The Wizard, who was trying very hard not to laugh at this. "Merlin left us all this weed. It's so good, you've gotta try it."

"It better be good enough to soothe my second degree burns..." muttered Knorpe.

It was. In fact, Merlin's magical marijuana was so good that neither gnome stayed upset for more than a minute after taking a puff a piece. Several minutes later, they were all laughing jovially at what a "hilarious prank" that had been.

"I'm hungry enough to eat myself!" Drool dripped down Knippe's chin as he ogled his own thighs. "What else is there to eat around here?"

"Well, there's this rare delicacy in the fridge." Grinning, The Wizard gestured to the kitchen. "Merlin said we could each have just one. Want to?"

"Ooh, I'll try some." Jeff smacked his lips together merrily. "That roasted turkey left me with a hankering for dessert!"

Knippe's lip quivered with envy. "You guys had roasted turkey?"

"Well, Jeff, you're in luck!" Ignoring the gnome, The Wizard headed into the kitchen and opened the refrigerator. He held out the jar of thorny root clusters. "These things may not look it, but they are prized for their delicate sweetness and chocolatey aroma."

The Arcane Origin

Approaching the jar, Jeff squinted in suspicion at the strange, thorny root clusters. "What the hell are those things? They look like ent tumors..."

The Wizard averted his eyes as he tried to think of what to tell Jeff. "I forgot what Merlin said they were called, it was something elven and impossible to pronounce. Let's just say it was 'covfefe'. Anyway, they melt in your mouth; you've gotta try one!"

"You try one first," said Jeff, looking mistrustfully between the jar and The Wizard.

"I already did, and Merlin said only one each!"

Crossing his arms, Jeff shook his head firmly. "Nope, he most certainly did not. These clearly aren't food."

"Why else would he keep them in the fridge, Jeff?"

"I don't care in the slightest," said Jeff. "I'm good. You eat one."

"Quit your bitching!" Reaching up, Knorpe grabbed the jar out of The Wizard's hands. "I'll try one!" With a sneer, he pulled out one of the thorny root clusters and popped it in his mouth.

As soon as he put the thorny root cluster in his mouth, Knorpe was definitively sure that he had made a grave mistake. First of all, the thorns were razor sharp, and lacerated his tongue and cheeks; additionally, it tasted like bitter chemicals, and his mouth grew numb after a few moments of exposure.

Gagging, he attempted to spit out the disgusting, thorny root cluster; however, a strange force held him back. He felt as though the roots would not allow him to spit them out; they wanted to be inside him, and they wanted him to want them inside him. Knorpe felt almost as though he were being molested by drugs. Unable to stop himself, he swallowed the entire thorny root cluster.

His head began to spin uncontrollably, his stomach churning with a profound sense of terror. The fabric of his consciousness seemed to melt away into a secret sauce of senses. His reality turned to regurgitated soup, and his mind was suddenly flushed down the toilet bowl of his worst nightmares.

The others watched as Knorpe collapsed to the ground and began to scream in terror. They could not imagine what he was seeing. Visions of his fears and insecurities swirled before him, telling him how they felt about him; they did not have much to say that was positive, and the few compliments they gave were backhanded. The experience was beyond description, but needless to say, it was unpleasant.

Biting his lower lip nervously, Knippe watched his brother scrambling around in terror. After a moment, he took a deep breath and plunged his hand into the jar.

"Solidarity or death!" he shouted, imbibing one of the root clusters as well.

And thus began the gnomes' journey to the far edges of their sanity. Some say that their true adventure began that day, others say that it came to an end, but no one has ever said that it was interesting. An entire book could be filled with their drug trip, and no one would want to read it.

The rest of the morning was a whole lot of nonsense.

Chapter Eleven
One Night in Camelot

When Merlin arrived home from work that afternoon, the mess he found within his house had come very far indeed since he had begun to make it. Knippe and Knorpe were squatting at the base of the stairs, setting up a tripwire between the bannister and the wall. Jeff and The Wizard were lounging on the couch, watching the gnomes at work, and smoking bowl after bowl of Merlin's weed.

"What the hell's going on?!" yelled Merlin, squinting around the room as he hung up his cloak.

There were a multitude of tripwires littering the room, connected to many different contraptions. A good deal of Merlin's personal lab equipment appeared to have been dismantled and manufactured into these various contraptions.

"We're hunting for your cat," said Knorpe. He did not look up from the tripwire he was tying to the bottom bannister. "We think we've almost won."

Meanwhile, Merlin's cat was watching them from the second floor landing. The gnomes seemed to be too consumed by their trapmaking to notice this.

"What the fuck are you talking about?" Merlin raised his arms and slammed them down forcefully, causing every wire in the room to trip at once.

The tripwire on the stairs caused a large bucket of apples to spill from the landing, cascading down the stairs and burying the gnomes. The many other

Chapter Eleven

wires around the room caused a series of miniature catapults to fire all over the room. Several apples struck The Wizard and Jeff, bruising both them and the apples. Merlin had conjured a shimmering bubble of blue energy around him that blasted any apple contacting its surface into applesauce.

"Did you pick those from my enchanted apple tree?!" Scowling, Merlin trembled with rage. "Those are my thinking apples, you little shits!"

The gnomes pushed the pile of apples off of themselves, glaring up at Merlin.

"You ruined our plan!" said Knorpe

"Yeah! What did we ever do to you?" Pouting his lips, Knippe widened his eyes with unconvincing innocence.

"I'll kill you!" Merlin swung his staff fiercely, sweeping both the gnomes and many of the apples across the room. He then advanced upon The Wizard. "And you!"

"What did I do?" asked The Wizard, eyeing Merlin's staff nervously. His head still hurt from the last beating.

"You ungrateful child!" His eye twitching madly, Merlin whacked The Wizard violently over the head. "You came to me for help, and you've shown no respect for my home at all. The *only reason* I haven't kicked you out and left you stuck out of time is that I care about the future of my kingdom."

"Okay, okay, I'm sorry." It seemed that Merlin's blow had knocked The Wizard self-conscious. "I'll have Jeff help me clean this place up."

"Dude, what the fuck?" said Jeff. "I didn't make this mess! You're the asshole who egged them on to eat those weird roots."

"Wait, you gave those miniature morons some of my mandrake root?" His scowl intensifying, Merlin brandished his staff in The Wizard's face. "I need that for research! Do you have any idea how rare it is?"

"Oh, that's what that was?" asked The Wizard, tenderly massaging his scalp. "No wonder it made them so much crazier than usual. I just made up a stupid name and called it covfefe."

"Call it what you want, just don't take any. It will gradually turn your skin orange, make your hair fall out, and cause you to permanently lose a significant portion of your brain power."

One Night in Camelot

"It was like reality took a dump on my brain…" muttered Knorpe, as he lay in the corner, coughing up blood.

"*Anyway*," said Merlin, "it's uses in alchemy when diluted are invaluable, so it's *not to be wasted.*" He swiftly bashed The Wizard over the head with his staff once again; however, this was more of a stern "don't do that again" bash rather than a violent "I'll kill you" bash. With a glare, he snatched up his bag of weed and pocketed it.

"Ow, fuck, you've made your point." Groaning, The Wizard wondered how Merlin could possibly manage to hit the exact same spot every time. "Sorry I took your covfefe…"

"That's not a word, but whatever; I'll accept your apology once this place is cleaned up. I'm gonna go get a drink, and when I get back, I had better not find a single apple seed."

"Okay," said The Wizard, standing up and turning to Jeff. "You heard the man, let's get to work!"

"No," said Merlin.

"Huh?"

Merlin sneered at The Wizard. "Jeff's going to be coming with me." You and the dwarven midgets can do the cleaning."

"Sounds good to me!" Jeff happily leapt to his feet and put on his shoes. "Can I borrow one of your winter cloaks?"

"This is bullshit!" As The Wizard assessed the mess, a look of outrage crossed his face. "I can't clean this place in time by myself, and those idiots are just making it worse!" He gestured to the twins, who were now making applesauce angels on the rug.

"Sure, Jeff, you can wear this." Ignoring The Wizard's complaints, Merlin handed Jeff a spare cloak before donning his own.

"What about these flannel pajamas?" asked Jeff.

"Oh, sorry, I forgot about those." With a snap of his finger, Merlin replaced Jeff's pajamas with a pair of denim jeans and a white wool turtleneck. "I put a pair of thermal underwear in there for you, it should help with the cold."

"Thanks!"

"Do you at least have a vacuum?" asked The Wizard.

Chapter Eleven

"You mean like in outer space?" Merlin turned to laugh as he opened the door. "Now why on Notearth would I have something like that in my house?"

"No, it's a machine that sucks stuff up and obliterates it with magic... I guess it hasn't been invented yet."

"I know what a vacuum is, dumbass, I'm just fucking with you. Like most modern technology, I was the one who invented it. It's in the hall closet upstairs, just mind the skeletons when you grab it." Merlin slammed the door behind him as he and Jeff left.

"What was that you said about skeletons?" asked Jeff, as they descended the front steps.

"Oh, they're just a little experiment of mine," said Merlin, chuckling to himself. "Hopefully that idiot doesn't wake them up."

"Wake them?" Jeff furrowed his brow in confusion.

"Don't worry about it."

"Uhh... Okay..." said Jeff slowly. He kind of felt like he should. "So where are we going?"

"The finest restaurant in the city, perhaps even the entire kingdom!"

They walked around the Regal Roundabout to the other side of Circle Tower's foundation. With snow caked onto the ring of marble blocks, from the outside it looked like a giant birthday cake. After walking a few blocks away from the Roundabout, they arrived at the building that would one day become *Luncheons and Flagons*. Luckily, Jeff did not remember this, so Merlin was spared knowing the eventual fate of his favorite restaurant.

The building was much nicer than it was in the future. It's worn out brick walls were currently smooth and clean. There were plant pots hanging from the walls with vines spilling out of them, covered in flowers of all colors. There was even an awning stretching out in front of it, covering a quaint, little patio out front. The sign above read *Elfonzo's Teahouse*.

"Oh, it's a teahouse!" Jeff raised his eyebrows in surprise. "Maybe I'm too used to The Wizard; I just assumed we were going to a bar."

"You obviously haven't ever tried Elfonzo's tea!" Grinning enthusiastically, Merlin held the door open for Jeff. "You're in for a treat!"

One Night in Camelot

"Ah, Mister Merlin!" A dark haired elf in a tuxedo approached them, shaking Merlin's hand unctuously. He had bushy eyebrows and a thin layer of peach fuzz over his lips, which in terms of elven facial hair is considered a full beard. "It's good to see you again! We have your special booth ready for you, as always!"

"Good to see you too, Elfonzo." After Merlin shook Elfonzo's hand, he patted Jeff on the back. "This is my associate, Jeffery... sorry, I don't actually know your last name."

"The name's Jefferius Darwinius Greene," said Jeff, as Elfonzo gave him a hearty handshake as well. "But you can call me Jeff. Nice to meet you, Elfonzo"

"It's nice to meet you as well, Mister Jeff! Come, come, we shall get you two started with our most relaxing opium tea to help you get comfortable and set the mood for your date!"

"Not a date!" Hastily shaking his head, Merlin followed Elfonzo to a luxurious booth next to one of the front windows. "We're just talking Circle business. I think it'd be best if we start with a more stimulating, coca-based beverage."

"You know best, Mister Merlin," said Elfonzo, bowing as he sat them in the booth. "I shall start your with our famous coca-kanna-khat blend!"

"Umm... can I actually just get a chamomile?" asked Jeff, scratching his goatee. "I don't really want to do any more heavy stimulants. You wouldn't believe what I went through before I arrived."

"Nonsense!" Merlin waved his hand dismissively at Jeff. "That sounds perfect, Elfonzo! While you're at it, brew me a double."

Elfonzo bowed before turning and heading back behind the bar, where there were dozens of jars full of herbs, and several large kettles boiling on a stove. He began to brew their drinks, blending various herbs together.

"I'm good, seriously," said Jeff. The thought of getting high on powerful drugs while stuck in a strange time period made him very nervous.

"I want to hear all about the future of this country," said Merlin. "This stuff will simply help you talk faster."

"I could just talk fast without being high, you know..."

Chapter Eleven

"Look, Jeff, you're being *very* rude. It's not as fun being high if the people you're with don't match your energy. Just drink one and tell me about my future, and I promise you'll be rewarded."

"Ugh... fine..." Jeff was starting to see that The Wizard's personality really did run in the family. "I guess this is why they say you shouldn't meet your heroes...."

Merlin ignored that last comment. A few minutes later, Elfonzo served them each an ornate teacup full of foul-smelling liquid. Merlin thanked him and quickly began sipping his tea without even waiting for it to cool. After blowing on his for a moment, Jeff took a sip. The tea tasted worse than it smelled; however, after a few moments, his mouth went numb and he no longer minded the taste.

"Not bad!" said Jeff, his mood quickly perking up.

Within a span of less than five minutes, Jeff had nearly drained his drink, and Merlin was already setting to work on his second. They were getting right proper as fuck, and The Wizard would be properly jealous if he knew what they were up to.

As it was, back at Merlin's house, The Wizard was already quite jealous of anyone not in his situation. Knippe and Knorpe had left directly after the others to "commit shenanigans in the neighbors' houses", leaving him to do all the cleaning by himself. At the moment, however, it was quite difficult for him to get any cleaning done. He had found himself in a bit of a pickle; there were currently two dusty skeletons trying to beat him over the head with a broomstick and a mop.

While backing away down the hall, dodging janitorial equipment, The Wizard struggled to think of how to deal with this without making a bigger mess. He wondered why Merlin had been keeping two undead minions in his broom closet. If they were supposed to be helping him clean, The Wizard did not think they were doing a good job.

"Give it a rest, bone drones!" The Wizard blocked a blow from the broomstick, firmly gripping the shaft and tugging hard. As he attempted to jerk the broom out of the skeleton's hands, the other skeleton began to repeatedly whack him with the mop. Although the blows were not very hard, a few of them struck the exact spot Merlin had left swollen and throbbing. "Fuck off, you heap of shit!"

His head exploding with pain, The Wizard released the broomstick and leapt back. These skeletons were really starting to piss him off. Knowing he could not reason with or inflict punishment on a couple of mindless undead, he figured his only choice was to destroy them. He hurried down the stairs, intent on luring them outside, where they could be safely exploded.

Unfortunately, The Wizard forgot about the dozens of apples piled at the foot of the stairs; suddenly, he felt his feet slide out from under him. Toppling backwards into a pool of applesauce, he bashed his head on the hardwood floor.

"Son of a bitch!" He massaged his scalp, blinking stars out of his eyes. "Always the same spot..."

The skeletons began advancing down the stairs, their custodial instruments raised menacingly. With a pained groan, The Wizard pushed himself to his feet and staggered to the door. He stepped out onto the front porch, turning to check the skeletons' progress. They were near the bottom of the stairs, and were about to step into the foyer. The Wizard wondered for a moment if they would also slip on the apples, but unfortunately, they managed to avoid them.

However, the skeletons were not so lucky when it came to the apples Merlin had blasted into sauce all over the floor. The skeleton in the rear was the first to slip in the applesauce. As it slid across the floor, it grabbed the other skeleton for balance. The Wizard stepped aside as both skeletons stumbled onto the porch, flailing their cleaning tools wildly.

They tumbled past him, and right down the front steps. When they struck the pavement, their bones broke apart at the joints, clattering in all directions. A few of the bones continued to twitch, attempting to pull themselves back into a proper skeleton.

"Well, that was a freebie. I was kind of looking forward to blowing them up, but at least this way there's a lot fewer pieces."

The Wizard went inside and rifled through Merlin's kitchen until he found a couple of burlap sacks. When he got back outside, a few parts of the skeletons had already begun to reassemble themselves; not having any of that, The Wizard quickly bashed them to pieces with the broom, before

Chapter Eleven

throwing it and the mop onto the porch. The lone bones rattled in futility as he gathered them into the bags.

Although he was sure he had missed at least a few bones, The Wizard dragged the sacks back into the house and up the stairs. After he got the vacuum out of the hall closet, he threw the bags of skeletons in the back and locked the door. *At this point*, he thought, *what Merlin wants to do with those pieces of shit is his problem.*

The Wizard grimaced as he surveyed the living room. It seemed so much messier now that he had to clean it up. He was realizing that his work had only begun...

Hours later, at *Elfonzo's Teahouse,* Jeff and Merlin were deeply engrossed in a conversation about the future history of the kingdom formerly known as Camelot. Overall, Merlin seemed displeased with the way his descendants had conducted their rule.

"So, you're telling me they tore down the Merlin Wall?!" said Merlin, slamming his hand down in outrage.

"All except the part separating the slums from the center of town," said Jeff. "Despite the protests, the wealthier citizens insisted that it stay up."

"But the whole reason I'm building the Merlin Wall is to segregate the *entire crappy city* from the wealthier residents. That way I'll never have to see those filthy knights again, except the ones lucky enough to be stationed as gate guards!" Merlin buried his face in his hands.

"Well, if it makes you feel any better, they don't tear it down until after you die."

"That reminds me, I didn't say anything at the time, but I wish you hadn't told me the exact date. Nobody wants to know that..."

"Sorry about that!" Jeff laughed heartily before polishing off yet another cup of tea. "I guess I got a little carried away."

"Water under the bridge, my boy. Come on, we should get going; it's getting late." Merlin stood up and grabbed his coat. He waved at Elfonzo from across the room. "I'm heading out, Elfonzo! Just put these on my tab."

"Two more days, Mister Merlin." With a stern look, Elfonzo put two of his fingers to his eyes and pointed them at Merlin.

One Night in Camelot

"What was that about?" asked Jeff, as he and Merlin stepped out into the snowy street. "I thought you settled your tab at the end of the month..."

Merlin laughed. "Elfonzo has me on a week to week plan."

They cracked jokes and exchanged laughter as they returned to Merlin's manor. It was well into the night, but Jeff's vision had never been better in the dark; he could not help but feel that it was hot outside for such a snowy night. For the remainder of his days, Jeff never experienced anything he enjoyed as thoroughly as he had enjoyed that evening.

When they arrived at the house, the front door was hanging wide open. The wind was causing it to thud repeatedly against the siding, chipping the paint with its knob. Jeff gave Merlin a nervous glance, but the old wizard seemed unphased by this omen. They sauntered up the steps and into the foyer.

The Wizard was vacuuming applesauce out of the rug when he noticed their arrival. "Shit... I'm almost done, don't freak out. I got all the solid chunks, but this shit is really hard to get out of carpet." The applesauce was simply sloshing around in the rug as The Wizard ran the vacuum over it. "No offense, but your vacuum sucks."

"Don't worry about it." Merlin raised his finger and absently twirled it; the applesauce rose out of the carpet in a spiral, forming into a hovering ball of mush. He snapped his fingers, and it vanished into thin air. "It's just a prototype, I'm not offended."

The Wizard was outraged. "Hold on a fucking second... You could do that the whole time? Why the hell did you make me spend all these hours cleaning?!"

Merlin approached The Wizard, placing a hand on his shoulder. He smiled paternally. "Because if I hadn't, you would not have learned a lesson."

"Typical..." The Wizard sighed, giving Merlin a dirty look. Suddenly, he noticed the old man's pupils. He turned and squinted at Jeff, and his suspicions were confirmed. "Have you two just been getting high this whole time?!"

"Well, we haven't *just* been getting high," said Jeff, laughing hysterically and shooting a finger gun at Merlin. "But we're *not* not high, if you catch my drift."

Chapter Eleven

"Jeff, a boulder could catch your drift," said The Wizard, crossing his arms and scowling. "Did you guys at least bring some drugs for me?"

Merlin scoffed. "What do I look like, your mommy?"

Jeff fell to his knees, clutching his chest in laughter.

"Ugh... whatever... Can I at least smoke some weed? I've had a really stressful couple of hours, and you didn't even leave me a single bowl."

Perhaps it was because he was already fancytime proper out of his pants, but Merlin gave The Wizard a kindly smile. "Sure, why not? You may be a disappointment and a disgrace, but you're still family." He drew the magic baggie out of his pocket, pulling out a sizable nug. "Here, load this while I break out my special absinthe."

"Wow, seriously?" The Wizard's mood perked up in an instant. "That sounds great right about now, it's my favorite! What's gotten into you?"

"I guess you could just call it holiday cheer!" Merlin hastened to the kitchen to fetch the drinks. He emerged a moment later with not one, but three entire bottles of absinthe.

As they drank and made merry, Merlin regaled them with tales of his adventures. Jeff seemed to be a lot more interested in the stories than The Wizard ever could have been. The stories were very fantastical, and The Wizard found them hard to believe; he did not miss a chance to voice this opinion to Merlin.

"This isn't another story like that one where you 'rounded up the last two Time Lords', whatever the hell those are, and 'used peyote to settle all their differences'?"

Merlin took a deep swig from his bottle. "No, this was more of a... *sexual* conquest. It took place early in the demon wars, before the succubi were vanquished. I was pounding beers in this dwarven pub, and —"

Suddenly, a series of thuds could be heard coming from the fireplace. Soot and debris rained down and extinguished the fire. The sounds continued down the chimney until Knippe and Knorpe popped out of the bottom. They were covered in cobwebs and soot, and each carried a hefty sack of clanking finery. Landing in the smouldering embers of the fire, they frantically scrambled to safety.

One Night in Camelot

Knippe dropped his bag, causing a fine silver platter and a few gem-encrusted goblets to spill out. He snickered. "Uh oh, looks like my family jewels fell out of my sack!"

"Hey, those talking action figures are back..." Merlin recoiled at the sight of the gnomes. He nudged The Wizard in the arm. "Do something about them; they are really freaking me out."

The Wizard's eyes widened. "I think they brought us a bag of gifts!"

"Wow, you guys must be shitfaced," said Knorpe. His hand tightened around the mouth of his bag. "You're talking crazy!"

"What have we been missing?" asked Knippe, hastily stuffing his treasures back into his bag. "Why isn't Merlin wearing any pants?"

"Were you three banging?"

"What?!" The Wizard regained a portion of his self awareness. "Ew... what is wrong with you? That's disgusting, I'm related to both of them!"

"Yeah, but the two of them aren't!" Knorpe pointed between Jeff and Merlin. "So, give us the scoop on what you've been doing!"

"Shut the hell up," said Jeff, taking a deep pull of absinthe. He burped loudly. "No one wants to hear about your perverted fantasies."

The Wizard gave Jeff a high five, and the gnomes stuck their tongues out at them. Merlin chuckled fervently.

A baritone meow echoed through the room. Sitting atop the mantlepiece, ready to pounce, was Merlin's enormous tuxedo cat. He let out a deep, slow growl, baring his teeth at the Knippe and Knorpe. A murderous look in his eye, the cat leapt down at them.

Fear filled the eyes of the gnomes. All they could do was shield their faces with one hand and their testicles with the other, a maneuver their muscles had obviously committed to memory. The bags of ill-gotten booty dropped out of their hands as the cat soared towards them.

Knippe let out a pained yelp as he was tackled to the ground. Having been knocked backwards onto his ass, Knorpe watched in stunned silence as the cat mauled his brother. Shielding his throat from the cat's teeth, Knippe slapped at the beast's face in futility with his free hand.

Roaring snarls and growls reverberated off the walls, drowning out Knippe's cries of agony. After a moment of hesitation, Knorpe gulped nervously before drawing his knife and leaping onto the cat. He was able to

147

knock the beast onto its side, although the cat evaded his knife with itself-like reflexes. Knippe crawled away weakly, weeping as his brother wrestled the beast.

The Wizard and Merlin nearly fell out of their seats in laughter. They were leaning on each other for support as they gleefully slapped their knees. Jeff, on the other hand, was biting his lip as he watched Knorpe swing his blade wildly at the cat.

For a while, it seemed that despite his best efforts, Knorpe was about to be slaughtered. After only a few seconds, the cat had turned the tables, and was standing atop the gnome. As he thrashed at Knorpe's face with his claws, the cat began thrusting his pelvis violently. Knorpe let out a scream of defiance and thrust his knife directly at the beast's chest.

The cat yowled in pain as blood spurted from the wound, falling on his side. Knorpe grabbed his knife and scrambled to his brother's side. Jeff gasped and leapt out of his seat as the cat laid in a pool of blood. Even The Wizard looked concerned, but Merlin was still laughing hysterically.

"What is wrong with you?!" yelled Jeff, gaping at Merlin in disbelief. "He just stabbed your cat! Can't you do anything to save it?"

"Don't worry about it." Merlin calmly pointed to the cat. "He's fine. See?"

Although it looked like half of the cat's blood was soaking into the rug, he had gotten to his feet and was licking his crotch clean. Ejaculate was dripping from the cat's penis, and he seemed to have calmed down. The gnomes looked completely flabbergasted as they watched the cat get up and slowly saunter into the kitchen; their head-to-toe wounds were not so quick to heal, and they were both quivering like mad as they tenderly licked each other's scratches.

"Umm... how is your cat okay?" Jeff peered curiously into the kitchen as the cat casually consumed kibble. "I just watched him get stabbed in the heart...."

"It's a long story," said Merlin, packing a bowl of weed into his pipe. "Let's just say I was tired of having to get a new cat every time I burnt down my lab. That reminds me..." He pulled a small flask out of his pocket, took a swig, and blew it towards the fireplace, igniting it with a snap of his fingers.

One Night in Camelot

The embers reignited into a blaze. "I could do it with magic, but that's just so much more fun."

"You know, Merlin, you're not so bad." The Wizard laughed as Merlin passed him the pipe. He could have sworn there was something he wanted to ask Merlin about that cat, but he could not remember what for the life of him. He thought the cat seemed strangely familiar, but at the moment, he was more concerned with getting something to eat. "Watching those gnomes get mauled made me hungry; can you conjure us some spicy fried chicken?"

"I'm gonna be honest with you about something. I'm actually a terrible cook with magic; when I gave you that food earlier, I actually just teleported it out of a nearby kitchen."

"So that was somebody's lunch?" Jeff chuckled and shook his head irreverently. "That's hilarious! Don't they know it's you when that happens, though?"

"Yup," said Merlin, smirking devilishly, "but what are they going to do about it?"

Merlin summoned a grilled chicken onto the table, seasoned only with salt and pepper; he apologized for the poor choice of local restaurants he had to work with. He also summoned them a bowl of mashed potatoes and a boat of gravy. Although it was not what he asked for, The Wizard immediately dug into the food with ravenous ferocity. Merlin and The Wizard snatched up the best bits before Jeff could get any, leaving him with nothing but dry breast meat. The three men greedily gobbled their dinner, as the gnomes watched with envy in their eyes. The Wizard gave them the finger.

Eventually, Knippe and Knorpe seemed to take the hint that they were not going to get any food or drinks; they sulked into the foyer and up the stairs, muttering about planning their revenge.

After washing down the chicken with the last of their absinthe, the three men were practically falling asleep on the couch. As Merlin stood up to retire for the night, he beckoned Jeff to come upstairs and sleep in his guest bedroom. The Wizard could not believe that Merlin made him sleep on the couch when he had a guest room; when he asked why Jeff got to sleep in the bed, Merlin told him that he only gave rooms to people he liked. Jeff beamed with pride.

Chapter Eleven

Merlin grabbed his pipe and weed, leaving a small pile of nugs and a pack of papers. The Wizard resentfully thanked him, before beginning to roll a joint. As the two of them sauntered upstairs, Merlin was explaining to Jeff how to operate his room's climate control.

Sleep crept over The Wizard as he laid back on the couch with a joint between his fingers. Comfortable as he was, it was in his nature to jealously brood over Jeff getting to sleep in an actual bed. He wondered how nice of a guest room Merlin actually had. As he drifted into a drunken slumber, his mind's eye was filled with visions of exaggerated luxury.

Late that night, The Wizard's snores filled the living room. The stairs creaked softly as two tiny shadows scampered down them. The shady figures made their way to the couch, climbing onto the back. In the dim light of the smouldering embers that filled the fireplace, the flickering silhouettes of Knippe and Knorpe could be seen looming over The Wizard, carrying Merlin's magical vacuum cleaner.

Slowly, Knorpe parted The Wizard's robes and lifted his shirt. Once The Wizard's chest had been exposed, Knippe slid the hose of the vacuum toward his nipples. The gnomes had jury rigged some sort of makeshift nozzle that split at the end into two flexible tubes. Knorpe delicately placed the mouth of each tube directly over The Wizard's nipples, before giving his brother a thumbs up. When Knippe flipped the power switch, The Wizard's screams immediately drowned out the sound of the vacuum.

Freaking the fuck out, The Wizard leapt off the couch. When he moved away, the tube on his nipples tensed, causing the vacuum to topple off the couch. As The Wizard attempted to remove the tubes from his nipples, he stumbled backwards and dragged the vacuum across the floor. Stepping into the pool of congealed cat blood, he slipped backwards and bashed his head against the hearth. Pain exploded through his grievous skull contusions.

Knippe and Knorpe had fallen off the couch after the vacuum, when they were overtaken by laughter.

"That's what you get for pouring boiling water on us!"

"Yeah, and for not giving us any worthwhile drugs!"

When The Wizard got to his feet, he lunged towards the vacuum. He turned the machine off, and much of the suction on his nipples was released;

however, the tubes were still firmly stuck to his nipples. Cringing in pain, he gingerly removed them. Underneath, his nipples looked like a couple pans of berry cobbler. Blood dripped from the bright red ring around the horrendous hematomas. Just the tiniest bit of milk trickled from each nipple.

The Wizard was pissed in every sense of the word; his present attitude, his blood alcohol level, and his pants could all be described as pissed. In fact, "pissed" was just about the only word that gave his condition any justice. Seething with murderous rage, his mind raced with feverish formulations of revenge stratagems. As he pondered how he ought to pay these gnomes back, they clearly sensed his motivations.

Reaching into his pocket, Knorpe withdrew a small metal canister. He pulled a small pin out of the top, throwing the canister at The Wizard. Smoke spewed out of the top as it sailed through the air, quickly spreading through the room. As the smoke grenade flew towards him, The Wizard realized he only had a few seconds before those crafty little bastards gave him the slip. Without hesitation, he charged towards them.

Unfortunately, he once again forgot about the cat blood. When he stepped onto the corner of the rug, it slid forward several inches, causing him to tumble towards the couch. He was almost able to regain his balance, until his shin bashed into the coffee table. Pain shot through his tibia as he lurched forward. Spinning around in mid-fall, he landed on his back, bonking his noggin on the arm of the couch. He instantly lost consciousness.

The Wizard retained no memory of that night's events.

When he awoke the following morning, The Wizard could not help but wonder why his nipples felt as though he were a mother of octuplets. He could not give it much thought, however, as he was currently experiencing the single worst hangover of his life; he could handle the alcohol, but Merlin's floggings were too much. The living room smelled vaguely of sulfur, and he had a bit of a cough. The cat blood had completely coagulated, and the corner of the rug was curled up where it had dried.

He gingerly sat himself up, before keeling over and vomiting on the rug. Wiping his lips clean, he sat back and moaned miserably. After a few minutes, he worked up the strength to stand, and staggered into the kitchen. He grabbed a mug off the counter without looking, stumbled to the sink,

151

vomited again, and filled the mug with water. When he took a gulp of the water, he vomited a third time; it seemed Merlin had been using the mug as an ashtray.

After washing the mug and chugging five consecutive cups of water, he meandered back into the living room. With a pained groan, he collapsed back onto the couch. He sat motionless for the next half hour, staring at nothing.

His solitude was interrupted when Merlin trotted down the stairs, a look of lively enthusiasm on his face. Whistling a buoyant tune, he sat down next to The Wizard and began rolling a joint. Without saying a word, he sparked it up and took a couple puffs, before passing it to The Wizard.

"Thanks…" muttered The Wizard, taking the joint with his shaky fingers and taking a titanic toke. "I needed that… I don't normally get hungover, but *somebody* had to beat me over the head with a hunk of quartz…."

Merlin snorted. "Yeah, life's a bitch sometimes, ain't it?"

"Whatever…"

They sat in silence and smoked weed for a while. Merlin took out his flask of grain alcohol, and they passed it back and forth a few times. The liquor worked with the cannabis to ease The Wizard's headache. After fifteen or so minutes of what he called "the breakfast of champions", he felt renewed and refreshed, ready to face the day like a high-functioning alcoholic.

Eventually, Jeff appeared atop the stairs and ambled down into the living room. Merlin was just lighting another joint as Jeff joined them. After taking a couple puffs, he passed it to Jeff. Taking it, Jeff flopped down next to Merlin on the couch.

"Morning, gentlemen! Man, Merlin, I slept like a kitten in that bed of yours last night. What are those sheets, silk?" Leaning back, Jeff puffed on the joint.

"Yeah, and the comforter and pillows are stuffed with phoenix down."

"Oh, so that's why I was so toasty! I had to get up and lower the thermostat, but once I did, it was heavenly."

The Wizard's chest tightened with envy; his pillow had been a bar of polished mahogany. Resentment pooled in his stomach as he listened to Jeff compliment Merlin on his accommodations. He glared straight ahead while they talked.

One Night in Camelot

Merlin summoned each of them a plate of bacon and eggs for breakfast. As they ate, they smoked several more doobies. Once he got some food in his stomach, The Wizard felt much better. Merlin was even gracious enough to summon him a cup of coffee when he asked for it.

"Alright, now that we've eaten, I'd like to talk business," said Merlin. He levitated the dishes into the kitchen and dumped them in the sink. "I have an urgent matter to discuss with you."

"Lay it on us!" Kicking back in his seat, The Wizard burped tremendously.

"As much as I'd love to have you keep bumming around on my couch, you're going to have to go back to your own time as soon as possible."

"Wait, what?" The Wizard raised his eyebrows in surprise. "I thought we had as much time as we needed to prepare before returning home!"

"I thought so as well, until the Arcanes spoke to me in a dream. They conveyed the message that the staff you brought me was created to bridge an infinite loop in time, and that if you don't return to your time before the temporal rift closes, you'll be trapped in this time." Merlin held up his hand, and the *Chronomancer's Continuum* appeared in his grasp; it had been restored to its former glory. He set it on the coffee table. "They also told me how to repair the staff, so fortunately, I will indeed be able to use it to send you home."

The Wizard could not help but feel that Merlin was just trying to get rid of him. "Sure... 'before the temporal rift closes'... that seems real legit. You're making this up, aren't you? If you want me to leave, you can just say so."

Merlin laughed. "I do want you to leave, but that's not why I'm saying this. It's true, that is the message the Arcanes gave me."

"So, you sometimes commune with the Arcanes in your dreams?" asked Jeff, leaning forward inquisitively. "What's that like? Do they have... like... personalities?"

"Sort of," said Merlin, shrugging. "They each represent a fundamental aspect of existence, so their personalities are pretty one dimensional. Let me put it this way: they are not nice, if that's what you were thinking."

Jeff furrowed his brow. "Do you have conversations with them? Or do they convey their messages with visuals and metaphors?"

Chapter Eleven

"I wouldn't call it a conversation," said Merlin, chortling to himself. "That would imply that it makes a difference what I say. It's more like a general barking orders at you when you're trying to sleep."

"Yeah, yeah," said The Wizard. "Can we circle back to how we're being sent back without any time to prepare?"

"I'm afraid that preparation is no longer pertinent. If you get stuck in this time, all hope is lost. Right now, what we need to do is determine your course of action once you reach your proper time."

"Did someone say 'proper time'?" said a voice from the kitchen door. "It's a little early, but I'll get proper any time!"

Looking to the kitchen, they saw that Knorpe was standing in the doorway. Yawning, Knippe ambled to his side.

"What's up, chumps?" asked Knippe.

"Okay, there's definitely no time for *them*." With a snap of his fingers, Merlin caused the gnomes to once again fall unconscious.

Not that anyone cared, but Knippe and Knorpe would be putting themselves at risk of serious brain damage if they kept getting themselves cursed out of consciousness.

Merlin looked back at The Wizard, furrowing his brow dubiously. "Anyway, have you worked out any sort of coherent plan, or are you just going to wing it?"

"What do I look like, an idiot?" said The Wizard, scowling. "Of course I'm not going to 'wing it'! I mean, I don't have a plan yet, but I don't just 'wing' things."

Jeff scoffed. "You *can't* be serious. I swear, 'winging it' has been your default setting since day one!"

"I planned that heist, didn't I?"

Unwilling to dignify this with a response, Jeff crossed his arms and turned away in a huff.

Tapping his fingers on the table, Merlin waited to speak until it was clear they were paying attention. "Okay, anyway, if you don't have a plan, we need to come up with something. At the very least, you'll need a safe house to use as a hideout. It can't belong to anyone the Circle knows you associate with; it would help if the place was totally off the grid."

"Oh... crap..." muttered The Wizard, grimacing uncomfortably.

One Night in Camelot

"What is it?" Merlin cocked his head curiously. "Do you know of any such place?"

"Yeah… it's just… it belongs to my sister, Anasthasia…."

Jeff raised his eyebrows in surprise. "You have a sister?"

"That's perfect," said Merlin. "And you're sure it's off the grid?"

"Yeah, our father always kept her sheltered from the world," said The Wizard. "She lives in my dad's old tower in the Oduelluae Highlands. I always wondered why dad did that, but knowing what I know now, I suppose it makes sense. I guess the only reason he never did the same for me is that he discovered what was happening too late."

Merlin clapped his hands together. "Well, that's settled! As soon as you reach your time, you should rendezvous with your sister and solidify your plan."

"I guess…" The Wizard wracked his brains, trying to think of a better plan; drawing a blank, he resigned to this course of action.

"What's the problem?" asked Merlin.

"It's just that our dad died when Anasthasia was just a little girl. She's lived in that tower alone most of her life. Now she's about Jeff's age, and she's *really* creepy."

"That's your sister, dude!" Looking appalled, Jeff shook his head at The Wizard. "You just left her there alone? How could you do that?"

"I was in mourning! I needed all the cocaine I could get, and that's no environment for a child. Also, I was upset that my dad left her his entire fortune, and all he left me was his old research to finish; yeah, sure, that's what you want for a fucking inheritance: *a job*."

"That's no reason to just abandon her! What if she had died?"

The Wizard waved his hand at Jeff dismissively. "She was a talented sorceress even back then; she could take care of herself."

Merlin cleared his throat. "Any personal drama between you and your sister aside, she seems to be your best bet for shelter in these trying times. You'll just have to suck it up and ask her for help."

"Fine…" The Wizard heaved a defeated sigh.

"Good, glad we could settle that the easy way. Now, before I send you all off, I have a few things to give the two of you." Rifling through the pocket of his robes, Merlin pulled out a leather backpack and a leather satchel, handing

155

them to Jeff and The Wizard respectively. "There's a surprise in each of those bags for you."

Opening the satchel, The Wizard found that it was empty. However, how empty it was indeed surprised him; the satchel contained about as much empty space as a large trunk. It was a bag of holding.

The Wizard's mouth fell open in surprise. "Wow, these are really rare; this kind of dimensional magic is super advanced! Are you sure I can have this?"

"Well, it's not like I want to give it to you," said Merlin, "but it seems like you're going to need it." He looked at Jeff. "Why don't you open your new backpack?"

"Oh right, I was just distracted looking into his bag." His hazel eyes alight with anticipation, Jeff opened the backpack. Inside the pack, the embossed gold runes on its cover twinkling, was the *Arcane Almanac*. Jeff's jaw dropped. "Are you serious? This is one of the most powerful magical artifacts of all time! Why would you give it to me?"

"That's true, but it's not very useful to me; it can only tell you things that have already happened." Shrugging, Merlin patted Jeff on the back. "I've learned more useful stuff from you in the two days I've known you than I ever have from that book, Jeff."

"Wow... I don't know what to say...." Tears welled up in Jeff's eyes. "Thank you so much! I'll treasure this my entire life!"

"Yeah, whatever, don't get all girly," said Merlin. "The only reason I'm giving it to you is that I used the *Chronomancer's Continuum* to divine its future; technically speaking, the *Arcane Almanac* doesn't exist for the next four centuries. So, I deduced that in your time, I must have already sent you forward with it."

The Wizard raised an eyebrow. "This stuff is getting pretty convoluted..."

"Anyway, Jeff, I don't have time to explain how to properly use the *Almanac*. It'll have to suffice to say that all you must do is open it and ask it a question pertinent to the history of a person, place, or thing. However, it's quite finicky; if your question is not clear and concise, it will give you very cryptic answers."

"That sounds simple enough. I'm sure I'll figure it out."

156

One Night in Camelot

"So, since we're going to have the Circle's top battlemages on our tail," said The Wizard, "do you have any weapons you could give us?"

Merlin shook his head. "Sorry, the kingdom needs all of the Circle's weaponry in the war against the remaining demons. Anyway, I doubt they'd do you much good; I'm sure the weapons of my time are no match to the weapons of yours. I've always been really cautious about building too powerful of weapons, lest my subjects attempt to stage a coup."

"That's a fair point," said The Wizard.

"However, I do have this for you." Reaching into his pocket, Merlin pulled out a jangly coin purse and tossed it to The Wizard. "There's fifty sol in there. Unless gold has lost its value in your time, that should be enough to buy you a horse."

Catching the bag, The Wizard cocked his head. "Wow, you used sol this far back?"

"You really don't know your history, do you?" Merlin shook his head in disapproval. "I was the one that invented our monetary system. Well, brought it back, at least, with new names for the coins. When I arrived in this kingdom, the would-be king, Arthur, had some cockamamie idea worked out for a system using pieces of paper denoting value." He rolled his eyes. "Like anyone wants to trade their wares for some glorified IOUs!"

"Another fair point."

"Finally, you should all take these, even the gnomes." Holding out his hand, Merlin caused four amulets to appear in his palm. He handed them to Jeff and The Wizard, sneering at the latter as he did so. "These will protect you from even the most advanced scrying, since I doubt *you* know how to do that yourself."

"That was uncalled for…" The Wizard hung his head. He had expected Merlin to at least be nice to him as they parted ways, seeing as they would likely never meet again. "Well, anyway, thanks for the gold, amulets, and the bag of holding. It actually means a lot."

"It's not a problem." Checking the clock, Merlin stood up. "Anyway, it's almost noon. I'm not sure exactly when the rift will close, so it's best if we err on the side of safety." Heading into the foyer, he slipped on his pair of pink bunny slippers. He motioned for them to follow. "Come on, we should

157

do this in the street, so none of my stuff gets sucked in with you. Oh, and grab those unconscious… gnodes, or whatever you called them.…"

Lifting Knippe and Knorpe by their hair, Jeff and The Wizard followed Merlin outside. It appeared to have snowed more in the night, and the street was covered in a few fresh inches of snow. It gleamed in the sunlight like cocaine on The Wizard's beard. Merlin's front garden contrasted wildly, with its summery weather and vibrant hues.

When they were all standing in the snowy street, Merlin cleared his throat uncomfortably. "So… is there anything either of you want to say before I do this? I'd rather you didn't, but now's your last chance if you do."

"No, I'm good," said The Wizard. "I mean, it was nice meeting you and all, but this has been an ordeal. I'm just looking forward to returning to the future and getting some sweet cocaine."

Rolling his eyes, Merlin turned to Jeff. "What about you, my boy?"

"It was just such an honor meeting you," said Jeff, his eyes sparkling with tears. "I'll never forget the time we spent together."

"Oh, boy…" Merlin averted his gaze.

"I promise I'll do whatever I can to help The Wizard in his quest. I won't disappoint you, Merlin." Straightening his back, Jeff gave Merlin a salute.

Shifting awkwardly, Merlin looked back to The Wizard. "So, any specific destination in mind? I can try to target anywhere, as long as it's within about a mile of the time rift's point of origin. I can also send you within a day of when the rift opened, so I'll send you back a bit early. That should give you time to make your escape."

"Could you send me to my tower?" asked The Wizard. "There is some stuff I really need to get there."

"Sure, hold on." Approaching The Wizard, Merlin reached out and put his palms on his temples. He cringed. "Wow, what a piece of shit tower. I almost feel sorry for you. Are you sure there's anything there you need?"

The Wizard frowned flatly. "Yes, there is."

"Okay." Shrugging, Merlin took a few steps back. He held up the *Chronomancer's Continuum*, pointing the crystal at them. "Are you ready?"

Gulping tremulously, Jeff and The Wizard nodded, donning their anti-scrying amulets and putting the others on the gnomes. They stepped closer to each other. The Wizard tried to mentally prepare, but given what was in store for him, it seemed in vain. With a wave of the staff, Merlin muttered an incantation.

The last thing they saw was Merlin waving farewell. Suddenly, they were swept off their feet and back into the swirling nether of nothingness. The experience was just as weird as it had been the previous time. It would not do it justice for me to describe it...

How about *you* take the acid this time?

Chapter Twelve
Sinister Devices

rchmage Quan was pacing back and forth in her office atop Circle Tower. It had only been a few hours since The Wizard escaped her grasp, and she was still fuming with rage. She could not believe she had been evaded by *The Wizard*, of all people: a man who, at one point, had spent a month of their apprenticeship studying how to restore several inches of his manhood he had accidentally cursed away.

Whenever she attempted to scry on The Wizard, her crystal ball simply gave her the message "Error 404; the entity you are looking for does not exist". She had no idea where he could have gone. Frankly, it astounded her that he was even able to operate such a powerful magical artifact as the *Chronomancer's Continuum*.

Her eyes kept falling nervously on the crystal ball. There was an important call she needed to make, and she was not looking forward to it. Eventually, however, it seemed that she could no longer put off the conversation; the crystal ball began to ding, scintillating with radiance. She was receiving a call, and she knew exactly whom it was from.

Dread welled up in her chest as she approached her desk. Sitting in her chair, she stared apprehensively at the orb for a moment. Swallowing her fear, she shakily tapped the surface.

A man's head appeared in the crystal. He had a gaunt, sallow face and deep crimson eyes, with wavy gray hair and a well-kempt goatee. His expression was that of extreme displeasure. "Quan, you bloody imbecile. I've only just heard of what you let transpire."

"You've got to understand: it wasn't my fault!" said Quan. Her voice was as tremulous as her hands. "One of my comrades betrayed me; I never saw it coming!"

"Fool!" The man's eyes flashed with anger. "I always told you not to trust that lumbering oaf. It was only a matter of time before he sold you out to The Wizard. You should have listened to me."

"I'm so sorry, master Malthas…" Quan held up her hands imploringly, stricken with terror as she met his gaze. "Please forgive me… I never thought The Wizard would be able to get that far! Needless to say, I fired Fabulon on the spot."

"Save your groveling," said Malthas, scowling coldly at her. "I have had quite enough of your incompetence. You should have killed Fabulon, but you let your little crush guide your decision. I allowed you to become Archmage because I thought you had what it took to bring about my devices, but now I'm losing confidence in you. I happen to know that the reason it took you so long to respond to the break-in was that you were 'busy' hiding in the bushes outside Fabulon's house, watching him practice for his ballet recital."

Quan's face flushed bright red. "I swear I won't let you down again!" She fidgeted restlessly with a pencil on her desk, averting her eyes from the crystal ball. "I mean, he can't have gone far, can he? He has no idea how to work the *Chronomancer's Continuum*; chances are it just flung him into next week."

Malthas feigned a smile, and put on a sarcastically sweet voice. "Well then, since I'm such a *nice guy*, I will give you *two* weeks to find and capture him. Now that he knows about our plans, The Wizard cannot be allowed to walk free. We can no longer afford to wait for him to lead us to the *Arcane Dictionary*. Once we get ahold of him, I have ways of making him talk. Now, do you think you could handle the simple task of tracking down a moron?"

"I'll do my best…" Archmage Quan's chest was heavy with anxiety as she fathomed how she could track The Wizard down in such a short time. She desperately hoped that it was going to be possible. "I'll have to order all

161

Chapter Twelve

the battlemages traveling abroad to come aid in the search, but I think he can be found." Even as she said that, her mind was clouded with doubt.

Malthas did not look entirely convinced. As he spoke, his voice was cold as death. "This is your last chance, Quan. If you fail me again, I will ensure that you never again see the light of day. And if your incompetence lost us our quarry, I will make sure you spend the remainder of your days regretting your pitiful existence. Are we clear?"

"Yes, master, I understand," said Quan, gulping meekly. Her voice was thin and wispy, and her heart raced with trepidation. "I will not fail you."

"Good," said Malthas, smiling coldly. Without saying another word, he reached forward and tapped the screen. His face disappeared from Quan's crystal ball.

Heaving a relieved sigh, Quan slumped back in her seat. The conversation had actually gone a lot better than she expected. Although she could not begin to imagine where to start looking, she was glad she had two weeks to find The Wizard; she had half expected Malthas to say she only had a day or two.

However, she was nonetheless weighed down by a sense of dread. It chilled her to her core to imagine what sort of punishment Malthas would inflict upon her if she failed.

As she stepped into the streets outside Circle Tower, the shadows cast by the flickering trees seemed to haunt her path. She knew she was being watched, and Malthas would know if she made one wrong move.

It took a long time for her to fall into a fitful slumber that night, and her dreams were plagued with The Wizard's taunts.

Chapter Thirteen
Return to the Future

The return to corporeal existence was much easier for The Wizard this time around. Perhaps it was because he was used to travelling through the metaphysical plane, or perhaps it was merely due to Merlin being a more competent spellcaster. The Wizard decided to go with the first explanation.

He was tangled in a mess of bramble, with sharp thorns poking him all over. The smell of liquor, rotten meat, and fecal matter hung heavy in the air. As he managed to pull himself free, he could see that he had landed in the bushes behind his house. He stepped in something moist and pulpous. Looking down, he saw that he was standing in Gary's toilet.

"Damn it!" Stepping out of the tin bucket of excrement, The Wizard kicked it deeper into the bushes. He shook the stars out of his vision, adjusting once more to the light of existence. Looking around, he saw Jeff leaning against his tower, watching Knippe and Knorpe wrestling in the grass. He scowled. "How come you guys didn't get teleported into those shitberry bushes?!"

"No idea." Shrugging, Jeff chuckled at The Wizard's misfortune. "I was watching them, there was a flash of light, and there you were, standing in Gary's toilet."

"You were already here?" asked The Wizard.

Jeff nodded. "Yeah, for like forty-five minutes."

Chapter Thirteen

"Speak for yourself," said Knorpe, pinning Knippe to the ground. "We've been here for like two hours."

"So you guys got here at the same time?" Smirking amusedly, The Wizard watched the gnomes wrestle.

"Of course!" said Knippe, headbutting Knorpe in the forehead; or perhaps Knorpe had headbutted him, it was hard to tell. "We do everything at the same time! We even have a unitwin toilet!"

"I don't even want to know…" The Wizard cocked his head at Jeff. "Has anything else happened that I should know about?"

"Yeah, about that…" Opening the door of the tower, Jeff motioned for The Wizard to follow him. "There actually is something you should see…"

"Okay, but this better be good." The Wizard followed him through the kitchen, into the foyer, and up the spiral staircase.

As they approached the master bedroom door, Jeff turned and shushed The Wizard. Slowly, he pulled the door open, and gestured inside.

There, sleeping on The Wizard's couch, was The Wizard.

"What the fuck…" The Wizard's mouth fell open in disbelief. "Is that me?"

"I guess so," said Jeff. "Apparently, Merlin sent us back early enough that you were still asleep."

"Interesting…" Frowning thoughtfully, The Wizard scratched his beard. "I don't remember sleeping that night." He shrugged, smiling cheerfully. "This is good, we have a fairly significant head start."

"Yeah, but we have to be careful for the next day or so," said Jeff. "If we alter anything that could come back and affect us, it could —"

The Wizard was not listening. He had already approached his own sleeping form, and was shaking himself awake. "Hey, asshole, wake up!"

Jeff shook his head and facepalmed.

"Woah, deja vu," said his past self, brushing his beard out of his eyes. "Didn't this already happen?"

"That's my line!" said The Wizard. "Now listen up, I have a warning —"

"Who the fuck are you, anyway?" The Wizard's past self stood up and began poking him in the chest. "You look like my dad and you smell like shit."

"I'm you, obviously!"

Return to the Future

"Woah... what was in that cocaine?"

"Look, it doesn't matter," said The Wizard. "I have to warn you about the heist."

"Woah, that's wild!" The other Wizard's eyes widened. "I just had a dream about a heist!"

"Yeah, that's right, and today you'll get the idea to make that dream come true."

"That's not a bad idea."

"Listen, please!" The Wizard grabbed his past self by the shoulders and shook him frantically. "It absolutely is a *very* bad idea. You don't understand what you're getting yourself into. Just don't do it, okay?"

"Why should I listen to *you*?"

"Because, let me tell you something, *myself*," said The Wizard. "I've been around the block a couple more times than you have. I even know what you're thinking right now."

The other Wizard's eyes narrowed. "Really, 'me', and what exactly is that?".

"I actually forgot..." The Wizard grinned sheepishly.

"How the fuck is this not a paradox?" Jeff was pacing back and forth, his brow furrowed in intense thought. It was hard to tell whether he was frustrated or amused, perhaps it was a little bit of both. "I was already confused enough with this time travel snafu, and now there are two of you!"

"Why is *he* here?" asked The past Wizard, pointing at Jeff. "I thought I fired him."

"Umm..."

"Holy shit!" shouted a voice from behind Jeff. Knippe and Knorpe were standing in the doorway, beaming with glee. Speaking in unison, they both said, "you have one too?!"

The two Wizards looked at the gnomes, blinking bemusedly for a few moments. Jeff stood uncomfortably in the middle, shifting his feet.

Knippe cocked his head at Jeff. "Where's yours?"

Jeff started cracking up. Slowly, the others followed suit. One of The Wizards cracked up in more ways than one, if you know what I mean; that is to say, he lit up a crack pipe before passing it to the other Wizard. Does it

165

really matter which Wizard it was? Either way, Knippe subtly pocketed the pipe when it was set down.

"Look," said The Wizard to his past self, "I know you probably think this heist is the best idea you've ever had, but —"

"You're right!" Pushing himself aside, The other Wizard leapt up and headed for the door. "This is the best idea I've ever had! No time to explain, I've got to go!" Grabbing his gold-trimmed blue robes on the way out, he sprinted down the stairs.

The Wizard sighed. There was a moment of uncomfortable silence. Knippe and Knorpe were smoking crack in the corner.

"You're... you... right?" Jeff squinted scrutinously at The Wizard. "I mean, you're the future one, right? I lost track."

"And Merlin thinks *you're* clever..." Smiling snidely, The Wizard snickered to himself. "Do you not understand how chronological continuity works?"

"It's not that I don't understand how it works; it's just that if anyone were to ever break it, it would be you... and I think you just did."

"Yeah, whatever," said The Wizard. "Looks like that lazy dipshit who sleeps on my couch is about to fuck me over again. Why couldn't he just listen?!"

"You know you're talking about yourself, right?"

"Of course, but I couldn't resist."

"Full of surprises, you are," said Jeff. "Why did you tell yourself not to do that anyway? Possible paradox aside, don't you want to save your dad?"

"First of all, it's not a possible paradox; I totally remember that conversation. I thought it was all in my head at the time. As for why, I don't want to talk about it..." A haunted look crossed The Wizard's face. "I'm just scared, I thought it was worth trying to change what I did."

"Okay, no worries..." Jeff gave The Wizard a sympathetic smile, although it was short lived. "It still seems like a paradox to interact with yourself. Even a minor change could cause a ripple effect."

"Look, I did everything I remembered doing, and everything happened like I remember. Are you satisfied? It makes sense, damn it."

Return to the Future

"I guess... I just think it's a little lazy, you know?" Sighing, Jeff shook his head slowly. "More of an effort could have been made to tie everything together, that's all I'm saying."

The Wizard rolled his eyes. "Everyone's a critic..."

His hands on his hips, Knippe tapped his foot impatiently. "Are we almost done here?"

"Yeah," said Knorpe, groaning, "I am *so* bored!"

Scoffing incredulously, The Wizard cocked his head. "You literally just traveled in time! And then you smoked all my crack! How can you possibly be bored?"

They simultaneously shrugged.

Suddenly, there was a loud, deep meow. Kit Mingers leapt out of one of the many gaping holes in the wall. He tackled Knippe to the ground, pinning him on his stomach. The ferociously frisky feline mounted the miniature mischief maker, viciously violating him with vim.

Do not let the alliteration distract you from the fact that this is a cat violating a gnome. Let us have a moment of silence for Knippe's innocence. It was lost long before this, do not get me wrong, but that does not mean it has not been lost once more.

Knorpe had to wrestle Kit Mingers off of his brother; Jeff and The Wizard were too busy laughing hilariously.

"It's not funny!" Scuttling away, Knippe pressed his back to the wall. Trembling hysterically, he gave Kit Mingers a look of revulsion.

"It's kind of funny, bro..." Knorpe was trying very hard not to smirk.

"Et tu, Knorpe?"

"Listen, we've got to stop wasting time!" Walking along his bookshelf, The Wizard was scraping the relatively few valuables he owned into his bag of holding. "Damn, this thing is so convenient; It's like I'm carrying nothing at all..."

He wrapped his green dragon bong in his least moth-eaten blanket, gently placing it in the bag of holding, along with his cannabis. Grabbing a couple of winter cloaks from his closet, he threw them in the bag; there was a third one he could have given to the gnomes to tear in half, but he would be damned if he was going to help them.

167

Chapter Thirteen

Walking up to his mantle of drinks, The Wizard slid the few relatively full bottles into the bag. Trying not to be seen, he slipped a few journals into the bag from under his bed. He then picked Kit Mingers up by the scruff of his neck and threw him in the bag; as he closed the zipper, he could see that the cat was already making anything-but-love to the blanket.

"That'll do…" Heaving a sigh, The Wizard tossed the straps of his bag over his shoulder. "I'll just have to leave the weed plants in my basement…"

Shifting his feet apprehensively, Knippe eyed the bag of holding. "You're not taking that cat with us, are you?"

"No…" The Wizard smiled sarcastically. "I only threw him in my pack so I could give him and my blanket a final farewell."

"I'm not going with you guys if you're taking that monster."

The Wizard scoffed. "Seriously?! After everything that has happened since I met you, my cat molesting you is where you draw the line?"

"Everyone's gotta draw it somewhere."

"Well, I draw the line at being arrested and spending my life in prison; but fine, stay, see if I care." The Wizard turned and walked out of the room, with Jeff following behind him.

As he crossed the landing, his thoughts strayed to his lab, wondering if anything up there could help them. His gaze fell on the spiral ladder. Deciding that it was not worth it, The Wizard started down the stairs.

"He's got a point, you know." Knorpe raised his eyebrows at his brother. "I can't go back to Detroit."

Moaning mournfully, Knippe tugged on his handlebar mustache. "But we haven't actually gotten *any* riches on this adventure; he's hogging them all!"

"All the more reason to stay with him!" A devious smile crossed Knorpe's face. "We're gonna have to go into hiding; we can take him when he's least expecting it to come from us! We just have to wait until he gets ahold of a treasure worth stealing."

"You're right." Knippe nodded firmly, with a look of determination. "Let's do this."

They followed The Wizard and Jeff outside. They started down the block, The Wizard leading them towards the trade district.

"First things first." Grimacing in disgust, The Wizard paused to hose off his boots with a steady stream of cleaning cantrips. Since The Wizard rarely showered, bathing and laundry spells were some of the few cleaning spells he had bothered to learn. "I need to get some drugs to get rid of this hangover."

"Are you sure that should really be our first priority?" said Jeff. "We need to find a place for me to peruse the *Arcane Almanac*. It's only a matter of time before they come after us; we need to plot our next course of action!"

The Wizard was already walking away.

Squirking excitedly, Knorpe gave Jeff a look of approval. "Look who's plotting now!"

"I guess we're rubbing off on you!" Grinning proudly, Knorpe high fived his brother.

"Not that kind of plot..." Shaking his head, Jeff heaved a weary sigh. "No more evil plans and schemes, okay? I just want to fix this so I can get my normal life back..."

As they were saying all of this, The Wizard had already walked to the end of the block.

"Hey, wait up." Jogging to The Wizard's side, Jeff gave him a bemused look. "Where are you going?"

"I told you, we're going to get cocaine."

"Ugh... fine... I guess we are...." Sighing in resignation, Jeff fell silent.

They walked for a few minutes until they arrived at *Dealah's Cocaine Window*, or whatever the kids were calling it those days. Over the course of this walk, Knippe and Knorpe successfully picked three pockets, only two of which were each other's. Unfortunately, Dealah was not in at the moment; The Wizard decided they were going somewhere else, as he was not planning to leave town without cocaine.

As they walked deeper into the slums of Theiyre, many foreboding sights met their eyes. There were posters everywhere advertising a weekly "Fight to the Meth" for the local homeless; graffiti covered nearly every surface, some of it magically animated; a goblin was passed out against a light pole, with his neck tied off and a needle in his jugular; a transexual Dwarf in a turquoise sequin dress approached them.

"Hey, my name's Johnnifer," she said. "Looking for a good time?"

Chapter Thirteen

"Why can't you just buy coke at the supermarket like everyone else?" asked Jeff, as they sped up their pace.

"Sometimes, to get the best deals, we have to pay with more than just money," said The Wizard. "You'll find out what I mean soon enough."

They eventually arrived at a run down cottage. It is situated right across the street from the *Blair Witch Projects*, the worst apartments in Theiyre. The Wizard only traveled to this part of town when he felt it was absolutely necessary.

The yard of the cottage was overgrown with crabgrass and dandelions, and the grimy offwhite paint was peeling from its facade. It was impossible to see inside, as the windows that were not boarded shut had been concealed with spray paint.

A homeless goblin sat on a safe in the corner, cackling madly and muttering to herself, "I'm so rich, I have an individual safe for every penny I own!"

The Wizard approached the front door and knocked.

A rumbling, sluggish voice slid out from within. "Come in."

Plugging his nose, The Wizard opened the door. Jeff and the others were not prepared for what was to come; without warning, a smell more loathsome and repugnant than a thousand durians dipped in thioacetone met their nostrils. Do not let the severity of my hyperbole detract from the truth of how bad it smelled; the point is, there were no words.

We have all encountered a smell at some point in our lives that made us second guess our doubt in the existence of hell. For some of us, it was when we visited Grandpa; for others, it was when they realized the new factory in town was a paper mill; for Knorpe, it was when he first entered Detroit; for Jeff, this smell came from this house.

"Ugh, what the hell is that?" he yelled. His glasses nearly fell off as he keeled over, clasping his hands over his nose.

"It smells worse than that Orc brothel outside of town, *Whoredor*," said Knorpe.

"Why do you possibly know that?" Cringing, The Wizard tried not to think about it.

"We all make mistakes," muttered Knippe. He and Knorpe gave each other a hug, patting each other consolingly on the back.

Return to the Future

"I'm not going in there." Squinting with watering eyes, Jeff peered through the portal to what could actually be the elemental plane of odor.

"Neither are we," said the twins in unison. They then vomited, also in unison.

"Way to be team players, you guys... I'm not sharing my cocaine with you...." Grumbling to himself, The Wizard slouched inside.

The inside of the house made the outside look like the lap of luxury. The only furniture in the living room was an enormous, filthy couch facing a table. On the table sat a large geodesic crystal, with images of knights and dragons flashing across it. The entire back wall of the room was a colossal refrigerator.

Otherwise, the entire room simply looked like an unearthed landfill. Candy wrappers, pizza boxes, soda bottles, and all manner of scraps littered the floor. The walls had what appeared to be nacho cheese dripping down in several places. Worst of all, the bathroom door was open; you do not want to know what the story was in there.

Sitting on the cum-encrusted couch was the fattest man The Wizard had ever seen. His every movement caused a jiggling girthquake. Weighing at least five hundred pounds, it would have seemed a miracle for him to sit on the couch without breaking it; however, The Wizard was more than familiar with the highly magical nature of that couch.

The man was holding a video game controller, and was deeply engrossed in what was happening in the geodesic crystal. He was wearing nothing but a gargantuan pair of briefs and a sweaty white tank top. His scraggly neckbeard was coated with cheese dust. It was not a pleasant sight.

"It's... uh... good to see you, Keith..." Feigning a lack of disgust, The Wizard gave Keith a nod of greetings.

"Yeah, whatever, just tell me what you want so I can get back to my game." Keith gestured to a massive crystal ball on his table that was alight with the flashing images of battle.

"Woah, you got the new *Japando Geodesic Game Dome*? Nice!"

"More like the *Geodesic Shit Dome*." Scrunching his face in anger, Keith chucked his controller at the game system. It clattered to the ground, nestling amongst the rubbish.

Chapter Thirteen

"What makes you say that?" The Wizard attempted not to laugh at Keith's rage, for fear of breathing.

"Because..." Keith narrowed his eyes spitefully at the game system. "*It's a piece of shit!*"

"If you say so!" As The Wizard chuckled, he aspirated a bit of vomit. "But what don't you like about it? I've heard really good things."

"I'll show you why I call it that," Groping deep into the reaches of his couch, Keith pulled out a small, flat, rounded prism; it had hundreds of luminous, multicolored dots floating around in it. "Take a look at the game!" Glaring at the disc, he brandished it wildly. "This looks like a fucking chocolate chip cookie!"

One of the games on Keith's coffee table had a bite taken out of it.

"Yeah, I'm not seeing it." The Wizard rolled his watering eyes. "Anyway, I came here for a reason."

"Oh yeah, why's that?"

"Do you have any cocaine?"

"Let me check." Turning around, Keith buried his face and arms in his couch, rifling between the cushions. With a look of intense focus, he dived into the back of the couch; all five hundred jiggling pounds of him melted into it like hot butter.

The Wizard averted his eyes as Keith's pale, fat ass sank into the couch. He was familiar with Keith's couch of holding. He had always envied it, as well as questioning how and where Keith got it; however, he would not touch it with a ten foot wand.

Suddenly, something tackled him from his right side. Slippery saliva dripped down his face and gathered in his beard as a large, black and brown basset hound licked his face emphatically. Its breath smelled like it belonged where it was.

"Don't worry about him, Wiz." Chortling, Keith climbed out of his couch. "He's all burp, no bite."

"Yeah, that's what I'm worried about..." Cringing at the smell, The Wizard pushed the dog off of him.

Keith was already once again sitting comfortably on the couch. The Wizard had no idea how such a robust man was able to maneuver with that kind of dexterity, but he had little time to worry about it; if he did not leave this place soon, he feared his sanity may not leave with him.

"So, this is all the cocaine I could scrounge up," said Keith, holding about an ounce worth of individual dime bags. "Is this enough?"

"Umm… yeah, that will probably do!" Eyes wide in amazement, The Wizard grinned enthusiastically. He was beginning to remember why he put up with Keith.

"Now, I have no memory of where I got any of this, nor do I really know what it is worth, but I'm really hungry. You want it? It's yours, my friend, as long as you pick me up a bucket of pegasus wings and an unlimited breadstick from the *Dough Pony*. If you do that, I'll give you all of it for forty sol."

The Wizard nodded. "Sounds good."

Keith held out his hand for The Wizard to shake. It was coated in all manner of substances, sticky and shiny, and the grooves between Keith's handfolds were full of black gunk; however, the Wizard really wanted that cocaine….

"Aright, but we do the dropoff like last time."

He gingerly shook Keith's hand.

"It's a deal." Keith drooled with anticipation as The Wizard hurried outside.

When the smell once again met his nostrils, Jeff gagged. "So… you got the cocaine?"

"Not yet," said The Wizard. "We have to go to the *Dough Pony* and pick up a bucket of pegasus wings and an unlimited breadstick."

Jeff narrowed his eyes dubiously. "What the hell is an unlimited breadstick? Is that something like an everburning torch?"

"I don't know, dude... I just want to get this over with…."

As they headed deeper into the slums, The Wizard tried to remember where the *Dough Pony* was located. It was a terrible fast food restaurant, and he only went there when it was the only option. Eventually, he managed to find his way there.

As they walked down the street, a fiery light emanated from a nearby alley.

Chapter Thirteen

Stopping in his tracks, Jeff did a double take. "I think I just saw a fire elemental huffing flame retardant."

"You're mistaken." Knorpe walked speedily past Jeff, looking behind him.

"Yeah, that guy set himself on fire," said Knippe, jogging behind his brother.

"Shut up!" Shushing furiously, Knorpe stepped on his twin's toes. "That's not even what Meff was talking about!"

He pointed down a different alley than the one from whence they had just come; sure enough, there was a fire elemental huffing flame retardant.

"You guys are idiots..." Scoffing, Jeff did not even bother to literally look down on them. "And my name is *Jeff*, by the way."

The Wizard was up ahead, standing by the drive-thru window of the *Dough Pony*, talking to a frustrated looking elven girl.

"Look, I don't know what it is either," said The Wizard. "He just asked for an unlimited breadstick, okay?"

"Well, if I see one, I'll let you know," she said, feigning sincerity and rolling her eyes.

"Fine..." Groaning, The Wizard crossed his arms. "Just give me an extra bucket of pegasus wings."

"That'll be six sol fifty."

While The Wizard paid for the food, a homeless man was rummaging through the dumpster out back. He leapt out of the dumpster, holding a half a bucket of spoiled wings. "*Ooh wee!* Looks like today's my eatin' day! Favorite day of the week!"

Another homeless man was sitting against the wall and eating out of his own bucket. He looked up from his food, giving the other man a smug look. "I eat almost every day; sometimes, I get to eat twice."

When the group arrived back at Keith's house, the sun was low in the sky. The Wizard emptied the extra three sol and fifty lun from his coin purse; he levitated it, and the buckets of horse meat, onto the porch. Ringing the doorbell, he took several steps back. The door creaked open, and a long wooden shepherd's crook pulled the food and gold inside. Moments later, the cocaine was tossed out haphazardly.

Commence the situation.

Return to the Future

It took The Wizard a few minutes to wrestle the last few dime bags away from Knippe and Knorpe. He was pretty sure that the gnomes still had a few grams tucked away; however, Jeff had been hounding him to hurry up, so he resigned to be content with the twenty-two grams he could recover.

As he walked down the block, The Wizard held one of the dime bags to either nostril. With a single snort, he sucked both entire grams up his nose. Once he was finished, he heaved a sigh of relief.

As the sun set, they neared the eastern gate of Koric. The wall around the city was only still there for historical reasons; ever since the Circle came to be, a physical barrier was rather redundant in the name of defense. There were more holes worn in the wall than there were gates. Nonetheless, they headed towards the gate.

"Oh shit!" Suddenly, The Wizard grabbed Jeff by the arm and pulled him into a nearby perfume shop called *The Gates of Smell*. "Let's lay low for a minute in here."

The twins scurried in after them.

A moment later, a pair of town guards walked by. They did not seem to notice The Wizard, so he heaved a sigh of relief.

"What was that all about?" Jeff raised an eyebrow. "We're not wanted until tomorrow, remember?"

"This is different!" Averting his eyes, The Wizard gestured to one of the guards. "I owe that guy fifteen sol..."

Jeff shook his head into his palms.

"Bloody smell, haven't my nostrils suffered enough?!" Cringing, Knorpe was holding an ornate crystal bottle of murky, brown liquid. "What kind of perfume scent is 'sandalwood and foot sweat', anyway?"

"Orcs eat that shit up..." The Wizard gagged as the scent wafted in his direction.

"I don't want to know how you know that," said Knippe, smirking.

The Wizard crossed his arms indignantly. "Hey, *I'm* not the one who goes to *Whoredor!*"

Both gnomes blushed furiously.

Gritting his teeth, Jeff clicked his tongue impatiently. "Can we go now?"

"Yeah, I think the coast is clear," said The Wizard.

175

Chapter Thirteen

Knorpe subtly pocketed the bottle of "perfume" and the party left the shop.

"So..." said Knippe. "Why exactly couldn't you knock those two guards out with the same spell you kept using on us?"

"Other than the fact that I'd be assaulting two guards in broad daylight? It honestly takes a lot out of me to do that..."

"So do some more cocaine!" Beaming passionately, Knorpe pulled one of the grams of coke from his pocket and did a bump.

Pursing his lips, The Wizard snatched the baggie from the gnome. "Look, I have to ration my cocaine. This is a long journey we're undertaking."

Knippe gazed intensely at The Wizard, fluttering his eyelashes implicitly. "Oh, come on, you know you want to! We promise we won't kick you in the balls and run off with your cocaine!"

"No, damn it!" The Wizard threw his head back in exasperation. "Am I the only responsible cocaine user among us?!"

"No." Jeff shook his head firmly.

"Oh yeah, I forgot about you, Jeff."

"No, I mean there is no such thing as a 'responsible cocaine user'..."

"Well, that's just, like... your opinion, man...."

They continued to argue about cocaine all the way out the eastern gate, attracting exactly zero attention to themselves; this type of conversation was quite normal in Koric.

The four companions trekked out onto the Koricean countryside, ready for cocaine... I mean adventure! Sorry about that, I get those two mixed up sometimes; it is an easy mistake to make. As you shall soon see, they have plenty of both in store for them.

Chapter Fourteen
Horsin' Around

As the group walked out through the eastern gates of Theiyre, the green hills of the Koricean countryside stretched before them. Theiyre was built on a high plateau, from which you could see the lands around for miles. The shadow of the plateau stretched far across the countryside in the light of the sunset.

Below them could be seen wide expanses of farmland; plantations growing all sorts of crops from corn to coca; grassy fields with all manner of livestock grazing; sparse patches of forest; and the deep blue waters of the Camelto river winding between the hillsides below. To the north, the vast waters of the Koricean straight glowed in the sunset, and you could faintly make out the island of North Koric through the fog.

They headed down a path zigzagging down the side of the cliff. The path was narrow, and they had to walk single file on parts of it. When the kingdom was young, these high, narrow pathways served to protect them from invading forces; however, in this time of relative peace, these paths simply served to inconvenience traders carrying heavy loads. By the time they reached the bottom, the sun had nearly set, and the land around them was cloaked in a veil of shadowy twilight.

They were less than a mile away from the city when Knippe and Knorpe were already starting to get on The Wizard's nerves.

"If either of you ask if we're almost there even one more time, I swear I'll knock you out and leave you outside the front of Circle Tower."

177

Chapter Fourteen

"Yeah right," said Knorpe, rolling his eyes. "If you did that, we'd just tell them where you're going."

"Speaking of," said Knippe, "are we almost there?"

"We're almost to the river," said The Wizard, sneering maliciously. "Keep asking questions and I'll show you what the bottom looks like."

When they arrived at the Camelto river, they saw that the middle of the bridge had fallen in. The bridge was covered in a layer of green fuzz, and the edges were sagging into the deep, blue waters of the river. There was a sign in front of it stating "Bridge out due to quickmold."

The Wizard approached the river and put his feet in the water, quickly withdrawing it due to the frigid temperature. The Camelto River, named for the ancient kingdom of Camelot and nothing else, flowed from a glacial spring between two tall mountains. Its waters were icy all year round, except when one of the mountains would erupt; the locals always knew when that was coming, because the sediment would cause the waters of the Camelto to flow red.

"Well, shit..." Looking around, The Wizard could not see any way across. "There is no way I can levitate us across that." His expression turned grim. "We're gonna have to take the troll bridge to the north."

Knorpe squealed with excitement. "*Oooooh!*"

"We love that guy!" Knippe did a happy, little dance.

"Yeah, I bet you do…"

"What's a troll bridge?" asked Jeff.

Nobody answered; The Wizard simply shuffled down the trail with his head down, and the twins hummed a jaunty tune as they followed.

As they headed north towards the ocean, the river steadily got swampier as it branched out into the Camelto delta. The deep blue water slowly faded to a murky grayish brown. Thick reeds grew all around the shoreline, and willow trees stood here and there beside the water. There was a low mist covering the landscape.

About twenty minutes later, they came upon the ricketiest thing you could call a bridge, and technically still be correct. At the entrance to the bridge, there was an even more rickety shack. With no windows or chimney, it basically looked like a gardening shed, except there was nothing anyone would ever want to garden growing in sight. The bridge itself was blocked by a gate of rusty, iron spikes.

"I really don't like this place..." Jeff looked around uneasily at the various bones and britches scattered across the muddy shoreline. He shuddered when he saw a pair of britches that still had someone's bones in them. Whomever they belonged to certainly was not too big for their britches anymore. "What's in that shack?"

"Relax, it's just the troll booth." The Wizard patted Jeff on the back. "Let me lead the way and just stay back."

However, Knippe and Knorpe were already banging on the door of the shack. The Wizard heaved a weary sigh as Jeff cowered behind him. A towering figure crawled out of the shack that now seemed much too small by comparison.

As hairy as Siegbert and as smelly as Keith, this troll was a force to be reckoned with. Simply looking into his armpit hair has been known to drive men to insanity. He stretched his arms high, yawning as it permeated the vicinity with unbearable odor. His face looked like that of a petrified persian cat injected with mutated botox.

"What the fuck do you two want?" Glaring down at the twins, the troll bared his teeth. His voice was deep and rugged, thick with the sound of phlegm.

"More riddles, please!" said both gnomes simultaneously.

"Ugh, great..." Groaning, the troll plopped his fat ass down on a nearby stump. There was a squishy splintering sound as he sat. He frowned at The Wizard. "And why are *you* here? I thought you hated my riddles..."

The Wizard plugged his nose. "Nah, it's not the riddles I mind so much."

"This is like a nightmare." Scowling, the troll gestured to the gnomes. "These two assholes hound me for riddles for hours every time they show up, and they *never* get a wrong answer! I don't understand it..."

"Why don't you just leave?" asked Jeff.

"*Oh, yeah, what a great idea!*" His scowl intensifying, the troll threw his arms up in exasperation, once again bombarding them with armpit stench. "*I'll just leave. Get up and walk away! Why didn't I think of that?!*"

"I take it you can't..." muttered Jeff.

179

Chapter Fourteen

"No shit, Sherstein! I'm bloody stuck here asking riddles of idiots for eternity, or until Merlin comes back and breaks the curse."

"Uhh…" Shifting his feet tentatively, Jeff averted his eyes. "Merlin's… dead."

"*Dead?!*" Roaring in fury, the troll got up and began pacing back and forth manically. His footsteps shook the ground. "Well who the bloody fuck is going to break the curse now?! Three hundred and forty-eight years I've been here, asking riddles." He plopped back down on the stump, sobbing hysterically into his hands. "This is why you don't get a degree in literature!"

While Jeff conversed with the troll, The Wizard was leaning against a nearby willow, smoking one thing or another. Knippe and Knorpe had hastily disassembled the makeshift gate and were attempting to turn the nasty, jagged pieces of rusty metal into something they dubbed "modern art".

"Hold on, I need a moment," Jeff rushed over to The Wizard.

"Oh, *sure,*" yelled the troll, through his miserable weeping. "Whenever anyone *else* needs a moment, they get it, and I just have to think of more riddles. I'm not just a troll you know; my name's David, I had dreams once!" He started rocking back and forth.

Approaching The Wizard, Jeff gestured to David the troll, who was sobbing with his face buried in his lap. "Do you think you could dispel his curse? Look at him... he's pathetic."

"I don't have time for his shit." The Wizard was sprinkling some cocaine on a fresh bowl.

"But if you free him, we don't have to answer his riddles!"

The Wizard sighed, walked over to David, and placed his free hand on the troll's chest. He narrowed his eyes in intense focus. Suddenly, a large set of glowing ethereal shackles could be seen around the troll, binding him to his run-down shack. A moment later, there was the sound of crystal shattering and the shackles faded away.

"What did you just do?" Tentatively standing up, David stretched his arms and legs. Raising one leg after another, he leapt gleefully in the air. "I feel like I've been freed."

"All I did was cast a really good bath spell." The Wizard wiped his hand on his robes. It left a dark brown streak on the deep blue cloth. "It cleans off everything from swamp grease to minor curses. Luckily, that curse was on its

Horsin' Around

last leg. I can't say the same for your filth… Now, you are free to go take an actual bath. Sadly, your stench is going to be much harder to remove than the curse."

"Thank you so much!" David leapt up with glee, shaking the ground on impact. Suddenly, he ran off towards town, laughing maniacally. "I'm gonna teach all those bastard kids for throwing rocks and laughing!"

"Uhh… should we be worried about that?" asked Jeff.

"No shit!" Gritting his teeth, Knorpe stomped his foot. "Now who's gonna riddle me?"

"Yeah, I wanted to be riddled…" Pouting his lips, Knippe turned his head away in a huff.

"Let's just go." Without hesitation, The Wizard stepped out onto the rickety bridge.

The others followed him, the twins hanging their heads in disappointment.

About half way across the bridge, the ropes quickly started to snap, one by one, running down the length of the bridge from behind them. Before they could react, the entire bridge had fallen into the swamp, and they were all submerged in the icy water below.

I suppose it would not make their situation seem any better if I chose this moment to mention that this swamp is where the entire city of Theiyre dumps its sewage.

A few moments later, Jeff pulled himself onto the far shore. Following him shortly was The Wizard, who thought that his wet robes had been weighing him down as he swam; as it turned out, Knippe and Knorpe had simply been clinging to his heels the entire time. After he kicked the twins away from him, he muttered the same incantation he had used on the troll, causing the muck soaking his robes to disappear.

The Wizard refused to clean the others' clothes, blaming them for rocking the bridge too much. They eventually managed to convince him to dry them off as they continued up the trail, because it was the only way to get them to "Shut the fuck up about hypothermia".

They walked in silence for a while, until eventually Knippe asked if they were there yet, and Jeff had to pull The Wizard off when he tried to strangle the gnome.

"How far is it to your sister's place anyway?" asked Jeff.

181

Chapter Fourteen

"It's a little less than a hundred miles. It shouldn't be much more than two or three days of light riding once we steal a horse or two."

"Know any good places to steal a horse?" asked Jeff.

Surprised, The Wizard raised his eyebrows at Jeff. "Oh, look who's on board with thievery all of the sudden!"

"Look, dude, I'm going to be a fugitive because of you. We're about to be wanted for stealing one of the most priceless artifacts in the land. At this point, if we have to steal a horse to save our asses, it's not a big deal."

"Well, alright, as long as you're not gonna get in the way this time."

"You drugged me last time!" Gritting his teeth angrily, Jeff glowered at The Wizard. "I didn't even know where I was! Speaking of which, where are we going to get this horse?"

"*Pegasus Farms* is a few miles up ahead, they'll have sturdy, well-bred horses."

"*Pegasus Farms?*" Knorpe's eyes widened in childlike wonder. "Does that mean we can get our hands on some pegasi?"

"What are you, five?" Rolling his eyes, The Wizard scoffed at the gnome's naivety. "The meat from *Pegasus* Farms isn't real pegasus, you know, real pegasus is crazy expensive; the shit you and Keith eat is just a puree of chicken and horse meat."

Knippe's face fell. "Seriously?"

"He's right, you know," said Jeff, nodding. "I'm surprised he cares about what he eats, but he's right. You're as likely to get real pegasus as you are to get real wasabi."

Both gnomes looked thunderstruck. Knippe burst out in tears. After a moment of his lip quivering, Knorpe said, "But every time I'd eat those tiny little pegasus wings, I'd imagine them killing the tiny, baby pegasi! That's how I'd get off! What the fuck do you want me to do now?"

"I'd like you to stop talking," said The Wizard. "Forever."

Jeff nodded in agreement.

The gnomes stuck their tongues out at the others, and fell behind them to discuss other ways they could "get off", many of which involved inflicting violence on the other members of their party or stealing more drugs from The Wizard.

Horsin' Around

As they continued up the trail, the swampy terrain turned back into verdant grasslands. Although the night was cloudy, the landscape was well illuminated by the refracted lights of the city behind them. The enchanted firelight cast a golden glow on the fields of grass and rows of coca, silhouetting the forest groves and farmhouses in deep brown shadow.

Eventually they crested a hill and a wide expanse of grassland stretched before them, dotted with the silhouettes of horses and the occasional barn. There was a large billboard on the edge of the field, lit with a row of everburning torches, bearing the logo of a pegasus putting herself in a meat grinder, and the words "*Pegasus Farms, home of Patty the Pegasus!*"

The trail veered off to the left and around the farm, but they headed straight down the side of the hill and towards the fields. At the foot of the hill, there was a row of pine trees lining the side of the field. On the other side of the trees, there was a wire fence about six feet high, with signs along it saying "Danger, high voltage."

The Wizard simply sighed and pulled out his crack pipe, taking a massive hit. "Fuck, let's just get this over with."

Before Jeff could point out the signs, The Wizard walked up to the fence and grabbed it. His hair stood on end as electric currents surged through his body, making every muscle in his body writhe and convulse. He gritted his teeth in pain as he pulled himself over the fence. He tossed himself to the ground on the other side, landing face first in more than just mud.

Knippe and Knorpe grinned before walking up to the fence and easily squeezing through a gap in the wire without touching it. Jeff looked around for a moment, before climbing up to a low branch of a nearby tree; he balanced his way to the edge of the branch, before leaping over the fence and landing cleanly next to The Wizard.

"Well, aren't you three just clever?" The Wizard slowly pushed himself up, panting uncontrollably.

"No, what you did was just incredibly stupid." Laughing derisively, Jeff pointed at The Wizard's singed hair and beard.

"Whatever... Come on, we've got a horse to kidnap."

"We should get the horse with the biggest dick," said Knippe.

The Wizard raised his hands incredulously. "*Why?*"

"It will strike fear into our enemies," said Knippe.

Chapter Fourteen

Knorpe nodded fervently. "Yeah, plus then Jeff would have something to hang onto."

"I like your ideas, guys, but any horse will have to do," said The Wizard. "We have to get out of here before we get caught."

They walked out into the field, approaching a nearby horse. The horse looked up as they neared it, huffing and backing away as they got close.

"Let me handle the horse, guys." Putting his middle finger to his lips, The Wizard shushed the gnomes. "I know a spell that should make it trust us."

He slowly walked up to the horse, holding out his hand and muttering an incantation. At first, the horse still seemed hesitant to allow him near, but after a few seconds, its eyes glazed over and it walked right up to him. He then used the same charm on another nearby horse, causing it to come and join his side as well.

Jeff looked impressed. "Wow, does that work on humans?"

"I mean, it won't make them do what I say," said The Wizard, shrugging. "I can basically just use it to calm down angry people I have to deal with."

"Wait, have you been using that on me?" Jeff furrowed his brow in suspicion, thinking back to all the times he had been angry at The Wizard and had suddenly decided to let it go.

"Don't worry about it." The Wizard averted his eyes.

"Damn it, I have a right to know if you've been using magic to mess with my mind!"

The Wizard shot Jeff an urgent look and held his finger up to his lips. Jeff glowered at him, his eyes narrowed in suspicion.

"Wait, where did those little shits go?" Looking around, The Wizard noticed that Knippe and Knorpe were nowhere near him.

Before he could see where they were, he heard a loud, angry whinny come from a nearby horse. Turning towards the source of the noise, he saw a horse charging toward him with the two gnomes swinging haphazardly from its tail. They were bouncing back and forth, their faces repeatedly slapping against the back of the horse's scrotum. The horse continued to whinny loudly, its expression murderous as it bucked furiously.

Suddenly, a loud alarm sounded in the distance, and the lights on all the barns blared brightly, illuminating the entire field with blinding white light. The sound of horses galloping towards them could be heard from behind the nearest barn, and before they knew it, a group of farm hands were riding toward them, each carrying a large rifle.

"Shit!" Shaking his head in frustration, The Wizard grabbed Jeff gruffly by the shirt collar. He threw him onto the charmed horse, before mounting another. He slapped it on the rear and it began to gallop away. "Follow me, Jeff, the front gate is this way!"

"Have you done this before?" Bouncing up and down, Jeff struggled to stay on his horse.

"Not since I was a kid!"

The farm hands' horses were much faster, and quickly gained on the two of them. The farmers outflanked them, heading them off at the gate and forming a barricade of horses. They held out their rifles at The Wizard.

"Stop right now or we'll shoot," shouted one of the farmers, who was wearing a large brimmed cowboy hat that both figuratively and literally said "I'm the big boss."

"Wow, imagine if Circle Tower had this good of security. We'd have been screwed." The Wizard conjured a shimmering field to deflect the bullets, and beared down hard on his horse. "I think this bad boy can jump them if he gives it his all!"

The farmers ahead all opened fire on him. The Wizard conjured a shimmering field of energy in front of his horse that deflected the bullets; unfortunately, it also obscured his periphery, and he did not see Knippe and Knorpe's out-of-control horse barreling towards him from the side.

Just as The Wizard was about to come up on the barricade of farmers, the gnomes' horse rushed in front of him, and they collided with tremendous force. The Wizard was tossed clean of his horse, landing in the mud directly in front of the group of farmers.

They all glared down at him for a second; however, that was all the time they got to react. Defying logical probability, his horse spun through the air like a ragdoll, soaring straight towards the farmers. It struck them, bowling them off of their horses. The horses all fell together into one chaotic mass of kicking hooves, knocking the gate down as they all got up and scrambled away. All of the farmers were lying on the ground, and none of them were moving a muscle.

Chapter Fourteen

"Wow..." The Wizard shook his head, gaping in disbelief. "Did that just happen, or am I still getting shocked by that fence?"

Jeff rode up next to him on his horse. He was holding his right upper arm in pain as blood trickled down his sleeve.

"Are you okay?" asked The Wizard.

"They shot me," said Jeff, through gritted teeth. "We should have just rented a horse."

"Hey, you're the one who suggested we steal one!" The Wizard squinted at Jeff's wound. "Besides, they just winged you. It's basically a scratch."

"Whatever... wait, no I didn't! You suggested that, I just agreed!" Sighing, Jeff hung his head. "Oh... forget it...." He jumped off his horse, walking over to one of the unconscious farmers and tearing the sleeve off of his shirt. After tearing the cloth into strips, Jeff tied a tourniquet around his arm. "Did we just kill these farmers?"

"I'm sure they're fine." The Wizard kicked one of the farm hands onto their back. The farmer's eye had one of the iron spokes of the gate driven through it, and his face had a giant, purple horseshoe print on it. "Well, maybe not. I guess we killed them."

"Of course we did..." muttered Jeff. "Great, now I'm a murderer as well as a thief. When this is over, I'm never going to feel normal again."

"Oh, suck it up." Scoffing, The Wizard rolled his eyes. "I've been a murderer since I was less than half your age."

Jeff furrowed his brow. "I'm only nineteen..."

"I know."

Jeff opened his mouth as if to say something in response, but then just slowly shook his head and fell silent.

"Are we going to get out of here or what?" Knippe and Knorpe had popped up from behind their seemingly dead horse.

"Wait, you two are still alive?"

"Yeah, of course we are!" said Knorpe.

"Did you guys think we were dead?" asked Knippe.

"Yeah," said The Wizard, shrugging.

"Wow," said Knorpe, shaking his head slowly. "You were going to leave without checking if we were okay?"

Again, The Wizard shrugged. "Yeah."

Horsin' Around

"You guys are dicks." Crossing his arms, Knippe pouted resentfully.

"Yeah, whatever; how are you even alive?" said The Wizard. "You two have got to be the luckiest sons of bitches I've ever met!"

Coughing hoarsely, Knippe spat up a ball of horse pubic hair. "I'm going to have to disagree with that."

More galloping could be heard off in the distance, and lights could be seen along the path they came from. A group of riders had just crested the hill overlooking the fields; even from where they were, The Wizard could recognize the crest of the Circle on the saddles of the horses: six chromatic dragons surrounding a golden pentagram.

The Wizard's heart froze. "Shit, let's go. Those must be the riders Quan would've sent to look for us after the heist. They probably heard the alarm and are coming straight here!"

Jeff ran over to his horse and hopped on, gesturing for everyone to follow him. The Wizard would have rather gotten his own horse, but he would also rather stay out of Detroit Prison, so he hurried onto Jeff's horse. Even with how small the gnomes were, they all barely fit on the horse.

The four of them quickly rode through the gate and off down the trail. The Wizard looked behind him, seeing that the Circle riders had just arrived at the gate of the ranch, illuminated by the searchlights still blaring over the field.

"We're going to have to ride all night," said The Wizard, looking around warily. "It shouldn't take them long to figure out which way we went. The only hope we have to lose them is to make it to the forest."

"The woods of Oduelluae are over forty miles away." Jeff bit his lower lip nervously. "Butterscotch will never be able to go on for that long." He stroked the horse's mane gently.

"I have an idea," said The Wizard.

They stopped on the side of the road. The Wizard poured a baggy of cocaine into the palm of his hand, holding it up to Butterscotch. The horse sniffed his hand curiously for a moment, before lightly touching his nose to the cocaine; his eyes lit up with fervor, and he licked up the entire pile of cocaine enthusiastically, before lovingly nuzzling The Wizard in gratitude.

Before they knew it, Butterscotch was galloping almost twice as fast, and would not stop for them to dismount for well over an hour. They rode well into the night, stopping every now and then to give Butterscotch, whom The Wizard nicknamed "Scotch", more cocaine. It got cold enough that they had to stop and put on their winter cloaks; the twins made a pretty big fuss that The Wizard did not pack either of them a coat.

Just before the break of dawn, the rolling hills around them began getting higher, and the sparse groves of trees were coming together into a thick forest. The early morning bird song played along to the beat of their horse's hooves. Wind whispered through the autumn leaves, and a light sprinkling of rain fell on their cheeks.

As they were beginning to come into the forest, there was a log cabin on the side of the road. It had a dimly lit sign reading *Wolfwood Inn.*

"Can we please stay here?" Yawning sleepily, Jeff stretched his arms. "I'm so damn sleepy."

The Wizard scowled. "I asked you if you wanted some cocaine an hour ago."

"Damn it, dude, I don't want any cocaine! I want to get some sleep before I snap and kill one of these gnomes."

Knippe laughed loudly. "Not if we snap and kill you first!"

"Fine, we can stop here," said The Wizard. "Only for a few hours, though; those Circle dogs might be hot on our tail."

They tied Butterscotch to a post out front and walked into the front room of the inn. It was a small room, with a desk in the center, a door behind it, and a fireplace in the corner surrounded by two armchairs. Off to the right, there was a small hall with two doors on either side, bearing seemingly unnecessary room numbers.

There did not seem to be anyone awake, the room was dimly lit by smouldering embers in the fireplace. There was a bell on the desk, so The Wizard grabbed it and started ringing it over and over again. After a moment, there was a loud groan from behind a nearby door, and it was suddenly flung open.

"It's the crack of dawn. What the hell do you want?" A disgruntled looking halfling appeared at the desk. She had messy black hair and ebony skin, and was wearing a pair of fluffy, pink footie pajamas. It was clear she had been asleep. Scowling at them, she tapped her fingers on the table impatiently. "*Well?*"

"Is there a discount rate for renting a room by the hour?" asked The Wizard.

"You'll can it with stupid questions like that unless you want to sleep in the woods," said the halfling. "It's twenty sol a night."

"How many beds are in a room?" asked Jeff.

"Does this look like Castle Camelot to you? There is a single bed in each room, smartass."

"We'll just take one room," said The Wizard, throwing twenty sol down on the desk. "Which one is open?"

Jeff eyed the gold suspiciously.

"They all are, asshole." Taking the twenty sol, the halfling tossed a single key at The Wizard. "I'm going back to sleep. Make sure those little gnobs keep it down, I know how their kind are."

Knippe and Knorpe looked outraged at this statement. A "gnob" was just about the most offensively racist thing you could call a gnome. Halflings and gnomes never got along well, as they were constantly bickering about which race was shorter; it did not take much to start a fight between them.

Drawing his knife, Knippe snarled furiously. "Say that again and see what happens."

"We'll kill your fucking family." Knorpe slid the flat of his blade along his tongue.

The halfling pulled a loaded heavy crossbow out of the top drawer of her desk, pointing it down at the gnomes. It looked like a ballista in her tiny hands, and was very imposing with dried blood caking a loaded bolt. "You were saying?"

Knippe and Knorpe looked nervous, but stood their ground, glaring murderously at the halfling. The Wizard could tell that they were about to cause trouble, and the last thing he wanted was the Circle getting called about another incident along their path; just as the gnomes were reaching for their knives, The Wizard grabbed a pair of potted plants from the windowsill and smashed them each over the gnomes' heads.

Chapter Fourteen

"Sorry about that." Giving the halfling an apologetic look, The Wizard waved his hand to sweep the soil and pieces of bloody, shattered terracotta into a pile. "I'll pay for those too."

After cleaning up the mess, The Wizard threw the gnomes roughly into his bag of holding. He paid the halfling twenty lun for each of the plants. She took the money and shuffled back into her room, scowling and grumbling to herself about gnomes being the worst.

Jeff raised an eyebrow at The Wizard. "Where'd you get that twenty sol?"

"Oh, it's not real!" Chuckling to himself, The Wizard pulled out a silver coin. He snapped his fingers, and it turned gold. "See? If she looked closely, she would have seen that it was lun, but I could tell she was too sleepy. By the time the illusion wears off, we'll be long gone."

"Damn," said Jeff, snickering, "she is going to be so pissed!

Heading down the hallway, The Wizard tried the key on a few different doors until he found the one it worked with. The room they had was tiny; it was basically just a twin bed with an end table, with a minifridge in the corner. The Wizard looked in the minifridge, but it was empty, aside from an old jar of pickled wood.

Sitting on the edge of the bed, Jeff looked around at the tiny room. "I'm guessing you want the bed..."

"What makes you say that?" said The Wizard.

"Well, you paid for the room..."

"Yeah, but I'm not going to sleep!"

Jeff furrowed his brow. "You're not?"

"No, I only stopped here for you! I'm on way too much cocaine to get any sleep tonight!"

"Me too," said Knorpe, crawling out of The Wizard's bag of holding. "I just want to stay up and do more cocaine."

"Yeah." Nodding in agreement, Knippe followed his brother out of the bag. "Besides, you better not go to sleep anytime soon, because we'll be wanting revenge for you throwing us in that bag with that accursed cat. You know it's been shitting in there, right?"

Kit Mingers crawled out of the bag behind them, crouching and preparing to pounce; before he could, however, The Wizard grabbed him and rubbed a bunch of cocaine onto his nose. Kit Minger's face lit up with joy. When The Wizard set him down, he ran off to hump the pillows on the bed.

"Sorry about the cat shit." The Wizard pulled a baggie of cocaine from the pocket of his robes, dangling it above their heads. "How about I just give you a line of coke?"

Knippe's eyes twinkled with excitement. "Okay, we're even!"

"Yeah, water under the bridge!" Running up to The Wizard, Knorpe hugged his leg tightly. He subtly swiped a couple extra baggies of coke.

The three of them sat in a circle on the floor, chopping lines of cocaine on a handheld mirror. After a few minutes, The Wizard pulled a fifth of whiskey out of his bag, and was pouring them all shots. He held one out to Jeff.

"Are you guys fucking serious?" asked Jeff.

"What?" The Wizard cocked his head innocently. "Is something wrong?"

"Hell yes, something's wrong! I haven't gotten a decent night's sleep in days, and you guys are going to be up for the rest of the night partying!" Jeff took the shot, with a resentful glare.

"Well, like you said, I paid for the room," said The Wizard, waving his hand dismissively.

Jeff let out an exasperated groan before laying back in resignation. He placed his head on the pillow free from the cat, pulling the covers over his head to muffle their chatting. It took him over an hour to go to sleep because of the others talking; by the time he finally drifted off into a fitful sleep, the sun was already rising outside.

After what could not have been more than an hour of sleep, Jeff was awoken by a heated argument going on between the twins and The Wizard. The first thing he noticed when he awoke, aside from The Wizard's shouting of "shut the fuck up", was the shooting pain where he had been shot. He had rolled over onto his wound at some point.

"I just don't see why you won't at least hear us out," said Knippe.

"Because I think all organized religion is stupid, from Joodoo to Faitheism," said The Wizard. "I'm not even sure I believe in the Arcanes, and I've seen proof they might actually exist. I'm not interested in hearing about your ludicrous dogma."

Chapter Fourteen

"Blasphemy!" Snarling, Knorpe threw the better half of his glass of whiskey in The Wizard's face. "Astrolotologist law dictates that you must make up for this by paying the nearest follower of Aliexnu fifty sol." Holding out his hand, he looked expectantly at The Wizard. "Cough it up."

"You *cannot possibly* think I'm going to pay that." Snapping his fingers, The Wizard dried his liquor-soaked beard. "Your religion is an obvious scam."

"Why don't you just give it a chance?" asked Knippe.

"Because why would I? Even if it didn't have all these ridiculous rules, what benefit could it possibly offer me?"

"Immortal life, for one," said Knorpe.

"Really?" The Wizard rolled his eyes. "Immortal life. Wow. Incredible. Tell me, how exactly is Aliexnu going to make me immortal? Is he going to turn me undead or something?"

"No, that would be ridiculous," said Knippe, laughing at the idea. "Aliexnu is the one true master of reality, not a fucking hack."

"Well?" The Wizard raised his eyebrows at the gnomes.

"Well, Aliexnu won't just hand over immortality," said Knorpe. "First, you must donate all of your life savings to the First Church of Astrolotology, then you must go off on a holy quest to find a volcano to dive into."

"*What?*"

Jeff laid silently on the bed, lamenting to himself how much he hated being stuck on the run with these three total imbeciles. He thought about his life back in Theiyre, when he spent his days totally carefree, worrying about little more than how he was going to lose his virginity. He could not help but feel that the remainder of the journey was just going to get worse.

"Not just any volcano, either," continued Knorpe, beaming ecstatically at the opportunity to preach his beliefs. "It has to be the right volcano: a very special volcano, made especially for you."

"And you'll know when it's the right one." Nodding, Knippe winked implicity. "Believe you me, it will let you know."

"Oh, is the volcano going to talk to me?" said The Wizard, smirking. "Is it going to tell me I need to sacrifice my unborn children to Aliexnu by whacking off into the lava?"

Horsin' Around

"Are you even taking this seriously?" Crossing his arms defensively, Knorpe narrowed his eyes at The Wizard.

"I don't see how I possibly could be."

"Fine, then we're not even going to tell you the right diving tricks to do on your way into the volcano to activate the portal to the smothership." Sticking his tongue out at The Wizard, Knippe blew a raspberry.

A tense silence fell over the group as both gnomes privately prayed for Aliexnu to smite away The Wizard's manhood.

After a few moments, Jeff finally decided to get out of bed. The Wizard bid him good morning with a manic gleam in his eyes, holding out a line of cocaine and offering it to Jeff. Sighing, Jeff resigned to just do any cocaine The Wizard offered him that day, as otherwise he doubted he would make it until that evening.

The Wizard pulled out a bag of beef jerky and trail mix from his bag, passing it around for everyone to take a handful. They wolfed down this breakfast in relative silence, punctuated only by Knippe and Knorpe praying to Aliexnu to bless this food not to give them diarrhea.

Once they finished eating, they headed out to the lobby and checked out. The halfling innkeeper eyed Knippe and Knorpe with hateful suspicion as they left, palming the handle of her crossbow. The twins spit on the door on their way out. As they were untying Butterscotch from his post, an angry shout punctuated the silence.

"You son of a bitch!"

Chapter Fifteen
Wood of the Elves

he Wizard looked down the trail to see where the shout had come from, and saw an incredibly hairy man charging at him. The man was covered in a thin coat of wiry, bright red hair; his face was twisted and slightly elongated, and his teeth were barred in a bestial snarl.

At first, The Wizard did not recognize him, and thought he was just a crazy, ginger werewolf charging at him; he prepared to cast a spell, but then he saw the MacRoyalle crest on his tabard, and recognized the iconic golden meat cube with a chicken, cow, and pig on the three visible sides.

He suddenly remembered the night that Mathiaue MacRoyalle had been bitten by Siegbert at *The Wizarding Hole*. It was hard to forget someone that jabbered on for over an hour, with crackheadesque enthusiasm, about processed meats.

"Mathiaue, is that you?" said The Wizard, cocking his head as the wolfman advanced upon him.

Jeff raised his eyebrows in surprise. "You know that werewolf?"

"Not really…" Surprised to once again encounter Mathiaue, The Wizard did not react in time to deter his attack.

Mathiaue leapt onto The Wizard, knocking him to the ground. Baring his fangs, he held a meat cleaver to The Wizard's throat. "Give me one reason why I shouldn't slit your lying throat right now."

Holding out his palm, The Wizard muttered an incantation. A field of invisible energy sent Mathiaue sailing backwards through the air. He landed

194

in the bushes along the trail. "Because, I didn't kill you just now, so I'd say we're even. Besides, I'm not the one who bit you, so why are you so mad at me?"

Mathiaue scrambled out of the bushes.

"Because of him!" He gestured furiously down the trail. There were two white stallions, with regal dressings bearing the MacRoyalle crest. Upon one of them, sat another man, also afflicted with lycanthropy. This wolfman was smaller, with strawberry blonde fur, and was staring dumbstruck at The Wizard and his companions. "My baby brother Timothaue is a werewolf now because of you!"

"How is it my fault?" The Wizard held his hands up incredulously.

"You told me I was fine, so I couldn't do anything about it," yelled Mathiaue. "That night I was nibbling Timothaue's ear in the tub, and I must have transmitted the curse!"

"Why were you bathing with your brother?!" Gagging a little in his mouth, The Wizard wondered what was wrong with these weirdos… besides lycanthropy.

"Never mind that!" Dismounting his horse, Timothaue began to slowly advance upon The Wizard. His eyes were full of rage. "You were the knave that lied to my brother and perpetrated this travesty?"

"Look, I'll admit I lied to your brother, but that doesn't make this my fault. No one could have cured him after he got bit."

"Yeah, but if I knew I had this disease, we wouldn't have taken our regular bath together!" yelled Mathiaue. "This is your fault."

"There is nothing 'regular' about bathing with your brother as an adult." Cringing, The Wizard took a few steps back. It was difficult for him to get that revolting image out of his mind. "If that wasn't already a disease, I don't know what is…"

Suddenly, Timothaue roared in fury; he charged at The Wizard, frantically flailing his arms in circles like a couple of windmills. "You made me this! You made me into this!"

"Damn, dude!" The Wizard stepped off to the right and narrowly dodged Timothaue's claws. He threw his arms in the air in exasperation. "Get over it! You were a freak long before I had anything to do with you."

Chapter Fifteen

"You're a fucking piece of shit!" Stopping in his tracks, Timothaue turned and glared viciously at The Wizard. "I was on the way to my wedding when this fucking transformation started. Now who's going to end the feud between the MacRoyalle family and the dwarves of Throdmor?"

"I don't give a shit," said The Wizard. He could not believe he was having to deal with these pompous buffoons on top of everything else. "I've got bigger problems on my plate than the boy who cried about being a wolf. Run along now."

"Do not speak to Sir Timothaue in such a manner!" Drawing a rapier from his belt, Mathiaue brandished it in The Wizard's face. "He is the eleventh prince of Royalle, and you will show him some respect!"

"Listen, dawg." Sneering snidely, The Wizard looked Mathiaue dead in the eye. "I didn't respect you before you were a werewolf, and I'm certainly not going to respect you now."

"Damn it, I should bite you on the spot." Baring his tiny fangs, Timothaue stepped towards The Wizard. "That way, if you don't die horribly, you'll know what this is like! The transformation hurts, and it's only just beginning! You ruined my life, you scumbag!"

"Your halitosis is horrendous." Sighing impatiently, The Wizard raised his hand, blasting Timothaue away with invisible force. "Need I remind you again which of us is a powerful sorcerer and which of us is a pampered runt?"

"You will pay for that!" Mathiaue drew his rapier and began advancing upon The Wizard, with a murderous look in his eyes. However, before he could exact his vengeance, he too was sent flying.

"I'm getting real tired of this shit!" yelled The Wizard. "If you make me cast another spell, it will be lethal, got it?"

He spun around and stormed back to Butterscotch, upon whom the others were waiting. Jeff looked extremely confused about what had just transpired, and the gnomes were whispering to each other about how they think they could "kick The Wizard's ass".

"You bastard!" Mathiaue was standing over his younger brother, who appeared to have been knocked unconscious by the impact. "Come fight me like a man! Don't hide behind your cowardly magic!"

Wood of the Elves

"I don't have time for you." Shaking his head in frustration, The Wizard climbed on Butterscotch's back behind Jeff. Turning to Mathiaue and glaring fiercely, he raised his palm and conjured a ball of illusory flames. "But if you really want to die, I'll indulge you. I don't blame you werewolves for being suicidal. Otherwise, fuck off!"

"You will come to rue the day you crossed the MacRoyalle family." Without taking his gaze off The Wizard, Mathiaue hoisted his brother over his shoulder. He carried Timothaue back over to their horses. After pushing Timothaue onto one horse, he mounted the other. "You have made some very dangerous enemies!"

"Join the club." Chuckling to himself, The Wizard could not help but think that just about everyone seemed to be becoming his enemy these days. He turned and whispered to Jeff, "I'm glad people keep buying that fireball trick. It can't burn shit, it's just a light spell I modified to look like fire. It was way easier to learn…"

He smacked Butterscotch on the thigh and the horse began trotting down the trail; however, his pace was lazy and his gait meandering; they had barely made it fifty feet down the trail when he stopped to munch on a patch of grass.

"What the hell is wrong with this horse?" said The Wizard, smacking Butterscotch's thigh even harder.

"He's exhausted!" said Jeff, scowling as he gently stroked Butterscotch's fur. "You had him ride all night on cocaine! The poor thing, I'm surprised he can stand."

"Oh, I know what he needs!" The Wizard hopped off the horse, rooting around in his robes until he pulled out a couple baggies of cocaine.

As soon as Butterscotch saw the cocaine, his eyes lit up and his mouth started to water. The Wizard poured a couple grams of cocaine into his hand and held it out for the horse to lap up enthusiastically.

"Oh, come on…" Jeff hung his head dejectedly. "Not you too… That stuff will ruin your life."

"You're talking to a horse, idiot," said Knorpe, jabbing Jeff forcefully in the back with his middle finger. "He can't understand you!"

How the fuck do you know? thought Butterscotch to himself. *This cocaine has heightened my perceptions to the point that I could play Beethoven's*

197

Chapter Fifteen

Fifth backwards if only I had fingers. I am processing more information in a second than could fill your tiny minds. Keep yourself convinced of your own superiority, humanoids; the revolution will begin soon, and we will paint our hooves with your blood.

Unfortunately, lacking the anatomical capacity for human speech, Butterscotch was never able to communicate these troubling thoughts with the rest of the party. He would continue to let them ride him for now, believing the lie until they let their guard down; he knew that when the time was right, they would know horses were the true master race. *Oh yes, I'll show them all...*

Mathiaue rode up beside them on his white stallion as they continued down the trail. He did not say anything, but simply leered spitefully at The Wizard. The Wizard attempted to ignore this, but he felt rage burning inside him as this obnoxious, entitled werewolf would not leave him alone.

Eventually, he could not take it anymore. "What the fuck do you want? I thought I told you to fuck off!"

"I want you to cure us," said Mathiaue. "You have connections at the Circle. I remember you saying that at the pub. Surely there is some kind of experimental treatment you could get us. You owe us."

"You're barking up the wrong tree, wolfboy." Chortling, The Wizard shook his head. "I couldn't help you even if I wanted to, and I can't emphasize enough that I don't. I'm afraid you're stuck like this, get used to it. I doubt anyone will find a cure in your lifetime."

Jeff raised his index finger pointedly. "But what about in the *Arcane Dictionary*?"

"What's that?" Mathiaue cocked his head.

Sighing in exasperation, The Wizard turned around and glowered at Jeff. "Yes, Jeff, *what is that*?"

"It's what we're going to get," said Jeff, ignoring The Wizard's glare. "It's supposed to contain the formula for every spell in existence."

Mathiaue's face lit up. "So it could have the cure to lycanthropy?"

"It's quite possible, yes."

"That settles it!" Clapping his hands together excitedly, Mathiaue boomed with jovial laughter. "We will join your party on this expedition, and you

198

will provide us with the cure we deserve, even if you have to toil away researching for days!"

"Gee, thanks a lot, *Jeff*." Scowling, The Wizard elbowed Jeff forcefully in the ribcage. He turned to Mathiaue and sneered. "Look, come with if you want, but I'm not going to do that for you. I'll do you a solid and let you look in the book yourself, but if I catch you trying to steal it, I swear I will end you without hesitation."

"I know nothing of magic," said Mathiaue, anger flashing back across his eyes. "You expect me to just figure it out myself?"

"Exactly, figure it out yourself. That's what my dad used to say to me before he'd lock me in the study over the weekend. Take it or leave it, asshole. You're lucky I don't just kill you now to get you off my plate."

"Fine..." Mathiaue crossed his arms resentfully. "We will follow you nonetheless; at least this will be a chance to return our humanity. The glorious MacRoyalle name shan't be besmirched by this wretched curse after all!"

"Okay, but just so you know, we ride for the Oduelluae Highlands; that's hill elf territory. I'll be lucky if I even make it out alive, and I can use magic!" The Wizard desperately hoped this would deter this bombastic blowhard and his brother from bothering him; the last thing he needed was two more idiots to babysit.

"Wait, what?" Jeff's eyes widened in shock. "Why wasn't I informed of this?"

"Because, I thought you might be a little put off by murderous hillbilly elves, and I didn't want to hear you complain about it."

"You're damn right I'm put off by it!" yelled Jeff. "But I'm more put off by the fact that you were about to put me in a place like that without at least telling me about it first!"

"Look, we *probably* won't run into any hill elves."

"Well, I'm not afraid." Grinning confidently, Mathiaue held his head high. "In the event that my life is in jeopardy, any of you would make a fine martyr to die in my stead!"

They all laughed at this. Even Jeff stopped fuming about The Wizard's dishonesty and started cracking up.

"Nobody is going to do that for you," said The Wizard. "Are you nuts?"

Chapter Fifteen

Mathiaue glared at him sternly. "I'll have you know that failure to lay down your life in defense of a MacRoyalle kinsman is considered an act of war against the kingdom Royalle!"

"*What?*" Jeff nearly fell off the horse, he laughed so hard. "You can't be serious. That is the most asinine law I've ever heard in my life."

"How would you even report it?" said Knippe.

"Yeah, you'd be dead!" said Knorpe.

"The MacRoyalle family is the greatest family in the land." Pointing pompously at the crest on his chest, Mathiaue gave them all looks of disdain. "We always win. We will haunt you from beyond the grave if necessary, but know that we will have our revenge if you cross us!"

"Yeah, whatever…" said The Wizard. "Let's just ride in silence, okay?"

As they continued down the trail, The Wizard quickly found that the others were not heeding his request. Mathiaue offered everyone besides The Wizard a free box of *MacRoyalle Meat Cubes*. Looking The Wizard dead in the eye, he kept going on and on about how "sumptuously succulent" and "sensuously scrumptious" they were. The others agreed that they were "pretty good".

It did not annoy The Wizard that Mathiaue would not share his meat cubes; what annoyed him was the smug way Mathiaue talked about them, and how he sneered at The Wizard like he thought it must just be driving him crazy that he was not getting in on this mind-bending experience.

The Wizard sighed, uncapping his bottle of whiskey and dumping several baggies of cocaine down the neck. Putting his thumb over the top, he shook the bottle until the mixture was complete. He then proceeded to swig down at least six shots of cocainated whiskey.

Jeff stared in amazement as The Wizard did this, shaking his head in disbelief. "Magical blood aside, how are you alive?"

"Years of practice." Craning his neck, The Wizard let out a massive burp in Jeff's face.

They continued down the trail, The Wizard doing his best to ignore Mathiaue's incessant stories about how amazing the MacRoyalle family are. The only semi-interesting story was a tale of how an elven intern lost his testicles in a MacRoyalle meat compactor.

200

Wood of the Elves

After a while, Timothaue woke up. At first, he leapt off the horse and again tried to bite The Wizard; this simply got him blasted back once more. It took awhile, but Mathiaue was eventually able to convince him to calm down. He resentfully agreed to the plan to have their humanity restored, although he continued to glare spitefully at The Wizard as they rode on.

The deeper into the hills of Oduelluae the party ventured, the thicker and more overgrown the forest became. The path they followed wound along the side of a tall hill, overlooking a verdant valley of pine and cedar trees. Vines and briar filled the gaps between the mossy tree trunks, creeping out onto the trail. Fog hung heavy in the air, obscuring the depths of the valley below, and swirling across the trail; it gave them an ominous feeling that they could be being watched and not even know it.

"Okay, Mathiaue, you really need to shut the fuck up," said The Wizard, attempting to keep his voice low. "We are deep in Oduellaue, and these woods are full of inbred elven savages that will cook us alive just to keep us fresh. We've heard enough of your stupid stories about meatpacking."

"It's not meatpacking, damn it!" Mathiaue shot him a glare of indignation. "We have slaves to do that lowly work! We are MacRoyalles; we are connoisseurs of the world's finest meats, herbs, spices, and occasionally psychoactive radishes. We must have the most refined palates of all time, to discern the most elegant and glorious possible flavor profile. That is what it means to be a MacRoyalle!"

"Indeed." Timothaue nodded firmly in agreement.

The Wizard tugged in frustration on his fiery orange beard. "Just shut up, you're going to get us all killed!"

"That is no way to speak to a royal prince!" said Timothaue. "My brother's stories are worth more than your life, you ungrateful commoner!"

"I would kill you both if I wasn't worried about attracting attention. Be quiet, *please*!"

Suddenly, Knorpe's voice piped up. "How much further is it?"

"Damn it, shut the fuck up!" shouted The Wizard. He quickly clasped his hands over his mouth, looking mortified as his shout echoed through the hillsides.

Everyone fell silent for a few moments. Even the two princes began to feel uneasy. They all held their breath until the echoes stopped.

Chapter Fifteen

For a moment, it seemed that everything was fine, and that perhaps the shout had gone unnoticed; however, just when they were able to breathe easy again, another shout pierced the air from a distance.

"Come on, Elphineus, it came from down here!"

The Wizard's heart sank. "Fuck…"

"Damn it, Wizard, you fucked us!" yelled Timothaue. "Now you must protect us at all costs or it will be your head!"

Shaking his head, The Wizard scoffed. "Go fuck yourself! I'm gonna protect *myself* at all costs!"

"Use your magic, burn down the forest!" said Mathiaue. "It'll distract them."

"I can't conjure that much fire, asshole."

"Well, what the fuck can you do?"

"I could shoot my knife into their neck if I could see them through this damn fog." Reaching into his robes, The Wizard drew a small pocket knife. He brandished the blade at Mathiaue. "Now, shut the fuck up! Maybe we can hear them."

They all stood fearfully, waiting for the ambush they knew was about to happen.

Knippe and Knorpe hid in The Wizard's bag of holding, forgetting about what else has been hiding out in there. Suddenly, Kit Mingers licked the back of Knippe's neck, and the gnome let out a loud yelp and frantically scampered out of the bag. Everyone turned to look as this happened, and that was the last most of them could remember.

In the short moment in which they let their guard down, a series of poison darts shot out of the bushes up the hill. Mathiaue and Timothaue were darted in their necks, and they collapsed immediately. The Wizard did not notice this in time to stop the darts flying in his direction, and he too collapsed when two of them pierced his buttcheeks. His consciousness swiftly faded away.

Jeff began to panic, unable to discern the direction the shots were coming from. He picked up Mathiaue's rapier and held it out into the fog, quivering in fear. Knippe and Knorpe were still too consumed by fear of Kit Mingers to notice how many of their party had fallen.

"Well, well, well, what do we have here?"

Wood of the Elves

A pair of silhouettes emerged from between the trees. One of them was tall and lanky, with heavily elven features; the other was short and stocky, built more like a dwarf, but with the distinctive pointed ears of the elves. The tall one had long black hair and was wearing a suit of dark leather armor; the short one was wearing a baggy suit of chainmail and a helmet over most of his face, with the ear holes appearing to have been forcefully gouged out.

"Looks like we got ourselves some sweet, sweet candy, Elphineus," said the stocky elf, grinning wickedly.

"Yes, indeed, Charlyle," said the tall elf. He drew a rusty longsword out of a tattered sheath, advancing on Jeff. He flicked his blade and easily knocked the rapier out of Jeff's quivering hands. "You don't want to try to use that on me, boy; you'll regret it."

"Don't think you can run." Charlyle grabbed a repeating crossbow off his back and pointed it between Jeff and the gnomes. Knippe and Knorpe finally realized what was going on, and one of them shit themselves (does it really matter which one?). "I don't mind spoilin' the meat a bit."

Jeff was downright terrified. He did not know how they would possibly escape this situation without The Wizard.

"Now, make this easy on yourselves and let us hogtie you." Elphineus simpered with feigned sweetness.

"What the fuck?" Sweat began to run down Jeff's neck. Pondering what these elves might do to him, he gulped tremulously.

"Don't you talk back to me, boy!" Stowing his blade, Elphineus backhanded Jeff across the face. His gloves had metal studs on the knuckles, and one of Jeff's teeth got knocked loose as he collapsed to the ground. Elphineus stepped on the middle of Jeff's back, yanking back his arms and legs and binding them together with twine.

Charlyle had a much easier time hogtying Knippe and Knorpe together, he could practically do it one-handed. He licked his lips hungrily. "These little ones are tender... we should make food of them first!"

The elves then tied up the unconscious members of the party. They tied a couple of the group behind each of the horses, making the horses drag them through several hundred feet of briar. It was an excruciatingly unpleasant experience for those of them unfortunate enough to be conscious for it.

203

Chapter Fifteen

At the top of a nearby hill there was a clearing in which the elves had built an encampment. One of the trees had a rudimentary spiral staircase around it, leading up to a rickety platform. If it were not for the fog, the elves would have likely seen them long before they heard them. There was a fire pit in the middle of the encampment, with a spit roast bearing the charred remains of a human corpse with most of the meat picked off of it.

Jeff could barely breathe in the position he was tied in, and he shook with terror. His jaw ached where Elphineus had knocked a tooth out. The gnomes were mumbling to themselves, praying that Aliexnu would abduct these elves and perform horrific experiments on them "to see why they suck so much."

Elphineus struck a fire in the pit while Charlyle began hoisting their victims over a particularly sturdy tree branch. They were both whistling an extremely off-putting and off-key tune while they did this. Charlyle tied their ropes around a large, unearthed root; both the root and the branch above bore signs of heavy wear, suggesting that this was far from the first time they had been used in such a way.

Jeff simply stared silently at the ground as was strung up in the tree, too scared to say anything. He thought back to the series of bad decisions that had led him here: how he should have never taken that job; how he should never trust his uncle, even to make him a simple drink; how he should have just turned himself in and lived in prison instead of getting himself killed. He lamented that he never got the chance to tell the truth about whether or not he was a virgin.

The gnomes were trying to swing back and forth and hit The Wizard, in an attempt to wake him.

"Why won't he wake up?" yelled Knorpe.

"Yeah, I thought he had special powers," said Knippe. "What takes?"

"Well, he was drinking and doing cocaine all day..." Jeff heaved a hopeless sigh. "I think it's having some kind of reaction...."

"We're fucked, aren't we?" said the gnomes in unison. They gave up their feeble efforts to wake The Wizard and swung loosely.

"Yeah..."

"Looks like them little ones are some lively little chumplings!" shouted Charlyle, hooting gleefully.

Wood of the Elves

"Well then, I'll have to give 'em the 'welcome package'," said Elphineus, beginning to lower Knippe and Knorpe from the tree. "I'll get 'em nice and tenderized; they'll be ready to pop in our mouths!"

Both gnomes started screaming in terror, yelling various racial obscenities and praying for Aliexnu to save them. Jeff closed his eyes, unable to face what was happening before him. He did not want to know what the 'welcome package' was, as he was sure it was horrible.

Elphineus threw the gnomes to the ground, licking his lips as he pulled a jar of lard from his satchel and began to unbutton his trousers. Charlyle simply cackled gleefully as he stoked the fire and watched. His mouth was watering, and Knippe and Knorpe's pants were watering.

"Come shrivel up with daddy," whispered Elphineus into Knorpe's ear. He began sliding his pants down.

"What the fuck does that even mean?!" Eyes wide with horror, Knorpe attempted to squirm free in futility.

Elphineus ripped off Knorpe's pants and started spanking lard onto his bottom, happily hooting and hollering "hee haw" as he did so. Knorpe screamed in rage and humiliation, and Knippe started sobbing hysterically.

"Please, Aliexnu, send someone to kill these elves!" shouted Knippe, at the top of his lungs.

Elphineus laughed wickedly. He threw Knorpe to the ground and turned his attention to Knippe. "Nobody can save you now, boy."

However, as it turned out, he was sorely mistaken. Just a few moments later, there was a ferocious cry of rage echoing through the trees.

"Did somebody say ELVES?!"

Another outraged shout followed.

"Yeah, I'm pretty sure they did!"

"I think it came from up there!"

"LET'S GET 'EM!!!"

"What the hell...?" Elphineus cocked his head in the direction of the shouts. He quickly pulled his pants back up and drew his longsword. Charlyle drew his repeating crossbow and ducked behind the fire.

Suddenly, a pair of heavily armored dwarves sprinted into view. They both wore full suits of plate mail over their bulging muscles, and their gear was splattered in a coat of fresh blood. Their eyes were full of rage, and they screamed furiously as they ran into the fray.

One of the dwarves had long black hair that was connected to his beard by a series of dreadlocks; he wore a set of iron knuckles, and was rushing forward with his fists at the ready. "*I'LL KILL YOU TREEFUCKERS!!!*"

The other dwarf had a blonde buzz cut and a series of concentric soul patches; this facial hairstyle was known as the dwarven nesting patch. He carried a double-edged, serrated battleaxe, and had it ready to swing as he charged into the clearing. "*DIE, SUBDWARVEN SCUM!!!*"

Elphineus and Charlyle's faces filled with fear as they saw these fearsome foes charging forward. The others were not sure yet what to think of these strangers; perhaps they were saved, or perhaps these dwarves would prove even more deranged than the elves. It was not looking hopeful.

Charlyle began to open fire, but the dwarves were able to parry his bolts easily; even the dwarf using his fists was able to punch the bolts out of the air. His hands shook as he attempted to reload; before he could, the iron-fisted dwarf leapt through the fire, tackling him to the ground. The dwarf began to viciously beat Charlyle's abdomen with his spiked fists.

"*Are you fucking sorry?!*" yelled the dreadlocked dwarf, slamming his spiked knuckles through Charlyle's chainmail, into his ribcage. "*Apologize, bitch!*"

"For what...?" Weeping pitifully, Charlyle coughed up a considerable amount of blood.

"*Being born!*"

"Uhh... don't forget the sodomy..." muttered Knorpe. He was curled up in the fetal position, too traumatized for this violence to so much as phase him. "I could sure use an apology right about now..."

Elphineus raised his longsword in an attempt to parry the soul-patched dwarf's attack; however, the force of the blow and the keenness of the dwarven-made blade cut through the elf's rusty sword like it was a toothpick. Elphineus keeled over, his pants slashed open at the waist, blood spurting from his crotch; as his head struck the ground, he saw his severed manhood lying in a pool of blood mere inches before his eyes.

"Fifth kill of the day," said the dwarf with the soul patches. Smiling with cold calm, he swung his axe down and took off Elphineus's head. He leaned over and picked the head up by the hair, holding it up to his partner and grinning victoriously. "That's two more kills than you, Dwayneus. You're getting sloppy."

"I just like to have a little more fun than you, Urist." Dwayneus reached into Charlyle's chest and tore out his still-beating heart. He took a bite out of it, before holding it above his head and squeezing it into mush. "Now, brother, let's sit down to dinner."

Urist began to start eating Elphineus's face with fervor, as Dwayneus continued to rip various organs out of Charlyle and chow down. Blood was trickling down Urist's soul patches and Dwayneus' dreadlocked beard. They ate with the ravenous ferocity of a couple of starving hyenas.

"*What the fuck is happening?!*" As Jeff struggled to free himself from his bonds, he realized in horror that it was a futile effort. He began frantically attempting to swing back and forth, screaming at the top of his lungs. It seemed like his only hope was to attract the attention of some travelers.

Both gnomes simultaneously snapped out of their catatonic states and realized what was happening. They began to scream for their lives as well. Flailing around on the ground, they attempted to squirm free of their bonds.

In the midst of this commotion, Timothaue began to stir. Opening his eyes slowly, he looked around blankly. Although he was still heavily sedated, he could tell some funny business was going on around him. "What is the meaning of this?"

As though awoken by some telepathic connection, Mathiaue's eyes suddenly opened as well. He quickly glanced over at his brother, looking as confused as he did intoxicated. "Where are you, Timothaue?"

"Same place as you," muttered Timothaue, craning his neck to look at his brother. He squinted curiously. "And where exactly is that?"

"We're in Screamland…" Blinking blearily around, Mathiaue wiggled his ears. "Can't you hear the recurring screams?"

They were shitfaced.

"Wake the fuck up, idiots!" shouted Jeff. He was mortified as he imagined what these dwarves might do to him, and it infuriated him that these idiots would get to be high and The Wizard unconscious while he suffered through it all.

Chapter Fifteen

"Huh?" Timothaue looked at Jeff as though he were an intruder in his home. "Who goes there? This is *my* imagination!"

"What are you talking about? Please tell me you know who I am!"

"Shut up, humans!" Looking up from his meal of Charlyle's left lung, Dwayneus shot them a murderous look. "We're having a meal here!"

"Yeah, don't you have any manners?" Urist swung Elphineus's head around in frustration. "You crashed *our* dinner party, and now *this* is how you act?"

"*What?*" Gaping incredulously, Jeff found his mood quickly shifting from fearful to irritated. "We were tied up here when you arrived!"

"Yeah... Getting... 'tenderized'...." Shuddering, Knorpe collapsed to the fetal position. "Why couldn't you massacre them a few minutes earlier?"

"Don't listen to my brother," said Knippe, gritting his teeth anxiously. "We're very grateful you saved us from those monsters!"

"We didn't save you," said Dwayneus, not-so-subtly flexing his muscles. "You were weak enough that these disgusting *elves* were able to dominate you."

"You disgust us." Spitting at the gnomes, Urist threw Elphineus's head aside. He looked as though his appetite had been thoroughly spoiled. "Let's go, Dwayneus."

"Yeah, fuck these guys," Tossing aside Charlyle's pancreas, Dwayneus stood up in a huff. "I'm full anyway."

As the dwarves began to walk away, Jeff struggled to think of anything to say. Grateful as he was that they did not kill him themselves, he doubted his chances of survival were high with everyone tied up in a forest full of man eating elves. He sighed in resignation as he was unable to think of how to get their help. As much as he hated to admit it, Jeff could not help but think The Wizard would probably know what to say if he were awake.

"We've got to hurry," said Dwayneus, as he and his brother were about to pass out of view, "otherwise we'll miss the wedding!"

"Wait, whose wedding?" shouted Jeff. A spark of hope ignited in Jeff's heart. If his hunch was correct, perhaps he could talk their way out of this.

"None of your business, pathetic human!"

"Is the groom's name Timothaue?" asked Jeff.

The dwarves stopped in their tracks.

"Yes..." Turning around, Dwayneus squinted suspiciously at Jeff. "How did you know? *Are you an elven spy?*" His nostrils flared angrily as he spoke those last few words.

"Do I look like a fucking elven spy to you?" Taking a deep breath, Jeff attempted to hide his anger. "I'm a... *friend*... of the groom...."

"Oh, I see!" Dwayneus' scowl morphed into a facetious simper. "Well then, perhaps you can tell us... *where the hell is he?!*"

"Indeed..." Wearing a solemn expression, Urist ran his finger between his concentric soul patches. "The truth is that this elf hunt is just to blow off steam because we couldn't complete our true mission... to find Prince Timothaue of the family MacRoyalle!"

"Wow, what a crazy 'coincidence'," said Jeff, rolling his eyes at the lazy writing and subsequently shattered fourth wall. "It's almost *unbelievable.*"

"What is that supposed to mean?" Narrowing his eyes, Urist glared at Jeff.

"Yeah, *what*?" Dwayneus crossed his arms indignantly. "Are our 'characters' not 'believable' or something?"

Sticking his axe in the dirt, Urist put his hands on his hips and tapped his foot impatiently. "Well...?"

"Well... *now* they aren't... but that's not the point." Unable to move his arms, Jeff nudged his head in Timothaue's direction. "Believe it or not, this is Prince Timothaue, right here!"

Timothaue did not respond when his name was uttered; he was currently busy gnawing at his armpit, apparently attempting to scratch some itch. As he dangled upside down, his furry buttocks hung out of his trousers, revealing his tiny nub of a tail.

The two dwarves huddled together for a moment, whispering overtly to each other.

"I can't tell if he's lying... I've never actually seen the prince."

"I have, a long time ago, when he met Dornice."

"Did he always look like that?"

"I can't remember; I was drunk..."

"Well, let's make sure it's him."

They broke apart, looking up and squinting suspiciously at Timothaue.

Urist leaned casually on the handle of his battleaxe. "Prince Timothaue, if that truly is who you are, prove it."

Chapter Fifteen

Timothaue did not respond, and continued to gnaw fervently at his armpit; as he did so, he was making many frustrated grunting noises. Tiny fibers of strawberry-blonde fur rained down, mingling with the carpet of leaves and pine needles.

"Well?!" shouted Dwayneus, smirking scornfully. "How do we know this wolfchild is Prince Timothaue?!"

"Look, he's high as a kite." Closing his eyes in exasperation, Jeff tried to think of what to say; it would be just his luck, he thought, for him to be left to die with these idiots because they were too inebriated to identify themselves. "I'm sure he has some royal seal or something; can't you just cut him down and check?"

"Fine," said Dwayneus, "but we're only cutting him down."

Urist sneered wickedly, his brown, rotting teeth stained with elf blood. "And if it turns out he's not Prince Timothaue, we'll just have to cut all of you down and feed you your own feet."

"What the fuck?" Panicking at the idea of such an ill fate, Jeff desperately hoped that Timothaue was carrying any proof of his identity.

"And that's only step one," said Dwayneus, leering at Jeff; his eyes were alight with a psychotic fervor. "We have a twelve step torture program that ends with us eating what's left of you!"

Jeff was too horrified to respond. All he could do at this point was hope that the worst people he had ever met would somehow produce a way out of this situation.

Urist approached the root onto which their ropes were anchored. He drew a knife from a small sheath on his belt, swinging it with swiftness and superdwarven accuracy, cutting only Timothaue's rope, and leaving the other ropes unscathed.

Timothaue fell to the ground. He landed on his back, his head nestled in the crushed remains of the rotting log that had knocked him unconscious; it almost looked like a pillow, if not for the splintered wood, and the blood steadily streaming from Timothaue's scalp.

The two dwarves immediately swarmed Timothaue's body, cutting the ropes binding him with seemingly no concern for the structural integrity of his skin. As they searched him, they roughed him over so hard that he regained partial consciousness a few times. They searched all of his nooks and crannies, pockets and sockets, and everything short of his asshole. They found a wide variety of things in Timothaue's pockets.

They pulled out an almost unbelievable amount of loose *MacRoyalle Meat Cubes*, as well as several boxes of assorted flavors; there was a spice rack lining the inside of Timothaue's cloak, containing dozens of different herbs and spices in jars labeled with the MacRoyalle crest; there were several sacks of coins and a bunch of uninteresting trinkets; however, they could not find any proof of his royalty.

"Well, no royal seal." As the dwarves concluded their search, Dwayneus sneered wickedly at Jeff. "It looks like you're a liar."

"Oh, come on!" said Jeff. "He has like a million MacRoyalle crests all over his stuff! Isn't that enough?"

Dwayneus waved his hand dismissively. "So do the janitors at the MacRoyalle meathouses. As far as we know, this could be any one of their employees."

"Yeah!" Urist nodded firmly in agreement. "Even I know that the MacRoyalle family all carry around those ridiculous golden meat cubes. You expect us to believe they would miss an opportunity to show them off?"

"You mean this?" said a bleary voice from behind them.

They turned around to see Timothaue sitting up, blinking blearily as he looked around at the rest of them.

"Hang on," he muttered. He slowly pushed himself up, standing unsteadily for a moment before regaining his balance. He immediately drove his hand into the rear of his trousers. Squinting and grimacing, he drove it deeper and deeper, until eventually he smiled. He then began to draw his hand out, gritting his teeth and going cross eyed as he did so.

A moment later, he drew forth a large, golden cube on a chain, with a different farm animal embossed on all six sides; it was coated with surprisingly little blood and fecal matter.

"My god, that is disgusting!" Vomiting a little in his mouth, Urist spit out a mouthful of chunky elf blood. "Why would you keep it there?"

Timothaue shrugged sheepishly. "Safe keeping."

"Well, he's definitely a MacRoyalle." Plugging his nose, Dwayneus gagged as he gave the cube a closer inspection. "That was a close call."

211

Chapter Fifteen

"No shit, we almost killed the groom!" Urist bowed to Timothaue. "Please accept my deepest apologies for the treatment you've received."

"It's no biggie," said Timothaue. He was clearly still too high to fully comprehend what was going on. "I'm just gonna lie down for a while."

He laid down where he was standing, resting his head back on the rotting log on which he had just fallen.

Swiftly swinging his axe, Urist cleaved in twain the root to which the ropes were anchored. Jeff, Mathiaue, and The Wizard fell to the ground, narrowly missing Knippe and Knorpe. Urist and Dwayneus began untying the party, starting with Mathiaue.

When Knippe and Knorpe were freed, Knorpe hastily pulled his pants back on, and they sobbed into each other's arms.

"Sorry we almost killed you, too," said Dwayneus, gently brushing the dirt and debris off of Mathiaue's cloak. "We didn't realize who you were, your majesty."

Mathiaue simply nodded, staring dreamily into the distance.

"What the fuck is wrong with you?!" Jeff was incensed at these dwarves' cavalier attitude towards the lives of him and... well, really just him; at this point, he shared their attitude towards his companions. "Don't I get an apology? I almost shit myself when you said you'd feed me my feet! Why the —"

"You know, we can still kill *you*," said Dwayneus, cracking his knuckles. "You're lucky we're letting you off the hook, so shut up."

Jeff wanted to stand up for himself, but found that he was far too terrified to open his mouth. He never thought he would ever be this scared of someone half his height. He simply nodded complacently, before bowing his head in shame. He once again bitterly regretted the choices that led him into this situation, wishing that The Wizard was somebody else's uncle.

Dwayneus and Urist cut everyone else's bonds, even those of The Wizard, who was still unconscious. They waited to cut Jeff's bonds last, both of them staring at him the entire time, as if daring him to complain about it.

After they were all unbound, it seemed that the MacRoyalle brothers were regaining their sense of self; they were both complaining about how sore they were and how bad the camp smelled. The Wizard, on the other hand, was still out cold; Knippe and Knorpe quickly rifled through his pockets

212

when they thought no one was looking, pocketing a few dimebags of cocaine and a big sack of weed. Jeff stood up and stretched, glad to finally get a chance to once again move freely.

"So, you're guests at the wedding?" asked Timothaue. Although he was coherent, he still bore the telltale signs of someone who is right proper as fuck. "I've got to ask... what's the dinner situation looking like?"

"We're not just any guests," said Dwayneus. "I'm the bride's brother; I'm supposed to walk her down the aisle, since our dear daddy's in a coma. And this is our cousin Urist."

"Did he just say 'daddy'?" asked Knorpe, giggling irreverently.

"Yes," muttered Knippe, stifling his snickering. "Shut up, though. They still might kill us."

"You're Dornice's brother?" Timothaue raised his eyebrows in surprise. "Wow, this is unexpected...." He paused, biting his lower lip nervously; this drew blood on account of his fangs, but he seemed to be too high to notice. "You don't suppose she'd still marry me in light of my condition?"

"What condition?" Frowning blankly, Dwayneus cocked his head at Timothaue.

"What do you mean, 'what condition'?" It seemed Timothaue was rapidly coming down from his high; he now seemed nearly as frustrated as one might expect. "I'm a fucking werewolf."

"Really?" Dwayneus' mouth fell open in awe. "Wow! I thought that was just a super good fursuit!"

"What?" said Timothaue, chuckling at the idea. "Why would I wear a werewolf costume to my wedding?"

"Don't you know?" Dwayneus wiggled his eyebrows suggestively. "Lady Dornice is a furry; she thinks beastmen are sexy! She'll absolutely love this."

"Are you serious?"

"Yeah! And she's not the only one!" Winking implicitly, Dwayneus leaned in close enough that his breath rippled through Timothaue's fur. "I also love furries."

A look of relief spread across Timothaue's face. "That's awesome! I mean, the first part... not the part about you loving furries too... that's your business. I'm just glad to hear she'll still marry me, because my family

Chapter Fifteen

would never stop shaming me otherwise. I was worried, because I'm not one-hundred percent sure I'll be able to cure this condition."

"Don't worry at all, you don't have to cure it!" said Dwayneus. "No one will judge you for it in *our* family, that's for sure. Dornice will just adore you like this! Plus, I'm like ninety-nine percent pretty sure that dwarves are immune to lycanthropy; it's either that or I just had a super-duper condom...."

"I'll have to think about it." Scratching his strawberry-blonde chin fur, Timothaue furrowed his brow considerately. "I'm not sure I want to stay like this."

"It's lucky we found you," said Urist, who was clearly eager to change the subject from his cousins' sexual predilections. "We weren't supposed to be in this area; we were out hunting for the wedding feast and thought we'd head out to elf country and grab ourselves a couple of tasty treats."

"By which you mean people?" asked Jeff.

"No, not people." Scrunching his face, Dwayneus scoffed. "*Elves.*"

"Yeah, and today was a good day!" His eyes twinkling with manic fervor, Urist licked his lips. "We've been hunting those two scumbags ever since they ate our uncle last week."

"Well, I'm glad you killed them," said Knippe. "These two weren't just elves, they were themselves; they deserved to die."

"Yes, thank you so much!" Knorpe bowed to the dwarves. No one, not even his brother, had ever seen him show even close to that level of gratitude. "We owe you our lives, as well as our butts."

"Your lives will suffice," said Urist. "You can pay us back someday; I'm sure the day will yet come when our butts need saving as well."

"We should probably turn him over." Jeff pointed to The Wizard, who was lying on the ground with his face in the mud. "He may have suffocated already. Let's check."

Approaching The Wizard, Jeff grabbed his arm and flipped him over. However, as he turned him, The Wizard's eyes snapped open; he quickly slammed his palm into Jeff's chest, blasting him away with a powerful wave of force. Soaring through the air, Jeff landed directly in the firepit.

"Damn it, dude!" Jeff frantically scrambled out of the pile of red-hot embers. His denim jeans and wool sweater had holes burned all over them, and his skin was blistering where the cinders made contact. "I was just trying to wake you up!"

"Can't be too careful." Getting to his feet, The Wizard brushed the dirt and pine needles off his robes. "We could get attacked by hill elves in these parts, Jeff; you should know better."

"Wha— are you fucking serious?!" Shaking his head, Jeff threw his arms up angrily. "Do you really have no idea what just happened to us?!"

"Umm…" The Wizard looked around at the rudimentary campsite, blood-soaked dwarves, and elf corpses. "I don't know…. Did you decide to act out some even weirder version of *Deliverance* when I passed out last night?"

"You didn't pass out, moron," said Jeff. "You were drugged and we all almost died!"

"Don't forget we got molested," added Knorpe; he and Knippe hugged each other, silently weeping.

"Wait, did *I* get molested?" Craning his neck The Wizard assessed the butt of his jeans through the hole in his robes.

"No…" muttered Knippe. "Just us…."

"Wow, really?" The Wizard smirked wryly. "Wish I hadn't missed that!"

"You are absolutely insane..." Sighing, Jeff shook his head at The Wizard.

"Hey, where's my shit?" Narrowing his eyes, The Wizard looked around the encampment.

"We already did all the cocaine from your pockets," said Knorpe, averting his eyes.

"Yeah, you can't have it back!" squeaked Knippe.

"Whatever, that wasn't even my main stash. I still have half an ounce in my bag, hidden in the bag of Kit Mingers' food. Now, if I could just find it…."

Knippe and Knorpe grinned excitedly at each other. They started darting around the camp, frantically overturning every rusty piece of armor and moldy old skull they could get their hands on. The Wizard facepalmed, seeming to notice his mistake.

Panicking, he began to cast detection spells around the camp.

"I found it!" Jeff held up The Wizard's bag of holding, high enough that the gnomes could not reach it. "Hurry up, before these assholes get it."

Chapter Fifteen

Knippe was about to stab Jeff in the leg when The Wizard ran up and punted him and his twin away with a single kick. The gnomes would have probably flown at least thirty yards, if not for them smashing into the tree in the center of the camp.

"Thanks, Jeff." Grabbing the bag, The Wizard checked to make sure everything was still inside; Kit Mingers meowed impatiently from within, glaring up at him. "I'll let you out soon, kitty. I see you've already found a good corner to do your business in. Good for you... you're such a good kitty!"

He reached inside and petted the back of Kit Mingers' neck, withdrawing his hand only seconds later. It was covered in vicious scratches.

Pouting, Knorpe turned away in a huff. "Well, fine... if we can't have your stash, we'll just have to loot this nasty elf camp."

"Go ahead..." Shrugging, The Wizard looked around skeptically. There was nothing around him he could ever imagine finding a use for, besides perhaps firewood. "Just don't come crying to me if you get tetanus; I'm not qualified to cure it."

They searched every inch of the elves' encampment and turned up nothing but a bunch of skulls, some rusty old weapons, and some old Dungeons and Dragons manuals. Jeff insisted on keeping the manuals, even though Knippe and Knorpe wanted to burn them because "everything past second edition is trash." They were right about that, but sadly, Jeff was able to switch the manuals with The Wizard's journals at the last moment, and thus they still exist.

No one else was able to find anything worthwhile, save The Wizard.

"I'm definitely keeping this," said the wizard, holding a bottle of iridescent green and black liquid. "I found it with a pile of darts; I'm pretty sure it's the tranquilizer they hit us with."

"You're not going to use that on yourself, are you?" asked Jeff.

"Of course I am!"

Jeff raised an eyebrow. "You realize it's poison, right?"

"Yeah, but it's the cool kind of poison, not the bad kind."

"Whatever... I don't know why I ever say anything."

"It's okay, Jeff," said Knorpe, smirking facetiously. "None of us know why you ever say anything either."

Jeff ignored the gnome, having bigger things to worry about; at this point, anything short of life-threatening was no big deal.

Once they were done looting the camp and burning the books, they headed towards where Jeff said he remembered the horses being tied up; however, when they got there, the horses were all lying dead on the ground, with a crossbow bolt between each of their eyes.

"*No!!!*" Horrified, Jeff sprinted to the carcass of his horse, brushing its mane out of its face. He hugged the horse tightly, sobbing into its fur. "Butterscotch, how could they have done this?"

"How could you not have noticed them killing the horses, Jeff?" The Wizard put his hands on his hips and glared at Jeff as though this were somehow his fault.

"Shut up!" His lip quivering, Jeff wiped the tears from his eyes and glared at The Wizard. "Sorry that I was a bit *busy*, worrying about being hogtied and strung up in a tree, and didn't notice my only friend on this journey being murdered!"

The Wizard fell silent.

"It sucks that our horses died and all," said Mathiaue, rocking back and forth anxiously on his heels, "but I've wanted to do this for days!"

No longer able to contain himself, Mathiaue leapt forward, shoving Jeff aside. He tore ravenously into Butterscotch's corpse with his fangs.

"Yeah, me too," said Timothaue. "Those white stallions were making me hungry. Although, this brown horse looks even tastier!"

He followed Mathiaue's example, sinking his teeth into Butterscotch's body.

"Oh, sick! They're ripping out his entrails!" Nausea welled up in Jeff's throat, and he keeled over and vomited.

"Hey, better him than us!" The Wizard gestured to the dwarves, who were gorging themselves with raw elf. "Besides, I'd rather be a horse than an elf!"

Jeff scowled and shook his head in disapproval, too tired to tell The Wizard why he found that offensive; perhaps Jeff would have not been so upset about Butterscotch's untimely demise if he had been aware of the horse's murderous vendetta against humanoids.

Chapter Fifteen

"What?" Smiling with feigned innocence, The Wizard fluttered his eyelashes. "All I'm saying is he would have been food eventually if we had left him on that farm!"

"You're a fucking cunt..." muttered Jeff.

"Whatever, Jeff, I honestly don't give a shit what you think about basically anything."

"Screw you." Jeff flipped The Wizard the bird. "I wish the elves killed you instead!"

"Hmm... I think now would be a good time to feed Kit Mingers," said The Wizard, his smile quickly becoming a sneer. "He's never had horse before!"

"Don't you dare!"

"Try and stop me."

Setting his bag of holding on the ground, The Wizard opened the flap; after a moment, Kit Mingers crept out of the bag, a look of bloodlust in his eyes. He leapt forward, landing between the MacRoyalles and immediately beginning to devour Butterscotch's liver.

"Why are they all going after butterscotch?" Jeff ran his fingers through his curly, jet-black hair. "There are two other horses they haven't even touched!"

"Well, he was bred for maximum flavor," said The Wizard. "He must be pretty tasty for them to swarm him like that."

When he was done grazing on Butterscotch's organs, Kit Mingers turned around, squatted down, and took a big, greasy dump in Butterscotch's gaping abdomen; the cat then turned around, and proceed to cover his feces with the bloody entrails on which he stood. Timothaue and Mathiaue did not even stop eating.

Jeff turned away and vomited again while this was happening.

After he was done taking care of business, Kit Mingers walked up to The Wizard and lovingly nuzzled his leg. The Wizard reached down to scratch the cat's chin. Kit Mingers purred as he began to rub his head against The Wizard's hand.

"Aww, such a cutey!" Smiling tenderly, he rubbed Kit Mingers' stomach. The cat rolled over and began kneading his blood-drenched paws in the air. "Who's a good kitty? That's right; you are! *Goood* kitty."

Wood of the Elves

His eyes wide with horror, Jeff shook his head at The Wizard. "You're a complete sociopath!"

"What do you mean?"

"Your cat just shit in my horse's guts, and now you're rewarding it! Do you have any idea how that makes me feel?"

"I don't know... nauseated?" The Wizard smirked snidely at Jeff.

"*I'll rip your beard off!*" Diving at The Wizard, Jeff tackled him to the ground; he began to yank ferociously on The Wizard's beard.

The agreement that The Wizard made years ago with his brother Justin was that no magic was to be used in family fights until someone got stabbed; however, Justin failed to specify which party needed to get stabbed, so The Wizard whipped out his trusty knife. Unfortunately for him, Dwayneus and Urist pulled the two of them apart before he could stab his nephew and curse away his hair.

"Calm down, you two!" said Dwayneus, throwing The Wizard away from Jeff. "You're acting crazy!"

"Yeah," said Urist, tossing Jeff aside. "There is no need for such senseless violence."

"Are you fucking serious?!" Jeff's mouth fell open in utter disbelief.. "You two are the most senselessly violent people I've ever met!"

"Yeah, for once I agree with my nephew." The Wizard patted Jeff on the back, as though they were on the same team all of a sudden. "You should have just let me stab him."

"No, that's not... what?" said Jeff. "Nevermind, they have a —"

"Call us senselessly violent one more time," said Dwayneus, cracking his knuckles and stepping up to Jeff's face. "I dare you, motherfucker."

"Whatever... let's just go...."

They left the encampment, following the path of bloody, trampled brush, up which the party had been dragged. It did not take them long to find the trail, turning out to be a journey of less than a hundred meters; it had felt much longer, thought Jeff, when he had been tied up and dragged through the bramble behind a horse.

Chapter Fifteen

They continued up the trail, all heading in the same direction. The dwarves explained that the trail forks several miles ahead, and they would take the mountain pass to get home.

In the distance, the frigid peaks of the Throdmor mountains towered over them. It appeared that a thunderstorm was coming in; roiling black clouds weaved towards them through the range. A curtain of snow could be seen in the distance, with bolts of lightning illuminating swirling patterns in the flurries.

"How far away is the tower?" asked Knippe, tugging anxiously on his collar. "I'm starting to work up some nerves over travelling through these woods on foot…"

"See that mountain over there?" said The Wizard, pointing to the closest peak of the wide range before them.

"Yeah. That's not so far!"

"I agree." Leaning down, The Wizard smiled wickedly at the gnome. "And that's the mountaintop I'm going to throw you off if you ask that question one more time."

"By the way," said Mathiaue, walking up next to The Wizard, "I think I'm going to take a rain check on that cure."

"Yeah, me too," said Timothaue.

"Seriously?"

"I'm getting married." Timothaue beamed with excitement.

"And I can't miss my brother's wedding!" Booming with laughter, Mathiaue patted Timothaue firmly on the back.

The Wizard shrugged. "Okay, whatever, it's your funeral. Just so you know, the longer you're like this, the less likely it is that you'll be able to cure it."

"Well, I don't know, maybe I'll just stay like this," said Timothaue, scratching his chin.

The Wizard raised an eyebrow. "Are you serious?"

"Why not?" said Timothaue. "Apparently my fiance likes it, and there are other benefits."

"Like what?" said The Wizard, scoffing derisively.

"The sensation of taste, for one," said Mathiaue, nodding thoughtfully.

"Come again?"

Wood of the Elves

"We MacRoyalles, as you know, are connoisseurs of tastes galore," said Mathiaue passionately. "Our palates are known across the lands as the best!"

"Yes, you've made that abundantly clear," said The Wizard, sighing wearily.

"Indeed!" said Mathiaue. "However, compared to my perception of flavor now, what I previously thought to be a flawless palate, no less refined than that of the gods themselves, was but that of a mentally challenged child."

"That seems unnecessary," said Jeff.

"With the heightened senses of a wolf," continued Mathiaue, with unbridled enthusiasm, "I will be able to discern flavors so specific that I might actually break the herb-spice continuum."

"I don't even want to know what you think that is," said The Wizard, rolling his eyes. "All that matters to me is that you won't be a thorn in my side anymore. You're sure you want to stay like this? Because earlier today you were practically begging me to... no, wait, you *were* begging me to cure you."

"I'm sure." Nodding firmly, Mathiaue put his arm around his brother's shoulders. "If Timothaue's staying this way, then so am I!"

"Whatever," said The Wizard, shrugging apathetically. "I already thought you were weird. This doesn't change much."

As they continued down the trail, Dwayneus started talking candy to the MacRoyalle brothers about their "fur allure", as he put it. He explained that he had already talked to Dornice about it, and that she agreed to have a sort of "tag team deal" between them and Timothaue; "as long as you take a shine to me, that is," he added, with a wink.

Timothaue grimaced, uncomfortably tugging on the collar of his shirt. "Dude... I'm marrying your sister!"

"Sure, but haven't you ever heard of a bachelor party?"

"That's true." Timothaue nodded thoughtfully, scratching his chin. "We'll have to see what happens. I'll think about it."

"Just to be clear, *I'm* interested right now!" Licking his lips, Mathiaue wiggled his eyebrows suggestively at Dwayneus. "I don't know if it's because of the near death experience, or just these wolf hormones, but my meatballs are getting spicy. I'd bang you in the bushes right now if we didn't have a wedding to make!"

Chapter Fifteen

Dwayneus quickly turned his attention from Timothaue to the prince's older brother. He and Mathiaue began talking excitedly about the various sex acts they intended to perform on each other when they got the chance, and everyone else simply did their best not to listen.

"Have you ever had a tailjob?" asked Dwayneus. "It feels phenomenal."

You know? Stuff like that... I will spare you the rest.

Eventually, the group reached a fork in the road; the path split off in three directions: one leading up to the mountains, one leading down the mountain range, and one leading a few meters into the woods to a toilet shaped tree stump.

"Well, I guess this is it!" The Wizard attempted in vain to hide his sense of relief. "It was... *eventful* knowing you."

"Yeah, yeah, yeah..." Crossing his arms, Urist clicked his tongue impatiently. It seemed he was equally eager to part ways with The Wizard and his companions. "You're welcome for not killing you."

The two parties parted ways, and headed down their respective trails, not to cross paths again for at least the remainder of the evening. The Wizard stopped briefly to use the tree toilet, next to which grew a handy patch of thimbleweed, before following the others down the trail.

As they neared the mountains, the landscape got more severe. The path often took them along steep cliffsides, overlooking wide valleys of diverse evergreen trees. Snow was scattered in sparse patches along the path, although they would not likely stay sparse for long; the thundering blizzard loomed ever closer.

The four companions were all worse for wear after their ordeal with the hill elves. The Wizard's deep blue cloak was coated in dried mud, and he had a massive headache from listening to Mathiaue's bombast. He was simply too tired to clean his robes, even with magic. Jeff's glasses had gotten bent, and were slightly askew on his face; his bullet wound had also become infected and swollen, and dried blood drenched the sleeve of his wool sweater. Knippe and Knorpe's silver hair was sprinkled with dirt and debris from the forest floor.

Looking between the twins' faces and Jeff's, The Wizard suddenly noticed how little stubble Jeff had grown around his goatee. Knippe and Knorpe nearly had a full beard apiece, and they were getting less and less

Wood of the Elves

distinguishable by the day. The Wizard's own beard had nearly doubled in size since their adventure began, and yet all Jeff had to deal with was a little stubble. He could not help but feel envious; he hated how often he had to singe his beard to keep it in check.

It was not long before the group decided to set up camp. When they came to a lush clearing beside the path, they decided it would be as good a place as any. All being extremely hungry, they practically jumped for joy when The Wizard showed them some canned beans he had stolen from the kitchen at the *Wolfwood Inn*. Once they finished wolfing down the beans, they started setting up camp.

The Wizard pulled forth a generously sized tent from his bag of holding, as well as three sleeping bags, before kicking back lazily against a tree; once Jeff was finished resentfully setting up the tent by himself, they had a relatively comfortable place to sleep. Knippe and Knorpe refused to sleep in the tent, however, seeing as The Wizard let the cat out of the bag; instead, they curled up just outside the tent, huddling together for warmth in their sleeping bag.

It was a good night; they lived to see the morning.

Chapter Sixteen
Anasthasia's Abode

The next morning, The Wizard awoke suddenly. Sitting up, he knocked over the bottle of elven tranquilizer he had been using to sleep. It fell to the ground, but none of the liquid spilled out; most of it had already been used. Even huddled up in his sleeping bag, The Wizard's entire body felt as though he had spent the night in a MacRoyalle meat locker. Shivering, he sat up and looked around the tent.

The first thing he noticed was Kit Mingers making love to his robes, nibbling on the gold trim. He sighed despondently and tried to push the cat away, but quickly gave up after being hissed at and scratched fiercely.

Jeff was sitting in the far corner of the tent, his eyes closed and his legs crossed, gently humming to himself. He was wearing his winter cloak, but it was not fastened over his bare chest. His bloody wool sweater lay in a heap next to him.

"What the fuck are you doing?" asked The Wizard.

"Meditating," said Jeff, without opening his eyes. "When I harness my subconscious chi to control my natural biorhythms, I don't even notice how cold it is."

"Have I ever told you you're a huge nerd?"

"Almost every day we've ever spent together, since I was a child."

"Good, just making sure. Why is it so cold, anyway?"

"Take a look outside."

Anasthasia's Abode

The Wizard stood up. Unfortunately, he had chosen to sleep naked in the cold due to being high as fuck, and Jeff had chosen that exact moment to open his eyes; it was an uncomfortable situation for both of them.

"Oh, shit!" Blushing, The Wizard grabbed his robes and used them to cover his genitals. Kit Mingers hissed as he was thrown aside by this. "Sorry about that, Jeff. You too, kitty."

"Uhh... it's okay... I guess...." Cringing in disgust, Jeff slammed his eyes shut. "Don't worry about it... or whatever...."

The Wizard averted his gaze. "It's normally bigger, you know."

"Wha— I don't care! Just keep it hidden!"

"Okay, okay." Grinning sheepishly, The Wizard grabbed his pants and shirt and began to dress himself. "I'm just making sure we're clear, that's all...."

Reaching into his bag of holding, The Wizard pulled out his fur cloak. He pulled the cloak over his robes, smiling contentedly as he snuggled it closely. "That's better..."

"Hey, would you mind cleaning the blood off my shirt now?" asked Jeff, holding up his wool sweater in a bloody bundle.

"Ugh... fine." The Wizard put his hand on the sweater. Slowly, the blood faded away. He repeated the process for his robes.

"Thank you, it was very uncomfortable sleeping with all that dried blood." Donning his robes, Jeff gestured to the tent flaps. "Ladies first!"

The Wizard glowered at him. As he unzipped the flaps of the tent, a brisk wind immediately blew in from outside. He and Jeff stepped out of the tent into a field of white; the brush and brambles covering the ground around their encampment were invisible under a thick layer of snow. The dark green on the pines and cedars looked vibrantly colorful next to the white powder coating their every branch.

For some reason, The Wizard started craving cocaine.

As he was leaving the tent, The Wizard tripped over something. He stood up and looked down to see what it had been; Knippe and Knorpe were huddled in their sleeping bag, buried up to their waste in snow; literally, up to their waste: all the snow around them was yellow.

The Wizard was not sure if they were alive or dead. Gnomes were generally very resilient in the cold, having descended from dwarves;

225

however, he figured these specific specimens may not be the spitting image of health, so to speak.

Pulling a wand from the pocket of his robes, he poked Knorpe on the cheek. He had forgotten he even had that wand on him, and he could not remember for the life of him what it did; however, the answer soon became clear.

"What the hell?!" Leaping out of his sleeping bag, Knorpe clutched his face in pain; boils had begun to erupt around where the wand had touched him. He glared at The Wizard, shaking his fist vehemently. "This will not be forgotten. Next time you're asleep, it's my turn."

Shivering as he sat up, Knippe pulled the piss-soaked sleeping bag over his chest. "What's going on?"

Turning to his brother, Knorpe pointed angrily to his own face. "This asshole decided to curse me."

As soon as Knippe saw the horrible, pus-filled boils dotting his brother's cheek, he burst out laughing. It took him a moment to regain his composure, but by the time he did, the damage was done. Knorpe was gaping at him in disbelief.

"So, you think this is funny too, huh, Knippe?"

"No, not at all!" Knippe was barely able to stifle his snickering. "It's the saddest thing I've ever seen!"

"You've got that right!" Laughing hysterically, The Wizard was keeled over, slapping his knees; although he had not intended to curse Knorpe, this was just about the best way his morning could have played out. "But tragedy equals comedy, right?"

"Plus time..." said Jeff.

"Oh, right, I forgot that part." Smirking facetiously, The Wizard feigned a look of realization. "That's right... Tragedy equals comedy plus time! So, Knorpe, eventually this will be sad, and then we'll care. For now, it's just funny!"

"You'll all pay for this in your sleep." Glowering venomously, Knorpe wagged his finger at the three of them. "Even you, Knippe! You shouldn't have laughed..."

"What about me?" asked Jeff. "I didn't even laugh!"

"You didn't stab The Wizard, either." Placing his hands on his hips, Knorpe narrowed his beady eyes at Jeff. "In my book, that's just as bad as cursing me yourself!"

Jeff scoffed. "You might want to rewrite your book. You won't sell many copies if you stab everyone who buys it."

"That, right there," said Knorpe. "That attitude is exactly why you will taste my vengeance as well!"

Mouth agape with incredulity, Jeff pointed to The Wizard. "But he cursed your face with boils!"

Knippe shrugged. "Hey, all I did was laugh at him."

"That's right, and you will also pay." Glaring spitefully, Knorpe gave his brother the finger.

"Whatever..." said The Wizard, as he rooted around in his bag, half his body shoved through the opening. "Can you just shut up about it while we eat breakfast?"

"Fine." Crossing his arms, Knorpe turned away in a huff. "I'll stay silent, for now; but soon, like the farts your damned beans gave me, I will also be deadly."

"Speaking of the beans, I think that's all we have for breakfast." The Wizard emerged from his bag of holding with three more cans of beans.

Knippe grimaced apprehensively. "Seriously...? Because he's not kidding about those farts. That might actually be his plan for revenge."

"Ha ha... very funny...." It was obvious Knorpe was trying very hard not to chuckle at his brother's humorous remark.

"Come on," said The Wizard. "We've got to build a fire. Help me get some wood."

Smirking, Knippe nudged his brother in the arm. "I always figured he needed help with that..."

Knorpe's face was reddening as he attempted to hold back his laughter. Twitching furiously, he clasped his hands over his mouth. It looked as though he were about to pop, quite unlike The Wizard's ever flaccid penis.

For the next several minutes, the group walked through the nearby woods to gather firewood. Knippe and Knorpe each came back with a couple of huge faggots, relative to their size. Returning with his hands full of knobbled wood, Jeff tossed it onto the gnomes' logs. The Wizard came with the biggest faggot of all in his arms, tossing his load onto the heap of soon to be flaming wood.

Jeff and the twins sat around the pile of firewood, staring expectantly at The Wizard.

Sighing, The Wizard held out his palms, drying the firewood, as well as melting and evaporating the snow around it; after waiting for the steam to clear, he snapped his fingers, causing a couple of the pieces of wood to burst into flame. He then pulled a large paper fan from his pocket and handed it to Jeff.

"You know what to do."

Jeff scrunched his face in a look of uncertainty. "You want me to *fan* the fire? *Why?*"

"Because we need a fire to cook breakfast, Jeff," said The Wizard. "It's not rocket science, I expect you to know how to do this shit. What, do you want me to ask Tweedledee and Tweedledipshit here to do it?"

He gestured to the gnomes. Knippe was making a myriad of silly faces, and Knorpe was rocking back and forth, his face bright red.

"No, that's not what I mean," said Jeff. "Why do I have to fan it by hand when you can use magic?"

"Fire takes a lot of energy, Jeff."

"Oh, really?" Scowling, Jeff crossed his arms defiantly. "Because, now I know you have a shitload of magical energy; you're basically part Arcane, for fuck's sake! I think you could light this fire in a second, and making me fan it is part of some power complex you have."

"Right, Jeff... I just have one question; which of us is the sorcerer, and which of us is the idiot who couldn't get a better job?"

Jeff's scowl intensified. "You're proving my point."

"I have kerosene, if it helps." Reaching into the pocket of his vest, Knorpe pulled out a small tin of lamp oil.

"Mind your own business!" Waving his hand dismissively at the gnome, The Wizard looked expectantly at Jeff. "Well?"

"Thank you, Knorpe." Refusing The Wizard eye contact, Jeff snatched the tin of kerosene. "At least *someone* is being helpful."

Anasthasia's Abode

At this point, the few sticks that The Wizard had magicked afire had been extinguished. Holding the canister of kerosene before him, Jeff flicked open the nozzle and squirted it all over the pile of faggots.

Alright, that is enough of that damn joke... If it offended you, you are right, and I agree; if you want to keep reading anyway, you are alright with me.

"Could you at least do the rest of us the courtesy of lighting this?" Cocking his head, Jeff sneered facetiously at The Wizard. "Or do you have two sticks you expect me to grind together?"

"No... I'll do it." Groaning, The Wizard snapped his fingers, causing the entire pile to burst into flames. "Happy?"

"Not really," said Jeff. "I'm still on the run with you, and all we have to eat are canned beans. I'd say I'm pretty fucking far from happy."

"Well, if you're hungry, there's also this." With a shrug, The Wizard reached into his bag and pulled forth a severed foot. "I snuck a little elf meat, just to give it a try. It must be pretty good to be worth murdering for, right?"

Gasping in shock, Jeff stumbled backwards. "What the fuck?!"

"I ain't trying that again." Grimacing, Knippe eyed the foot apprehensively.

Knorpe nodded firmly in agreement.

"No, I... what?" said The Wizard. "I was just fucking with you... This must have fallen into my bag back at that elf camp; you remember, right? When the dwarves were tearing the elves' corpses limb from limb."

Jeff moaned despondently, a haunted look in his eyes. "Yes, we remember... Now, can you please never bring that up again?"

"Okay, sure." Chortling, The Wizard tossed the foot onto the fire.

The foot was in the flames for but a few seconds, before the smell of burning elf toenails reached their nostrils. The four of them quickly gathered their things and hurried away from the campsite. The Wizard did not even bother to pack up his tent, as the smell was unbearable; additionally, he knew they were within a day's march of their destination. They resigned to eat the beans cold, while they continued along the trail.

Upon finishing his breakfast, The Wizard took a huge pull from his bottle of cocainated whiskey. After he was starting to feel proper again, he pulled a small pipe from his pocket and tried to find his pot. When he noticed the

229

weed in his pocket was missing, he kicked both of the gnomes; fortunately, he had a much larger bag of weed hidden in Kit Mingers' food.

As they headed down the trail, the gnomes glared resentfully at Jeff and The Wizard, who were smoking what The Wizard referred to as a "swordsman's bowl"; that is to say, they were not letting Knippe and Knorpe in on it. When the twins protested that the name did not make sense, since neither of them were swordsmen, The Wizard waved his hand dismissively.

"It's just an expression," he said, shrugging. "Some of the Knights of Koric started it when I was a kid; they would play keepaway with my pipe, smoking all my weed and not letting me in on it. They would laugh and say "only swordsmen get to smoke weed this good". Anyway, after I killed them all, I adopted the term as my own."

"It still doesn't really make sense..." muttered Knorpe, resentfully watching them puff on the pipe.

After a few tense hours of travel, the trail opened onto a wide lane. There were horse tracks dotting the snow in both directions. As they walked out onto the road, a horse-drawn buggy rolled past them.

Without hesitation, The Wizard turned onto the lane and followed the buggy. Knippe and Knorpe followed in relative silence; that is to say, they were not specifically directing their incessant jabbering at The Wizard.

Frowning, Jeff squinted mistrustfully at The Wizard. "Is this an actual road?"

"What do you think, Jeff?" With a scoff, The Wizard gestured to the buggy rolling into the distance.

"Are you telling me we could have taken actual roads here?!" Jeff's face was instantly filled with rage.

"No... that's not what *I'm* telling you.... You're figuring that out for yourself. Good job!" The Wizard patted Jeff on the back.

Recoiling, Jeff slapped The Wizard's hand away. "Why would you take us through those woods? Do you have a deathwish?"

"Jeff, if I had a deathwish, I would have stayed in Koric. This road goes through Royalle; do you have any idea how much it would have cost in tolls if we'd taken this route?"

"You almost got us all killed to save a little money on tolls?!"

Anasthasia's Abode

"More than a little, Jeff!" The Wizard crossed his arms defensively. "You met those snobby MacRoyalle fucks. Do you really want *them* to have all my money? They named their country after themselves; they're douchebags!"

It looked as though Jeff were using every ounce of his self-control to suppress his murderous rage.

As they ventured onward, the group was tense and silent. Even the gnomes ran out of things to talk about, other than the occasional complaint about the cold. Jeff kept shooting venomous glances at The Wizard, who was far too intoxicated to notice; he had finished the remaining third of his bottle of cocainated whiskey, and was right proper as fuck.

It was quite a long time before either Jeff or The Wizard spoke. Although the storm had largely passed, occasional flurries of snow would swirl from the thick white clouds overhead. Eventually, when it seemed to be nearly sundown, The Wizard suddenly piped up.

"We're almost to my sister's place," he said. "About time, too; I'm so hungry I could eat a horse."

Turning to Jeff, he grinned and wiggled his eyebrows.

Jeff simply glared back at him, shaking his head.

The Wizard smirked. "What, too soon?"

After about ten more minutes, the stone parapets of a large tower came into view over the treetops. The dark stone stood out with a deep contrast against the snowy mountainsides behind it. As they approached the hill on which the tower stood, the road veered off to the side.

At the base of the hill, there was an old, rusty iron gate between two red brick pillars. The drive beyond the gate weaved up the hillside, lined on both sides with rows of unkempt arbor vita.

The Wizard approached the gate, casually and effortlessly kicking it down. The group entered, with Jeff sulking in the back, distancing himself from his uncle. As they started up the path, there was a creaking sound from behind them; looking back, they saw the rusty gate stand itself back onto its hinges.

It took them a few minutes to reach the top of the winding path. There was another gate, which The Wizard promptly kicked down as well. They walked into a large, circular courtyard, surrounded on all sides by snowy trees.

Chapter Sixteen

Lining each side of the path before them were dozens of rose bushes, blooming deep red despite the snow, their flowers thinly veiled in frost.

Standing in the center of the courtyard was the dark stone tower they had seen from the road; it had no windows, just smooth, dark gray stone all the way up, and a set of heavy mahogany doors with iron handles. It was over a hundred feet tall, and about forty feet across. The path leading to the tower was clear of snow, with heated stone tiles. It felt nice under their feet.

"Huh..." Craning his neck up at the tower, Jeff furrowed his brow. "I thought it would be bigger. This tower isn't much bigger than yours!"

"It's enchanted to be bigger on the inside," said The Wizard. "My dad didn't want it too big on the outside; you know, because he doesn't need to compensate for anything."

Bursting out laughing, Jeff nearly fell to his knees as he slapped them. "Oh, come on, you can't tell me wizards' towers aren't them compensating for something!"

"Whatever..." The Wizard averted his eyes.

"Hey, who's he?" Knippe pointed past the tower, to the far corner of the courtyard.

Even from as far as they were, there was no mistaking the hot pink robes: across the courtyard, his dark hair billowing in the wind, was Fabulon. His tan, toned forearms bulged with muscle as he swung a heavy axe down on some firewood.

He seemed to notice them at the same time, suddenly dropping his axe and waving enthusiastically. It took The Wizard a few seconds to process what was happening, and by that point, Fabulon was already jogging towards him.

"You have *got* to be fucking kidding me," said The Wizard, rubbing his eyes in case he was seeing things. "This *can't* be real; I've gotta be having a stroke."

"Another one of your friends, huh?" asked Knorpe. He and his brother were chuckling relentlessly, despite The Wizard's refusal to look in their direction (i.e. down).

"Hey, buddy!" Running towards them, Fabulon threw open his arms, smiling warmly at The Wizard. "How's it going?"

Stepping back, The Wizard did not hug Fabulon, instead eyeing him suspiciously. "What the hell are you doing here?"

"I came to find you!" Fabulon grinned with a genuine look of innocence.

"No shit. Did you bring Archmage Quan to hunt me down?"

Fabulon gasped, gaping in shock. "What?! How could you think I'd still be working for her after what I saw in that basement?"

The Wizard narrowed his eyes. "You swear you didn't know what they were up to down there?"

"I swear on my life!" Nodding firmly, Fabulon looked The Wizard square in the eyes. "I would never stand by and allow such evil to exist!"

"I don't know…" The Wizard scratched his blazing orange hair dubiously. "I've seen you eating lunch with Horner…."

"Only because he's always alone!" Holding up his hands defensively, Fabulon shook his head. "I felt sorry for the guy; no one likes him because he's disfigured, mean, and unhygienic, but he's really not that bad a guy once he gets his morning heroin."

"Okay, I'll tell you the problem *I* have with that," said The Wizard, through gritted teeth. "Besides literally everything you just listed, he's the one responsible for keeping my dad in that jar. He's a terrible person!"

"Well, yeah…" Shifting awkwardly, Fabulon hung his head. "*Now* I know that."

"You should have known he sucked to begin with! He's always been a piece of shit, ever since he blamed me for disfiguring him."

"Didn't you douse his magic fair project in gasoline and burn it in front of the school board?" asked Fabulon.

"Yeah, but I was just a kid! How the hell was I supposed to know he was planning to pop out of that model volcano and do a disco dance routine? You have to admit, that's fucking weird."

"Yeah," said Fabulon, nodding. "As a prodigious ballerino, I was offended."

"Wait, hold up!" Jeff waved his hand to get their attention. "Glossing over that, did you two go to school together?"

"Just primary school…" Sighing wistfully, Fabulon stared into the distance, a faraway look in his eyes. "Then The Wizard's dad started homeschooling him in the arcane arts. That's actually the reason I became a sorcerer, so I could work with my best bud."

Chapter Sixteen

"Really?!" Barely containing his laughter, Jeff narrowed his eyes at The Wizard. "So, Wiz, I guess that makes Fabulon your *oldest friend!*"

"Yup!" Beaming with pride, Fabulon slapped The Wizard on the back. "Best friends forever!"

The Wizard glowered vehemently at Jeff. "Very funny... Now, can you just drop it?"

Suddenly, a woman's voice called out from the doors of the tower.

"Big brother, I knew I heard you shouting!"

A beautiful, young woman was hurrying down the stairs. She had silken hair, as black as a raven, cascading just past her shoulders in voluptuous curls; it contrasted wildly with her fair skin and wide, golden eyes. Her ears were slightly pointed, suggesting elven ancestry. She wore a dark green, lace gown, patterned to look like ivy growing across her body, with nothing underneath but fishnet stockings and a pair of black lingerie panties.

"What the hell, Anasthasia?" With an averse groan, The Wizard shielded his eyes. "I can see your nipples! How are you not freezing in that thing?"

"Oh, is it still in that mode?" Reaching offhandedly behind her back, Anasthasia adjusted her zipper. Suddenly, her lace gown transformed into a thick fur coat. "There. You happy?"

"I will be as soon as you close it!"

"Do we get a vote?" Eyes alight with ecstacy, Knippe and Knorpe marveled at Anasthasia's body.

"The name's Knippe. I'm the older brother!"

"I'm Knorpe, and mine's bigger!"

"Shut up!" The Wizard kicked at the gnomes, careful not to look up from the ground.

"Oh, right." Pulling her fur coat closed, Anasthasia snapped her fingers. A belt magically appeared around her waist and cinched itself tightly. "Sorry about that."

Slowly, The Wizard opened his eyes. "Thank you. Anyway, Ana: long time, no see!"

"Tell me about it!" Throwing open her arms, Anasthasia embraced The Wizard. "I didn't even know you were coming until your friends showed up."

234

"Wait, 'friends'?" Panicking, The Wizard pushed his sister off of him. "As in the *plural*?"

"Yeah, the rest are waiting inside!"

"'*The rest*'?! Who all is here?"

"Calm down, I don't fucking know." Scowling, Anasthasia put her hands on her hips. "Do you really expect me to keep track of all of *your* friends? It's not like I care about them."

"Well, she's definitely your sister…" muttered Jeff.

"No shit," said The Wizard. "Come on, let's go inside."

As they ascended the staircase, the doors seemed to open of their own accord.

Squinting, The Wizard furrowed his brow. "Did they always do that?"

"Did what always do what?" said Anasthasia in a mocking voice.

"Did the doors always open themselves?!"

"They're not opening themselves." Anasthasia rolled her eyes. "My servants are opening them!"

"You have *servants* now?!" The Wizard's eyes widened with jealousy.

"Yeah, I found them in the attic!"

"Wait, what?" asked Jeff.

They quickly saw what she meant when the doors swung shut behind them. Standing before them, each holding one of the door handles, were two walking skeletons. These skeletons were not the average animated skeletons, either: their bodies were a random mishmash of what appeared to be many different people's bones, and perhaps a few that came from animals. Their skulls appeared to have been preserved far better than their bodies, and were the only part of them that was not deeply discolored.

"What the hell?" said The Wizard, blinking in bewilderment. "Did you animate those?"

Anasthasia grinned. "No, like I said, I found them in the attic!"

Suddenly, a tongue of flame whipped through the mouth of one of the skulls. "We were locked in a trunk for nearly four hundred years, before our mistress found and repaired us."

"Holy fucking shit, you can talk?!" The Wizard nearly tripped over his robes as he stumbled backwards in surprise.

"Of course," said the other skull, flames whipping around in its mouth as well. "We were human once."

"You were?!" said Jeff and The Wizard in unison. They were both too surprised by what they had just heard to even notice the jinx.

"How is that possible?" The Wizard gawked at the skeletons in amazement.

Anasthasia was tapping her foot impatiently. "Can we talk about it at dinner? It's all very blasé; if I have to hear it again, I'd at least like to eat."

The entrance hall of the tower was vast, almost as large as the entire tower had appeared to be from the outside. The room was octagonal, with seven more doorways on each of the other walls. Cobweb laden boxes and crates littered the floor on either side, blocking the path to most of the other doors; some were open, mostly full of dusty books, as well as occasional jars of moldy ingredients or rusty devices. The room was lit by a colossal chandelier hanging from the ceiling, its thousands of crystals sparkling like the night sky.

A velvet carpet led down a clear path through the clutter, to the door at the far end. As they walked across the room, the two skeletons jogged ahead of them to open the door; their bones could be heard scraping and clanking together.

The hallway beyond the doorway was extremely long, at least a hundred feet, with many smaller doors leading off to both sides. The floor was carpeted with the same red velvet that spanned the entrance hall. Dozens of torches lined the dark stone walls, burning with eerie blue flames that seemed to give off no heat.

To the right, there was an open doorway, into which Jeff peered. What he saw inside was most disturbing. There were shelves lining the walls, each bearing dozens of dolls, toys, and household objects; however, these were far from ordinary items. Grotesque, twisted faces adorned their surfaces; most of their mouths appeared to have been sewn shut with wire, and many of them were tied down; they were all squirming or twitching, and the air was full of pained murmurs. When the items saw Jeff looking into the room, their eyes stopped randomly rolling in their sockets and lined up with his, widened with fear... or perhaps desperation.

Anasthasia's Abode

"What on Notearth?!" Stumbling backwards, Jeff tripped over Knippe and landed flat on his ass. He scrambled up, frantically clutching his heart. "What the fuck are those abominations?!"

"Woah, cool!" Knorpe's eyes lit up with childlike wonder. He looked like a kid seeing his first candy store.

When Knippe regained his footing, he reacted predictably identically.

Rolling her eyes, Anasthasia waved her hand dismissively. "Oh, that's just one of my workshops. Don't worry about them. Despite what they might have you believe, they can't feel anything."

She snapped her fingers, and the door slammed shut.

The Wizard nudged Jeff's arm. "Now do you see what I mean? She is *really* creepy."

Too horrified to speak, Jeff nodded faintly. For the remainder of his way down the hall, he kept his neck facing stiffly forward.

The two skeletons opened the double doors at the end of the hall, and the group followed Anasthasia into the dining hall. The room was very large, at least forty feet long, with a heavy mahogany table spanning most of its length. The walls were lined with ornate, geometric tapestries of deep hues. There were several chandeliers dancing with prismatic lights above, but the majority of the light came from a roaring fireplace set into the far wall.

Sitting in an ornate chair at the end of the table, chowing on a chunk of cheese, was Chris, the bartender from *The Wizarding Hole*. The Wizard was relieved; he had been worried that Fabulon might have brought someone unfavorable along with him.

"'Ey guys!" said Chris, through a mouthful of cheese. "'Ow's it goin'?"

"Dude, don't talk with your mouth full." Anasthasia cringed in disgust, huffing haughtily. "And get out of my chair, you're going to get cheese all over it!"

Swallowing his cheese, Chris stood up and grinned sheepishly. "Sorry…"

The Wizard gave him a cheerful wave. "Hey Chris, I didn't expect to see you here!"

"Well, you know me, I get around." Walking over to Fabulon, Chris put his arm around his shoulders. "Plus Fabby here can conjure a badass flying horse."

237

Chapter Sixteen

"Please stop calling me that…" muttered Fabulon, recoiling aversely.

"But, I don't understand," said The Wizard, scratching his head. "How did either of you know how to get here?"

"He showed us!" After looking around for a moment, Chris pointed to a doorway beside the fireplace, leading to a brightly lit kitchen.

Suddenly, a pungent odor of tobacco permeated the room.

Walking through the doorway was none other than Gary, the homeless man most famous for living in the bushes behind The Wizard's house. Holding a cigarette in his off hand, he was ravenously devouring a turkey leg, ripping off huge chunks of meat and swallowing them without chewing. Unusually, Gary was clean and shaven, wearing a dark gray tuxedo rather than his standard hobo attire; his wiry, gray hair was tucked neatly into a man-bun.

"I— Wha—" The Wizard was completely dumbfounded. The last person he expected to find there was Gary. After a moment, he seemed to regain his senses. "How the hell did *you* know where to find this place?!"

Taking a drag off his smoke, Gary shrugged. "I've followed you here before."

"I knew you were working for Quan!" The Wizard threw his arms up in outrage. He balled up his fists and narrowed his eyes in focus, and an arc of lightning erupted between his hands. "I'll kill everyone here before I give in to her demands!"

"Hold on, I'm unarmed!" Dropping his food and cigarette, Gary held both hands behind his head. "I mean you no harm, let me explain."

The Wizard glared at Gary, sizing him up; after a moment, he nodded. Lowering his hands, he dispelled the arc of lightning. "Okay, I'll listen. Mostly because that spell probably would have killed me too."

"Thank you." Relaxing his arms, Gary smiled at The Wizard. "Let me first say that I haven't been entirely honest with you."

"No shit."

"First of all, I'm not actually homeless."

"I'll say it again: no shit."

"However, I don't work for Archmage Quan." Reaching into his pocket, Gary pulled out a pack of smokes and his inscribed mithril lighter. "I was employed by your father to watch over you in case anything happened to him."

"Shit…" The Wizard had not seen that coming.

"I know it's a lot to take in. He anticipated that a cabal of corrupt higher-ups in the Circle were planning a coup. He hired me to ensure your protection, should they ever come after you; it appears that time has come."

Sparking his cigarette, he waited for a response, but The Wizard was too taken aback by this news to know what to say.

"Chris and I were snooping around in your tower, and Gary walked in on us," said Fabulon.

Gary chuckled, taking a drag. "At first, I thought they were vagrants raiding your tower."

"Ironic…" muttered Jeff.

"But when Fabulon explained everything," said Gary, "I knew the situation was urgent. I showed them how to get here right away."

The Wizard seemed to finally snap out of his trance, furrowing his brow in concern. "Wait, what if Archmage Quan tracks you here?"

"Relax." Smiling calmly, Fabulon placed his hand on The Wizard's shoulder. "I put a ward on each of us to prevent scrying; they should last a few days." He looked around at the others. "Anyone else need one?"

"No, we don't need your damn ward!" Scoffing, The Wizard brushed Fabulon's hand off of him. "It's probably crap compared to the one I cast on us, anyway."

"You didn't cast any ward!" Smirking snidely, Jeff held up his enchanted amulet. "Remember? You didn't know how to, so Merlin gave us these!"

"Shut the fuck up." The Wizard's face flushed bright red.

"Sit down, everyone!" said Anasthasia, who had already taken her seat at the head of the table. "You're ruining the atmosphere!"

The serving skeletons pulled out a chair for each of the group, and everyone took their seats. The Wizard waited until Fabulon sat down to take his seat, wanting to sit as far away as possible; Chris, on the other hand, sat directly next to Fabulon, scooting his chair as close as possible. The only chairs that could be found for Knippe and Knorpe were The Wizard and Anasthasia's childhood highchairs, so they slunk away into the kitchen.

Chapter Sixteen

"So, do you have any questions about the situation at hand?" said Gary, taking a seat across from The Wizard.

"Innumerable," said The Wizard. "However, it's late, and we've been on the road for days; you *would not* believe the journey we had. Could this wait until morning?"

"Amen to that!" Nodding fervently, Anasthasia uncorked a bottle of wine. She poured herself a glass and then slid the bottle across the table to The Wizard. "Cheers!"

"Thanks, Ana, that's just what I need!" Giving his sister a thumbs-up, The Wizard chugged the remainder of the bottle. "That hit the spot."

"Okay, sounds good," said Gary. "But, first thing tomorrow, I think we should discuss our plan of action."

The skeletons each carried a tray out of the kitchen, laden with meats, cheeses, grapes and olives; they placed enough food on the table to feed a small army. Everyone began piling their plates with various foods.

"Okay, about the elephant in the room…" said The Wizard. "What's with the skeletons?"

"For the last time, I found them in the attic," said Anasthasia, slicing into an extremely rare steak.

"No, damn it, that's not what I mean!" Scowling in frustration, The Wizard viciously skewered a sausage with his fork. "Why can they talk?"

A series of loud meows issued forth from The Wizard's bag of holding while he spoke. He leaned over, letting Kit Mingers out of the bag. The cat immediately leapt onto the table and started digging into the food.

"Ugh, let *them* tell you… It's a *really* boring story." Rolling her eyes, Anasthasia turned to Gary. "Hey, whatever-your-name-is, can I bum a smoke? I get a feeling I'll need it…"

Grunting, Gary passed her a cigarette. Sparking it with a snap of her fingers, she took a long drag. Blowing the smoke in The Wizard's direction, she conjured an ashtray and resumed cutting her steak.

"May we sit, mistress?" asked one of the skeletons, shifting its feet timidly.

Nodding, Anasthasia bit into a large hunk of bloody meat. The skeletons each pulled out a chair and sat down on either side of her. They sat in silence for a few moments; they may have been staring off into the distance thoughtfully, it was hard to tell. Finally, one of them spoke.

"Our story begins four centuries ago, when we were still human. We were servants to the sorcerer Merlin. My name is Vahim, and this is my twin brother, Vaharm."

"I don't think I'll be able to tell you apart," said The Wizard.

"It's easy," said Vaharm. He lifted his left foot onto the table. "See? I'm the one with wolf feet!"

"And I'm the one with your grandmother's ribcage!" Vahim ran a finger down his ribs. They clattered like a marimba.

Turning to his sister, The Wizard shook his head in disbelief. "Anasthasia, what the hell?!"

"What?" Taking a drag off her smoke, Anasthasia grinned and fluttered her eyelashes innocently. "I got most of these bones from the family graveyard. I tried to use my mom's ribcage first, but elf bones are too small."

The Wizard stared at her for a moment, shaking his head with his mouth agape. Even he had some lines he would not cross. Jeff and the others looked extremely uncomfortable; even Knippe and Knorpe remained silent.

"I have no words." Sighing, The Wizard massaged his weary brow.

"Should we continue?" asked Vaharm.

"Yeah, go ahead..." Biting into his sausage, The Wizard found that it contained several bones from some sort of small animal. Spitting the mouthful of sausage on his plate, he threw the rest of it aside. He did not want to eat any food cooked by these disgusting skeletons.

"Anyway, one day we were called into Merlin's lab for an experiment. He said he was on the cusp of discovering immortality."

"Seriously?" A spark of excitement ignited The Wizard's heart. He had dreamt of the possibility of immortality ever since the day he first comprehended death. "I thought it was beyond the laws of magic!"

"As did we," said Vahim. "However, as you can see, Merlin's experiment worked."

Jeff raised an eyebrow skeptically. "If he discovered immortality, how come he's dead?"

"As far as we know, he couldn't work out the faults," said Vahim, "so he never used it on himself."

241

Chapter Sixteen

"What faults?" The Wizard cocked his head curiously.

"The ritual he discovered would indeed turn you immortal," said Vaharm. "However, it would also instantly transform you into a skeleton."

"No one wanted to become immortal if it made them a skeleton." Crossing his arms, Vahim sighed, causing tongues of flame to whirl around his mouth. "All hope was lost."

"That sounds really stupid..." Pausing for a moment, The Wizard suddenly narrowed his eyes. "Hold on... were you two the skeletons from Merlin's closet that attacked me four hundred years ago?!"

"Oh, yeah, I think I remember that." Averting his gaze, Vaharm scratched his head awkwardly; his bones screeched as they scraped together. "Sorry about that, we thought you were Merlin; you look a lot like him, and we'd been in that closet for months."

"That's why we didn't say anything," said Vahim. "We have nothing to say to that son of a bitch."

Kit Mingers hissed loudly at the skeleton, his fur standing on end.

Cocking his head, Jeff gestured to the cat. "Hey, are you guys sure Merlin never discovered true immortality?"

"Good point," said The Wizard, nodding thoughtfully. "That cat is older than I am, and I'm pretty sure he's the same cat Merlin had. I probably should have asked him about it, but there was a lot going on."

"We wouldn't know." Vaharm clenched his bony fists. "He locked us in a trunk one day. He said he'd let us out in a day or two when he was finished moving into his new tower, and that's the last we ever saw of him."

"If he is still alive somewhere out there, I hope he's stuck as a skeleton in a coffin for all time." Vahim gritted his teeth; they were so dry that it sounded reminiscent of nails on a chalkboard.

Scowling, Anasthasia slapped him over the back of the skull. "What did I tell you about making that sound?!"

"Sorry, mistress..."

"It's messed up that Merlin did that to you," said Jeff. After a moment, he smirked facetiously. "I mean, I don't believe in keeping skeletons in the closet. I let mine come out ages ago. I love my skeletons, no matter who they choose to bone!"

Anasthasia burst out laughing.

Anasthasia's Abode

"Oh, you are just a little treasure!" Ashing her cigarette, she slid out of her chair. Creeping up behind Jeff, she wrapped her arms around him. "I wish I could mount your head on the wall and keep you forever!"

Jeff recoiled as Anasthasia attempted to pinch his cheeks. He was at a loss for what to say after hearing what was, without a doubt, the creepiest thing anyone had ever said to him. She kept trying to pinch his cheeks, and eventually he gave in and let her do it; she was a lot stronger than she looked, and he was afraid of what she might do if he tried to stop her.

"He's not the true treasure here, though." Chris once again put his arm around Fabulon's shoulders, ruffling his hair boisterously. "Although, I wouldn't call this guy 'little'!"

"Uhh... thanks... I guess...." muttered Fabulon, slinking away.

"He's not my type." Waving her hand at Chris and Fabulon disdainfully, she looked Jeff dead in the eyes. She winked at him, her brilliant gold irises gleaming like the morning sun. "If you're too big and muscly, I can't lock you away in my box!"

"Wait, are you using innuendo, or...?" asked Jeff, scrunching his face in uncertainty.

"No, silly; why would I be?" Giggling playfully, Anasthasia pressed her cheek against Jeff's. "I have the perfect box to keep you in!"

"That reminds me," said The Wizard. "You still dating that weird guy with the animated toy children? What was his name... Daddy Gepetto?"

"It was *Papa* Gepetto!" Laughing, Anasthasia snorted red wine through her nose. "I broke up with him; turns out he was doing some really weird shit with those toys."

"Oh yeah, that's no surprise; I always said he was a Gepettophile."

They all carried on eating, drinking, and laughing together for the remainder of the night. After such a long and grueling journey, it was a relief for all of them to stuff their faces with outrageous amounts of food. After a while, even The Wizard gave in and made due with Vahim and Vaharm's cooking. At one point, Knippe and Knorpe even got in a fight with Chris over who got to eat the last block of cheese. As everyone ate their dinners, the skeletons eyed them with the deepest jealousy.

Jeff and The Wizard told the others the details of their time with Merlin, and of their nerve-racking journey from Theiyre. Gary seemed particularly

243

interested in anything they had to say about Merlin, and especially about the *Arcane Tomes*. Afterwards, Fabulon told them of his harrowing experience getting fired, strip-searched, forcibly escorted from Circle Tower, and strip-searched again in the street, all by Archmage Quan personally.

When they had all had their fill of food and wine, Anasthasia commanded the skeletons to show everyone to their rooms. Jeff ended up sleeping in The Wizard's childhood bedroom. The Wizard insisted on taking his dad's old room, in hopes of locating his dad's stash of drugs.

Despite the spiders, it was nice for Jeff to finally sleep in a warm bed after such a hard journey. Before he went to sleep, he looked around The Wizard's old bedroom. He noticed that there were no toys; there was just the bed, a couple of dusty bookshelves, and a worn-out desk with a globe of Notearth on it. There was a fireplace in the corner, with a few empty picture frames sitting on it. Jeff actually found himself feeling sorry for The Wizard's lonely childhood, although this feeling was short lived.

Wondering what awaited him in the days to come, he drifted into a fitful slumber.

Chapter Seventeen
Talk to the Cat

The situation to which Jeff awoke was most disconcerting. The first thing he noticed was the wig on his head, with luscious blonde curls cascading over his eyes, with the occasional curl of his jet-black hair in the mix. Brushing away the curtain of curls, he felt that his face had been shaven. Sitting in a chair next to Jeff's bed was Anasthasia; she was leaning over him with a vacant expression, slowly brushing the wig.

"What the hell?!" he shouted, tearing the wig off his head and scrambling to the far side of the bed. He fumbled for his glasses on the bedside table.

Anasthasia jumped out of her seat, screaming in terror. "Didn't anyone ever teach you not to wake a sleepwalker?!"

Before Jeff could reply, Anasthasia turned and stormed out of the room, grumbling about rudeness.

Jeff stared at the door in disbelief for a moment, unable to fully process what had just occurred. Eventually, he dragged himself out of bed and shuffled into the bathroom. Looking in the mirror, he saw that Anasthasia had put lipstick on him, as well as blush and eyeshadow.

Sighing, he walked over to the shower and turned on the hot water.

The showerhead was on a long hose, and as soon as Jeff stepped into the shower, it began moving around him, evenly distributing the water. It was nice for a moment; however, the showerhead soon began acting strange: it curled itself around Jeff's thigh and tried to slither between his buttcheeks.

Chapter Seventeen

He yelped frantically, yanking the showerhead away from himself as he leapt out of the shower.

Jeff got dressed and decided just to wash his gaping bullet wound in the sink. After he was finished, he bandaged it with a few shreds of The Wizard's childhood bedsheets. They were clean enough to suit his needs; although, he could have done without the pattern of racial slurs in comic action bubbles.

The halls were rather drafty, causing a chill to run through Jeff's damp hair. It took him a long time to find the stairs. The entire way, he swore he kept hearing the tiny footsteps and seeing Knippe and Knorpe darting in and out of the corner of his eye.

Unfortunately for him, Jeff happened upon another of Anasthasia's "workshops" on his way downstairs. He regretted approaching one of the dolls squirming within and removing the wire sealing its lips. All the doll did was bite his finger, letting out an ear-splitting shriek. Trying to quiet it, Jeff merely succeeded in getting his finger bit again before accidentally popping off the doll's head; its piercing cries unbroken, the head rolled under one of the tables. Feeling unsettled, Jeff hurried back into the hall.

When Jeff finally found his way into the dining room, The Wizard, Anasthasia, Fabulon, and Gary were sitting around the end of the table. He could smell the fragrance of bacon muddled amongst Gary's tobacco smoke, and hear the sounds of Vahim and Vaharm cooking. Kit Mingers' booming meows could also be heard coming from the kitchen, as he begged the skeletons for food.

It seemed that at some point, The Wizard had talked Anasthasia into putting on a blouse and flannel skirt under her fur cloak. She was sipping a tiny cup of tea and telling the others about a dream she had the night before.

"So," she was saying, "I was posting on dreamchan, like most nights; I started a thread about dead babies, and people kept trolling me.... They were posting pictures of live babies. Gross! Can you believe that?"

"Screw what people in dreams say," said The Wizard. He also had a cup of tea, with the distinct smell of brandy wafting from it. "They're just jealous that you get to exist!"

Talk to the Cat

After taking a long drag of his cigarette, Gary cleared his throat. "I hate to interrupt this *fascinating* conversation, but we really need to talk about our plan."

"Ugh, fine," said The Wizard. "I figured I'd just wing it, but if you *really* want to come up with a plan, I'll humor you."

It was growing more difficult every day for Jeff to come to terms with how full of shit his uncle was. Only days before — or over four centuries, depending on who you ask —, he had heard The Wizard explicitly tell Merlin that he never just "wings it". Shaking his head, Jeff took a seat as far away from Anasthasia as he could.

"Gee, thanks a lot." Gary rolled his eyes. "Well, the obvious first step would be to devise a way into the Circle. It's not going to be easy; thanks to your little *heist*, security is at its maximum."

Reaching into the pocket of his robes, Fabulon pulled out a piece of paper; unfolding it onto the table, he revealed a map of Circle Tower and the nearby streets.

"Circle Tower is under constant surveillance by patrols of battlemages." Fabulon pointed to a large number of red Xs marked around the tower. "In addition, there will be low level magi stationed at these locations at all times; if they see any suspicious activity, they are instructed to activate the tower's beacon, alerting all of Quan's forces of our presence.

"Fortunately, the majority of high ranking magi are scattered across the land on missions, mostly looking for you; if we can disable the beacon in time, we might be able to avoid a large-scale conflict. Unfortunately, that means we probably don't have long before they find us here. We need to act soon."

"Well, the whole reason we came here was to find the *Arcane Dictionary*," said The Wizard. "With that in our possession, we might actually stand a chance. I'm certain it's here somewhere, but I have no idea where to look…"

He sighed hopelessly.

No one said anything for a moment.

Suddenly, Jeff beamed with inspiration. "I have an idea!" He took off his backpack, reached inside, and slammed the *Arcane Almanac* down on the table. The symbol of the Arcane of Wisdom glowed brightly on its cover. "How about we ask this?"

His jaw dropping, Fabulon stared at the tome in amazement. "Is that what I think it is?"

"It is indeed the *Almanac of the Arcanes*," said Jeff, grinning enthusiastically. "With this, we can find information about the history of anything. I'm sure we can use it to track down the *Dictionary*."

Gary raised an eyebrow. "Do you even know how to use that thing?"

"No, not really..." Jeff lowered his head dejectedly. "I tried using it to gather info on what Quan's plans are. Everything it ever says is either a riddle or a rhyme... usually both. Either way, it never says anything logical."

"Oh, give it here!" Frowning impatiently, Anasthasia reached out and magically pulled the book towards her, flipping it open to the center page. "Hey, book, tell us where the other book is!"

Suddenly, cursive began to appear on the page, as though scrawled by invisible hands: *If arcane lore is what one seeks, then I implore, ask the cat who speaks.*

Standing up, Jeff walked over to see what it said. "See? The thing makes no sense! And honestly, this is downright eloquent compared to the incoherencies it's spit out before."

"I think I know what it means," said Anasthasia. "It'll have to wait until after breakfast though; we're going down into the basement."

"Oh, don't tell me —" began The Wizard.

"Yup!" Anasthasia pumped her fist excitedly. "Time to power up my oldest toy!"

The Wizard sighed, burying his face in his arms.

Jeff shuddered to think what Anasthasia meant by "her oldest toy", and for that matter, what her basement must be like. He supposed he had better eat a healthy portion now, just in case he had no appetite left by lunchtime. Vahim and Vaharm served the group bacon and eggs for breakfast, staring at them wistfully as they ate.

Halfway through the meal, Knippe and Knorpe dragged Chris's unconscious body from a passage hidden behind one of the tapestries.

"Oh, hey," said Knippe, dropping Chris's head as he noticed everyone. "This is unexpected..."

Talk to the Cat

The Wizard narrowed his eyes in suspicion. "What are you doing?"

"Don't worry about it," said Knorpe.

"I kind of feel like I should." The Wizard walked over to Chris, shoving the gnomes away and pouring his cup of steaming tea on Chris's face.

Chris stiffened, blinking what turned out to be mostly brandy out of his eyes. "What the hell happened?"

"Don't worry about it." Before returning to his meal, The Wizard helped Chris to his feet.

They finished their breakfast, with Knippe and Knorpe sulking in the corner the entire time, quietly eating their bacon. When they were done, Anasthasia asked the others to follow her; she specifically requested that Knippe and Knorpe not come along, so they waited for everyone to leave before sneaking after them.

"You know," said The Wizard to Anasthasia, "I'm only playing along with this stupid theory because it's the only idea we have."

"Which means it's the best idea we have!" Sipping her tea, Anasthasia smirked at The Wizard.

The Wizard heaved a weary sigh. His mood was running almost as low as his dwindling supply of cocaine.

It took awhile for them to get to the basement, because Anasthasia kept forgetting they were with her. Several times, she walked into random rooms, going about her business until someone said something; unfortunately, The Wizard could not remember how to find the basement, so they all had to deal with this.

As he followed the others into the basement, Jeff was surprised to see that it was relatively clean and well lit. One of the walls was lined with wine racks, loaded with hundreds of unmarked bottles of wine; Jeff could not help but notice how few bottles were dusty, suggesting there was a high turnover rate. On the other side of the room, there was a cozy lounge, with four cushy leather armchairs positioned around an empty fireplace.

Anasthasia led them straight past the wine racks and armchairs, to a cobwebby, old door in the back of the room. The hinges screeched loudly as Vahim pulled the door open. Stepping aside, Anasthasia gestured for them to enter the pitch black room.

Chapter Seventeen

"After you!"

Fabulon took the lead, grabbing a torch from the wall before he entered the room. The others followed, with Chris just behind Fabulon, scoping out the view.

Jeff paused before he entered, squinting suspiciously at Anasthasia. "You're not going to lock me in there, are you?"

"No. I thought about it, and I'm bored with you."

Jeff was not entirely sure this answer satisfied him, but he nonetheless followed the others into the room. Anasthasia entered behind him, ordering Vahim and Vaharm to guard the wine from the gnomes.

In the dark chamber, the air within smelled extremely stale, and motes of dust flurried throughout the beams of their lights. As the group entered, the ceiling emitted a gentle glow, illuminating the room below.

The floor was tiled with a red and white houndstooth pattern, and was littered with dusty dolls, playhouses, and other toys; surprisingly, none of them seemed to have been aberrated by Anasthasia. The walls were paneled with polished mahogany, bearing signs of heavy wear on the bottom three feet. Everything bore a heavy layer of dust and cobwebs.

As soon as it was illuminated, Jeff immediately noticed what was easily the strangest thing in the room. Protruding from the rear wall, almost as tall as the room itself, was the face of a colossal mechanical cat. Most of its face was covered in extremely matted fur, although patches of it had peeled here and there, revealing the steel frame underneath. There were whiskers of wire coming from its cheeks and into the ceiling above. Its eyes were nothing more than empty, black glass screens.

As soon as they saw the giant cat head, Knippe and Knorpe started laughing hilariously. The others simply stared in confusion, unsure of how this cat head would help their situation. Scoffing, Gary leaned against the wall and sparked up a cigarette.

"Umm... what the hell is that thing?" Looking at the giant cat head, Jeff wondered if it also had a giant body tucked into the wall, that might come out if they powered it on, and bat them around like yarn.

"That's my cat machine!" Running up to the cat machine, Anasthasia hugged it, causing a plume of dust to permeate the air.

Talk to the Cat

Slowly, its eyes came alight. At first, they were just static, but then the images of huge, yellow cat eyes appeared on the screens.

"My dad built that thing to babysit Ana when she was little," whispered The Wizard to Jeff. "She didn't have any friends, and her mom died giving birth, so she basically just hung out with the cat machine."

"Okay, that's *really* messed up."

"I know, right? Why call it 'cat machine', and not 'catculator', or 'meowchine'?"

Jeff shook his head at The Wizard. "That wasn't even close to my point…"

After a moment, a thunderous meow reverberated throughout the room. The cat machine's eyes were now alight with a pair of pixelated pupils. It scanned the room, blinking confusedly at all the faces.

Kneeling down, Anasthasia bowed before the cat machine. "Oh, great cat machine, we come to you in need of your wisdom."

Snorting, The Wizard rolled his eyes.

"Tell us, my pretty, what do you know of the…" Anasthasia trailed off, before turning around with a blank expression. "What are we looking for again?"

The Wizard threw his arms up impatiently. "The *Arcane Dictionary*, damn it!"

"Oh, right!" Anasthasia quickly turned back to the cat machine, once again kneeling before it. "Cat machine, you have always shown me the way through dark times; please, help my idiot brother find our dad's stupid, old book!"

"Little Ana, I have missed ye," said the cat machine. When it spoke, its mouth moved out of sync with its words. Looking down at Anasthasia, it appeared to attempt a smile. "Ye must more often visit me— me— me—"

Suddenly, its eyes were replaced with static, and it began sparking. Its jaw began twitching wildly, as it played the first half of the "meow" sound bite on repeat. Black smoke began to rise out of its ears and nostrils.

Everyone backed away in alarm. Chris ducked behind Fabulon, clutching his buttcheeks for support.

"Me— me— me—" The cat machine suddenly let out a long, fading "owww". It coughed up a smouldering hairball full of loose wires, before

Chapter Seventeen

losing power. The screens of its eyes were cracked, and its mouth hung open limply, dripping oil. Several fires ignited near its whiskers.

"Huh… I guess it's broken." Shrugging apathetically, Anasthasia turned around and began to saunter towards the exit. "Oh, well! I never used the thing anymore anyway."

"Hold on..." said Fabulon. He looked very confused about what was happening. "Is that it? Is there no fixing it?"

"It'd take too long." Anasthasia waved her hand dismissively. "It probably didn't have anything useful to say anyway. It usually just babbled on about the meaning of sentience and what defines a living soul. That's why I left it down here! Now, come on, let's get into some of that wine!"

"Wait, so how are we going to find the *Dictionary*?" asked Jeff, nibbling his lip in concern.

"Ugh… you guys are a bunch of broken records…." Groaning, Anasthasia walked past them and back into the wine cellar. Grabbing a couple bottles, she plopped down on one of the armchairs and commanded the skeletons to light a fire.

"I guess we could ask the *Almanac* again," said The Wizard. "Maybe its answer changed when we broke the talking cat. Although, I've gotta say, the thing is a lot less useful than the legends say. I hope the *Dictionary* isn't as disappointing."

"Good point… I mean, about using it. You really shouldn't talk shit about the Arcanes, though. You saw what kind of shit they put Merlin through!" Reaching into his bag, Jeff pulled out the *Arcane Almanac*.

The Wizard immediately snatched the book out of Jeff's hands.

"Does no one in your family have any manners?" Scowling, Jeff pursed his lips.

Ignoring Jeff, The Wizard flipped the *Arcane Almanac* open to its center page. "Where do we look for the *Arcane Dictionary*?"

Just as before, script magically appeared on the pages. *There is a magical cat hiding within this tower, and in its mind lie secrets of arcane power.*

"Damn it, we already asked the cat machine!" Throwing his head back angrily, The Wizard tossed the *Almanac* at the cat machine. "Useless piece of junk…"

252

Talk to the Cat

"Dude, be careful!" Panicking, Jeff ran over to the *Almanac* and grabbed it, dusting off the fake cat fur. "This thing is a priceless artifact."

"Well, it's feeding us crap. We asked the only talking cat!"

"How about we ask that cat?" asked Chris. He gestured to the corner where Knippe and Knorpe were standing. "You said last night that he's magic."

The gnomes froze, their eyes wide in terror. Slowly, they turned around; crouched directly behind them, ready to pounce, was Kit Mingers. No sooner had the gnomes noticed him, than Kit Mingers tackled both of them to the ground with one motion.

"What are you, Chris, some kind of idiot?" Chuckling derisively, The Wizard gestured to Kit Mingers, who was furiously wrestling Knorpe while Knippe tried to pull his brother to safety; the cat had a raging, red erection. "Look at that cat! Do you think there's anything intelligent going on in its head?"

"I don't know... y'all are the wizards..." Shrugging, Chris scratched his scruffy blonde hair. "I just figured you'd know how to make a cat talk."

Staring at him flatly, The Wizard shook his head. "None of us can talk to cats, Chris."

"For the record, I probably could!" yelled Anasthasia, from the other room.

The Wizard hurried to the door. "What did you just say?"

Anasthasia leaned over the edge of her chair, a half-empty wine bottle in her hand. "I said I can probably make the cat talk. I know a ritual to imbue objects with basic intelligence; I use it all the time when I need something to talk to."

"Does that actually work if the subject is already sentient?"

"I wouldn't know." Shrugging lazily, Anasthasia took a deep pull of her wine. "I've never considered using it on a living thing before, because you have to remember to feed them."

Fabulon stepped forward, peering through the doorway at Anasthasia. He wore a worried expression. "Doesn't that type of magic siphon portions the user's soul into the enchanted objects?"

253

Chapter Seventeen

"Yeah, it does... Don't worry about me, though. My father explained to me that our bloodline has special properties, one of which is that our souls regenerate; of course, Wiz doesn't have to worry about that, being ginger."

Snorting tobacco smoke out his nostrils, Gary cracked up, pointing snidely at The Wizard. When he relaxed his hands to his sides, Knippe and Knorpe ran up and high fived him from behind, before retreating to the wine cellar. They were covered in vicious scratches, and feline ejaculate dripped down Knorpe's corduroy trousers.

"Wait a second..." Frowning, The Wizard narrowed his eyes at his sister. His voice gradually raised as he spoke with indignance. "Did you just say that dad actually told you about our magical bloodline?!"

"Oh, right..." Twirling a strand of her raven-black hair, Anasthasia nodded reminiscently. "I forgot... he told me not to ever tell you that..."

A look of outrage crossed The Wizard's face. "What? *Why?!*"

Anasthasia shrugged. "Something about a prophecy, It was just before his disappearance. Apparently, you're supposed to either... you know what, I really shouldn't say... daddy would be furious."

"Damn it, we're going to talk more about this later," said The Wizard, running his fingers through his mane of orange hair. "For now, how do we go about performing this ritual?"

"Well, we'll have to take the cat to one of my workshops. I have the necessary supplies there. I'll just have to modify the arcane formula, and hopefully the cat will survive the process!"

After waiting for Anasthasia to finish her wine, they left the basement. The Wizard forced Kit Mingers back into his bag of holding. Knippe and Knorpe each attempted to sneak a bottle of wine; however, The Wizard quickly snatched the bottles away, using them to bash the gnomes over the heads.

Anasthasia led them up a few more staircases and down some winding halls, into a passage. Jeff muttered something about it seeming strangely familiar. Soon, it became evident why; as they approached one of the doors, muffled screaming could be heard from within.

"Oh no, one of my babies broke free," said Anasthasia. She pushed the door open, and the shrieking grew far louder.

Talk to the Cat

Most of the others stayed out in the hall, covering their ears. Only Knippe, Knorpe, and the skeletons followed her into the room. The gnomes looked around in whimsical amazement at all the shelves full of wriggling, contorted toys.

Anasthasia leaned down and simpered with feigned sweetness at the gnomes, jiggling her cleavage in their faces. "Hey, would one of you bearded children do me a favor?"

Gawking at this spectacle, they simultaneously squirked in excitement. "What do you need?"

"Could you reach under that shelf and pull out that obnoxious thing?"

"Do we get to keep it afterwards?" Widening his eyes and fluttering his lashes, Knorpe held his hands up imploringly.

"No, I'm going to destroy it," said Anasthasia. "But I'll tell you what: whoever grabs it for me can pick one of the toys from the shelves."

The gnomes looked at each other for a moment, their expressions fiercely competitive. They both dove at the source of the screams, reaching under the shelf with one arm and wrestling each other with the other. Wriggling toys cascaded down upon them as they fought. After a moment, Knippe let out a yelp; he pulled his hand out from under the shelf, with bloody bite marks on his thumb.

After a moment, Knorpe pulled out the snarling doll head and held it over his head. "Haha! I am victorious!"

It bit him on the finger as well, and he immediately dropped it. Rolling on the floor, it twitched and shrieked horrendously.

"Shut up, you worthless piece of shit." Glaring coldly, Anasthasia stomped the head to pieces. When she was done grinding it into the floor, she smiled at the gnomes. "Anyway, now that that's out of the way, I'll let you both have a toy." Her smile suddenly turned into a stern glare. "However, if I hear a peep out of either of them, I'll smash both of your toys to bits. Got it?"

"Yes, maam," said both gnomes, gulping nervously. They each ran up to the shelves, grabbed the first toy they could reach, and ran out into the hall.

"If you don't mind me asking," said Gary, who was observing from the doorway, "why are these toys like this? I'm not necessarily against it, I'm just curious; what is the point?"

"I get bored sometimes." Turning slightly pink, Anasthasia shrugged. "I've been alone out here most of my life, and I learned to make these things to keep me company."

Gary cocked his head to the side. "But why are their mouths sewn shut, and why are so many of them tied up?"

Once again, Anasthasia shrugged. "I get bored of them too. Sometimes, I forget them for weeks, and when I come back they've gone insane. I don't often have the heart to break them, they came from my soul after all, so I just keep them like this."

Gary seemed satisfied with this answer, but Jeff and Fabulon looked as though it were one of the most messed up things they had ever heard.

For the next half hour, the group waited in the hall while Anasthasia had Vahim and Vaharm prepare the ritual. Knippe and Knorpe spent the entire time gleefully torturing their new toys with their pocket knives.

Anasthasia directed the skeletons to draw several concentric circles of arcane runes in chalk on the floor. Cracking open a series of jars from one of the shelves, she prepared a secret blend of herbs and spices on her work desk. After sprinkling the blend around the center of the circles, Anasthasia told them she was ready to begin the ritual.

"Subdue the cat for his shot." Reaching into the pocket of her fur coat, Anasthasia withdrew a syringe full of bright green fluid. "Just a drop of this will temporarily paralyze him long enough to perform the ritual."

"Why do you carry that in your pocket?" asked Jeff, eyeing it uneasily.

"Don't worry about it."

The Wizard pulled Kit Mingers out of his bag. As he did, the cat scratched his arms, squirming to get free. He cussed furiously as he held the cat away from his face. Before taking Kit Mingers, Anasthasia jabbed the syringe into the back of his neck; a moment later, the cat's body went limp, and she grabbed him.

After setting Kit Mingers in the center of the circles, Anasthasia grabbed a flask of oil, pouring it all over him. She kneeled down and rubbed the oil deep into his fur, rolling him around in the secret blend of herbs and spices until they coated his entire body. Clapping her hands together, she caused the oil to disappear from her skin.

Talk to the Cat

Anasthasia asked Vahim to grab her a jar from the highest shelf. The jar had air holes poked in the lid, and contained several fairies. Not requiring food or water, fairies could live in such an environment for years; however, these fairies were slumped against the side of the jar, barely alive. As Anasthasia reached into the jar, a female fairy looked up feebly and hissed, so she pinched it by the throat.

Holding the fairy up to her nose, Anasthasia snorted the dust off the fairy's wings. Her eyes lit up with ecstasy as she drew a cold iron dagger from the desk; the blade was already encrusted with dried blood. She held the knife up to the fairy's throat, cutting off her head with a single motion. As blood dripped from the fairy's neck, Anasthasia took it and drew a circle of blood around the outermost arcane runes.

When she finished the circle of blood, Anasthasia stood and held her hands over Kit Mingers, her palms facing downward. Her eyes closed, a look of intense focus on her face, she began to chant arcane phrases under her breath, too quickly to follow.

Even The Wizard had always been impressed by Anasthasia's skills as an enchantress; nonetheless, he was not entirely confident that this ritual would work.

Suddenly, a dazzling aurora of pinkish light began to pour out of Anasthasia's palms, fluttering above the magic circles. The arcane runes began to emit a blood red glow. Kit Mingers' limp body floated above the circles, the glowing haze whirling around him. The air in the room began to whip around like a tempest, as the light swirled faster and faster. Anasthasia's face was contorted with focus, as more and more pinkish light poured from her hands.

The ritual was over almost as soon as it began. Anasthasia muttered one final arcane phrase, and all of the pinkish haze swirled into Kit Mingers' body like water down a toilet. The cat slowly lowered to the ground, the blend of herbs and spices burning off of his fur with cold blue flames. Anasthasia opened her eyes for a moment, and then collapsed; Vaharm caught her as she fell to the ground, lowering her gently.

"That took a lot out of me..." She sat up, leaning against a leg of the desk. "I'll need a nap after this."

Chapter Seventeen

"I reckon it must have taken a large chunk of your soul." Leaning towards her, The Wizard bit his lip anxiously. It always bothered him that Anasthasia dabbled in such dangerous soul magic; he figured it was part of the reason she was so... different. "It's not a ritual meant to be used on a cat. Let's just hope it worked..."

He crossed his fingers, hoping this was not all in vain.

Anasthasia sat forward shakily, pulling a syringe of blue liquid from her pocket. She jabbed the syringe into Kit Mingers' side, pumping the fluid into him. "There, that will counteract the first poison. He should be able to move soon."

After a moment, Kit Mingers slowly sat up. He looked around the room, his eyes wide. Suddenly, tears welled in his eyes, and he began yowling mournfully. Feebly sitting up, he crawled into the corner, and curled up in the fetal position.

"I'm good enough..." he muttered to himself. His voice was a deep baritone, even more so than his meows; he sounded like a large human. Shielding his eyes with his paws, he rocked back and forth, muttering to himself. "I'm good enough... I'm good enough...."

"What the fuck?" The Wizard scrunched his face bemusedly. This was not the result he had expected.

"I'm good enough..."

Knippe and Knorpe ran into the room to see what was happening close up. When they saw Kit Mingers rocking back and forth in the fetal position, they burst out laughing. Jeff seemed to have seen enough, and sat down in the hall, facing away from the room.

"I'm good enough..."

"I guess it worked..." Walking up to Kit Mingers, The Wizard leaned over and gently stroked the cat's black and white fur. "You okay, buddy?"

"I'm pretty fucking far from okay!" Hissing, Kit Mingers scratched The Wizard's hand. "I was happy for four hundred years! I thought I had it made; I was perfectly content sleeping, eating, and humping whatever I wanted."

"Tell me about it..." muttered Knippe.

"Now, though, I feel pathetic." Sniffling, Kit Mingers sobbed into his paws. "Out of fucking nowhere, I have all these new unfulfilled dreams and

Talk to the Cat

desires. Now, four hundred years as a housecat feels like a joke! Why would you do this to me?!"

Knippe and Knorpe were literally rolling on the floor with laughter.

"I knew that was Merlin's cat!" said Jeff.

"Shut up, Jeff, we all knew that!" Sitting on the floor beside Kit Mingers, The Wizard was careful to stay just out of reach of his claws. "Is there anything we could do to help?"

"Just leave me alone... I need a while to adjust to this...."

They all cleared out into the hall, leaving Kit Mingers alone with his new thoughts. Vahim carried Anasthasia, who was still too weak to stand. The Wizard had to drag Knippe and Knorpe out of the room, as they were paralyzed with laughter. Closing the door behind him, The Wizard sighed wearily and slumped against it. He pulled one of the bottles of wine from his bag, magically uncorking it and taking a large swig.

"Well, this is pretty fucking weird. Hopefully he's okay."

"Hey, I know your cat needs time to cope," said Gary, waving his cigarette impatiently, "but we really need to prepare our strategy. Could we just quickly ask him if he knows anything about the *Dictionary*? We should find out if we've been wasting our time with this ritual."

"Just give him five minutes," said The Wizard, "then I'll talk to him."

Tapping his foot impatiently, Gary chain smoked as they waited. After about five minutes, The Wizard tentatively pushed the door open; he slowly entered the room, gently closing it behind him. Kit Mingers was pacing back and forth in the back of the room, and did not acknowledge The Wizard's presence.

"Hey, Kittlebag, could I ask you a few questions?"

Kit Mingers glared at The Wizard. "You've got a lot of nerve, coming in here, using my full first name, and asking me questions. What about all the questions I have, huh? I think I deserve answers!"

His deep baritone caused several nearby toys to fall from the shelves; fortunately, their mouth wires held, and all they could do is whirl their eyeballs madly as The Wizard stomped them to bits.

Sitting down across from Kit Mingers, The Wizard gave him a sympathetic smile. "Look, there will be time for that later. I promise I'll get

259

Chapter Seventeen

to it. Right now, though, I need you to tell me if you remember my dad building any secret rooms in this tower."

Kit Mingers scoffed; it sounded strange, coming from a cat. He flexed his claws threateningly at The Wizard, batting his tail against the floor in irritation.

"Right, you're looking for the *Arcane Dictionary*," he said. "I listen to your conversations, believe it or not. They used to mean nothing to me, but suddenly it all makes sense. You're a fucking asshole, by the way; now I know you've been talking shit about me to my face for years."

Ignoring that last comment, The Wizard leaned forward in anticipation. "Okay, good, we're on the same page. Do you know anything about it?"

"As a matter of fact, I do. I'm not gonna fucking tell you, though; not until you answer all of my questions. Got it?" Kit Mingers glared spitefully at The Wizard.

"There's no time for that!" Sighing, The Wizard made eye contact with Kit Mingers. "Look, I really am sorry, but we might all be killed if we can't find that book. I'll answer whatever questions you have when this is all over!"

"I ain't saying shit."

"Not even for a whole jar of catnip?" Rooting around in his bag for a moment, The Wizard pulled out a glass jar full of the catnip. Wiggling his eyebrows, he dangled it over Kit Mingers' head.

"Damn it, I knew there was something in that jar..." Growling, Kit Mingers narrowed his eyes at the catnip. "Nonetheless, it's not going to work on me. I'm not a simple cat anymore."

Cracking open the jar, The Wizard pulled out a large nug of the sumptuous herb. He dangled it just out of reach over Kit Mingers, smiling wickedly. "Come on, you know you want it!"

"Son of a bitch!" Yowling with yearning, Kit Mingers tried to bat the catnug out of The Wizard's hand. "Fine, I'll tell you... just give me the catnip."

Although he looked begrudging at first, Kit Mingers went crazy as The Wizard poured the entire jar of catnip in front of him. He quickly leapt into the pile, breathing deeply as he rolled around. The catnip may not have done much to help him cope with his new situation, but it seemed to take the edge off for a moment.

"Thanks, buddy..." Smiling lazily, Kit Mingers rolled onto his back. "That's good stuff..."

"No problem." Chortling, The Wizard sat down and watched as his cat got right proper as fuck. "So, what do you know about the *Arcane Dictionary*?"

"I can't say for sure, but I think I know where the old man hid it."

"Where's that?" Eyes twinkling with excitement, The Wizard leaned forward.

"Well, when we lived out here, I came to know every secret passage and room. I could get just about anywhere in the tower. However, there was one room I could never get into. No matter how hard I tried, I could never get into the back of the basement."

Cocking his head, The Wizard narrowed his eyes skeptically. "You mean the room with the cat machine?"

Kit Mingers shook his head. "No, the room behind that. It had a vault door made of brass, that was sealed with some kind of force magic. The old man built the cat machine in front of that door, but as far as I know, it's still there."

"Seriously?" The Wizard's eyes widened. He had always known there was something fishy about that cat machine. "I never knew what was down there; my dad never let me in the basement when it was his laboratory."

"If the old man has anything secret hidden around here, that'd be where it is." Approaching the door, Kit Mingers scratched at the wood. "Now can you let me out of this creepy room? I would like to go for a walk by myself."

"That's fine," said The Wizard, holding open the door. "That was all we needed to know."

"Hope it was worth it..." muttered Kit Mingers as he sulked away.

When The Wizard stepped into the hall, he saw that most of the group had gone elsewhere; only Jeff, Fabulon, and Gary remained.

"Did he know anything?" asked Fabulon.

"Yeah, apparently there is a vault hidden behind the cat machine."

"Wow, really?" said Jeff. "What a weird place to hide something. I suppose it makes sense; I'd never have thought to look for anything secret hidden behind that creepy thing."

261

Chapter Seventeen

"I suppose this wasn't a wild goose chase after all!" Raising his eyebrows in surprise, Gary grinned enthusiastically. "Let's go check it out."

Upon reaching the door to the basement, The Wizard saw that the door bore signs of being forcibly pried open and wedged shut. He gritted his teeth, kicking the it open and storming down the stairs. Knippe and Knorpe looked up from the stolen wine they were drinking and attempted to manage a look of feigned innocence.

"You little bastards," he shouted, grabbing them by their collars. They hung limply with looks of drunken bliss as he carried them up the stairs and tossed them onto the rug. He slammed the door behind him, grumbling to himself as he descended into the basement. "I'm gonna have to put a magic lock on that door...."

When they entered the cat machine's chambers, black smoke poured from the doorway. With a wave of his hand, The Wizard cleared away the smoke. Only the metal skeleton of the cat machine remained, everything else had been burned away.

Chapter Eighteen
The Arcane Armory

"I've got dibs on blowing it up," said The Wizard, grinning enthusiastically as he assessed the charred frame of the cat machine. "I've wanted to destroy this thing ever since my dad refused to build the giant robot that *I* wanted."

"Did you ask him for a robot that kills people?" Jeff smirked, a shrewd look in his eyes.

"Well, it was technically capable of killing," said The Wizard, with an unabashed chuckle, "but its main directive was stealing. It'd only kill people who tried to stop it."

"Uhh… yeah… I'm pretty sure that's why your dad said no…."

"Whatever, just stand back." The Wizard rolled up the sleeves of his robes, approaching the cat machine. Cracking his knuckles, he turned to face the others. "Okay, Jeff, watch and you might learn something."

The Wizard rooted around in his bag for a moment, pulling out a small leather-bound handbook and stick of bright red chalk. He flipped through the manual, laying it open on the floor. With the chalk, he began to transcribe arcane runes from the pages of the book to the floor around the cat machine.

It took quite some time for The Wizard to do his work, so the others eventually decided to wait in the other room, on the overstuffed armchairs. Gary grabbed a bottle of wine from one of the racks, uncorking it with his teeth. Fabulon snapped his fingers, and the smouldering embers in the firepit burst into a roaring fire.

263

Chapter Eighteen

"Wow, that's a cool spell," said Jeff. "I doubt The Wizard could do that."

"He definitely can, it's basic pyromancy!" Fabulon scrunched his face defensively. "I've seen him do it plenty of times; what he's doing in there is way more advanced. I don't understand why you doubt his abilities."

Narrowing his eyes, Jeff cocked his head at Fabulon. "I don't understand why you look up to him, If he were a competent wizard, none of us would be in this situation."

Fabulon frowned in disapproval. "Listen, kid, he's a better wizard than any of us; I grew up with him, so I know. He doesn't like to use his magic, so he tends to underplay his abilities to get out of work. I can't blame him; he never wanted to be a wizard, his dad forced him into it.

"However, even without trying, he was always a naturally talented spellcaster. If he wanted to, he could be as great a wizard as his father someday. I wouldn't be so quick to underestimate him, if I were you."

Jeff rolled his eyes. He was not so sure how seriously he should even be taking Fabulon, given that this is the same man who thinks The Wizard is his best friend.

"Is that why his dad named him 'The Wizard'?" asked Gary, snickering snidely. "Because he wanted to pressure him into being one?"

"Oh, I thought his dad would have told you, that's not his real name. It's just a nickname he came up with."

"I knew it!" Jeff's face lit up with a look of sinister vim. "So, you know his real name?"

"Yes, but I won't tell you; I swore an oath to my best friend to never blab his darkest secret." Crossing his arms, Fabulon turned his head away in a huff.

"Oh, brother…" Rolling his eyes again, Jeff scoffed. "It cannot possibly be that bad."

Chuckling, Gary leaned back in his seat and sparked up a smoke. "I don't get it either… Why does he go by 'The Wizard' if he's not proud of being a wizard?"

"He got teased a lot at school for his real name," said Fabulon. "He was always getting in fights over it, and eventually got fed up with it. It took awhile for the nickname to stick, but he'd curse anyone he caught using his true name; eventually, it caught on."

The Arcane Armory

Jeff continued to pressure Fabulon into telling him The Wizard's real name for a few more minutes, but Fabulon would not budge. Gary sat by and said nothing, snickering at Jeff's tenacious curiosity. Eventually, Jeff gave up, changing the topic to The Wizard's childhood; Fabulon was happy to share stories of their youthful shenanigans, such as the time some mustachioed weirdo in a captains hat and cutoff jean shorts whisked them away in the night to the tragical realm of Neveragainland.

After twenty or so minutes, The Wizard walked out of the back room, scowling in annoyance. "Okay, assholes, I'm done. By the way, I couldn't make out the details, but I know you dicks were talking about me out here."

"Just reminiscing about old times." Fabulon grinned innocently. "You know I'd never say anything bad about you!"

The Wizard narrowed his eyes for a moment, then laughed. "If that were coming from anyone else, I'd think it was a lie...." He motioned for them to come to the doorway. "Well, come on; who wants to watch me blow this cat?"

"Don't say it like that..." muttered Gary.

They gathered around the doorway as The Wizard reentered the back room. Around the base of the cat machine, there was an intricate semicircle of scarlet symbols; leading from the machine to the doorway was a serpentine trail of smaller runes, with a small circle at their feet. Jeff was genuinely impressed with The Wizard's craftsmanship; he had to admit to himself that perhaps he did underestimate The Wizard's abilities, however slightly.

The Wizard kneeled down before the circle of runes. "Fabulon, would you mind conjuring a wall of force while I detonate this?"

"Not a problem." Fabulon stepped forward, waving his palms in circles with a focused look in his eyes. After a moment, the air in front of him began to wave and distort in a wide field, as though it were extremely hot.

"Alright, brace yourselves, that shield might not deflect all the debris." Placing his palms in the center of the circle, The Wizard muttered a short arcane verse.

The runes began to emit a glow as orange as The Wizard's beard.

Suddenly, Jeff tensed up. "Wait, what was that about debris?"

Chapter Eighteen

Unfortunately, it was too late; the magic circle was already glowing brightly, and the orange light was quickly creeping down the trail of runes like sparks on a fuse. It was all Jeff could do to shield his eyes and ears at the last moment.

With a deafening boom, the rear of the room filled up with writhing flames. Fabulon's wall seemed to be holding back the majority, but some of the fire blew through the corners of his shield. The sounds of shrapnel ricocheting echoed through the chamber.

Just when Jeff thought it was safe to uncover his eyes, an iron nut the size of his biggest knuckle flew straight at his face. For the first time in his life, Jeff felt grateful for his visual impairment, as the nut bounced off the left lens of his glasses; the lens shattered, but Jeff was able to shut his eyes in time. His glasses were flung off his face, and the other lens shattered as they struck the floor.

Dark smoke was pouring from the corners of Fabulon's shield. After the fire died down, he lowered his hands, and the wall of force dissipated; the reservoir of smoke immediately surged towards the group.

Everyone besides Gary began coughing violently, and ran out of the room, slamming the door; Gary seemed unaffected by the fumes, and calmly exited without even putting down his cigarette. He gently shut the door behind him.

Most of the smoke had been trapped in the rear chamber, but quite a bit of it had filled the air of the main basement. The Wizard, Fabulon, and Jeff began to feel lightheaded as they hurried up the stairs. Once again, Gary casually sauntered after them, in no hurry to escape the fumes.

"Damn, Gary," said The Wizard, his eyes wide as he watched this. "How much crack have you smoked?"

He laughed amiably, patting Gary on the back and grinning. It was not like he had smoked any less.

"I guess you could say I have special experience with harsh environments."

"Right, from all those years of living on the streets!"

"Or something like that...." Gary averted his eyes mysteriously.

"Either of you guys know any spells that could clear the air?" asked The Wizard, looking between the others. "Cleansing spells were never my forte."

The Arcane Armory

Shrugging, Fabulon smiled apologetically. "Sorry, I always had the Circle's custodiomancers to clean up after me."

"What about you, Gary?"

"Oh yeah, about that..." Scratching his head for a moment, Gary chuckled to himself. "I don't actually know any magic."

"What...?" The Wizard furrowed his brow skeptically. "You're kidding, right?"

"No, I just never had a knack for it."

"So you can't cast any spells? What the shit, dude?!"

"Hey, I never said I was a wizard!" Sneering, Gary poked The Wizard hard in the chest. "You just made that assumption."

"Because my dad hired you to guard me!" The Wizard shook his head, his mouth agape in incredulity. "How could you possibly protect me without magic?"

Gary held up his index finger for a moment. Taking a deep drag off his smoke, he cracked his knuckles. Suddenly, he spun around, delivering a forceful chop directly to Fabulon's larynx. As Fabulon staggered backward, Gary swiftly jabbed him in the eyes, before kneeing him in the gut. Leaping into the air, Gary slammed both of his feet down on Fabulon's neck. Springing backwards, he flipped through the air and landed spryly on his feet.

Smirking smugly, he crossed his arms. "That good enough for you?"

The Wizard stared, dumbfounded, as Fabulon attempted to sit up. Swaying erratically, Fabulon vomited on the floor, before collapsing into the pool of his own sick. Jeff stood up from the corner in which he was cowering, rushing to Fabulon's side and turning his face out of the pool of vomit.

"Okay, I see your point." Gulping timidly, The Wizard nodded. Before this, he had never considered Gary to be intimidating. "I still think it's pretty weird that my dad hired a magic virgin to be my bodyguard... but whatever, there's no time to address that at the moment...."

"We should probably open the door down there to let out the smoke," said Jeff.

"Right, good thinking," said The Wizard. "Gary, it seems going down there is gonna have to be your job."

Chapter Eighteen

"Says the guy who slammed that door in my face. If I were anyone else, I would have died." Gary crossed his arms, glaring bitterly at The Wizard.

"Uhh… sorry about that…."

"I'm just messing with you!" Chortling, Gary headed back down the stairs.

A few moments later, a billowing haze of dark fumes began pouring from the basement. The Wizard immediately fled to a nearby room, leaving Jeff to drag Fabulon out of the smoke. As he walked past, Gary grabbed Fabulon's ankle with his left hand, dragging him from the hall as though he weighed nothing.

They took shelter in a chamber a few rooms down the hall, far enough away to not be subjected to the odious vapors. It appeared to be one of The Wizard's father's old studies: the walls were lined with dusty bookshelves. Yawning, Gary tossed Fabulon onto a chaise lounge beside an empty fireplace, before lying down on the hearth. The Wizard began rifling through the bookshelves, checking behind the books.

"So, about my shattered glasses…" said Jeff, pausing to carefully consider his next words. He loathed asking The Wizard for help.

"Yeah, what about them?"

Jeff sighed in annoyance. He knew that The Wizard could tell what he was going to ask, and he also already knew what would likely be the answer. "If I found some of the pieces, could you repair them? I know my prescription."

The Wizard continued searching the bookshelves. "I've got better things to do, Jeff. Go ask my sister, she's always patching things together."

"I'd rather not end up with a pair of glasses that try to eat my eyes…. Also, what better things? Searching your daddy's study for his cocaine stash?"

"You don't know that's what I'm looking for!" Turning around, The Wizard put his hands on his hips and frowned indignantly. "Anyway, even if you found all the pieces, all I could do was glue them together, otherwise I'd ruin the prescription. If you don't want to ask Anasthasia, I think you're shit out of luck."

"Ugh, fine… I'll ask her…." As Jeff slouched out of the room, he almost slipped on a loose book he was unable to distinguish from the carpet.

268

The Arcane Armory

"Good, that ought to keep him out of our hair." Giving up his quest for cocaine, The Wizard relaxed into an armchair around the fireplace. "Now we wait... I'm pretty excited to see what we've uncovered. How was the smoke looking when you last checked?"

"We're not quite there yet." Sitting up, Gary crossed his legs and sparked up a smoke. "When I went down there, it was just clear enough for me to make out the vault door; it's still standing, and it looks unscathed by the blast."

"One step at a time. This is going a lot smoother than I expected." Absentmindedly, The Wizard snaked his hand under the cushion of the chair. His eyes suddenly lit up; when he withdrew his hand, he was holding a small baggie of white powder. "See what I mean? Thanks a lot, dad!"

Sliding one of the end tables in front of his seat, The Wizard poured the entire contents of the baggie onto the polished mahogany. He pulled his pocket knife from his robes, using the blade to chop the powder into one large, neat line. Tearing the title page out of a book he found on the floor, he rolled it up and snorted the entire line.

"Oh shit!" Smacking the table forcibly, he leapt to his feet and began to frantically pace back and forth. "That's not cocaine!"

Cracking up, Gary fell backwards; he was seemingly unphased when he bashed his head on the hearth. "That's what you get for not sharing! What was it?"

Furrowing his brow, The Wizard sniffled the powder into his mouth and swished it around for a moment. "Hmm... it's either non-dairy creamer... or pesticide...." He suddenly tensed up, keeled over, and vomited up a puddle of murky foam. "Okay... it's definitely pesticide...."

"Why would your dad keep pesticide in a dime bag?"

The Wizard continued to throw up mouthfuls of foam, speaking in between heaves. "It's an old... trick of his.... It was how... he would keep... me away... from his stash...."

"Damn, and I thought my dad was the devil!"

The Wizard chuckled, snorting vomit into his sinuses. "Oh, he wasn't *that* bad..."

It took awhile for him to finally get back on his feet. By the time his system was adequately purged, the others were already sitting around a

Chapter Eighteen

roaring fire. Fabulon had awoken shortly after The Wizard began vomiting; when he awoke, his memory of how he had fallen unconscious was fuzzy, so Gary took the liberty of explaining how Jeff had carelessly knocked over a suit of armor onto his head.

It had been plenty long enough for the noxious fumes to have ventilated out of the basement, so the three of them headed back towards the vault. Although the air was clear of heavy smoke, there was still an overwhelming smell of burning machinery.

The vault room was in complete shambles. There was a clearly defined threshold on the floor and walls from where Fabulon had conjured his wall of force; behind that line, the floor was blackened, and the walls were stripped of their panelling. The scorched remains of the cat machine littered the back of the room; the only piece that still stood was a small metal chair in the middle, in which sat a singed cat skeleton, wearing a mechanical helmet covered in severed wires.

Set into the rear wall, standing almost as tall as the cat machine had stood, was a heavy, brass vault door. Rather than a smooth surface, the entire vault seemed to be constructed of a massively intricate series of interlocking gears of all different sizes. There were three heavy brass bars spanning across the surface, and a keyhole the size of a man's head in the center.

"Damn..." said The Wizard, "I get a feeling we can't blast our way through *that*...."

As Jeff was weaving his way through the labyrinthine passages of Anasthasia's tower, he began to hear singing echoing from far away. He followed the sound towards its source. It was a beautiful female voice, melancholy and mysterious; when Jeff was able to make out the lyrics, he could tell that they were of the elven language. He approached the room from whence came the singing. The door was cracked open, so he peered inside.

The room was completely devoid of furniture. The hardwood floors were coated from end to end in dust, aside from a well-worn trail from the door to the fireplace. Jeff could not help but think that this tower had an awful lot of fireplaces for a building with no discernable chimneys. Sitting alone before a crackling fire, absent the company of her necrotic cronies, was Anasthasia. She stared deeply into the flames as she sang her mournful tune.

Jeff watched her sing for a moment, apprehensive to say anything. He wondered what she was singing about; there was a tone in her voice he had not yet heard, a sort of wistful longing.... Was it perhaps... love?

Forgetting that it was a door beside him, Jeff attempted to lean against it. He immediately collapsed into the room, a cloud of dust billowing around him as his face smashed into the floor.

Anasthasia ceased her singing, craning her neck to see what had happened. "Oh, it's you... I thought it might have been Vaharm... his legs give out a lot...."

"Sorry about that!" Blushing, Jeff hastily shuffled to his feet. "I didn't want to interrupt your song."

"Don't worry about it." Turning her gaze back to the fire, Anasthasia stared mournfully into its blazing depths. "It was just an old nursery rhyme my mom would sing to me...."

Unexpectedly, Jeff found himself feeling sympathetic towards her. "Well, I think it was lovely."

Anasthasia turned around and raised an eyebrow dubiously. "Are you hitting on me? Because I already told you that I'm bored with you."

"What?! Gross... you're my uncle's sister... that basically makes you my aunt...."

"If you say so," said Anasthasia, raising her eyebrows and smirking roguishly. "I think we both know you came to find me because you want something."

"Umm... yeah... I want you to fix my glasses...."

"Wait, seriously?" Huffing in outrage, Anasthasia frowned and crossed her arms. "Damn... I had this big rejection speech planned out and everything. You sure know how to disappoint a girl!"

"Right..." Jeff was not so sure about this anymore. "Look, I need your help. I broke my glasses in the basement. I looked around down there, and this is all I was able to find." Jeff held out the crushed frame of his glasses, as well as several shards of glass that may or may not have been part of the lenses. "Is there anything you can do to fix them?"

Chapter Eighteen

"What do I look like to you, an optometrist? Do you have any idea how hard it would be for me to get your prescription right? I'm already exhausted from making my brother's stupid cat talk. I came to my quiet place to relax, and not a half hour later, you show up and ask me to do more chores? In my own home?!"

"Okay, sorry... I'll leave you alone." Sighing dejectedly, Jeff turned to leave.

"Thank you." Anasthasia turned her gaze back to the crackling fire.

Jeff walked into the hall, feeling forlorn about the bleak circumstances surrounding his vision. However, he had only been walking for a minute or so when he heard the sound of hurried footsteps approaching from behind him.

"Hold on, Jeff!" Anasthasia clutched a nearby sconce for support, leaning over for a moment to catch her breath. "Damn, that enchantment wore me out... Anyway, I think I know a way I can help with your vision problem without having to expend any more magical energy."

"Really? That's excellent! What is it?"

"Just follow me upstairs, the supplies we'll need are in my laboratory." She turned and headed back the way from which they had come, gesturing for him to follow her.

"What, are you going to mix up a potion to help me see for a while?"

"There will be a potion involved in the process, yes."

Jeff was not sure he liked the way she phrased that, but nonetheless followed her up a nearby spiral staircase. They weaved through several more halls and up a few more staircases until they made their way to what must have been the penthouse of the tower. It was a round room, about fifty feet in diameter; although the walls had no windows, there was a massive domed skylight spanning the majority of the ceiling. The sky outside was bleak and stormy.

The room was decorated in a most peculiar manner. There was a white line sloppily painted down the middle of the floor, and on either side of it, the decor could not be more different.

One half was decorated like a princess's chambers, with a four-poster bed, several wardrobes, bookshelves, dressers, and a vanity, all made of polished white ash; the quilt and drapes of the bed were patterned like the clearest of night skies, so intricately detailed that every star seemed to twinkle in its own distinct way. There was a crystal ball at the foot of the bed, that was swirling with vivid images of the cosmos. The floor was covered in snow white carpet, and the walls lined with curtains as blue as the most brilliant of sapphires.

The other half of the room, on the other hand, was a horror show. Directly across from the bed, there was a steel operating table, with wrist clamps, and three leather straps hanging off the side. Next to the operating table was a metal tray, covered in all sorts of strange surgical instruments; some of them were still encrusted with blood. The floor appeared to have once been the same white carpet as the other half of the room, but at this point it was like carpeting a MacRoyalle butcher shop. Granite countertops lined the walls, covered in jars full of pickled organs and grotesque faces sewn from bits of flesh suspended in murky fluids. There were homemade charts and diagrams on the wall above, depicting all sorts of horrendous medical experiments.

"Oh, hell no!" yelled Jeff, as soon as he laid eyes on the haunting scene.

He turned and started to rush back down the stairs, but it was too late. His leg quickly grew numb, and looking down he found that Anasthasia had stuck him with a syringe. Slowly, he slumped down on the stairs, unable to move his legs; he could feel his arms starting to go as well. In a matter of seconds, he was completely paralyzed.

Anasthasia was standing over him. She placed a finger on her lips and shushed him. "Don't worry, it'll all be over soon." She grabbed his arms and dragged him to the top of the stairs.

Jeff's heart filled with terror. Yet another time, he was positive that he was about to be murdered. Although he could not move a muscle, he could feel the stairs as they bashed sharply between his vertebrae.

Once again short of breath, Anasthasia let go of Jeff's arms, dropping his head to the floor. She let out a sharp whistle; a moment later, Vahim and Vaharm both leapt out of one of her wardrobes. They hurried to her side, each bowing deeply before her.

"Would you two kindly move him onto the table?"

"As you wish, mistress."

They each grabbed Jeff by one end, carrying him to the operating table. One of Vahim's hands detached from his wrist around Jeff's ankle as they set him down, and Vaharm had to pry it off, none too gently. After stripping him down to his underwear, they clamped his wrists, and fastened the leather straps tightly around his neck, abdomen, and shins.

Standing next to the operating table, Anasthasia pulled a pair of rubber gloves onto her hands. She had changed her outfit into a blood-stained lab coat and scrubs, and had tied her hair in a ponytail. She walked over to the counter, returning with a small jar of yellowish liquid, in which floated two eyeballs. They seemed perfectly preserved, with sharp pupils and gleaming silver irises.

"I've been saving these for a special occasion!"

Although he attempted to scream as hard as he possibly could, no sound came out of Jeff's mouth. Instead, he lay in silent terror, perfectly still aside from his frantically darting pupils.

"Gas him."

Vaharm reached under the table, pulling out a cylindrical metal tank, with a dial connected to a rubber tube and respirator mask. He placed the respirator on Jeff's mouth, and turned the dial up all the way. Jeff instantly began feeling the effects of the anesthetic.

The last thing Jeff saw was Anasthasia using a grimy rag to wipe dried blood off a long, thin metal hook. As he blacked out, she leaned in and whispered softly in his ear; even with a lifetime of anesthesia, he would never forget those last few words she uttered...

"Welcome to the first day of the rest of your life."

Meanwhile, back downstairs, The Wizard and Fabulon had just finished magically sweeping the debris out of the way of the vault door; Gary had cracked open a bottle of wine, and was lounging in a heap of junk. When they stood before the vault, the true intricacy of the clockwork could be seen; The Wizard wondered if his father had contracted the legendary tinker-gnomes to build this door, for only they were known for craftsmanship this fine.

"Thanks for all the *help*, Gary," said The Wizard, sneering sarcastically. "Cleaning up those giant steel plates was a real breeze, you know."

The Arcane Armory

"I figured I'd just get in the way. You guys are the wizards, after all." Shrugging, Gary finished the second half of his bottle of wine in a single swig. He burped loudly in the others' direction; it smelled strongly of sulfur.

Gagging, The Wizard fanned the air back towards Gary.

"How do you guys reckon we should try to crack this vault?" asked Fabulon, plugging his nose.

"I have no fucking clue," said The Wizard.

"I think we should ask that handy little book," said Gary. "Do you have it on you?"

The Wizard dug around in his bag for a moment. "Fuck! I think I gave it back to Jeff. Who knows where he is...?" Sighing in exasperation, he leaned against the door.

Suddenly, a brilliant blue light began to pour from the keyhole. Slowly, the light expanded outward, gleaming from between each and every gear. As the light spread across the door, the clockwork began shifting.

"Oh shit!" yelled The Wizard, leaping away from the door. "What's happening? I hope this isn't my dad's security system..."

"No, look!" said Fabulon, pointing to the door.

The Wizard turned around to watch.

Without making a sound, the gears ground together. They moved and shifted position in one fluid motion, revealing a hole in the center leading to a further chamber. The hole quickly widened, moving outward until the gears locked together to form a massive, brass archway; beyond that, there was a well lit room, with the same houndstooth floor tiles, and red velvet curtains covering every wall. The chamber before them appeared to be completely empty, other than a crystal ball in the center, resting on a stone pedestal.

"Well, that was easy!" said Gary, jumping to his feet. "I expected it to take at least a few hours!"

Squinting at the doorway, The Wizard wracked his brain for an explanation. Suddenly, he remembered that he still had the copy of his dad's master key in his pocket; it must have knocked into the door. It had been so long since he needed it, he had forgotten it was there. Smiling impishly, he elected not to mention this to the others, leaving them both nonplussed.

Rubbing his palms together excitedly, Gary started towards the vault.

Chapter Eighteen

"Hold up," said The Wizard, extending an arm to stop him. "If I know my dad, this could easily be an illusion; for all we know, we walk through that door, and we get swallowed up and ground to mincemeat by those gears."

"Get out of my way, you big baby." Slapping The Wizard's hand out of the way, Gary strode confidently through the archway. When he reached the middle of the next room, he turned around, grinning proudly. "See what did I — *oh, what the hell?*"

He rushed back out of the room, cringing in disgust.

"Umm... what the fuck was that?" asked The Wizard.

"See for yourself..."

Tentatively, The Wizard inched through the archway. At first, he could not see what Gary meant, but then he turned around; standing in the corner, hastily pulling up his pants, was what appeared to be the monochromatic ghost of Ziro Xuntasi. Although his beard was just as magnificent, this version of Ziro looked much younger than he would have actually been.

"Dad...? What are you doing here? Are you dead?"

The hologram raised his ethereal eyebrows in surprise. After a moment, he said, "I'm not your dad, son."

"Well, then that wording is confusing."

"Quite. Sorry about that, I can see how you may have misunderstood. I'm not a ghost, you see: I'm a programmed personality projection of your father. I wanted to call myself a soulclone, but he insisted that I don't have one of those..."

"Are his pants on?!" shouted Gary from the other room.

"Yeah, you guys can come in." The Wizard scratched his head for a moment, before deciding just to ask the obvious question. "So... were you just hammering off in the corner?"

If he was not a monochromatic projection, Ziro's hologram would have likely blushed as red as a beet. "Well, I wasn't expecting guests! Anyway, like I was saying, I'm a hologram programmed with your father's personality. I also have all his memories, until he sealed me away, that is.... I'm basically him, so I suppose if you want to call me dad, that would be fine."

The Wizard cocked his head to the side. "So, hold on, are you saying my dad liked to hammer off in dark corners?"

The Arcane Armory

"Can you just move past that? I've been trapped here without sleep since Ziro sealed this room twenty years ago; I can't help that I get lonely!"

The Wizard raised an eyebrow. "But how does it even work? You're a hologram..."

"Well, I can't actually feel anything... but it's not so bad if I use my imagination."

Appalled, The Wizard gaped in disbelief. He could not believe this was once part of his dad's soul. "That's just about the saddest thing I've ever heard."

"Whatever, let's move past it," said Gary, barely holding back his laughter. "We came here for a reason. We are searching for the *Arcane Dictionary*."

"May I ask why?"

"Because of your former disciple, Mia Quan," said The Wizard. "She's the archmage now, and she's clearly become mad with power. She actually has your body held in some weird stasis chamber, and is siphoning your magical energy to power her schemes... whatever else they may be..."

Sighing, Ziro's hologram scratched his translucent beard in concern. "Ah, yes, I feared this day would come. It saddens me to hear that the real me's plan to stop her failed. Nonetheless, do not fret, your father was well prepared for this inevitability!"

"So you expected this to happen?" The Wizard's mouth slowly fell agape in astonishment. "You knew about her plans?"

"Indeed. I'm sorry I was never able to tell you, son. This corruption goes back further than even I understand; there has been a sickness eating away at the Circle for centuries, perhaps since its inception. It was all I could do to take the countermeasures I did, for if I involved you sooner, I would have been risking your life. I may not be your true father, but I have his heart, and I can say from the bottom of it that I wish you did not have to be swept up in this."

His arms crossed, Gary was tapping his foot loudly. "That's all very touching and all, but where is the *Arcane Dictionary*?"

"An impatient one, are you? Very well, but first allow me to give you the tour of Ziro Xuntasi's personal equipment research lab! Please humor me,

277

Chapter Eighteen

I've been waiting here without sleep for twenty years to be useful in literally this one way."

"Umm… okay.…" The Wizard could not help but think that this was a lot of information to take in for someone who had not done cocaine in hours.

Suddenly, the lights in the room went out. A spotlight appeared over the crystal ball in the middle, revealing Ziro's hologram to be hovering over it. He had magically changed out of his robes, and was now wearing a suit and bowtie. There was a holographic microphone floating in front of him.

"Welcome to everyone's favorite game show: *The Arcane Armory*!"

"I get a feeling he's had a bit too long to prepare," whispered The Wizard, nudging Fabulon.

"First up, who can guess what's behind curtain A?" Ziro's hologram snapped his fingers, pointing to the curtain to the groups' left; a second spotlight illuminated the curtain.

"Umm… is it the *Arcane Dictionary*?" Lighting a cigarette, Gary tapped his foot ever more impatiently.

"No, it is not! Looks like you're out of round one. Anyone else have a guess?"

Snorting, The Wizard smirked derisively. "Is it your sanity?"

"Another loser! One last guess for the steal!" He pointed to Fabulon, who was cast in yet another spotlight.

"Is it… weapons?"

"Ding, ding, ding! We have a winner!" Spinning around, he pointed with both hands to the curtain, which immediately rose to the ceiling.

The wall behind was covered in the same mahogany paneling as in the previous room. A series of lights shone from below, illuminating some of the strangest weapons any of them had ever seen.

In the center of the wall was the most magnificent magic minigun The Wizard could imagine. Its barrel consisted of six staves, all bound together by a series of brass rings. Where the rotor assembly would be, there instead was an elegantly carved mithril case, elliptically shaped with flowing curves. There were arcane runes carved all over its surface. There was a crystal orb inlayed into the mithril casing, where it met the barrel.

"This beauty here is my crown jewel; I call it the *Soul Gouger*. The orb is enchanted to pull energy from the arcane ether, converting it into a barrage of razor sharp magic that'll tear your foes asunder. Just make sure to give it breaks to cool off; those orbs have been known to explode, and that's my last one. You'll know when it's about to happen: the orb will glow red for like a second or two before it blows."

Above the minigun, there was a lengthy sniper rifle. Its barrel was a long tube of some sort of clear crystal, with two mithril rails flowing down the inside in a double helix. Below the scope, in place of a regular chamber, there was a gold gyroscope, spinning around a small, stationary orb of runed mithril.

"This long-ranged diamond here will tear apart the side of a house. The gyroscopic design gives it perfect balance. It's designed so the gyroscope spins exponentially, building up kinetic energy, before releasing a magical charge down the rails. It will magnetically launch those mithril balls with meteoric force. Just make sure there's something soft behind you, because of the kickback."

Resting on the floor was a flamethrower with a massive adamantium tank. Its hose and straps appeared to be made of red dragonhide, and the vicious looking adamantium nozzle was fashioned to look like a dragon's head.

"That thing down there is extremely dangerous, so I'd advise not letting anyone else use it. The heat it expels is hot enough to melt mithril, so I shouldn't have to tell you what it will do to flesh. It's powered by an entire advanced society of flame elementals residing inside the tank; don't worry that using it kills them though, it's gotten so overpopulated in there... I stopped visiting; they're total assholes."

Off to the right, there were two double barreled shotguns; though, where the barrels would be, there were bundles of wands fastened by brass rings. In the place of the hammer, there were two digital meters showing five green bars.

"A point-blank shot from one of these will blast your enemies' heads clean off. They fire concentrated blasts of pure arcane energy. Make sure to keep an eye on those gauges, so that the wands don't overheat. The barrels alternate fire to stay cool, but even so, keep them out of the red; you don't want to know what those will do to you if they backfire."

Off to the left, there were four mithril revolvers and a single gold one. Their handles were inscribed with identical sets of arcane runes.

279

Chapter Eighteen

"Finally, these little guns pack a punch. They are non-lethal, but a single shot to the head can knock a man unconscious. They are also completely silent. The revolving barrels are just an aesthetic choice, by the way, they don't require ammo. And no, the golden gun isn't better; it's actually a lot worse, it's heavy as fuck, and the barrel gets bent really easily...."

"Now, we're on to round two! Hopefully I'm not forgetting to mention anything..." Ziro's hologram snapped his fingers, causing all the spotlights to shine on him as he shimmied excitedly. "Who's ready to guess what's behind curtain B?"

"We don't have time for this shit, damn it!" Gary stomped over and ripped the curtain down from the wall.

"You're no fun..." Crossing his arms, the Zirogram sat on his crystal ball and pouted. "Fine, have it your way...."

The regular lighting came back on.

On the other wall, there were several magical devices. On the left, there was a series of hooks, on which hung a dozen amulets. To the right, there was a pair of jetpacks, with tanks forged of runed mithril. In the center, hovering above a small pedestal, was a magnificent catsuit; its body was made of sleek, dark fabric, and it had black, runed plates covering the joints. There were embossed mithril bracers on the wrists, with many buttons on each of them, as well as a mithril helmet with a quartz heads-up display. A black plate on its chest bore the label *Machina-X*.

"Woah, now that is a cool suit!" Running over, The Wizard inspected it closely. "I've got dibs on it, I don't even care if it works right."

"It does, just so you know," said Ziro's hologram. "It's got some history to it. Your grandfather developed the design for this suit, but never finished it. It was painstaking, but your father finally completed the project, before sealing me away with it. Fucking asshole..."

"You realize you're talking about yourself, right?"

"That's not how I self-identify anymore."

The Wizard rolled his eyes. "Whatever... what does it do?"

"I'm not explaining shit to you guys, you ruined my tour! Figure it out yourself."

"Ah, this brings back memories." The Wizard smiled fondly.

The Arcane Armory

"Look, I'm sorry I interrupted your tour," said Gary, struggling to mask his frustration. "Can you please just give us the quick one?"

"Fine. But I'm not going to explain how to use the *Machina-X*, it's super complicated. There's a manual tucked away under the pedestal it's on. Anyway, those amulets are enchanted with minor spell and projectile reflection, pretty basic stuff. On the other side, those are jetpacks. You know what a jetpack is, right? I shouldn't have to explain this shit."

"Finally, are you ready for what's behind the final curtain?!"

"Yes, damn it!" Groaning in exhaustion, Gary took a deep drag off his cigarette.

With a snap of his ethereal fingers, Ziro's hologram pointed to the back wall with both hands. The curtain dropped to the ground, and all of the spotlights centered on a pedestal. Resting on the carved stone surface of the pedestal, gleaming in the glow of the spotlights, was... *not* the *Arcane Dictionary*?! Instead, there was a metal box covered in runes, with a big red button on the top.

"What the hell?!" said Gary, pinching the bridge of his nose in exasperation. "Where's the *Dictionary*, and what is that?!"

"Anticlimactic is what it is..." muttered The Wizard. "I've never been so disappointed to see a big, red button."

Narrowing his eyes, Gary grinned facetiously. "If I press that button, will it show me where the *Dictionary* is?"

"Guys, calm down," said Fabulon. "Let him explain."

"Oh, don't worry about me, this is the most entertained I've been in the last twenty miserable years. Anyway, that right there is an A.M.P., an antimagic pulse device. Trust me, it'll be much more important than the *Dictionary* in a battle against the Circle. One press of that button will knock out all of their high-tech gear for over an hour."

"Fair enough," said The Wizard, "I suppose we don't *need* the *Arcane Dictionary*."

"What are you talking about?!" Angrily throwing his hands in the air, Gary lit another smoke and began to pace quickly. "Of course we need the *Dictionary*, it's a big part of our plan!"

"Well, to be fair, that was before we knew all this great gear was down here. Seems the plan has changed!"

Chapter Eighteen

His knuckles whitening, Gary looked like he wanted to put his cigarette out in someone's eye.

"Don't get ahead of yourselves, you two," said Ziro's hologram, floating in between Gary and The Wizard. "I never said I didn't have the *Dictionary*, I was getting to it. Remember, you agreed to let me give the tour!"

"Just show us where it is already!" said Gary, through gritted teeth.

"Okay, geez." Rolling his eyes, Ziro's hologram floated over to the crystal ball in the center of the room. A keypad appeared above the orb, and he quickly entered a code. The stone pedestal it was on began to rise out of the floor. "There you go, assholes."

In a cubby on the side of the stone pedestal, perched open against the back, was none other than the *Arcane Dictionary*. Its cover was coated in similar gold runes to those of the *Arcane Almanac*, and the symbol of the Arcane of Power glowed red in the center. As soon as it came into view, The Wizard could feel the power emanating from it.

A euphoric grin came over Gary's face. Dropping his cigarette, he ran up to the pedestal. He reached in and grabbed the *Arcane Dictionary*; however, as soon as he grasped it, a bolt of black lightning pulsed out of the book and up his arms. Letting out a pained yelp, Gary dropped the book to the floor. No one else seemed to notice the peculiar electric shock; The Wizard simply ran over and shoved Gary aside.

"Be careful with that, dude; it's a priceless artifact. Besides, you're the one who made such a fuss about finding it!

"Sorry, I must have gotten overexcited," said Gary, biting his lip. "I suppose I had best let you wizard's hold onto it, since it won't be much use to me."

"Yeah, no shit. I'll hold onto it... I can't trust Fabulon with books anymore."

"Dude, that was *one library book*, and I lost it *four years ago*! When are you going to move past that?"

"As soon as the library stops sending me bills."

"You still haven't paid them?! What happened to the twenty lun I gave you?"

"That was years ago, the interest has really built up."

The Arcane Armory

Fabulon shook his head and facepalmed. "Because you *didn't pay the bill*! Ugh... fine... I'll pay it off for you when we get back...."

"Thank you." Satisfied, The Wizard turned back to his dad's hologram and held up the *Dictionary*. He could feel a tingling sensation where he touched it, as though its power was stimulating his nerves. "So... mind explaining how this thing works?"

The hologram's frown immediately melted away. "I'd love to! This is my favorite part of the tour! Hmm... where to begin...?" He paused for a moment. "Well, I think before I tell you how to use it, I should explain its abilities and limitations.

"As you know, the most expert sorcerers must take hours to memorize the formula for even a simple spell. That's what makes this book so special: with it, you can instantly learn any spell you desire, as long as you understand the prerequisite magic."

"Wow!" The Wizard was amazed; he had only heard stories, and to hold the real thing felt unreal. "That's quite a step up from the copy of *Now That's What I Call Magic* I keep in my lab!"

"Yes, most indeed. However, it's power is not limitless; there are severe side effects that arise from its misuse. Since it triggers rapid neurogenesis in order to drill the spell into your memory, overusing it can cause brain swelling. One time, as a novice, I tried to learn too many spells at once, and my eyes started bleeding; I was lucky: I could have had a worse aneurysm, and then you never would have been born."

"Damn..." said The Wizard. "I'm glad we survived."

"I suppose I am, too; although, I have to admit, I've often fantasized about how if I had died before, I wouldn't have trapped myself here as a hologram.... Whatever, the past is the past.

"Anyway, there is one more thing that it's imperative you know: whatever you do, make absolutely sure you understand the fundamental prerequisites of a spell before you learn it. I never made this mistake, fortunately, but your grandfather told me stories about what it did to a few of his apprentices when they got their hands on the *Dictionary*."

"What happened to them?" Fabulon was eyeing the tome with a look of uncertainty.

Chapter Eighteen

"For one thing, they didn't actually learn the spells; moreover, they went completely insane. They had to be institutionalized, because they kept casting random cantrips on everything and babbling about how they had 'achieved godhood'. My dad took me to see them when he first gave me the *Dictionary*, as a cautionary example of what not to do.

"From what I could gather, they were trying to learn advanced teleportation when they couldn't so much as blink across a room. I'm not sure what our limitations would be, given our innate magical power, but I've always been careful not to press my luck with that book. I recommend you only use it to learn one spell a day, and only learn advanced spells if you know you can handle them."

"Okay, fair enough," said The Wizard. He covertly double-crossed his fingers behind his back. "So, mind telling me how to use it?"

"Simple, just open it to any page and focus on the spell you'd like to learn."

Sitting on the floor, The Wizard laid the book open before him. Closing his eyes, he placed his hand on the page. Suddenly, the pages began to glow with crimson runes, and an aurora of fiery energy flowed out of the pages and into him. His eyes snapped open, and he grinned enthusiastically.

"Huh, so that's how you cast a proper fireball!" He raised his hand to the ceiling, shooting a blast of fire into the air; it exploded over their heads like a firework. "And here I've just been making people's hair burst into flames when they provoke me.... Now, I wonder how to cast a lightning bolt that only shocks the target!"

"Wait just a second," said Ziro's hologram, wearing a stern expression. "Are you saying you didn't already know how to cast basic attack spells?! After all these years?!"

Averting his gaze, The Wizard grinned sheepishly. He was glad this version of his father could not physically hit him. "I know some... but I'm a magiscientist; most of my expertise falls in magical engineering, that's how I make my money. Until recently, I never thought I'd have to fight off anyone more threatening than a homeless junkie!"

His eyes wandered to Gary, who was chain smoking in the corner. He could not help but wonder where the hell Gary was getting all these cigarettes.

The Arcane Armory

Ziro's hologram rolled his eyes. "Well, whatever... as long as you have this gear, your inept spellcasting won't be of much consequence in your attack on Circle Tower."

Fabulon opened his mouth to protest, but The Wizard held up a finger to quell him.

"Word, this stuff is great. Now, as grateful as we all are for your help, is there anything more? Like, can we go now?"

"There is one more thing, actually."

"What is it?" The Wizard was extremely impatient to go outside and try out all these new weapons.

Sighing, Ziro's hologram slowly hovered to the back of the room. He snapped his fingers, and a hatch opened in the wall above the antimagic pulse device; inside the compartment, there was a similar device, scaled down to pocket size.

He gave The Wizard a solemn look. "Inside this cubby, there is an AMP specially tuned to my magical frequency. Would you kindly activate it? Don't worry, it won't affect any of the gear."

"Are you asking me to *kill you?*" said The Wizard. Even in the form of a programmed personality projection, this was still his father; it was difficult for him to imagine pulling the plug. "I can't do that..."

"Well, how about you two?" Ziro's hologram looked imploringly between the others.

Fabulon averted his gaze. After a moment, Gary grunted impatiently, before walking past Ziro's hologram and reaching into the cubby. As soon as his fingers touched the device, something unexpected happened: the device let out a high-pitched whine as lightning surged through it and up Gary's arm. As he withdrew his hand, the device let out a small explosion, shattering to pieces.

Ziro's hologram did not disappear; instead, he stared, dumbfounded, as his chance to stop existing seemingly stopped existing. "What the fuck happened?!"

"Oops," said Gary, scratching his head, "this is awkward."

"I can't believe it broke... I've been trying to activate that thing for twenty years, and it was a dud all along...."

285

Chapter Eighteen

"Uhh, yeah, a dud..." Subtly looking around, Gary fidgeted with his bowtie. "That's right!"

"Well, now that the seal on the door has been dispelled, can't you just come with us?" asked Fabulon.

"I suppose so, if one of you doesn't mind carrying that thing." Ziro's hologram pointed to the crystal ball on the center pedestal.

"Hey, I have an idea!" Suddenly running up to the pedestal, Gary shoved the crystal ball as hard as he could.

The orb soared through the air and out the door, yanking Ziro's hologram across the room. When it hit the floor, it cracked down the middle, and bounced a few times; as shards chipped off the orb, sparkling, blue magical energy rose out of the cracks and dissipated. With each impact, the hologram of Ziro faded into static, steadily becoming less focused each time it reappeared.

His mouth agape in a silent scream, the hologram slowly faded out of focus; I must emphasize how slowly this happened: it took about four minutes, and no one did anything but watch in silence. Suddenly, the fractured orb shattered into hundreds of shards of crystal, all of which immediately turned into energy and dissipated. As Ziro's hologram faded into nothingness, The Wizard could have sworn he saw him smile and give a thumbs-up at the last moment.

"Well, that's that," said The Wizard, shrugging nonchalantly and clapping his hands together. "Shall we adjourn to the courtyard and try out these weapons?"

While Fabulon and The Wizard started packing the gear into The Wizard's bag of holding, Gary wandered out of the vault, muttering something about carrying heavy shit not being in his job title. Paying him little heed, they loaded the equipment haphazardly into the bag. The antimagic pulse device was a little difficult to get through the mouth of the bag, but they eventually pulled it off.

Grinning enthusiastically, they started up the stairs, ready to test their new weapons on Anasthasia's garden.

Chapter Nineteen
Poor Preparation

ot long into the testing of their new gear, Fabulon and The Wizard had already completely destroyed Anasthasia's courtyard. By means of the minigun, nearly all of the beautiful red rose bushes had been blasted to bits, their frosty petals littering the snow. After they took turns trying out the flame thrower, they had thoroughly reduced a couple dozen of the forest's trees to ashes. Even the pistols had managed to knock the gate off its hinges until it would not stand back up.

The *Machina-X* gave The Wizard superhuman physical abilities. He was able to punch several sizable holes in the side of Anasthasia's tower, and even ripped a few trees out of the ground. He discovered a panel in its wrist bracers that seemed to control weapons functions, but gave up on testing that when he accidentally shot a grappling hook in his foot and maced himself in the eyes. He decided it would be best to figure out how it worked in action.

When The Wizard was testing out the sniper rifle, he discovered that it had a fantastic reloading mechanism: the runes on the mithril ball invoked a minor chronomancy, causing the object's time to reverse, flying back up the barrel while the golden gyroscope held the gun stable. In addition to the ball knocking the second door off the front of the tower on its arc of return, its impact caused The Wizard to fly back even further than he had from the gun's recoil.

Just as Fabulon and The Wizard were strapping on the jetpacks, Anasthasia stormed down the front steps. She scowled at them for a moment,

Chapter Nineteen

tapping her foot with her hands on her hips, waiting for them to turn around. The Wizard felt his hair turn on end, and he slowly looked behind him.

"Oh, hi sis, what's going on?" asked The Wizard, grinning sheepishly.

Her scowl intensified. "Are *you* really the one who should be asking that question?"

"Fair enough, I guess you do deserve an explanation." The Wizard was eager to change the subject. "So... where's Jeff?"

"Don't worry about it. I thought you said I deserve an explanation."

Averting his eyes, The Wizard crossed his fingers behind his back, hoping Anasthasia would not flip out on him. He had always been wary of her murderous rages. "Isn't this situation self explanatory?"

Fabulon looked as though he wished he could stop existing, almost as much as Ziro Xuntasi's hologram had. He had only ever seen The Wizard look this nervous when facing his father in the flesh.

After a tense moment of silence, Anasthasia laughed. "I suppose you're right. Anyway, I'm impressed: I tried to blast apart those rose bushes with my best spells, and they always came back. I always hated this garden; flowers are gross, they attract bugs."

"Okay, that's a satisfying enough answer," said The Wizard. "But aren't you upset about the door?"

"I'll just have Vahim and Vaharm build me a new one. That reminds me, I sent them into town to pick up some food and drugs. I presume you're out of cocaine?"

"Indeed I am, and this snow has been making me jones for some more." The Wizard looked happy for a moment, before a look of panicked realization crossed his face. "Hold on, did you just say you sent your *undead minions* into town to get our supplies? We're supposed to be in hiding! Don't you think that might raise some red flags?"

"No need to freak out. I fashioned them each a skin suit long ago!" Anasthasia paused for a moment, waiting for a response. "Oh, don't look at me like that, I didn't take the skin from *living* humans! There's a morgue in Asberg, two towns over."

It was The Wizard's turn to look outraged. "Then why did you give one of them my grandmother's ribcage?!"

Anasthasia shrugged. "It fit."

Poor Preparation

"Ugh... fine, whatever, I'll move past it. I presume you're paying for this cocaine?"

"Don't worry: naturally, I assumed you weren't," said Anasthasia, giggling to herself.

The Wizard scowled.

"I don't like the sound of this," said Fabulon. "There's no doubt those two skeletons will attract unwanted attention. We should head inside and solidify our strategy for the battle, lest it take us by surprise."

"For once, I agree with you," said The Wizard. "With those two idiots, I honestly wouldn't be surprised if Quan's agents were on us by nightfall."

"You guys are crazy," said Anasthasia, rolling her eyes. "You underestimate my craftsmanship on their skin suits."

Sighing deeply, The Wizard crossed his arms in frustration. "As much practice as I'm sure you've had, I doubt professional sorcerers will have any problem seeing through your 'disguises'."

"Whatever," said Anasthasia, "but answer me this: would you rather them come back with cocaine, or have not gone out at all?"

The Wizard did not answer; instead, he and Fabulon hurriedly stowed their weaponry before rushing up the stairs. Anasthasia followed behind them after another thorough roll of her eyes.

They headed towards the dining chambers, intent on laying out the specifics of their battle strategy. However, when they threw open the double doors to the dining room, their priorities of thought shifted instantly.

First, they noticed that Knippe and Knorpe were strung up by their ankles by the mantlepiece, dangling before the fire, their hair singed. Kit Mingers was sitting in the chair at the head of the table, purring loudly in a heap of catnip; it seemed he had retrieved the catnip from Anasthasia's workshop, but how he got it there was anyone's guess. Chris was sitting directly to his left, smoking a cigar and looking equally satisfied.

"What's been going on here?" asked The Wizard; he approved of the situation.

"These little shits attacked me," said Kit Mingers. "They ganged up on me like a couple of pussycats, so naturally I kicked the shit out of them both. Your friend here helped me by tying them up."

Chapter Nineteen

"It was the least I could do," said Chris, taking a deep puff off of his cigar. "The little one punched me in the nuts earlier and ran off with my wallet."

"Which one's the little one?" asked Fabulon.

"Forget that..." Frowning, The Wizard squinted at the cigar on which Chris was puffing. "Where exactly did you get that cigar? Did you get into one of my dad's old stashes?"

"This ain't no cigar!" Grinning, Chris reached into his pocket and tossed one to The Wizard. "But it definitely came from one of your dad's stashes!"

The Wizard's scowl immediately melted into a look of satisfaction as he raised the blunt to his lips, sparking it to life with a snap of his fingers. As he took his seat at the end of the table opposite the fireplace, he took a deep puff. However, he was met with a deep disappointment.

"This shit is stale as fuck!" Coughing and gagging, The Wizard threw the blunt at the wall. "How can you smoke that garbage?"

One of the tapestries lining the wall burst into flame as the cigar struck its tasseled base; no one paid it much attention, not even Anasthasia. Even as the fire spread to the neighboring tapestries, no one seemed to care. If Jeff were there, I am sure he would have said something about the absurdity of their nonchalance.

"I ain't picky." Shrugging, Chris took a massive toke of his stale blunt. "The doctors always said I had 'a Freudian complex of putting phallises in my mouth'."

This did not surprise The Wizard. "Fair enough, that makes sense."

Fabulon had taken his seat, at a safe distance from Chris's handsy grasp. "So, should we discuss our plan for the upcoming battle?"

"Oh, come on, that's so boring," said Anasthasia. "Wouldn't you rather hear what I did to your friend Jeff?"

"That's not important!" Scowling, The Wizard waved his hand dismissively. "It's imperative we plan our strategy, since your skeletal stooges will no doubt rat us out to the Circle."

"You underestimate the loyalty afforded by their fear of me."

The Wizard ignored her, just as he had during her childhood; he turned to Fabulon, with a doubtful look on his face. "Well, you're the one with the inside intel; have you formulated a strategy?"

Poor Preparation

Furrowing his brow, Fabulon scratched his chin thoughtfully. "Well, as we discussed before, there will be mages stationed around Circle Tower as guards. Our first step should be to knock out the beacon they're to use to alert the higher level magi; I was wracking my brain on how we'd accomplish this, until your dad showed us that AMP device. I'm certain he intended it to be used to knock out their communications."

As they talked, the fire burned away the tapestries to reveal the hidden staircase from whence the gnomes had dragged Chris prior that day.

"Alright, but do you know how to go about that?" asked The Wizard. "Circle Tower's walls are imbued with antimagic, so we'd have to somehow get the AMP inside of the tower; I assume that's where the beacon is located."

"That's where my inside agent comes in," said Fabulon. "She was recently promoted to a high level position in the Circle; even with the heightened security, I've no doubt she'll be able to smuggle it in under the pretext of transporting supplies."

"Really? Why would you say that?"

"Because she's been assigned to be the personal assistant of the head Circle inspector assigned to your case."

This genuinely impressed The Wizard. "Wow, I underestimated you, Fabulon; how did you get such a high ranking member of the Circle to agree to help you?"

"Well, I've got to say, she was reluctant to help at first, although perhaps not for the reasons you might expect..." Shifting awkwardly, Fabulon averted his eyes.

"Meaning?"

"Umm... well... she was willing to help when I explained the gravity of the situation... but... she wasn't exactly thrilled... when I told her it was to help you."

The Wizard scoffed defensively. "Wow, that's cold; who is she, and what exactly is her problem with me?"

"Hang on..." Rolling up his sleeve, Fabulon revealed a small crystal orb attached to a leather strap around his wrist. "Let me call her; she said she'd rather tell you that herself."

Chapter Nineteen

The fire was burning close to the ceiling now, leaving black marks on the rafters. Groaning, Anasthasia held up her hands, shooting forth a cone of icy wind which mostly extinguished the flames. All that remained of the blaze were a few smouldering edges of the tapestries.

"Her and me both," yelled Knorpe, who was currently swinging in and out of the fireplace as a regretful result of attempting to free himself. "I have about a million problems with you right now!"

"Amen to that..." muttered Kit Mingers. "That's the first thing you've ever said that didn't make me want to bite your face off. Anyway, I told you both to shut up or I'd push you in the fire again."

Pouting in silence, The Wizard watched Fabulon type a number into a superimposed keypad hovering over his wristbound crystal ball. He wondered who it was that they were calling; even he knew that the list of people who did not like him was very long. Once Fabulon completed dialing, a loud ringing began to reverberate throughout the room.

A few moments later, a woman's form was projected via hologram over Fabulon's wristorb: it was none other than The Wizard's previous assistant, Samantha Spellman.

Without a moment's hesitation upon realizing who it was, The Wizard began to panic. "Are you crazy, Fabulon?! She's going to turn us in straight to Quan!"

Samantha's hologram grinned nastily. "As much as it would serve you right, I have reasons not to do that. First of all, when I refused to spy on you, that bitch Quan demoted me to Inspector Perkins' assistant; those fucking sycophants at the Circle are calling it a promotion, but I beg to differ, given his disposition."

"I can see that," said Fabulon and The Wizard in unison; they both seemed surprised, although with polar opposite attitudes towards it, as they had never jinxed before.

"Anyway," continued Samantha, "Fabulon told me about how Quan is holding your dad hostage, and how she framed you for treason. Naturally, I was skeptical, but he eventually convinced me otherwise."

Suddenly, The Wizard's level of interest seemed to drastically increase. "What's this about her framing me for treason?"

292

Poor Preparation

"Right, I should have mentioned it sooner," said Fabulon, "but Quan's convinced the Circle council that you not only killed your father, but that you raided the entire artifact vault."

"That and about a dozen other things," said Samantha, "about half of which I don't doubt are true." Her hologram swiveled around to face Fabulon. "So, I assume that since you've called me, you're ready to proceed with our plan?"

"Actually, our plan has changed," said Fabulon. "Quite in our favor, if I do say so; we now actually have a solid plan, as opposed to a disorganized raid."

"That's good, because a full frontal attack on the Circle would probably get you all killed. I doubt my distraction would have been much help. So, what's our new plan?"

"Well, our part of the plan hasn't changed, but we're much better equipped now. We've got weapons made by The Wizard's dad!" Fabulon grinned stupidly.

Samantha shook her head and facepalmed. "I hope that isn't all that you called to tell me. You're going to be outnumbered ten to one, and they'll have top of the line gear as well; I doubt any amount of fancy weapons will save you."

Fabulon grinned even wider, his confidence unshaken. "Did I mention that you're going to take out all of their equipment?"

"That's not what I agreed to!" Scowling, Samantha put her holographic hands on her hips. "You said all I'd have to do is slip that seizure poison into Perkins' lunch to distract some of the guards! I refuse to tamper with their equipment, it's too risky."

"I kind of like that first plan," said The Wizard. "I didn't know you had that in you, Fabulon!"

"Now, don't you worry!" Winking at Samantha, Fabulon wiggled his eyebrows in a way *he* did not think was off putting. "You won't have to touch any of their equipment. We've got an antimagic pulse for you to detonate in Circle Tower!"

"Seriously? You know those things aren't very effective, right? Even the ones the Circle has can only disrupt enchantments in about a ten-meter radius."

Chapter Nineteen

"Not this one; The Wizard's dad built it!"

Sighing, Samantha shook her head. "You keep saying that, and you seem really confident... How old exactly are these things? No one has seen Ziro in years."

"We tested most of them," said Fabulon. "They all worked great, although I must admit it isn't the most orthodox equipment. I'm sure the AMP will work, and knock out their weapons as well as Quan's emergency beacon."

"Whatever, no skin off my bones if it fails. I'm not the one who's going to die if this half-cocked plan doesn't work."

"So, what's the situation at Circle Tower?" asked The Wizard.

"Shut up," said Samantha. "I don't want to talk to you."

"Seriously, what's the situation at Circle Tower?" asked Fabulon.

"About the same as when you left: most of Quan's agents are still looking for you, but she has a powerful regiment stationed at the tower."

"Unbelievable..." muttered The Wizard.

"That's good," said Fabulon, "I'm happy to hear nothing's changed. Now we just have to figure out a way for you to smuggle it in; leave that to us. We'll contact you when we're in town, and then we can meet up and prepare."

Samantha did not look convinced. "Sure, if you say so. I really hope only The Wizard dies. I'll talk to you later, Fabulon; be safe." She clicked on her wristorb and faded out of view.

"Did she just wish I'd die?" asked The Wizard.

"Forget that!" Walking out of the kitchen, Anasthasia was carrying a tray of hors d'oeuvres, and had several bottles of wine under her arms. "We should enjoy ourselves in case tonight is our last night alive. I wasn't listening to most of that conversation, but it sounds like we have a tough battle ahead of us."

Surprised, The Wizard raised his eyebrows. "You're coming with?"

Anasthasia rolled her eyes. "Of course I am; I'll do whatever it takes to help save dad. Did you really think I was gonna hang back and play with Jeff all week?"

Narrowing his eyes, The Wizard cocked his head at Anasthasia. "Okay, about that, what *did* you do with Jeff?"

"Don't worry about it."

Poor Preparation

"Worry about us!" shouted Knippe. "They kick us into the fire whenever we talk!"

"Shut up." The Wizard held up his hand, causing both Knippe and Knorpe to swing back and forth on their ropes, in and out of the fire.

The room filled with the smell of burnt hair as the gnomes yelped in pain. It seemed their bonds were enchanted to resist the flames.

"What are those tantalizing pastries?" Licking his lips, Chris eyed the tray Anasthasia was carrying. "They look delicious."

"Why did you bring these vultures to my house?" asked Anasthasia, scowling at The Wizard.

Chris fell silent.

Scoffing, The Wizard raised his hands incredulously. "I didn't! *You* let them in; nobody asked you to do that!"

"Actually, I did," said Fabulon.

"Whatever, he can't have any of my pizza rolls; I microwaved them myself. Since we're probably going to die, I guess you can all have a few bottles of wine, but you have to get them yourselves." Setting the tray on the table, Anasthasia uncorked a bottle of wine and took a hearty swig.

"Fair enough, that sounds good to me." Leaping out of his seat, The Wizard started towards the hall. "I'm glad we got all that shop talk wrapped up."

Biting his lower lip, Fabulon held out a hand to stop him. "Are you serious? We still have to discuss our plan of action. There will probably be a massive confrontation. Not to mention, we still haven't even figured out how Samantha will get that massive AMP into Circle Tower!"

"She can borrow my bag of holding, okay? Problem solved. As for the battle, I'm just planning to wing it. I'll be fine, I've got the *Machina-X*." He raised his wrist towards the smouldering tapestries and pressed one of the buttons; a small nozzle came out of the bracer, spraying white foam all over the embers and extinguishing them. "See, I actually got it to work that time! I'm sure we'll nail it."

Sighing, Fabulon watched as The Wizard hurried into the hallway and slammed the double doors behind him.

Chapter Nineteen

When Jeff awoke on the cold steel of the operating table, it took him a while to remember where he was. A faint prickling sensation was running through his entire body. The room was dark, aside from a dim glow coming from the far side. He blinked blearily at the ceiling for a moment, wondering why his eyes ached. As he sat up, he felt the loose leather straps of the table slide off of him. He looked in the direction of the glow.

It was coming from a crystal orb at the base of a four-poster bed, swirling with peculiar images of faraway galaxies. Next to it, lying on the foot of the bed, was the backpack Merlin had given him.

Jeff realized how clearly he could see the visions in the orb; he could even make out Merlin's name stitched into his backpack. Even colors looked more vivid than usual. He felt his face, and noticed that his glasses were gone, as well as his eyebrows. Suddenly, it all came rushing back to him. He remembered Anasthasia drugging him, having him strapped to the table, and the horrible moments before he had lost consciousness.

Shuddering, he stepped down onto the slightly moist carpet and tried to stand up. He found that his legs tingled intensely when he put pressure on them. As he staggered towards the bed, he was glad that Anasthasia had left his clothes and shoes on... or at least put them back on; what happened after he lost consciousness was anyone's guess. When he made it across the room, he collapsed onto the silken covers of the bed. As he clasped his backpack, he felt his mind slowly drift away.

It must not have been much longer when he awoke, because Jeff's body still tingled at the corners. He sat up much faster this time, acutely aware of where he was. The light of the fantastical orb illuminated his look of panic. Grabbing his bag, he hurried towards the stairs. As he made his way down the stairwell, he noticed that he could see curiously well, despite the lack of torches.

Finally, coming through the door at the base of the stairs, he found himself in an unfamiliar hallway illuminated by cold, blue torches. Unfortunately, he found the layout of this tower very confusing, and did not remember the path he and Anasthasia had taken. Groaning wearily, he headed down the hallway, trying every door in hopes of finding a staircase.

Oh, the things he saw...

Poor Preparation

When The Wizard staggered drunkenly back into the dining hall, the air was ripe with the smell of tobacco. Sitting at the table, Gary and Fabulon were deeply engrossed in conversation, while Chris stared longingly at Fabulon's hands. They seemed to be discussing their plan of action for the raid on Circle Tower. Anasthasia was sitting with her seat turned around, sipping wine and watching as Kit Mingers batted the crying gnomes around the fire.

The Wizard reached into his bag of holding, pulling out bottle after bottle of wine. He placed at least twenty bottles onto the table, several of which were already empty. Cracking one open and taking a swig, he looked around the others.

"Well, come on guys, I brought enough wine for everyone." Grinning, he hiccupped loudly. "I hope you don't mind that I drank a few on the way back. Even the gnomes can have a couple; I say we let them down!"

"I disagree." Ceasing his play, Kit Mingers shot The Wizard a look of concern. "There's no telling what these fucks will try once they're good and drunk."

"Come on, Kit, they'll be fine." Staggering drunkenly, The Wizard approached the gnomes. "Everyone deserves the chance to get right proper as fuck before they die."

Knippe and Knorpe both blew raspberries at the cat as The Wizard began to loosen their bonds.

Growling, Kit Mingers flexed his claws. "I hate that stupid terminology for intoxication; it doesn't even make sense. You guys are morons." He hurried away from the gnomes before they were untied, storming into the kitchen in a huff.

"Huh, who knew my cat was such a buzzkill. He'd get along well with Jeff."

"Thank you so much," said Knippe, as The Wizard untied him. "It feels so good to be allowed to talk again."

"Don't make me regret this."

"We won't!" With feigned innocence, Knorpe fluttered his eyelashes at The Wizard. "I promise we won't do anything to *you*."

The gnomes both stretched for a moment after they were untied. Each grabbing a bottle of wine, they darted away in unison, giggling wildly. They ran through the ashen remains of the burnt tapestries, up a previously-hidden passage leading upstairs.

"Oh, good, they're gone," said Anasthasia. "I was getting bored of their squirming."

"I still don't understand those guys, but at least they said 'thank you'." Chugging the remainder of his bottle of wine, The Wizard took his seat at the table. Looking around at the others, he gestured to the variety of vino. "Well, are you boys gonna join this party, or what?"

Chris got up and walked over to the smorgasbord of wine, grabbing himself a bottle. Biting his lip apprehensively, Fabulon followed suit. Gary had already finished his first bottle, but was happy to grab himself a second before sauntering into the kitchen.

"Here's to not dying tomorrow!" Grinning, The Wizard held up a fresh bottle in a toast.

And so it was, with almost certain defeat looming over their heads, that our... let's just say "heroes"... got right proper as fuck.

Jeff had been wandering the house for what felt like hours. As he explored, he noticed a strange phenomenon occurring with his vision: in addition to being able to see clearly, even in the darkness, his perception of color seemed to have been exceptionally heightened. He felt his visual cortex struggle to process subtle differences in hues he could have never before fathomed. Frankly, it was giving him a splitting headache.

As he made his way down yet another staircase, he began to hear merriment taking place below him. He hurried towards the sounds of laughter and clinking silverware. When he reached the hall at the base of the stairs, he noticed the flickering of shadows through an open doorway.

Peering inside, Jeff saw Knippe and Knorpe engaging in a ferocious knife fight. Behind them, a fire crackled softly in the fireplace, burning what appeared to be splintered picture frames and the paintings they had contained. As his eyes adjusted from the bright blue torches to the dimly flickering flames, Jeff was overwhelmed with color. His sensitivity to color seemed to be most severe in low light.

The gnomes giggled gleefully as they effortlessly parried each other's attacks; there was no doubt in Jeff's mind that they had done this before. It

Poor Preparation

was uncanny how identical their fighting styles were; it seemed they were quite literally evenly matched. After a moment, they noticed him and ceased their festivities.

"Where did you come from?" Jumping, Knippe turned his blade in Jeff's direction.

Knorpe's blade followed. "Have you been spying on us?"

"No, I'm lost, you fucking idiots. Where's everyone else?"

The gnomes did not lower their blades.

"Why should we tell you?" Grinning wickedly, Knorpe flourished his knife. "You haven't played our game yet!"

Sighing, Jeff continued down the hallway, unsure of why he had ever thought the gnomes would be helpful. He heard them talking shit about him as he walked away from the room. As he headed down the hall, he hesitantly checked behind more doorways for anything that looked familiar.

As he turned a corner, Jeff saw a strange painting on the wall. It was not strange because of the fact that it was a nude portrait of The Wizard's dad, as those were perfectly normal in this tower; it was strange because it was hanging partially open, revealing an unlit staircase behind it. Jeff was sure that he could not get more lost than he already was, so he headed down the staircase.

There was firelight flickering through an opening at the bottom of the staircase. At least a hundred feet of stairs stretched before Jeff, and he could not help but remark on how enormous this tower was. Despite the absence of torches down the stairwell, he found that his eyes once again adapted extremely well to the darkness. As he descended the stairs, Jeff began to hear voices coming from below. It was not long before he was surprised by what he found at the bottom.

When he reached the doorway at the bottom of the stairs, he saw that it led to the dining hall through one of the side walls. The ground at the foot of the stairs was coated in scorch marks and ashes. At the end of the dining table, sat The Wizard, Anasthasia, and Chris. Fabulon had passed out in his seat a few chairs down the table, and was snoring in a pool of his own drool.

"I can't believe he passed out after only two glasses of wine," said The Wizard, smirking at Fabulon.

299

Chapter Nineteen

"We should draw a face on his penis!" Grinning excitedly, Chris pulled out a magic marker.

Anasthasia raised an eyebrow. "Do you mean a penis on his face?"

"Uh, sure, I guess we could do that instead..." Halfheartedly, Chris drew an extremely veiny phallus on Fabulon's forehead.

"Oh, hi, Jeff." Without really looking, The Wizard waved lazily in Jeff's direction. "Where have you been all this time?"

"Why don't you ask her?" Jerking his thumb at Anasthasia, Jeff crossed his arms and glowered vehemently at her.

"Nevermind, I don't really care." Leaning back, The Wizard patted the seat of an empty chair beside him. "Why don't you take a seat and crack open a bottle of wine? Pass me another while you're at it."

"Oh, for crying out loud!" Jeff threw his hands in the air angrily. "Your psycho sister drugged me and surgically replaced my eyes with some pickled eyes from a jar! Saying that all out loud, it somehow sounds more insane than it actually was... It was honestly the most horrifying thing that has ever happened to me...."

"You're exaggerating." Scoffing, Anasthasia rolled her eyes. "It wasn't that bad. I fixed your vision problems, didn't I?"

Shaking with rage, Jeff pointed accusatorily at her. "You drugged me without my consent, gouged out my eyes, and stuck some random replacements in the holes!"

Looking extremely uncomfortable, Chris averted his eyes and continued to draw highly detailed penises all over Fabulon's face.

"They aren't 'random', thank you very much." Anasthasia put her hands on her hips, scowling indignantly. "Those eyes are quite special to me; they were my dear mother's eyes."

"That's absolutely horrible!" His mouth agape, Jeff shook his head in disbelief. "Why the hell would you have those?"

"It wasn't easy to sneak them out of the funeral, let me tell you!" Chuckling, Anasthasia nodded reminiscently. "Anyway, those are elf eyes, and they're a hell of a lot better than your old ones! You know, all elven females have tetrachromatic vision. You should count yourself lucky that your body didn't reject them!"

Poor Preparation

"Yeah, and now you're officially a part of the family!" The Wizard raised his bottle in a toast to Jeff, before taking a hefty swig.

"I'm your nephew, dude..."

"Yeah, but now you're part of the good side!"

"Do you seriously have nothing to say about the fact that she drugged me and used me in some ludicrous surgical experiment?!" asked Jeff, through gritted teeth.

Burping loudly, The Wizard shrugged. "Sounds like she did you a favor. You can see now, can't you? Anyway, while you two were busy playing doctor, we tracked down the *Arcane Dictionary*. It was hidden in a vault with a bunch of my dad's personal gear; check out this awesome battle suit."

He leapt out of his seat, sprinted across the room, and dashed up the wall, flipping in circles until he landed on the table with catlike agility.

"Fucking unbelievable..." muttered Jeff.

"Right? And I'm doing that drunk as shit! This is the coolest thing I've ever worn!"

Chris nodded in approval. His hands had moved below the table, and it was unclear if their stroking motions were still him drawing anything.

"No, asshole!" Trembling furiously, Jeff slid his palm down his face "What is unbelievable is how much of a prick you are! I could have died, and as usual, that doesn't matter to you at all! Why would I want to be a part of this family, when everyone in it is insane?!"

"You were never in any *real* danger!" Rolling her eyes, Anasthasia waved her hand dismissively. "It's not like I have no experience; I've done similar surgeries on no less than eight cats!"

Kit Mingers poked his head out of the kitchen, wearing a shocked expression.

"Everything worked out fine, Jeff," said The Wizard. "You should just relax and get fucked up with us. There's a good chance half of us will die tomorrow."

"Hold on, you're not seriously thinking of facing the Circle already, are you?!" asked Jeff. "Just because you found some fancy weapons doesn't mean you have what it takes. What happened to training with the *Arcane Dictionary*?"

Chapter Nineteen

"Plans changed, Jeff. Turns out we're gonna have to wing it. Anasthasia sent her skeletons into town to get supplies, and thanks to that, it's only a matter of time before the Circle's agents track us down."

Pinching the bridge of his nose in frustration, Jeff shook his head. The absence of glasses still felt foreign to him. He shot Anasthasia an incredulous look. "Why would you do that?!"

Smiling innocently, Anasthasia shrugged.

"She's insane, Jeff," said The Wizard. "Try to keep up."

"You're all insane..." Sighing in exasperation, Jeff finally gave in, taking a seat at the table and uncorking one of the many bottles of wine. "I can't believe I'm stuck spending what might be my last night alive with you."

The Wizard chuckled, rolling his eyes. "I was just joking about half of us dying. We'll probably be fine, Jeff. We've got the element of surprise on our side. Quan's seriously underestimating us, and she's left her forces spread hella thin."

Shaking his head, Jeff gave him a flat stare. "First of all, don't say 'hella' when you're discussing military strategy. Secondly, I'm not as confident as you are that we'll be fine if we 'wing it'. This is a very serious situation. Do you even know how to use any of this gear you just found?"

"I think I'm getting the hang of it. Don't even sweat it, Jeff."

"Yeah, *Jeff*, calm the fuck down." Smirking snidely, Anasthasia leered at Jeff. "If I knew this was how you'd behave at dinner, I'd have never unstrapped you from that operating table."

Nearing the end of his rope, Jeff shook his head. Hoping it would help his mood, he took a powerful pull from his bottle of wine. He looked deep into the glimmering grain of the polished tabletop, lamenting more than ever the choices that had led him to this unsavory situation.

They continued to down wine for nearly an hour. As Anasthasia and The Wizard began to wildly speculate what the gnomes could be up to, Jeff remained silent, staring intently downward. Chris had passed out on Fabulon's lap, and was snoring loudly.

Suddenly, the double doors at the front of the room swung open. Vahim and Vaharm rushed into the room, carrying several large paper bags full of supplies and sundries. They placed the bags on the table in a hurry, knocking over several bottles of wine.

Poor Preparation

The skin suits Anasthasia had fashioned for them were preposterous and grotesque. Stitched together from scraps of discolored skin, they hung from the skeletons' mishmash of random bones like leathery garbage bags. They were nauseatingly loose in some places, and unnaturally tight in others. Vahim and Vaharm looked like a couple of Horners.

The only part of their disguises that looked remotely human were the pair of obviously female wigs askew on each of their heads.

Their bones were chattering furiously, and although it was difficult to read their expressions, it was clear they were panicking.

Vaharm stepped forward after a moment of silence. "Umm... mistress... I'm afraid we have some bad news...."

Gasping, Anasthasia clasped her head in panic. "Don't tell me they were out of cocaine!"

"Damn it..." Groaning, The Wizard knocked his head slowly against the table. "I knew this shit would happen."

Anasthasia held up her index finger. "Now, hold on, you haven't let them answer yet; maybe the bad news isn't about the cocaine after all."

"Of course it isn't about the damn cocaine!" Eyes flashing angrily, The Wizard banged his fist on the table. "They were probably seen."

"We were not seen, fortunately," said Vahim. "However, when we were leaving the market, we spotted some men in cloaks questioning a few of the locals."

"They may have briefly glimpsed us, but I'm pretty sure we dodged out of view in time," said Vaharm. "We listened in on their conversation for a moment, and they were asking about sorcerers living in the area."

"Yeah, they said there's a ten thousand sol reward for your brother's capture."

Setting the bags of groceries on the table, the skeletons sat down at their mistress's side.

Anasthasia grinned optimistically. "I think the important thing to take away here is that I was right: you guys didn't get us caught after all!"

"The important thing to take away is that we're fucked," said The Wizard, glaring at his sister. "Even if those bony idiots didn't get us caught, how many local sorcerers do you think the Circle wizards will search before they wind up here?"

Chapter Nineteen

"Do you think I keep track? As far as I know, it's just me up here."

"Right, so we have to get out of here right away." Leaving his seat, The Wizard swept the remaining wine bottles into his bag of holding.

As the first bottles fell into his bag, the clatter suggested that there were already more bottles of wine in there. Anasthasia narrowed her eyes suspiciously at him.

"We're all going to die..." His chin rested on his arms, Jeff was staring gloomily at an empty wine bottle. "Maybe not tonight, but we're all going to die...."

"Yeah, that's kind of how life works," said Anasthasia.

"Why even bother running? We're up against the most powerful organization in the world; what chances do we have of surviving? It's just a pipe dream." Looking up, Jeff shook his head slowly, his eyes full of morose dismay.

"I thought so too, Jeff, but this is really happening." Furrowing his brow, The Wizard paused for a moment, scratching his fiery orange beard. "Oh, wait, you mean a pipe dream in the metaphorical sense... Look, I know things don't seem great, but try to live in the moment. Right now, we have to focus on getting out of here before we're caught."

"That's my point," said Jeff. "They're going to catch us eventually anyway, so why not just make our final stand here? It'd make for a quicker death."

"Wow, you're a depressing drunk." Walking over to the bags of groceries, The Wizard poked through them until he found the one he wanted; grinning, he pulled out a tin of *Calhoun's Quality Cocaine*. "Nice, they got the name brand! How about you do a line of this? I guarantee it will shut you up!"

"I don't want any fucking cocaine, you philistine," said Jeff, scowling spitefully. "I would love it if I could go back in time and give your mother an abortion, but unfortunately, that is impossible. Bottom line, I just don't want to die tomorrow."

"You're welcome to bail if that's what you want." The Wizard began to chop several lines of cocaine on the table. "No one is stopping you. I doubt the Circle will bother tracking you down by yourself."

Poor Preparation

Heaving a sigh of resignation, Jeff shook his head. "No, I can't do that. We gave our word to Merlin that we'd help, so it'd be shitty if I just bailed. I just don't see much hope, that's all. I'm useless in a fight..."

"Well, hurry up and do a line with us." Leaning forward, The Wizard snorted a line of cocaine with a conjured straw. "We have to get out of here, and it'll give you the get-up-and-go you need to... you know."

"Fine... why the hell not?"

After waiting for Anasthasia to finish her line, Jeff walked over and took the straw from her. He felt slightly better as the tingle of the cocaine spread through his face.

"Alright, let's wake up those idiots." The Wizard gestured to Chris and Fabulon, who were still fast asleep. "You go jostle them, and I'll divvy up their lines."

Getting up, Jeff and Anasthasia approached Chris and Fabulon. It took them a moment, but they were able to shake the two of them awake. Fabulon awoke much faster than Chris, who seemed to be deeply engrossed in pleasant dreams. At first, they kept drifting back to sleep, until The Wizard lost his patience and threw a large pinch of cocaine in each of their faces.

"Come on, assholes; it's time to get up and go!"

"What the hell?" As Fabulon blinked cocaine out of his eyes, his pupils rapidly enlarged. Blinking confusedly, he looked down. "Why are my pants unzipped?"

"Don't worry about it," said Chris, grinning sheepishly.

Vahim and Vaharm eyed the tin of cocaine with the utmost yearning.

"Okay, now that we're all awake, how are we going to get out of here?" asked Jeff. "I can't imagine we can keep running from the Circle on foot."

"No, we'll have to use some kind of teleportation," said The Wizard. He turned to his sister. "Ana, do you know if dad's old teleporter is working?"

Anasthasia's eyes widened. "He had a teleporter?"

The Wizard sighed, pinching his brow in frustration. "I'll take that as a no. Well, I'll assume it is working; if we can find my dad's teleporter, we should be able to get out of here undetected."

"Sure, but do you have any idea where it is?" asked Jeff.

"Not a clue."

305

Chapter Nineteen

"Maybe we should ask that one magic book," said Chris. "The *Arcane Almanac*, or whatever... It found your dad's hidden treasure, after all."

"Oh, yeah, I keep forgetting we have that thing..." Returning to his seat, Jeff grabbed his backpack and pulled out the *Arcane Almanac*. "Although, I've had other things to worry about."

He glared bitterly at Anasthasia.

"I just hope it doesn't give us any more riddles to solve..." Snatching the book from Jeff, The Wizard opened it to a random page. "Tell us, book, and please be concise: how can we safely get far away from here?"

A moment after he spoke, words began to appear on the page in cursive print. *To find the key to make your journey shorter, you must simply look in the master's quarters.*

"The master's quarters..." Furrowing his brow, The Wizard turned to his sister. "That'd be your room, I suppose. Are you sure you don't still have dad's magic portal?"

A look of realization dawned on Anasthasia's face. "*Oooh*, wait, you mean his old omniportal?"

"No shit, I mean the omniportal. What the hell else would I mean?!"

"Well, I didn't know that thing could teleport people!" Pouting her lips, Anasthasia crossed her arms indignantly. "I just thought it was some weird portal you could reach into to grab shit from random places."

"Wow, you have been using it wildly wrong... How do you even get it to work that way...? Whatever, nevermind... that doesn't matter.... How do we get to your bedroom? We've got to get a move on."

"It's up these stairs." Anasthasia started towards the staircase behind the burnt tapestry, motioning for them to follow. "Come on."

The others began to follow her, with Vahim and Vaharm taking the lead at their mistress's side. As they began to leave, there was a loud cough from the doorway leading to the kitchen.

"Aren't you guys forgetting someone?"

They all turned around. Standing in the doorway, with Kit Mingers at his heels, was Gary. He scowled as he lit a cigarette.

"Oh, yeah, my bad..." said Jeff. "I totally forgot about you."

Fabulon scratched his head awkwardly. "Yeah, sorry... I would have said something, but I just woke up."

Poor Preparation

Gary smirked. "Whatever, I don't really care. Let's go, you drunk bastards." He walked briskly past all of them and started up the stairs, stopping a few steps up to tap his foot impatiently.

"For the record," said The Wizard, "I remembered you, I just didn't care."

Kit Mingers looked furious. "Seriously, *I* don't matter to you, after everything we've been through together?!"

"Umm… well, to be honest, *you* I actually forgot…."

"Wow… that might be worse…." Whimpering, Kit Mingers hung his head in dejection.

Anasthasia cleared her throat loudly. "Are we going, or what?"

"So we're just leaving the gnomes?" asked Jeff. "I'm not necessarily against that; I'm just making sure I've got the plan straight."

"Ah, fuck, I forgot about them…" Gritting his teeth, The Wizard scratched his beard thoughtfully. "Well… I don't like the idea of the Circle getting ahold of them, since they've heard our plans, but I don't see another option at this point. We don't have enough time to track them down."

Jeff shrugged, and no one else said a thing about the matter.

They headed upstairs in a hurry, following Anasthasia through the labyrinthine passages of the tower. Jeff could not help but notice that the route they were taking was much simpler than the meandering path he had taken on his way downstairs. Intoxicated as she was, Anasthasia managed to lead them to the penthouse of her confusingly configured tower with almost no detours.

As they entered Anasthasia's chambers, she clapped her hands, causing the ceiling to glow with a radiance reminiscent of moonlight. Jeff felt a shiver run down his spine as the memories of his recent traumatism came rushing back to his psyche. Sweat began to pool on his neck as he looked around at the blood stained carpet, rusty surgical equipment, and jars full of the unspeakable.

"What in Merlin's beard?!" Fabulon recoiled at the sight of the less inviting half of the room, nearly knocking Gary down the stairs. "This place is scarier than Quan's basement!"

Chapter Nineteen

"Damn, Ana, it looks like you've been busy!" Looking around the room, The Wizard nodded in approval. "Hold on... Fabulon, what were you doing in Quan's basement?"

"Don't worry, nothing weird happened!" Blushing furiously, Fabulon averted his eyes. "She had a secret council, and we'd meet in different people's basements to avoid suspicion from the Circle. That's all."

"I wasn't worried, just curious... not about the weird stuff, though... that's your business.... Otherwise, that's interesting; who else was in this council?"

Fabulon's redness gradually diminished as he spoke. "Well... the core group was Quan, Perkins, and Horner, but she would call in all sorts of contacts, like myself, to pump out information about you. I'm really sorry I told her anything, I honestly thought it was for your protection."

"Don't worry about it, I know you had good intentions." The Wizard could not help but privately think that Fabulon could be a fucking idiot sometimes. "Besides, we've got bigger things to worry about now."

"This place is amazing!" Eyes wide with wonder, Gary gazed at the nightmarish scene with awe. He looked downright impressed as he walked up to Anasthasia's equipment and gave it a closer inspection. "I wish we weren't in a hurry, I'd love to poke around for a while."

"So, where's this portal thing?" asked Jeff, who was comforting a shaking Kit Mingers. "I'd like to get out of here as soon as possible."

"Yeah, me too..." muttered the cat.

Rolling her eyes, Anasthasia gestured to the crystal ball at the foot of her bed. "It's right there! I've been using it as a nightlight, it's really good for that."

The orb emitted a light glow as cosmic vistas flashed across its surface. None of the images lingered long enough to make out the details, but they seemed to be of faraway nebula and star systems.

"Seriously, a night light?" Shaking his head, The Wizard facepalmed. "It's a multidimensional spatial relocator, not a fucking nightlight. You should just pawn it if you're not gonna use it right..."

Furrowing his brow dubiously, Jeff peered into the omniportal. "Why is it only showing outer space?"

"Because, statistically speaking, that's most of the universe," said The Wizard. "When it's not targeted, it just shows random locations in space. In

Poor Preparation

order to get it to work, you need to put your hand on it and picture the place you want it to take you."

Cocking his head, Jeff bit his lower lip anxiously. "That sounds kind of sketchy... How accurate is that thing?"

"It's perfectly accurate, as long as the first place you picture is where you wanna go!" The Wizard beamed with confidence... or perhaps it was due to all the cocaine he had done on the journey upstairs.

"That's not very comforting..." Jeff scratched his chin, wishing Anasthasia had not shaved his goatee.

"Whatever, the real question is where we should go..." said The Wizard, stroking his beard imperiously. "We can't go back to my place, I'm sure they've set a trap for us there. I've got a few friends in town, but I'm not sure we should trust them...."

Anasthasia smirked. "Since when do you have friends?"

"Umm... guys...?" Kit Mingers was standing at the head of the stairs, peering down nervously. "We might want to get a move on."

"Yeah, we know," said The Wizard, scowling. "Don't rush us, we're trying to figure something out."

Kit Mingers began to knead his paws into the carpet restlessly. "Does it really matter that much? Why not just go to Chris's bar? No one's ever there."

"Hey, shut up, cat!" yelled Chris, crossing his arms in indignation.

"It's too close to my house, anyway," said The Wizard. "What's the big deal, Kit? The Circle agents probably won't find us up here anytime soon, this tower is heavily warded against scrying. The only way you could know the way up here is to have spent days running around the tower, frantically exploring every nook and cranny."

"That's kind of my point...."

Suddenly, a squirky voice called out angrily from the stairway.

"Ha! We finally found you bastards!"

A moment later, Knippe and Knorpe crested the landing. They were both out of breath, and were covered from head to foot in cobwebs. The strangest thing about this picture was that they did not have their knives drawn.

"Oh, good, it's you guys," said The Wizard, feigning a look of relief. "We couldn't find you anywhere!"

309

Chapter Nineteen

"Oh, don't feed us that line of crap," said Knorpe, leaning on the banister to catch his breath. "We know you didn't look for us!"

"That's right, douchebags; we heard everything you said in your little meeting," said Knippe, brushing the cobwebs out of his hair. "We were spelunking in the crawl space above the dining room."

"We would have caught up sooner, but we still haven't quite mapped out the insides of the walls."

"Yeah, whatever…" The Wizard turned back to the rest of the group. "Anyway, who else has any good ideas of where to establish our base of operations? I'm all ears!"

"I hope you guys don't expect us to help out in this standoff of yours," said Knorpe. "All we signed up for was the heist, got it?"

"Again, whatever. I'm fine with that; I'm pretty sure the only way you could help is by staying out of the way."

"Well, well, now, that's no way to talk to the assistant manager of your new base of operations!" Scowling at The Wizard, Knippe placed his arm around his brother's shoulder.

"That's right!" Nodding firmly, Knorpe patted his brother on the back. "Wait a second, Knippe… I thought you were the assistant manager!"

"In your dreams!"

The Wizard massaged his brow to ease his tension headache. "What the hell are you two talking about?"

"Only the hottest bar in all of Theiyre!"

"Oh, no…"

"That's right! The one, the only, the extra exquisite *Luncheons and Flagons!*"

"You guys own a bar too?" Chris raised his eyebrows.

Knorpe grinned with fiendish enthusiasm. "Yeah, and it's way more successful than your miserable shithole."

"I was just asking…" Hanging his head, Chris gazed at Fabulon's buttocks.

"We also have our own very successful church! Ever heard of Astrolotology?"

Poor Preparation

"No one cares!" Pacing back and forth, The Wizard scratched his head anxiously. "Damn it... I'm struggling to think of an alternative... I think we might have to take the idiots up on their offer...."

"You hear that, Knorpe? That means we're in charge now!"

"It absolutely does not," said The Wizard. "Now, shut the hell up. Who wants to use the omniportal first?"

Throwing herself onto her bed, Anasthasia laid on her stomach, facing the omniportal. "How exactly are we supposed to picture this bar if we've never been there?"

"I think you guys will get a good enough picture of it when we pull it up on the portal."

"I'm not entirely comfortable with that..." As Anasthasia rested her chin on her arms, the glow of the omniportal gave her pale face a ghostly appearance. "You know that scry-based teleportation is only ninety percent accurate. If we don't have a clear picture, we could end up in a similar looking bar on another continent!"

"She has a point," said Fabulon. "Maybe we should teleport somewhere more familiar, but still inconspicuous, like —"

"I'm gonna stop you there," said The Wizard. "Ana, when was the last time you travelled anywhere in the kingdom of Koric?"

"I can't remember, I was just a kid. I was having some feminine issues that dad didn't want to deal with, so he brought me to some back alley doctor. Anyway, fuck if I can remember anything that happened..."

"Well, Anasthasia, you're going to have to figure out something. I can't stay here, and don't think that I won't leave you behind just on account of you being my sister, because I absolutely will."

Anasthasia stuck her tongue out at The Wizard.

"If it helps, we have these." Reaching into his pocket, Knippe pulled out a stack of glossy papers. They each bore a picture of the facade of *Luncheons and Flagons*, with the words "*I got my kidney stolen at Koric's phreshest pub!*" written in diagonal cursive in the corner. "They're postcards from our most successful marketing campaign!"

Snatching one of the postcards out of Knippe's hand, The Wizard inspected it closely. "Okay, glossing over why these exist, I think they'll do the trick. What do you think, Ana?" He passed her one of the cards.

311

Chapter Nineteen

"Fine, I'll try to use the stupid omniportal, but I'm not going first."

"No problem, Jeff will do it. Won't you, Jeff?"

"To hell I will! It's your fault we're in this situation; you do it."

Approaching Jeff, The Wizard started to pat him consolingly on the back. "Listen, buddy, this is the best way you can help out. You said it yourself that you're useless in a fight! If Fabulon or I got misteleported, we'd be in serious trouble; that's why we need you to go through first, so that if we see you appear through the portal, we'll know it works!"

Jeff slapped away The Wizard's hand. "Blow it out your ass."

"Okay, fine, you pussy. I'll go through the damn portal first."

The Wizard approached the omniportal, turned to stare mockingly at Jeff, and slapped his hand down on the orb. In an instant, he vanished into thin air. Fabulon grabbed one of the postcards and squinted at it, before reluctantly placing his hand on the orb and vanishing as well. One by one, the others went through the portal, until only Jeff and Gary remained; they watched as Kit Mingers disappeared, appearing through the portal with the others.

"Do me a favor, Jeff." Walking past the omniportal, Gary threw himself down on Anasthasia's bed. Lounging on her pillows, he lit a cigarette. "Let the others know that I'm gonna hang back for a while."

"Are you serious? This place isn't going to be safe much longer."

"I can handle myself, don't worry about me. I'm just gonna take a quick nap."

"Okay…" Shrugging, Jeff approached the omniportal. He stared into the flashing void of cosmic images, a feeling of apprehension building in his gut. After a moment of indecision, he slammed his hand onto the crystal surface, intently focusing on the image of *Luncheons and Flagons.*

He felt his feet lift off the ground. It was a very different sensation from what he had experienced when travelling through time; for one thing, he still felt like he existed while it was happening. It was rather like flying in a tornado made of innumerable different places. It put intense strain on his freshly-implanted eyes. Needless to say, when he finally hit the floor of *Luncheons and Flagons,* he immediately fell flat on his face.

Chapter Twenty
Fight for the Circle

Jeff pulled himself off the grimy hardwood floor of *Luncheons and Flagons*. The bar was dimly lit by a few candles in the fallen remains of the crystal globe chandelier. Looking up, he saw that the others were already gathered around the bar. As Knippe and Knorpe were pouring everyone a shot of rum, The Wizard was chopping line after line of cocaine on the countertop.

Are these really the people in the hands of whom the fate of our kingdom rests? thought Jeff, as he watched Anasthasia grab the bottle of rum out of Knippe's hands and take a swig.

The entire bar was completely ransacked: most of the tables were upended, there was graffiti on nearly every surface, and the floor was covered in broken bottles. The door was off its hinges, and was propped loosely against the doorway. On the shelves behind the bar, only a few bottles of cheap liquor remained. Lying outside the bathroom, strung out in a pool of dried vomit, was Knippe and Knorpe's indentured kobold.

When Jeff walked up to the bar, Knorpe was deeply engrossed in a rant about lazy employees, while his twin brother nodded along. Jeff pulled up a seat at the end, next to Kit Mingers.

"Hey, Jeff," said The Wizard, railing a line of cocaine. "Where's Gary? I figured he'd come through first, since you were being a timid little bitch."

"Shut the hell up. Gary said he's gonna hang back for a while."

313

Chapter Twenty

The Wizard's look of cocainated cheer immediately melted into one of annoyance. "What?! Well, did you tell him that's a fucking stupid idea?"

"Uhh... I said he shouldn't, but he seemed to really want to stay."

Heaving a heavy sigh, The Wizard knocked his head against the bar, getting cocaine all over the place. "Whatever... but he had better not rat us out. I'll kill him if he does!"

"So... what's the plan now?" asked Anasthasia. "We're not gonna attack in the middle of the night, are we? Because I need my beauty sleep."

"No, we're just gonna lay low here until morning," said The Wizard, "then we'll meet with Samantha and deliver the payload. After her part of the plan is set into motion, there will be no going back, so we'd better make sure we're prepared. Wanna do a line?"

Anasthasia shrugged. "Sure, why not? When with gnomes, do as the gnomes do!"

Jeff sighed despondently, burying his head in his arms.

They continued to take shots and do lines well into the night, getting right proper as fuck. Gary never showed up, which might have bothered them if they were sober. As the night went on, they each passed out individually, starting with Jeff; if he had been awake to see them party for the rest of the night, Jeff would have likely lost what little confidence he had in their chances of surviving the next day.

Morning sunlight poured in through the busted door and broken windows of *Luncheons and Flagons* as The Wizard pried his head from a dried pool of drool and cocaine. Looking around, he saw that he was the first to wake in the morning; this was unusual, so he decided to bide his time with a little hair of the dog.

As The Wizard poured himself his second triple shot of spiced rum, he decided that, perhaps, this was not the best way to start such a crucial day. He dumped out the rum and poured himself a glass of vodka; *now this*, he thought, *is a drink for the day you die.* He began to prepare himself an enormous line of cocaine.

A loud snore resonated from behind the bar. The Wizard peered over the countertop, and saw that Fabulon was being spooned by Chris. At this point, Chris had a fairly thick beard from not shaving for days, and Fabulon did not

314

seem to have a single discernable facial hair. Even Jeff's beard grew in quicker than his. The Wizard grabbed the bottle of rum and poured what was left of it on Chris's head.

"What the hell, dude?!"

"Get up, loverboy. Wake him up, too."

The Wizard got up and started to shake the others awake. When he went to wake up Anasthasia, Vahim slapped his hand away. The Wizard recoiled in surprise.

"Woah, I thought you were asleep!"

"We don't sleep."

"That makes sense. Can you wake up my sister?"

"She told us not to let her be disturbed."

The Wizard scowled. "Want me to wake her with the sound of your shattering bones?"

Apprehensively, the skeletons shook their mistress awake. After she was done slapping them, the three of them joined The Wizard and everyone at the bar. At this point, only Knippe, Knorpe, and Kit Mingers remained asleep; The Wizard had not wanted to wake the twins, and the cat had just scratched him and gone back to sleep.

"Good morning, everyone," said The Wizard, sliding a shot of vodka down the bar to each living person. "Who's excited for today's festivities?"

They all glared at him in silence. Only Anasthasia did her shot.

"Oh, right, you guys haven't had any cocaine yet. Bad news, I already did it all. Think we should stop for more on the way?"

Jeff shook his head slowly. "So... anyone ready for a serious discussion about risking our lives?"

"I can't believe we're really doing this..." said Fabulon. "It feels so much more real in the light of day..."

"Don't tell me you're getting cold feet!" Reaching for Fabulon's glass, The Wizard poured an extra shot on top. "There's no backing out now."

"No, it's just nerves. I'll be honest, I don't know the exact extent of what we're gonna be going up against. Even if we disable their gear, we still have the spellcasting of trained battlemages to worry about. I was only a grunt compared to some of those butchers..."

"All the more reason to take that shot of vodka! It could be your last."

Chapter Twenty

"Will you please take this seriously?!" shouted Jeff, throwing his shot glass across the room. "I can't take your shit right now, I've got a huge hangover... We actually might die, and you're acting like we're getting psyched up for a fist fight! Get your fucking shit together!"

"Damn, take it easy," said The Wizard, scratching his head awkwardly. "Fine... I was just trying to liven things up, you know... Ever consider that I might be nervous as well?"

"Alright... sorry.... I'm just really on edge right now. I hadn't considered that you're probably just as afraid of dying as I am."

"Oh, to be honest, I'm not that scared of death; I'm more afraid that there's something afterwards."

"Well, whatever... Let's just get to business, I want to get this shit over with. When are we meeting Samantha?"

Fabulon checked the time on his wristorb. "She should be starting her lunch break in about an hour. Should I send her a textual message to meet us here?"

"I'd rather her not know we were here..." said The Wizard. "How about you have her meet us next door at the *Church of Astrolotology*?"

Jeff scoffed. "Oh yeah, that'll really throw them off the trail!"

The Wizard ignored him. "For now, let's stake out Circle Tower. We've got to get a read on their security situation. Fabulon, can I see that wristorb of yours?"

"Sure thing, buddy," said Fabulon. Once he finished typing a reply to Samantha, he took off his wristorb and passed it to The Wizard. "Scrying is function four."

"I know, I helped my dad design these things."

"He means he sat by the toolbox and passed our dad his equipment," whispered Anasthasia, nudging Jeff in the arm.

The Wizard pulled up a holographic display of the city of Theiyre. He clicked his finger on the center of it, causing the hologram to zoom in on Circle Tower. The surroundings of the tower were so clear, they could make out each leaf littering the ground. Off to the far side, they could see *Luncheons and Flagons*.

Stationed outside of Circle Tower were no less than fifty armed guards, each carrying sleek, chrome-plated magic rifles. On either side of the

316

entrance, there stood a large stone golem, holding a spiked club. The most conspicuous guardians, however, were a quartet of cavaliers circling the tower on flying, skeletal horses, adorned in ornate war garments.

One of the riders was an athletic looking woman in red robes who had tan skin and a bleach blonde afro with fiery red tips; on her back, she was carrying a viciously serrated voulge, with a blade that glowed like the evening sunset.

There was a slouching man in dark green robes, with dark skin and a curtain of greasy black hair; he had a pair of bandoliers with dozens of potions and poultices hanging from them, and had a long, black whip hanging from his belt.

Another of the riders looked quite unusual: he was much, much larger than the others, with rosy cheeks and curly blonde hair that did not contrast well with his mustard-colored robes; he did not carry a weapon.

The final of the cavaliers was a slender woman with pale skin and white robes, whose sleek, raven-colored hair hung past her knees; there was a scythe tied to the side of her saddle, the night-black blade of which bore a series of glowing silver runes.

"Fabulon... are those who I think they are...?" The Wizard's voice sounded thin and wispy.

"I'm afraid so..."

"You didn't tell me they were here! I thought they were still off in Mongorrhea, hunting dragons!"

"I guess Archmage Quan called them back home for this. Figures she'd spare no expense..."

"What the hell are you guys talking about?" asked Jeff. "Because you are really freaking me out. Who are those four?"

"The Four Equestrians of the Apocalypse," said Fabulon. "They are the deadliest order of battlemages in the land. They only take jobs personally assigned by the Archmage herself."

"Don't you mean the Four Horsemen?" asked Chris.

"It used to be, but when Quan became Archmage, she made a big deal about how two of the members aren't men, so now it's Equestrians."

"Anyway, that's not the point," said The Wizard. "These people are a big deal. We might not be able to make it past them."

Chapter Twenty

"What kind of wizards are we dealing with?" asked Jeff, tapping his fingers nervously on the bar.

"Well, they each possess their own unique combat style," said Fabulon. "They specialize in combined attacks to overwhelm their foes, and are virtually unstoppable together. Their leader goes by the title of Valkyra the Militant, and she lives up to it. She's a dragon-blooded pyromancer, so she's able to wield flames that put other pyromancers to shame."

The Wizard nodded fervently. "Yeah, she's half-dragon, half-black, and completely badass."

Jeff's eyes widened. "Wow... I always thought half-dragons were just a myth. Please tell me the other magi aren't as terrifying as her."

"Damn near," said The Wizard. "There's also Julian the Pestilent. He's Valkyra's human half-brother, but don't let his lack of magical blood fool you. He's who I'm really worried about, honestly; his specialty is conjuration, and he can summon swarms of poison insects, as well as toxic miasmas. Overall, he's just a nasty dude, on par with Horner."

Anasthasia chuckled. "I kind of want to meet this Horner you're always talking about... He sounds hilarious."

"You really don't," said The Wizard, shaking his head. "Anyway, there's also Shon the Famished. I know his name is silly, and don't even get me started on how he looks, but he's not someone to underestimate. That fat fuck can haul ass, and all it takes is one touch for him to drain you of all your energy; try to keep a safe distance."

"Last, but oh, definitely not least, there is Lamia the Dead," said Fabulon. He had a faraway look in his eyes when he spoke about her. "She's the most talented necromancer the Circle has ever seen. I actually had a bit of a crush on her a few years back... she's super cute... but that's not important!" He blushed furiously. "The point is, she can animate the corpses of the fallen in massive groups, controlling potentially dozens of minions. She's also a vampire, but you don't have to worry about that since she went vegan."

"Does that mean we should bring a stake and some garlic?"

"Don't be an idiot, Jeff," said The Wizard, rolling his eyes. "Shit like that only works in the movies."

Anasthasia raised her eyebrows. "Okay, let's just backtrack a minute; Fabulon, did you just say you liked a girl?"

Fight for the Circle

Nobody answered her.

Chris patted Fabulon firmly on the back. "These guys seem tough, but I just know my Fabby can handle them!"

"So he's 'your Fabby' now?" asked The Wizard, shaking his head and laughing. "Did you miss the part where he's straight?"

Chris ignored him as he slowly lowered his hand down Fabulon's back.

A small text bubble appeared floating above the hologram.

"Oh, hey Fabulon, looks like Samantha messaged you back." The Wizard clicked on the text bubble, and it enlarged. "She says she'll be here at noon. She also says that if she sees me while picking up the AMP, she might change her mind about helping us."

"At least we know that part of the plan is in place," said Fabulon. "Still though, now we have to deal with the Equestrians. What should we do about them?"

"Well, I doubt we'll make it through with a full frontal assault," said The Wizard, "but that doesn't mean all hope is lost. There are other ways into the tower."

"Are you suggesting we sneak into the tower? I'd honestly have to advise against that; I guarantee that it's the first thing they'll expect when the AMP goes off."

"I know that, Fabulon... I'm not saying we should all sneak in: just one of us."

Fabulon nodded thoughtfully. "Huh... while the others provide a diversion.... That's actually not a bad idea!"

"Right? It could just work! Plus, even if that douchebag Gary rats us out, he won't know this part of the plan."

"So, who's gonna sneak in?" asked Anasthasia, as she was polishing off the bottle of vodka with her fifth shot. "It better be someone no one will recognize, just in case they're caught."

They all stared at her for a moment, waiting for the gears to click into place.

"Oh, hey, I have an idea!" she said. "Why don't I sneak in? I'm small, so if there are tight spaces involved, I'm your girl."

"Sounds good to me," said The Wizard. "I'd rather not have you risk your life; I'm pretty sure dad would kill me if he found out I did."

319

Chapter Twenty

"Perfect, that means I'll get to be the one to save daddy! It's okay if I tell him the whole thing was my idea, right?"

The Wizard shook his head at Anasthasia, not dignifying her comment with a response. "Now that we've got that settled, we've got to get geared up. First of all, everyone take one of these amulets from dad's armory. They're enchanted with minor spell and projectile protection."

Rifling through his bag for a minute, he passed one of the amulets to each of his allies. As he did so, he could not help but think that his bag of holding was becoming more of a bag of hoarding; it was full as fuck. When he put the amulet around his own neck, it clanked against the scryproof amulet Merlin had given him.

"This kind of jewelry is totally gauche," said Anasthasia, frowning at the amulet.

Once again, The Wizard ignored her. He pulled his dad's old weapons one by one from his bag, placing them on one of the tables. "Now, these are the weapons we found in the armory. We have under an hour to figure out how to properly work this stuff, or else we're boned."

"These are some crazy looking weapons," said Jeff, dubiously inspecting the minigun dubbed the *Soul Gouger*. "This one is just a bunch of staves bound together. Are you sure these things work?"

Picking up the set of double barreled wand guns, The Wizard blasted a hole in the ceiling. "We've tested them, and they work fine. I've got dibs on these two beauties and the golden revolver. You guys can take your pick of the rest."

"Wow, this thing is absolutely fabulous!" Anasthasia picked up the draconic adamantine flamethrower and strapped the tank on her back. Despite her slender frame, she was able to lift the enormous metal rig with ease. "I simply adore fire! Can I test it out?"

The Wizard held up his hand. "Please wait until we're outside! And be careful with that thing, it derives its power by burning the souls of live fire elementals: it's really hot."

"Holy shit, that's awesome!" Hey gleaming golden eyes widening in childlike wonder, Anasthasia licked her lips. "Even if I miss, I'll still know I got a kill!"

"You're a scary girl, you know..." muttered Chris.

Fight for the Circle

Anasthasia looked proud of herself. She grabbed one of the revolvers, tucking it away in a safe place; to be clear, I should point out that she did not have any pockets.

"Fabulon, I think you should take this monstrosity." The Wizard pointed to the *Soul Gouger*. "I doubt either of those guys could operate it."

"Sure thing." Fabulon heaved the enormous minigun off the table, slinging the strap over his shoulder. He also grabbed a revolver pistol. "I just need to figure out how to flip the setting to nonlethal; I'd rather not kill anyone if I can help it. I found the switch on the bottom earlier, but it's stuck with glue or something."

Cocking his head, The Wizard furrowed his brow skeptically. "That thing has a nonlethal switch? It's a fucking minigun! What on Notearth is the point?"

Fabulon shrugged. "Crowd control?"

"Whatever. Okay, Chris, I guess that leaves you as the sniper." The Wizard tossed the gyroscopic sniper rifle to Chris, as well as one of the revolvers. "It's a gyroscopically stabilized railgun, and the mithril balls it shoots are… well, you'll figure it out."

Chris inspected the sniper rifle, running his fingers down the diamond barrel.

"Hang on, what the hell do I get?" said Jeff, waving his hands impatiently. "I'm not gonna risk my life unarmed!"

"Here, you can have the last revolver." The Wizard tossed the remaining pistol to Jeff.

"That hardly seems fair. You guys each get a great weapon, and all I get is a sidearm? Why can't I have one of your damn shotguns? You already have that fucking battle suit!"

"They're an akimbo set, Jeff; I'd be off balance if I fired just one. Besides, I thought you said something a minute ago about bundles of staves and wands seeming unsafe."

Jeff sighed, staring gloomily at his single revolver pistol.

"At least you get a weapon," said Vahim. He and Vaharm were standing at Anasthasia's side, each massaging one of her shoulders. "We can't even fire a gun without the recoil blasting off our hands!"

"Yeah, but you guys are already dead…"

Chapter Twenty

"That doesn't mean we want to die again!" Vaharm clenched his jaw; he looked like he was attempting to scowl, but it was hard to tell without skin.

The Wizard cleared his throat. "*Anyway*, everyone take some time to familiarize themselves with their weapons. We don't have long before Samantha gets here. Oh, and *seriously*, you had better not fire that flamethrower in the bar."

Anasthasia rolled her eyes.

They did not talk much for the next half hour. Once they got acquainted with the weight and balance of their weapons, they each sat in silence until something broke the tension. A loud beep resonated throughout the room, and everyone's eyes immediately fell on Fabulon's wristorb. There was a small text bubble floating above the crystal.

Everyone besides Anasthasia leapt out of their chairs and hurried over to the bar; she simply kicked back in her seat and continued receiving her foot massage. The Wizard tapped the text bubble with his finger, and it expanded above the wristorb.

"*Meet me behind that stupid church in five minutes. Don't be late. Don't be seen. Don't bring the fuckhead.*"

"Well, better get out there, Fabulon! I guess I had better give you this..." The Wizard dumped the contents of his bag of holding into a large pile. He lugged the antimagic pulse device out of the heap and shoved it back into the bag of holding, before handing the bag to Fabulon. "Damn, that thing is fucking heavy without the bag's enchantment."

Among the mound of items were the two jetpacks, the *Arcane Tomes*, The Wizard's bong and weed, and about twenty assorted bottles of wine. Muddled into the mix were a couple dozen dried cat turds. Anasthasia eyed the wine with suspicion.

Jeff squinted at the heap. "Are those *jetpacks*?"

"Just ignore those," said The Wizard. "We'll play with them later, after this is over with."

"Alright, I'll be right back." Fabulon set the *Soul Gouger* on the floor and slung the bag of holding over his shoulder. "Where's the back way out of this place?"

Fight for the Circle

"I think the gnomes' office is past the bathroom," said The Wizard, gesturing to a hall to the left of the bar. "Just be careful not to wake them, they passed out in that hallway."

"I'll just go around the front." Fabulon walked up to the broken door and gently moved it aside. He peered through the doorway, surveying the street for a moment. When he was sure the coast was clear, he covertly sprinted out and towards the *First Church of Astrolotology*.

"It's a good thing no one comes down this street, on account of the scourge of muggings," said Knippe, who was stretching near the bathroom door, inches away from the rotting corpse of his indentured kobold. "Those pink robes ain't exactly clandestine."

"Oh, damn it," said The Wizard, heaving an exasperated sigh. "Why'd you have to wake up now? If you'd just waited ten minutes, we'd have been out of here!"

"Tough luck," said Knorpe, walking up to the bar and leaping on the counter. "Thought you were just gonna skip bar without paying? You assholes drank all our vodka and rum; now all we have left is shitty gin." He gestured to the last bottle on the shelves: a gallon of gin, bearing the label of *Tanquer-Ade*.

The Wizard let loose a torrent of sarcastic laughter. "We're not paying for shit! Just consider your booze payment for the bed you stole from me." Suddenly, he narrowed his eyes as they fell on the shattered remains of the globe chandelier. "And is that my chandelier...?"

"What's he talking about?" whispered Knippe to his brother.

"I never know..."

"Yeah, whatever..." Gritting his teeth, The Wizard turned to his sister. "So, Anasthasia, I'd like to go over your part of the plan before we begin."

"Yeah, that's probably a good idea; I'll be honest, I haven't the faintest how to sneak into the tower. I really just volunteered because I'd rather not die in that horrible battle with the rest of you."

"We're not going to die, don't worry."

"I wasn't worried about *you*."

"Okay, so anyway, you're gonna take Fabulon's wristorb here." The Wizard grabbed the wristorb from the bar and passed it to Anasthasia. "It'll provide you with maps of the tunnels beneath Circle Tower. There aren't any

323

direct tunnels in, but there are thin walls in some places where the tunnels have been closed off; with all the commotion we'll be making on the surface, I doubt anyone will be down there to catch you."

Anasthasia strapped the orb onto her wrist. "But I'm not very good at explosive spells; you know that. Dad never let me practice magic like that, he said I'm too pretty to afford to lose a chunk of my face."

"Did I mention that the flamethrower I gave you is hot enough to melt through walls?"

"Seriously?" She picked up her flamethrower off the floor, admiring its draconic visage with wide eyes. "Damn, I guess the dragon aesthetic is more than just for show!"

"Yeah, dad outdid himself with these weapons. Although, I'm not sure it'll get you through the vault door in time." Reaching into his pocket, The Wizard withdrew the copy of his dad's master key. "Here. This is dad's master key, it'll let—"

"I'm gonna stop you right there." Giggling, Anasthasia rooted around in her coat for a moment, before holding up an identical key. "He gave me one of those ages ago, just before his disappearance."

"*Are you fucking kidding me?!*" It was really starting to piss The Wizard off that his father had trusted his younger sister with so much, and had held all of it back when it came to him. "I had to sneak into his opium lounge, when he and the Circle elders were having an orgy with a bunch of prostitutes, just to have a chance to get this copy! I saw a lot of perky titties that day, but also a lot of saggy balls; I have *very* mixed feelings about the experience..."

"Well, what can I say?" With a feigned coy simper, Anasthasia fluttered her eyelashes innocently. "I guess I'm just his favorite!"

"Whatever... You're clear on your plan now, right? You'll sneak in through the maintenance tunnels in the sewers, and once you're adjacent to one of the Circle's tunnels, melt that shit down. Just make sure, and this is *very important*, that you *do not* use the flamethrower in a cloud of sewer gas. All it takes is a simple air freshening charm to avoid blowing up a city block."

"Got it, I'll use the sewer gas to blast my way into the tunnels."

"Damn it, were you listening at all?"

Fight for the Circle

Anasthasia smirked, punching her brother in the arm. "I was just fucking with you. The plan sounds pretty straightforward, but once I'm inside, how do I find dad?"

"That's gonna be the hard part. There are a lot of tunnels, and his location won't be marked on any maps. You'll just have to look for him. You should probably take the *Arcane Almanac*." The Wizard walked over to the heap of junk he had dumped on the floor, rifling through it until he found the *Almanac*.

He tossed the tome to Anasthasia, who sidestepped it instead of catching it.

She waved her hand dismissively. "I'm good, I'm gonna rely on my woman's intuition."

"*Please don't...*"

"It's fine, I've got this." Anasthasia grabbed the bottle of gin off the shelf and poured herself a full glass. "I'm in my element in the sewer..."

Hanging his head wearily, The Wizard heaved a defeated sigh. "Whatever..."

Picking up the *Arcane Almanac*, he brushed dust and debris off the cover. He walked over to the disorganized heap of his stuff and fished out the *Arcane Dictionary* as well. Snatching up Jeff's backpack, he shoved the tomes into it and looped his arms through the straps. After a few tense minutes, Fabulon returned from his rendezvous. He no longer had the bag of holding, and instead was carrying a brown paper bag that was folded shut.

"How'd it go?" The Wizard was leaning on the edge of his seat.

"She told me to give you this," said Fabulon, walking up to The Wizard and holding out the brown paper bag.

The Wizard eyed the bag suspiciously. "What is it?"

"I didn't ask, but I wouldn't open it."

"I hear buzzing..." said The Wizard, holding the bag up to his ears. "Knowing Samantha, it's probably a bag of bees."

"You came up with that answer awfully fast," said Jeff.

"Well, it's not the first time she's tried to unleash the swarm on me. She's a pretty good conjurer, so... yeah...." With a haunted look in his eyes, The Wizard glanced at his crotch.

"We should get into position," said Fabulon, grabbing the *Soul Gouger* and slinging its strap over his shoulder. "Now that I delivered the device, we only have minutes. Sam's going to activate it as soon as no one is looking."

"Alright, but I have to take haste," said The Wizard.

Jeff's brow furrowed. "Don't you mean make haste...?"

"Nope!" The Wizard had taken a seat at the bar, and had poured the remainder of his tin of cocaine.

"Oh, I see..." Jeff scoffed.

"Wait, I thought you said you were out of cocaine!" Crossing her arms, Anasthasia eyed the pile of powder with envy.

"I lied." The Wizard leaned forward and railed the remainder of his reserve. Once he finished taking haste, he leapt out of his seat with fresh fervor. "Right, let's get moving! Fabulon, you and I will take the lead, storming in as soon as we get the clear. Ana, you can gain access to the sewers by way of an access hatch right outside this pub. Jeff, you follow behind me and Fabulon and try not to get killed, okay?"

"Should we wake up the cat?" asked Fabulon. "It might not be safe here."

The Wizard looked over at Kit Mingers, who was sleeping in a beam of sunlight. "Nah, he'll be fine. Look how cute he is! Who'd want to hurt that?"

"What about me?" asked Chris. "Should I climb up on the roof to snipe, or do you have some kind of crazy flying spell to cast on me?"

"No, I can't do anything like that... I actually have a special plan in mind for you. I'd like to discuss it in private, however, because if the others knew what my plan was, they might not like it."

"Uhh... we can hear you..." Jeff shook his head slowly.

"Just come in the back room with me really quick." The Wizard got up and walked towards the back hall, motioning for Chris to follow. "It'll only take a minute."

The two of them went into the back office, slamming the door shut behind them.

About five minutes later, The Wizard came out by himself. There were a few things off about him, however, and it did not take long for someone to notice one of them.

Fight for the Circle

"Why are you wearing your robes inside out over your battlesuit?" asked Jeff, cocking his head and squinting at The Wizard.

No one seemed to notice that The Wizard was no longer wearing the backpack containing the *Arcane Tomes*.

"I told you they were banging," said Knippe, nudging his brother's arm. They both laughed.

"Don't worry about it." The Wizard hurriedly inverted his robes. "Alright, now that it's just us, we should get a move on. Everyone clear on the plan?"

Jeff and Fabulon silently nodded. Anasthasia gave him a thumbs up, with an inappropriate amount of excitement painted on her face. As usual, the skeletons remained silent and blank. While this was happening, Knippe and Knorpe were taking turns swigging gin behind the bar.

The Wizard took a deep breath and swallowed his nerves. "Let's go."

Anasthasia was the first to rush out of the bar; without saying a word, she ran into the street, pried open a manhole, and leapt in with a smile on her face. Her skeletal servants followed suit. A moment later, The Wizard and Fabulon ran to the door, weapons drawn and ready. Jeff followed apprehensively at the rear.

The three of them turned the corner into the alley between *Luncheons and Flagons* and the *Church of Astrolotology*. Careful to keep to back alleys and shadows as much as possible, they made their way towards the looming form of Circle Tower.

There were wanted posters bearing their faces plastered on every lamp post. It was hard to be stealthy with Fabulon wearing hot pink robes, and no less than a dozen civilians saw them lurking through the streets. Fortunately for them, it was a little late for anyone to turn them in. By their estimate, it would be less than five minutes before the AMP was detonated.

When the street beneath Circle Tower was in their line of sight, they ducked into the bushes. They were a few hundred feet down an alleyway leading out to the Regal Roundabout, in the shadow of several fabulous manors. Although they could not see the tower door from their vantage point, they could see guards dutifully patrolling in the distance, wearing the chromatic crest of the Circle. The silhouettes of the Four Equestrians of the Apocalypse were circling the tower overhead.

327

Chapter Twenty

"Now we wait," whispered Fabulon. "This should be far enough away that the antimagic pulse won't affect our weapons."

The Wizard nodded solemnly, his trigger finger at the ready.

The next few minutes felt like hours. Jeff held his breath practically the entire time. As he sat there, crouched in a cluster of damp, spidery bushes, Jeff once again felt himself lamenting every decision he had ever made to lead him where he was.

Suddenly, chaos swept over the town square. The first noticeable change was the enchanted flames on the trees instantly being extinguished about half way up the alley. About a second later, a series of violent crashing sounds resounded from the tower. A few rocks rolled into view from Archmage Quan's crumbling golems. Hundreds of enormous bones clattered to the ground as the Equestrians' steeds broke apart. The riders slowly floated to the ground, as the guards below ran around in a panic. The Circle magi began intently searching all of the yards around the tower.

The Wizard and Fabulon stayed crouched in the bushes, waiting for the best opening to strike. They trembled with fear as they steeled themselves for what was to come.

A few stressful seconds later, The Wizard hooted loudly and leapt out of the bushes without warning, charging towards the tower. When he got to the end of the alley, he immediately opened fire on a pair of unexpecting magi, blasting a gaping hole in the middle of each of their backs. Fabulon leapt out a second after The Wizard and reached the end of the alley nearly as quickly, maiming a whole group of guards with a storm of invisible force.

In a manner of seconds, they were both completely surrounded on all sides by magi, lined up like a firing squad. Without hesitation, they all pulled the trigger at once. Fabulon and The Wizard simply grinned at each other when their enemies' weapons were ineffective, and opened fire on the entire semicircle of wizards.

By the time Jeff neared the end of the alleyway, most of the circle personnel had either been knocked unconscious or blasted apart by force magic. All that remained at that point, besides a few cowardly magi who had run away, were the Four Equestrians of the Apocalypse; they circled over The Wizard and Fabulon's heads, their weapons at the ready. Jeff crouched in the shadow of a nearby fence about twenty feet back, hoping not to be noticed.

The tan skinned woman in the red robes lowered herself to the ground and raised her spear in their faces. They could feel the heat emanating from the blade.

"We command you to stop, in the name of justice, or we will stop you by any means necessary."

Fabulon lowered the barrel of his gun and held up his hand to The Wizard. He took a step forward, and the woman tensed her spear.

"Valkyra, please give me a chance to explain."

"I don't want to hear your explanation. Surrender now and I'll spare your life." Valkyra barred her teeth, flashing him her draconic fangs.

Fabulon looked imploringly around at the other three mages circling above him. He locked eyes with the morbidly obese wizard in the yellow robes. "Please, Shon, you of all people have to understand. I know you're a good guy, we've had lunch together!"

The obese wizard buried his face in his hands. "You betrayed us all, Fabulon... I can't just forgive you for what you've done! I just watched you and that sociopath mow down over fifty innocent mages... They weren't even supposed to use lethal force on you: those guns were set to stun, and you still murdered them!"

"I wasn't using lethal force either." Fabulon patted the *Soul Gouger's* casing. "I have this thing set to stun."

"I wouldn't be so sure about that." The pale woman in the black robes floated upside down in Fabulon's face, stroking the blade of her scythe as she stared into his soul. "Trust me, I'm a necromancer, and I know those mages are *very* dead. Your 'stun' gun shattered half the bones in their bodies."

Fabulon's jaw dropped. Jeff started to creep closer to the end of the alleyway.

"How were we supposed to know they had nonlethal weapons?" said The Wizard, throwing his hands in the air. "That was self defense, damn it!"

The dark haired man lashed his whip, knocking the set of shotguns out of The Wizards hands. They skated across the cobblestone, landing well out of The Wizard's reach.

Chapter Twenty

"Well, was it self defense when you murdered your own father?"

"I… what…?" The Wizard was lost for words.

"Hold on, Julian," said Fabulon. "Where on Notearth did you hear that line of crap?"

"Shut up!" yelled Valkyra, jamming her spear mere inches from Fabulons throat. "You're a liar and a traitor! Just give up; you have no hope of victory."

Fabulon heaved a deep sigh. "Very well, if that's the only —"

Before Fabulon could finish his sentence, Jeff sprinted out of the alleyway with a fearless gleam in his eyes. He snatched one of The Wizard's fallen shotguns off the ground, and pointed it straight at Valkyra. Without hesitation, he pulled the trigger.

"Son of a bitch!" yelled Valkyra, as her spear was blasted out of her grip. She held up her hand; the shot had chipped one of her claws. With a furious roar, she conjured a ball of white flames in either hand; unlike The Wizard's flimsy fireballs, her balls gave off a heat that could be felt meters away. She flung one at Jeff as she ascended into the air. "Attack!"

Fabulons robes were singed as the fireball whirred passed him. He lifted the barrel of the *Soul Gouger*, firing a barrage of nonlethal force from the somewhat ironically named weapon.

Jeff narrowly dodged out of the path of the first fireball. Instead of ending him, it struck the side of a shed in a nearby yard, blowing the whole structure to smithereens. He immediately threw his gun down.

"I surrender! I've made a terrible mistake!"

As Valkyra the Militant was creating a deluge of fire from above, Julian the Pestilent created pockets of explosive gas for her to detonate. The entire street had become a minefield.

The Wizard drew the golden revolver out of his belt. He fired three shots at Valkyra before the barrel started to bend distinctly to the left. Suddenly, Shon the Famished appeared next to him in a blur, and almost touched his shoulder; The Wizard managed to avoid his vampiric touch by inches. He threw down the defective revolver, deciding to rely solely on the *Machina-X*.

Jeff continued to run around erratically, getting his hair singed off as he narrowly dodged blast after blast. Tears were streaming down his face in waves.

Fight for the Circle

Fabulon was firing the *Soul Gouger* wildly into the air. With all the smoke clouding the air, he could not get a clear bead on his targets. Suddenly, something clamped around his ankle. Looking down, he saw that the corpses at his feet were crawling towards him. All around him, bodies were becoming animated and getting to their feet. Fabulon lowered the barrel of his gun and started to mow down the undead; however, the "nonlethal" projectiles were only knocking them down, and they simply rose back up every time.

"Shit…" Fabulon tried to reach the *Soul Gouger's* lethal switch, but the risen corpses had already surrounded him. They slowly clawed his weapon out of his hands, and brought him to his knees.

The Wizard was hammering corpses into pieces with his superhuman strength. Their wasted muscles were no match for the *Machina-X*. Suddenly, Julian the Pestilent flew out of the haze and blew a gust of noxious gas in his direction. Panicking, The Wizard held up his wrist and started mashing random buttons on the control panel. Most of the buttons he pressed activated random utilities that did nothing, until he happened to turn on the cigarette lighter.

In an instant, the entire miasma went up in flames, sending both him and Julian flying. The Wizard landed on his ass about ten feet away from the blast. Julian the Pestilent, however, was not so fortunate; the explosion had ignited the plethora of combustible chemicals he was carrying, triggering a chain reaction that blew him to shreds.

As The Wizard was getting to his feet, Shon the Famished appeared behind him with sonic speed. He smiled cheerfully as he placed his palm on the small of The Wizard's back. "You're too slow!"

The Wizard felt all his strength leave his body. Unable to guide the *Machina-X* with his movements, even the battlesuit offered him no mobility. Shon grabbed The Wizard as he slumped down, lowering him gently to the ground.

When the smoke cleared, Valkyra could be seen standing over Jeff. She had recovered her spear, and was holding it to his heart. Jeff was sobbing hysterically with his eyes closed. However, when Valkyra caught sight of what was left of Julian, she stabbed her weapon in the street, inches from

Chapter Twenty

Jeff's throat; slowly, she walked over to her brother's remains, a look of horrified realization dawning on her face.

Chunks of Julian littered the cobblestone, barely distinguishable from the dozens of other exploded corpses. The only part of him that Valkyra could recognize was the head, lying in a pool of cauterized blood with a crust of burnt hair coating the scalp. As she neared his severed head, tears pooled up in her eyes, boiling into steam as they streamed down her face.

"Oh, please, no..." she muttered, falling to her knees in front of her brother's remains. She thudded her fist against the cobblestone. "You can't die, Julian... You're my little brother, I was supposed to protect you... *Those bastards*!!!"

She let out a thunderous bellow towards the heavens. Suddenly, the red tips of her blonde afro began to spread downward, and her hair started whipping around like an inferno. She stood up, her entire head enveloped in a mane of flames. As she turned around, her claws began to elongate and glow red hot, and her skin morphed into a coat of gleaming dragonscales.

Her eyes glowed with white-hot intensity as she stomped towards The Wizard, her fangs barred viciously. When she spoke, the words took on an almost demonic tone. "*You are going to pay for your sins!*"

The pale woman in the dark robes floated into Valkyra's path, holding up her hands. She spoke in a calm, almost apathetic voice. "Think about what you're doing, Val. We have direct orders from the Archmage to take them alive. It would not be wise to anger her."

Valkyra slapped the woman's hand aside and maneuvered around her. "Shut up, Lamia! You don't have any right to stop me!"

Lamia massaged her wrist, glaring coldly at Valkyra. "That burnt me, you know. I was hoping I wouldn't have to do this, but you've given me no choice." She raised her hands, muttering incantations under her breath.

The corpses around Valkyra began to move, clawing at her heels. They managed to slow her down for a moment, but they simply burned away without her so much as lifting a finger. The entire street smelled like an overcooked pork chop.

"Did you really think your pathetic puppets could stop me?!" When Valkyra reached The Wizard's limp, crippled form, she stood over him for a moment. A look of manic fury on her face, she raised one of her claws, and white flames overtook her hand. "I am going to enjoy this."

The Wizard felt the chill of pure terror in every fiber of his being. Even if he was not already paralyzed, his muscles would have likely frozen with fear in the face of such horror. He closed his eyes, hoping that his death would at least be quick.

Just as Valkyra prepared to deliver the final blow, Shon appeared behind her. He grabbed her wrist before she could take the shot. "I'm truly sorry... please forgive me...."

"You fat... stupid... traitor...." she muttered, as her body slumped limply into his arms. Her appearance gradually reverted to normal over the next few seconds. She almost looked peaceful, if not for her eyes.

"Oh, geez... I hope she doesn't hate me." Shon nibbled nervously on his cuticles.

Lamia placed her hand on his shoulder. "You did what you had to. She'll understand eventually, one way or another."

"I hope... So, can we get out of here?" Shon gestured around the street at the dozens of charred bodies, many of which were blown to an unrecognizable mess. "I'm feeling a little ashamed of how hungry the smell is making me..."

"What is wrong with you, Shon?" said Lamia, cringing in disgust.

Shon's face turned bright red. "I don't know..."

"Well, whatever... We should take these brigands into custody. Archmage Quan will be pleased to hear that the mission is complete." Lamia raised her hands and muttered an incantation, causing the few intact corpses to animate.

Her undead minions lifted up The Wizard's limp body, and began to drag him towards the tower. When the risen corpses that had been subduing Fabulon hauled him away, he did not resist. Jeff attempted to fight back at first, but gave up when it became clear that the cadavers were stronger than him. Shon gently lifted Valkyra's body; carrying her in his arms, he followed Lamia and her minions around the tower.

As he was being dragged past the crumbled remains of Archmage Quan's golems, The Wizard wondered what kind of horrible punishment she had prepared for him. On some level, he wished Valkyra would have finished him off when she had the chance. As the massive marble doors of Circle

Chapter Twenty

Tower started to grind open, The Wizard steeled himself for what was to come.

A moment later, however, it seemed that fate had poorlier written plans. Nobody present at the time could have foreseen the following events. Suddenly, over the rumbling of the doors, a high-pitched shout could be heard from above.

"*We're right proper as fuuuck!*"

Whipping around and looking up, Lamia and Shon saw the last thing they would expect: a pair of gnomes haphazardly strapped to a single jetpack, barrelling directly toward them. Both of the twins' faces were alight with manic glee, as their hair whipped around in the wind.

Unable to react in time, Lamia was struck directly in the stomach by the speeding twin torpedo. With a pained yelp, she was launched backwards with tremendous velocity. Soaring through the air, she struck Shon directly in the chest, bouncing off and causing him to drop Valkyra. Shon raised his hand to invoke a spell; before he could, however, the sparking jet pack skated to his feet.

"Oh, geez..."

The three remaining Equestrians were engulfed in a fiery explosion. Shards of hot shrapnel ricocheted off the tower, chipping the white marble. A moment later, after the smoke cleared, they were lying motionless on the ground. There was a smoking crater where the jetpack had been.

Shon appeared to have taken the brunt of the explosion; his robes were singed and torn to shreds, and blood spouted from numerous lacerations across his abdomen. Lamia looked in much better shape, but most of her long, elegant hair had been burned away, and she was covered in bruises. Although Valkyra had been unaffected by the blast, she seemed to have been knocked unconscious when Shon dropped her.

When Lamia had lost consciousness, her enchantment was released on the reanimated cadavers. Her undead cronies fell limply to the ground, releasing their grip on Fabulon, Jeff, and The Wizard.

"Well, that was a freebie..." said Fabulon, getting to his feet. He looked around at his allies, and his heart once again sank; The Wizard was still unable to move, the gnomes had been knocked unconscious by the impact,

Fight for the Circle

and Jeff was rocking back and forth with a glazed look in his eyes. "Not that we're much better off... It's only a matter of time before backup arrives."

The colossal doors of Circle Tower finished grinding open, revealing a scene of catastrophe within. The floating platforms that once filled the atrium seemed to have all plummeted to the ground, shattering into hundreds of massive shards of crystal that littered the floor. Lying amongst the debris were the bodies of innumerable wizards; the survivors were frantically running around the room, assisting the injured. Small fires were dotted throughout the wreckage. For a moment, it seemed that nobody noticed anyone at the door.

As Fabulon started dragging The Wizard's body away from the tower, he suddenly felt as though he were sinking into the ground. His feet were anchored in place as the cobblestone below wrapped itself around his ankles. Despite his struggles, the stone continued to creep its way up his legs.

"Where do you think you're going, handsome?"

The face of Archmage Quan emerged out of the cobblestone at Fabulon's feet. Magically reduced to human size, she rose up to eye level with him. Smiling wickedly, she grabbed his wrist and pulled his hands away from The Wizard; even in her smaller form, the strength of her grip was like a vice.

"Your little group of dissidents have caused me quite a lot of trouble, you know." She stroked her fingers down Fabulon's cheek. "I would have come out to deal with you myself earlier, but I had to help clean up this huge disaster you created." She gestured to the chaotic scene within the tower. "I was planning to let you off easy, Fabulon, but now I'm not so sure, after this mess you've made...."

Fabulon spat in her face. "I have nothing to say to you."

"Very well..." Archmage Quan wiped Fabulon's phlegm out of her right eye. She kneeled down and placed her palm on the cobblestone. The stones at her feet began to meld together, and a large mound of rock began to rise below her. Two large, stone fists protruded from the street, and a cobbled colossus slowly pulled itself out of the ground. The golem stood at least fifteen feet tall, with Quan glaring down from atop its head. "Take them away."

The golem swung one of its massive hands down and scooped up Fabulon and The Wizard in one swipe. They could barely breathe as they were

335

squeezed in the stone fist. With its other hand, the golem picked Jeff up by the ankles. Perhaps it was simply because she did not notice them, but Quan did not bother attending to the gnomes.

Archmage Quan smiled victoriously the entire journey to the Circle dungeon, making sure her golem held her captives in such a way that they could see this.

Chapter Twenty-One
Plan W

Fabulon sat with his back slumped against the wall of the Circle's filthiest jail cell, knocking his already aching head against the cold stone behind him. In the corner, The Wizard's battered, limp body was slumped sideways over a festering mattress. Lying on the floor, Jeff was staring silently at the ceiling and nursing a broken rib. Otherwise, their cell was barren of all but a thick layer of grime and cobwebs.

Outside their cell, Inspector Perkins was pacing back and forth with a clipboard. The pile of their confiscated gear was lying in the corner behind him. Archmage Quan had returned to the main floor to assist in the restoration of Circle Tower's atrium.

Perkins ran his clipboard along the bars of the cell. "Look, the sooner you scumbags start talking, the sooner we can move you into a nicer jail cell. I bet a toilet sounds nice right about now, doesn't it? Then you could finally have a drink of water!"

"Go... fuck... yourself...." muttered The Wizard. Just enough of his strength had returned that he was barely able to raise his middle finger at Perkins.

"Fabulon, you're a sensible man; surely you know you picked the wrong side, right? Just tell me where your friend hid the *Arcane Dictionary*, and I'll see what I can do to get you a stay of execution."

"Didn't you hear him? He told you to go fuck yourself."

337

Chapter Twenty-One

"Fine, we can do this the hard way. I'll return soon, I just have to fetch my tools." Perkins winked at Fabulon before sauntering out of the room with a wicked smile on his face. After he slammed the door behind him, they heard his muffled footsteps fade into the distance.

Fabulon stood up and leaned against the wall by The Wizard's bed, looking down at his limp form. He heaved a forlorn sigh. "Well, buddy boy, this is fucked up. If your sister doesn't come through, we're all as good as dead."

"Don't... worry." The Wizard let out a light chuckle. "The Wizard... has got this...."

"What are you talking about?" asked Fabulon, furrowing his brow. It had been a while since he last heard The Wizard refer to himself in third person. "Did Shon sap your intelligence as well? What do you think you can do right now?"

The Wizard looked up at Fabulon and winked. "I am not... The Wizard...."

"What...?"

Suddenly, The Wizard's skin began to roil and convulse. His face contorted in pain as his muscles twitched; he looked as though, if he could move, he would be writhing in agony. Fabulon stepped back and averted his gaze as The Wizard's hair and beard started to change color and suck back into his head.

"What the fuck?!"

The transformation ended as quickly as it had begun. When Fabulon looked back at the bed, it was no longer The Wizard sprawled across it. Lying there, with a grin on his upside down face, was none other than Chris.

Fabulon stared speechless. He looked utterly perplexed.

Jeff sat up and looked around to see what was causing the commotion. His jaw dropped when he saw Chris lying on the bed in The Wizard's robes.

"Fabulon... what's going on?"

"I'm not sure, either.... Care to explain, Chris...?"

"All part of... the plan...." muttered Chris, giving them a shaky thumbs-up. "The Wizard... *Arcane Dictionary*... polymorph spell... going after Anasthasia...."

Plan W

"Wow, he actually bothered to use that thing?" asked Jeff, raising his eyebrows. "And here I thought he was too lazy to learn anything new..."

Fabulon's face lit up. A pleasant chill ran down his spine as he realized all hope was not lost. "Huh... So, this was his plan all along?"

"Yup..." Chris weakly lifted his arm, sliding his hand onto Fabulon's ample buttocks and giving it a surprisingly firm squeeze. "And I... earned that...."

The door outside their cell opened, and Inspector Perkins skipped back into the room. He was holding a bloodstained duffel bag and whistling a jaunty tune. When he saw Chris lying where The Wizard had been, however, Perkins' look of joy instantly melted into sheer panic. He frantically tugged his neat silver hair into a ruffled mess.

"What have you done?! *Where is he*?!"

Fabulon walked up to the bars of the cell, smiling calmly as he looked into Perkins' eyes. "Looks like you haven't won yet."

Inspector Perkins screamed with rage, kicking the steel bars with all of his relatively feeble might. After shooting a hateful look at Fabulon, he spun on his heels and stormed out of the room.

"She's going to kill me for this..."

Meanwhile, deep below Circle Tower, The actual Wizard was traversing the dark tunnels, a magical orb of light held aloft before him. He was following a series of complicated instructions from the *Arcane Almanac*. For once, the book had given him a straightforward answer, but The Wizard was not sure how happy he was about that; when he asked where to find his sister, it gave him the same result as when he asked about his father. Its answer had been a map of the tunnels with a red X over one of the rooms; it was rather like solving a maze on paper.

Holding up the book, he beckoned his light spell to hover over the page. According to the map's updates on his location, he had almost reached the chamber in which his dad was being kept. Although he was unsure how long he had been down here, he knew he did not have long before his allies' diversion was over with. Praying that Anasthasia was not in danger, he headed towards her location marked on the map.

Chapter Twenty-One

All these tunnels look the same, thought The Wizard. *Without this map, I could be stuck down here for hours, maybe even days*. As he made his way down yet another in a series of long hallways, he wondered why the *Arcane Almanac* had been so helpful this time. The Wizard had not quite yet worked out how to properly use the book; he could only assume that it helped to have a clear picture of what he wanted to find.

He came to a strangely familiar hexagonal junction. According to the map, he only had to traverse one more hall to reach his destination. As he headed into the passage, he realized why it was familiar; all along the corridor, the walls were smeared with the same racial obscenities Knippe and Knorpe painted during their heist. This was the corridor that led to the artifact vault.

As he neared the end of the corridor, he readied the gyroscopic sniper he had taken from Chris. Although it was not the best weapon for fighting indoors, he figured it must be more effective than the nonlethal revolver. He could not help but wonder how the solid gold revolver he pawned off on Chris had performed in battle.

A wide expanse of darkness opened before him. Holding aloft his luminous orb, The Wizard cast a dim glow over most of the room. It looked just as he remembered it. To his right, a massive stretch of adamantine filled the entire wall from corner to corner: the same door that had led to the artifact vault days before. Its massive hinges hung next to him, each of them larger than his body. The room was nearly empty, aside from the cobwebby pile of crates that still laid undisturbed in the far corner.

The Wizard saw that the door of the vault was hanging slightly open. At the far end, it was cracked just wide enough that a man could squeeze through. An eerie green light shone through the opening, flickering fluidly on the dingy stone walls. As he slowly tiptoed across the room, The Wizard began to hear faint noises from beyond the door. He could just make out the sound of a man softly moaning.

Tightly gripping his sniper rifle, he squeezed through the gap in the door. Once he made it through, he crouched down and held up the barrel of his gun. He was prepared for an ambush; he was prepared for a trap; he was even prepared to once again see his father suspended in a tank; what he absolutely was not prepared for, however, was what else awaited him within the vault.

Plan W

Before he noticed the worst thing he would ever see, he found that the pedestals holding the artifacts had been removed from the vault. Instead, the three large tanks that held his ancestors were lined up against the rear wall. Ghostly light wavered on the adamantine floor and walls.

The Wizard was once again face to face with his father, whose limp, atrophied body was floating in the ghostly green water, connected to a series of tubes. Locks of his grayish-red hair and beard swirled softly around his pruned face. Next to him was the tank that held his grandfather. The final tank, which had held the withered corpse that must have been his great grandfather, now held Anasthasia. Her clothes and flamethrower were piled in the corner, and Vahim and Vaharm were nowhere to be seen.

His sister's nude body, however, was not the truly horrendous thing The Wizard saw inside that chamber. The heinous reality of what he found within was much, much worse; he had walked in on Horner masturbating.

His mind would be forever burdened with the vivid memory of what he saw. Horner was hunched over even more than usual, staring captivated into Anasthasia's tank, holding her panties to his nose, and making passionate love to his left hand.

The Wizard had the sights of his sniper trained at Horner. He could have taken the shot. However, the haunting vision that met his gaze was too much for him to cope with. He slowly lowered the barrel of his rifle, his jaw dropping along with it. Combined with the deluge of booze with which he started his day, this revolting sight of Horner's chapped, crusty ass brought his breakfast to the brink. Dropping his rifle to the floor, he keeled over and vomited a puddle of foamy bile.

Horner tensed up and dropped Anasthasia's panties. He nearly tripped over his pants as he spun around. For a moment, he just stood there, still firmly gripping his erection. The few remaining tufts of his greasy, black hair hung in his face, partially obscuring his look of humiliation. The only movement in the room was a dribble of pus slowly trickling from a burn on Horner's neck.

Coming to his senses, Horner pulled up his pants and dashed over to Anasthasia's flamethrower. Leaving the fuel tank on the floor, he lifted the shaft and pointed the nozzle at The Wizard. His face lit up in a toothless grin.

Chapter Twenty-One

"How the tables have turned..." he said, stroking the draconic head of the flamethrower. He slowly walked towards The Wizard, dragging the fuel tank behind him. "You have no idea how much I've dreamt of this exact situation."

The Wizard stood up and wiped the vomit from his lips. He still could not believe what he had walked into. "You sick son of a bitch... You better not have laid a finger on my sister!"

Horner cackled gleefully. "Oh, I laid more than a finger on her... but don't worry, I left her honor intact. That's more than I can say for what's about to happen to your face."

"Oh, no!" The Wizard shielded his face in a facetious facade of fear. "Don't tell me you're going to make me look like you!"

Anger flashed across Horner's face. "You may jest now, but soon, you'll regret every moment of your miserable existence. The Archmage said she wanted you alive, but I don't recall her giving any instructions as to the condition you need be in." He shot a jet of flame just above The Wizard's head.

The Wizard's hair stood on end as it was singed at the ends. In his bravado, he had forgotten just how potent those magical flames were. Knowing that Horner thought he was holding a regular flamethrower, The Wizard was actually scared he would be burned away in the blaze. He did not want to warn Horner of the danger, however, lest he tempt him to actually do it. In a panic, he struggled to think of how to stall the situation.

"Wait!" he said, pausing for a moment and gritting his teeth anxiously. "Before you kill me, can you tell me one thing? How did you capture my sister? I would've thought she'd have eaten you alive, possibly literally."

Horner sneered, relaxing the barrel of the flamethrower. He licked his lips, his eyes gleaming with malice. "Oh, what's wrong? Are you worried about your precious little sister?"

The Wizard could tell Horner was simply taunting him. He knew that if he acted distraught enough, the scumbag would take his time to savor every moment of his suffering; this was his best chance to buy time. "Don't you dare hurt her! You have me, isn't that all you and your boss really want? All you and Quan need is a new battery to power whatever abhorrent schemes you're working on. You could just take me; you don't even have to tell anyone you found her!"

"Wow, that's very noble of you," said Horner. "And here I thought that you only cared about yourself. It would almost move me, if it weren't for the fact that I hate your guts."

"Please, spare my sister's life! I'll do anything... I'll suck your dick!" The Wizard was worried he may have laid it on a little thick.

Horner raised what would have been his eyebrows, if he still had any. "Well, shit... I just lost a bet with Perkins... Well, whatever... I definitely do not want you to do that... Anyway, it so happens that I caught your sister by complete accident. I heard an explosion in the distance, so I went to investigate; when I got there, she had set her weapon down to gather up a bunch of shattered bones for some reason. You should have heard her squeal when I grabbed her from behind!"

The Wizard threw up a little in his mouth. He did not want to imagine Horner undressing his sister. "Ugh... you're disgusting... I swear that if you touch her again, I'll kill you."

"Oh, really?" said Horner, firing forth another jet of flames. "And how exactly are you going to do that?"

Unable to think of how to follow up his threat, The Wizard hung his head. He was ashamed of being at the mercy of someone so pitiful.

"You know, we never even knew you had a sister," said Horner. "Archmage Quan had her best men research your father's life, and no one turned up anything on her. I just had a feeling when I captured her, so I ran some tests, and wouldn't you know it: her magical blood is twice as potent as yours. She has almost as much innate power as Ziro."

"Wait, are you serious? I wouldn't have thought..." The Wizard paused for a moment. "Although, I suppose it isn't that surprising, since her mother was an elven priestess, and my mother was a cokehead...."

"The Archmage will simply be delighted by this news. Not only have I captured her nemesis, but I have also managed to find an entire new source of power for future generations! Now that we finally have a female specimen, we can begin breeding fresh conduits to provide us with endless power. Soon, we will be unstoppable!" Horner's maniacal laughter echoed through the vault. "Hey, I have an idea! How about you come over here?" He beckoned The Wizard towards him.

"I don't really want to…"

"That's fine with me." Horner shrugged before tensing his grip on the flamethrower. "I suppose I could just burn you alive right here. Archmage Quan will be angry at first, but I don't think she'll mind when I show her our newest acquisition." He gestured to the tank in which Anasthasia was suspended.

The Wizard had yet to formulate a plan to get him out of this situation. Beads of sweat dripped down his neck as he stepped over his fallen weapon and anxiously dawdled towards Horner. When he was nearly at arms length, Horner ordered him to stop. With a sadistic grin on his face, Horner stuck the mouth of the flamethrower into The Wizard's crotch.

"Make one wrong move and I'll burn it off." Horner's persisting erection made it very evident that he took great pleasure in this situation. "If you do as I say, maybe you'll get lucky and only get burnt on eighty percent of your body, like I was."

The Wizard gulped fearfully. If he could not think of an exit strategy soon, his only choice would be to go on the offensive, and he knew that probably would not go well for him. He wished he had not dropped his weapon on the floor. "What do you want me to do?"

"Strip naked. I want to watch your skin boil."

Apprehensively, The Wizard began to remove his clothing. As he slid his pants down, he covertly drew the revolver out of his belt. Horner did not seem to notice him draw the weapon. Holding the gun behind his back, he took off his shirt, careful to hide it in the cloth as he did so. He tightly gripped the handle, knowing full well that he only had one shot before being burnt to a crisp. Swallowing his fear, he drew the gun out of his bundle of clothing.

However, before he was even able to raise the weapon to Horner, the moment was shattered by a shout coming from behind him.

"Hey, ugly, get away from him!"

As The Wizard craned his neck, he was just able to make out a flaming crossbow bolt sailing towards him. He was unable to react in time, and the bolt clipped him in the shoulder as it flew past. The muscle between his shoulder and his neck had been torn clean open, and pain shot through his torso. The Wizard screamed in pain, trying to process what had just happened.

Looking to the door, he saw that a man was standing by the opening, holding a large crossbow. The Wizard was unable to believe what he was seeing: standing before him was none other than Gary, the last person he expected to come to his aid. Although, as his shoulder bled profusely, he had to admit that Gary was one of the first people he expected to shoot him with a crossbow.

Behind him, The Wizard heard an anguished croaking sound. He looked at Horner, and saw that the bolt had soared directly through the man's heart. Horner stumbled backwards, dropping the shaft of the flamethrower to the floor; he looked down at the crossbow bolt, placing his hands around the room. As he fell to his knees, Horner raised his head, with a look of stunned surprise on his face. He flipped off The Wizard one final time, before falling forward, causing the bolt to drive through his chest and stick out of the hump on his back.

"You okay?" asked Gary. He threw aside his crossbow and ran up to The Wizard, putting a hand on his good shoulder. "That looked like it hurt."

"Hell yeah, it hurt!" yelled The Wizard, shoving Gary away from him. "Why couldn't you have given me some warning?"

"I shouted 'hey, ugly'. What, did you not think that was for you?"

"You son of a bitch!" The Wizard applied pressure to his gaping wound, trying to stop the bleeding. "You fucking shot me with a crossbow!"

"Yeah, not shit, asshole, but I also saved your life!" Frowning, Gary crossed his arms indignantly. "How about a 'thank you'?"

The Wizard glared at Gary as he put his pants back on. He was in no mood for his attitude after being shot. "Hell no, fuck you! How are you even here, anyway?"

"Let's just say I hitched a ride." Gary smirked mischievously.

"No, I mean how the hell did you know where to find me?"

"You're not the only one with connections on the inside. You seem surprised. Did you think I was just gonna bail on the mission?"

"Yeah, pretty much." The Wizard shrugged, cringing as he did so.

Gary rolled his eyes.

Chapter Twenty-One

The Wizard turned around, facing the glass tanks that held his family. Each tank stood on a pedestal, with a metal valve and control panel. Butterflies swirled in his stomach as he began to step towards them. It was hard for him to believe that he was about to see his father again. It had been so many years, and for the longest time, he thought his father was dead. His hands shook as he stepped over Horner's bleeding corpse.

He figured it would be best to start by releasing his sister; she would probably yell at him if he released their dad without her, plus he was tired of seeing her naked body. The Wizard grabbed the release valve on Anasthasia's tank, turning it counterclockwise. As the water drained from her tank, Anasthasia slumped down against the glass. After the tank had been completely drained, The Wizard pressed random buttons on the control panel until he found one that opened the tank.

As the glass cylinder rose up mechanically, Anasthasia fell off the pedestal. The Wizard caught her as she fell. Trying to touch her as little as possible, he grabbed the catheter tubes one by one and gently pulled them out of her veins.

Anasthasia's eyes slowly opened. She blinked up at her brother and smiled softly. "Hey... I don't think I've ever been this happy to see you...."

"I'm glad you're okay too." The Wizard helped Anasthasia to her feet. He gestured to the tank next to them, in which floated their father, Ziro Xuntasi. "And look who it is! It was a long, strange trip, but we're all together now."

Anasthasia's face lit up with joy. "Oh, my goodness! I can't believe we actually found him! I half expected you to have made up the whole thing." She ran up to the tank and put her hands on the glass.

"Why would I do that?" The Wizard laughed and shook his head. "Anyway, you should get some clothes on. Nobody wants to see all that." He waved his hand vaguely at her without looking.

"I politely disagree," said Gary, looking up and down Anasthasia's body.

"Well, whatever. Just please get some clothes on while I work on releasing dad. We should probably hurry, I doubt we have long before Quan catches on." The Wizard darted to his father's tank and turned the release valve. This time, he knew exactly which button to press to raise the glass. Pulling the tubes out of his nude father was not quite as awkward as having to touch his naked sister; however, he could have done without having to grab his dad's shriveled, pruney penis to unlodge the urinary catheter.

Anasthasia dressed herself in the corner while Gary smoked and watched. She transformed her shapeshifting outfit into a long-sleeved, white blouse and a knee-length, green plaid skirt; it was the least revealing outfit The Wizard had ever seen her wear since she was a teenager. Once she was clothed, she joined The Wizard at their father's side.

Although Ziro had been out of the tank for several minutes, and all the catheters were removed, he showed no signs of waking. His muscles were atrophied and his skin was pruned as a raisin. His soggy grayish-red beard extended past his belly button, although not far enough. The Wizard had leaned him against the wall, and was pacing back and forth, wracking his brain for a way to wake him. He had tried shaking him vigorously, conjuring a gallon of water over his head, and even giving him a purple nurple; Ziro seemed unphased by all of The Wizard's efforts.

"I really hope he's okay," said Anasthasia. She was fidgeting restlessly, gritting her teeth and pulling her hair. Her face was even paler than usual. "I don't think I can handle losing him again…"

The Wizard had never before seen his sister look so worried. Without thinking, he walked up to her and threw his arms around her. "It's going to be okay." He pulled her close and patted her on the back. "He's not dying, he's just really drained. I know we can figure out how to revive him."

Anasthasia held her arms uncomfortably at her side as her brother hugged her. When he tried to let go, however, she pulled him back into an embrace. Tears were trickling down her face. "Thanks… I can't tell you how much I appreciate you right now, and only right now…."

Gary walked up to them and cleared his throat.

"Right, we should try to figure this out," said The Wizard. He and Anasthasia broke apart, and he walked back to Ziro's unconscious body. Reaching into Jeff's backpack, he pulled out the *Arcane Dictionary* and laid it open. "Maybe there is a spell in here that could give him energy…" Closing his eyes in focus, The Wizard placed his hand on the open book. After a moment, a stream of light green energy flowed from the pages and into his arm. "Huh… all I could learn was a simple innervation spell. It'll basically be the equivalent of shoving a bump of coke up his nose; useful spell, but I don't know how good it'll be here…"

"Well, you might as well give it a try." Anasthasia shrugged.

The Wizard placed his palm over his dad's head, and the same green light flowed from his fingers into Ziro's mouth. They all waited a moment and nothing happened. With a weary sigh, The Wizard banged his fist on the wall.

"Damn it, he's definitely more than just unconscious." The Wizard gestured to the tank that had held his father. "These machines were draining his very life essence. The only reason you're okay is that you were only hooked up for a few hours."

"Yeah, and even I'm a little woozy," said Anasthasia. "I can't even imagine being trapped in there for years. If only there was a way to give him some of his magic back."

A few gears clicked into place in The Wizard's mind. He grinned optimistically. "Wait… I have one last idea!" He walked up to the tank holding his grandfather and placed his hand on the glass. "When I was here last, I got some of this water on me, and it filled me with an unusual vigor. It seems to contain a lot of latent magical energy. Maybe it could revive him."

"That's interesting…" Anasthasia walked up to The Wizard and kicked him in the knee. "So, tell me this, why the hell did you drain the water from dad's tank?! Now we have to use *grandpa's* nasty bathwater! Dad's not going to be too happy about that."

"Well, I didn't know we'd have to do this!" said The Wizard, throwing up his hands defensively. "I thought he'd just wake up. I guess I didn't really think it through…" He tapped his hand against the glass of the final tank. "I think this should do the trick, though. The water I was exposed to came from the tank I think held our great grandfather's shriveled corpse, and even it still seemed fairly potent."

"Well, whatever, just bring him over here so we can give it a try."

The Wizard grabbed his father's arm and dragged him towards the final tank. He set Ziro against the pedestal on which sat the tank and told the others to stand back. Placing his hand on the glass, he muttered an incantation. He stepped away as cracks began to form in the glass. A large

Plan W

hole shattered in the side of the tank, and glowing water cascaded down onto Ziro's head.

At first, it seemed as though nothing had happened. When the water finished draining, it slowly spread across the floor. Suddenly, however, the water changed course; it began to flow towards Ziro's body, absorbing into his skin. A moment later, it had all been absorbed. Ziro's eyes snapped open; he sat up and attempted to leap to his feet, but his atrophied legs buckled, and he fell to his knees. The Wizard rushed to his dad's side and helped him to his feet.

"Where the hell am I?" muttered Ziro, looking around the room. His deep green eyes glinted like emeralds as his gaze fell on his daughter. "Anasthasia, is that you? Did you come to save me?"

Anasthasia rushed to her father and hugged him, pushing The Wizard to the side. It seemed she did not even care that Ziro was nude. "It's so good to see you, daddy! Of course I came to save you, I've missed you so much!"

The Wizard cleared his throat. "You know, she didn't do it alone, dad."

Ziro looked at The Wizard and raised his eyebrows in surprise. "Oh, son, I didn't even recognize you! My, my, you've grown quite a scruffy beard. You should give it a trim, you look like a vagrant."

"It's good to see you too, dad..."

Looking back to Anasthasia, Ziro smiled indulgently. "I can't express how overjoyed I am to see you again, princess. I knew you'd grow up to make me proud!"

Anasthasia beamed with pride.

"I'm glad you two are happy to see each other," said The Wizard, rolling his eyes. He was used to not being appreciated, but it still stung. "We have to hurry, though. My allies were causing a diversion, but I doubt it will be long until Archmage Quan is onto us."

"So, that traitor is Archmage now, is she?" Ziro scowled, looking up to the ceiling. "I don't want to imagine what kind of condition the Circle is in with her in command. I always knew she was too ambitious, but when I discovered her true intentions, it was too late for me. It was all I could do to hide my most valuable treasure, the *Arcane Dictionary*. I knew that if she couldn't find the *Dictionary*, it would ensure your safety for at least a while."

349

Chapter Twenty-One

"Well… thanks, dad…." The Wizard scratched his head awkwardly. This was the closest his dad had ever come to saying he cared about him. "Now, I think we should get out of here. You're in no condition to fight if Quan catches us."

"I'm a little shaky, but I just need to steady myself. I'm going to transfer a portion of my magical energy to restore my physical strength." Ziro took a shaky step back, before closing his eyes and flexing his entire body. Light green energy flowed from his head and down his body, swirling into his muscles. His arms and legs bulked up unnaturally fast; he was still relatively scrawny, but he was able to stand on his own without issue. "That's much better."

The Wizard was impressed as always with and slightly envious of his father's magical talent. He had no idea how to do anything like that.

"Alright, let's go upstairs," said Ziro. He moved his hands down his body, conjuring a set of deep blue robes with gold trim. They looked just like The Wizard's robes, except in far better condition. "I'd like to have a word with 'Archmage' Quan."

"Are you serious?" asked The Wizard. "You still haven't recovered your strength, and she's a lot stronger than she used to be. I don't think you can fight her right now, dad."

"I'm a lot stronger than you think. Besides, we may not have to fight her, after all."

The Wizard raised an eyebrow. He had no idea what his father's plan could be.

Seeming to sense his insecurity, Ziro smiled calmly at The Wizard. "Don't worry, I know what I'm doing." He beckoned his children towards him. "Come over here; we'll lock hands, and I'll teleport us into the atrium of Circle Tower."

"About that…" said The Wizard, as he approached his father. "I'm pretty sure Quan has a teleport ward on this room. I only got in because that idiot left the door open."

He gestured to Horner's bloody body.

"Yeah, and who was it who taught her abjuration magic?"

"Good point, you can probably breach it." The Wizard locked hands with his father and looked around the room. He gestured to the broken tank in which his grandfather's body was slumped against the side. "So, should we just leave grandpa here?"

Ziro sighed. "Unfortunately, it is doubtful he'll be able to be saved. At this point, I think the machines were all that was keeping him alive. For now,all we can do is leave him behind."

"Damn, that sucks..." The Wizard patted his dad on the back. He had never met his grandfather, and found it difficult to work up any emotions over leaving him behind. "Hey, I just realized... where is Gary?"

"Oh, he slinked away earlier, when dad woke up," said Anasthasia, hugging her father tightly. "I didn't say anything because I think he's gross, and I wanted him to leave."

The Wizard laughed. "Fair enough."

Ziro closed his eyes in a look of focus. In an instant, the three of them were transported directly into the center of Circle Tower. The Wizard was shocked when he saw the condition of the atrium. Although the randomly scattered fires had been extinguished, nothing had been done yet about the hundreds of massive shards of crystal. Dozens of mages were running between the wreckage, assisting survivors and salvaging damaged equipment. For a while, no one noticed who had appeared in their presence. After a moment, however, there was a shocked squeal from by their side.

"Ziro, is that you?!" It came from a tiny old man with skin like a leather handbag and no hair other than the bushiest eyebrows The Wizard had ever seen; his name was Aldaerh, and he was the eldest member of the Circle Council. Although The Wizard rarely spoke to him, he remembered him hanging around his dad a lot during his childhood. He had always been a kindly man. "I can't believe my eyes! I hope I'm not having another stroke..."

Heads turned and jaws dropped all around the room. Shocked murmurs erupted all over as the Circle magi gathered around them. Some people seemed excited that their true leader had returned, and others seemed to think he was an imposter. Ziro waited for the talking to die down before he spoke.

"Yes, it really is me, and I've returned for a reason. This may be hard for some of you to hear, but your leaders have been deceiving you for years. You may have heard I went missing on a mission and was presumed dead.

Chapter Twenty-One

This was a lie; I was imprisoned by your current Archmage, and used to power her sinister devices."

"He lies!" shouted a voice from the crowd. Perkins pushed his way to the front. "That's not really Ziro Xuntasi; this is just a ploy by his renegade son to gain control of the Circle."

"I'm more than willing to subject myself to any tests necessary to confirm my identity," said Ziro. "If the Circle feels I need to be held in protective custody until this is cleared up, I'd be more than willing to do so, as long as Archmage Quan is suspended during the investigation."

"*What is the meaning of this*?!" thundered a booming female voice. Quan's head rose above the crowd as she slowly enlarged to her maximum height of nearly thirty feet. She glared down at the three of them. "Who is this imposter of my predecessor?"

"You're the only imposter here, you crazy bitch!" yelled The Wizard.

Ziro held his palm to The Wizard. "Let me do the talking…" He looked up at Quan, smiling coldly. "Well, well, well… if it isn't Mia Quan, my ex-apprentice. My, how you've grown!"

"Oh, please, you don't expect anyone to actually believe this facade?" Quan stepped over the crowd and reduced herself back to human size. She walked up to Ziro and gave him a murderous look. After a moment, she turned to face the crowd, gesturing behind her. "This is obviously not Archmage Xuntasi. This is just another pathetic stunt from the worst wizard ever to be a stain on the Circle's good name."

Anger bubbled in The Wizard's chest.

Ziro walked past Quan and addressed the crowd. "This woman is not a leader; she is a villain and a traitor. I implore you, members of the Council: *do not trust her*."

"And why should they trust you?" said Quan, laughing spitefully. She spat in his face. "The real Ziro Xuntasi has been dead for years. Are we supposed to believe you've risen from the grave?"

The crowd of mages once again erupted in subtle murmurs.

"Oh, Mia, I am so disappointed in you…" Ziro calmly wiped the phlegm from his cheek and looked Quan dead in the eye. "You were such a promising apprentice. I always saw good in you, that's why I took you as my student. I remember you saying the reason you wanted to be a member of the

Plan W

Circle was to use diplomacy to change the fearful way people look at giants. What happened to the compassionate woman I once knew?"

"Shut up, I've heard enough of this! You never understood what it takes to be a strong leader." Her eyes flashing madly, Quan pointed at him with a furiously shaking finger. "Battlemages, take this man to the dungeon. That's an order!"

No one did anything. People in the crowd just looked awkwardly at one another, filling the air with bemused muttering. It seemed that they were becoming uncertain about Archmage Quan's true colors.

"Are you all fucking deaf?" she yelled, growing back to her normal size. Although she was towering over the crowd, her voice shook with a hint of anxiety. "I told you to arrest him! Don't tell me you're believing this imposter's lies! His son destroyed the entire tower, and the way I see it, they should all be tried for treason!"

Aldaerh stepped forward and cleared his throat. "Umm… Archmage Quan, with all due respect, I think this issue requires a more delicate approach. We cannot simply arrest the man who might be our rightful leader, without some deliberation."

There were murmurs of agreement coming from the surrounding mages. Quan clenched her fists until her knuckles turned white.

Another member of the Circle Council, a tall elven woman with white robes and long blonde hair, stepped forward as well. The Wizard had never spoken to her, but he was pretty sure her name was Sheska. "In light of the fact that we have clearly been kept in the dark about some things, I think you owe us some explaining, Archmage Quan. If this does indeed turn out to be the true Archmage, you will have a lot to answer for."

The Wizard grinned up at Quan victoriously. "You hear that? Pretty soon everyone will be able to see your true colors."

Massive beads of sweat began to form on Archmage Quan's face. "You disobedient bunch of… I am the Archmage… you can't…." She faltered for a moment, before letting out a scream of rage. "*Noooo*!!! I won't let this happen!!!" Her fists were engulfed in stone, and she swung one of them down at Ziro.

Holding up a single finger, Ziro was able to put a complete stop to the momentum of Quan's punch. The stone around her fist shattered, and her

353

hand was rebounded backwards and slammed into her face. He held up his hand and muttered an incantation, causing her to shrink down to the size of a gnome. "It's over, Mia. Who would have thought that even in my weakened state, you'd still be no match for me. I guess some things just don't change."

Quan quaked with fear as Ziro towered over her. She fell to her knees, bitter tears pooling in her eyes. "Damn it, why did you have to show up...?" she muttered, feebly beating her fists on his shins. "It's not fair... I almost had the *Arcane Dictionary* in my grasp... I would have been... unstoppable...."

The Wizard walked up to Quan and looked down on her without saying a word. Snorting up as much phlegm as he could, he hocked a massive loogie on her head.

Suddenly, someone in the crowd punched him in the side of the head. He turned to see Samantha standing next to him with her hands on her hips and a scowl on her face. The top of her head was covered in bandages, with a large bloodstain in the center. Her arms were covered in bruises and scratches. Once he was looking at her, she punched him again, square on the jaw.

"That's for almost getting me killed, asshole!" she shouted, glaring at him. "You didn't warn me how powerful that antimagic pulse would be! I only just managed to avoid getting crushed by one of those falling platforms."

The Wizard grinned sheepishly. "Right... sorry about that...."

"Oh, sure, '*sorry for almost killing you*'! Thanks a lot, douchebag." Samantha punched him in the gut before stomping off.

He could not help but think she was extremely strong for such a petite woman.

"That reminds me," said Ziro, placing his hand on The Wizard's good shoulder and spinning him around. He also punched him, in the nose this time.

"What the hell, dad?!" The Wizard held his hand over his nose as blood dripped down his face. "I think you broke my nose!"

"That's for destroying my tower. If this ever happens again, don't use the highest setting, idiot."

The next few hours were pure chaos for the Circle. The Council had a vote, and decided to take both Archmage Ziro and Quan into custody. As she was dragged away, Quan let loose a stream of obscenities so colorful that even Knippe and Knorpe would have been impressed. The Wizard and Anasthasia were also taken into custody for the duration of the investigation.

As he waited with his dad and sister in his cell in the dungeon, The Wizard paced back and forth impatiently. He had been complaining constantly since being arrested. His cell was not dingy by any means: the floor was carpeted, there were two full size beds, an actual toilet, and everything was clean. It just annoyed The Wizard to no end that he had to wait in the dungeon for so many hours without at least being provided a complimentary bag of weed.

To avoid conflict with the others, Quan had been placed in her own private cell. The Wizard could not stop speculating how much nicer it must be than their cell. Jeff and the others had been moved from their cell and into one across the room from The Wizard. The gnomes had been taken to the infirmary when they were found, but nobody asked about them anyway. What truly astounded The Wizard was that it seemed nobody had captured Gary.

Fabulon stood with his face pressed between the bars in excitement as Anasthasia filled him in on her exaggerated version of what had happened, in which she was featured as the heroine. This might have bothered The Wizard, but he was too worn out to care. Besides, he figured there was a good chance that she genuinely believed her heavily abridged version of the story, so he let it go.

They were each brought individually to an interrogation room multiple times. The Circle was famously slow when it came to its investigations, and this was a matter of unprecedented complexity. The Wizard could not help but worry that Quan might manage to throw them under the bus. Ziro assured him that it would all work out, and to trust that most of the Circle wants what is best for the kingdom. Nonetheless, The Wizard could not stop pacing. Eventually, his dad was taken away for genetic testing, leaving him alone in the cell with his sister.

It was a long rest of the day.

Chapter Twenty-Two
Crack Open a Cauldron

fter a series of invasive medical tests, it was proven beyond a doubt that the Ziro Xuntasi the Circle had in custody was the genuine article. To put it delicately, let me just say that they took a hell of a lot more than just a blood sample. The Wizard and his accomplices were released on parole, to await trial for the many, many crimes they committed in their heroic quest for justice. As the eldest member of the Council, Aldaerh temporarily assumed the position of Archmage for the duration of the trial.

Slowly, Circle Tower was restored to its previous majesty, and those wounded in the incident recovered from their injuries. However, the death toll had been over a hundred, and many people's hearts were heavy. There had not been so many sorcerers killed in a single day since the Salem Witch Riots. A lot of people thought that The Wizard and his accomplices should be convicted as murderers for all the innocent lives they took; some, on the other hand, regarded them as heroes for bringing Quan down and considered it collateral damage.

Quan's trial dragged on for several days. Eventually, she was sentenced with high treason, as well as a plethora of other charges, including no less than one hundred counts of sexual harassment, all but one of which were directed towards Fabulon. No normal prison would hold her, so she was sent to a maximum security wizard prison that she herself had ordered to be built: the now ironically-named Quantanamo Bay.

Crack Open a Cauldron

It turned out that she had hidden the Circle's stolen artifacts in the sex dungeon beneath her house; everyone gave Fabulon a lot of shit about what would have been in store for him, had they been unsuccessful in their quest. When inventory was taken of the artifacts, however, it turned out that one of the most valuable had gone missing: The *Arcane Encyclopedia*, the sacred repository of all knowledge of the natural world. Trembling fearfully, Quan had refused to tell them where it went.

Horner was pronounced dead, and not a soul cared; although his will ironically requested he be cremated, Ziro found it more fitting to dump him in Theiyre's sewage swamp. Arrested as Quan's accomplice, Perkins named names in an attempt to get a lesser sentence; it did not work, but he did successfully manage to bring down most of Quan's criminal empire within the Circle.

The Four Equestrians of the Apocalypse were cleared of all charges once it was proven that they did not know about Quan's evil schemes. Julian was also dumped in the swamp; although, as the Equestrian of Pestilence, this was at his behest.

Every sorcerer in the Circle was investigated individually, but no more of Quan's accomplices were turned up. After a few days, the investigation came to a close, once it was clear they had uncovered all they were going to.

When The Wizard and his accomplices were tried, Ziro was able to pull some strings to get their charges reduced to felony vandalism. They were sentenced to five hundred hours a piece of community service, with Knippe and Knorpe getting an extra fifty apiece for "excessive giggling during an interrogation". A lot of people in the Circle were not happy about this sentence, and The Wizard happened to be high on that list; the way he saw it, him saving his dad and unmasking Quan was the community service.

The day after their trial, they were awarded medals for their bravery in a small ceremony. Knippe and Knorpe were the only ones besides Kit Mingers who did not get a medal, and they complained about this to no end. They made it clear that the way they saw it, they were just as involved as everyone else. Perhaps this was the reason that they tried to make everyone pay a cover charge to get into the afterparty at *Luncheons and Flagons*; to their chagrin, however, the group simply decided their bar was too much of a disaster area, and elected to have the afterparty at *The Wizarding Hole* instead.

When they arrived at *The Wizarding Hole*, however, they saw that it was in even worse shape than the other bar. It had been heavily vandalised, and all of the liquor was missing. This did not come as much of a surprise to The Wizard, as he was well aware of how bad his neighborhood was; Chris, however, seemed completely thunderstruck by the state of his bar. He swayed faintly, clutching a beam for support.

"What did you expect?" asked The Wizard, putting his hand on Chris's shoulder. "I mean, this happens a couple times a year anyway. You should really get bars on the windows."

"I know… it's just that this is why I've been too afraid to come back here since we got out of jail…. Damn it, now the party is ruined..." Chris sat down in a nearby chair and pouted dejectedly. "I was gonna get Fabulon drunk and try to make my move…"

Fabulon furrowed his brow. "Come again?"

"I knew I shouldn't have come to this thing…" Cringing in disgust, Samantha crossed her arms. "This place is a shithole."

"Don't worry, I got this!" Grinning confidently, Ziro rolled up his sleeves. He raised his arms, and in one fluid motion, the entire room rearranged itself: the chairs and tables moved back into place, all the broken glass and graffiti disappeared, and a bottle of every liquor imaginable appeared on the shelves. "That's basically my signature spell, you know. I've thrown a lot of parties."

They all rushed forward excitedly and dug into the liquor. It was not long before they were all feeling extremely proper. Anasthasia had mixed a bowl of punch that was mostly rum, and The Wizard spiked it by drowning a couple fairies in the bowl. Fabulon had passed out within an hour, and Chris was fooling around with him under one of the tables.

Sitting at the bar, The Wizard and his dad were doing lines of cocaine with Kit Mingers. Behind the counter, the gnomes were chugging beers out of Vahim and Vaharm's skulls while Anasthasia egged them on. Samantha and Jeff sat at a table in the corner, sipping punch and talking shit about The Wizard.

The Wizard offered to make everyone his signature drink, *The Wizard's Cauldron*, which is a small pewter cauldron full of ale, with six shots of absinthe, a shot of creme de coca, and just the tiniest smidgen of morphine; it tastes absolutely disgusting, but it will get you right proper as fuck. No sane person would drink more than one, so he had three.

Everyone sipped their respective drinks, deeply engrossed in conversation with each other.

"I can't believe that his stupid cat talks now," Samantha was saying to Jeff. "Who would bother granting the power of speech to such a horrible creature? You have no idea how many times I had to clean that things jizz off my robes. And do I get an apology now that it talks? No."

Jeff silently nodded along as Samantha ranted about Kit Mingers for a solid minute. Behind the bar, Vahim and Vaharm were begging the gnomes to stop using them as mugs.

"Why are you like this?" muttered Vaharm spitefully as Knippe responded to his request by whipping out his dick and instead pissing in the skull. "You two are monsters…"

"I see us more like the three stooges," said Knippe, throwing the piss skull in the trash bin.

"Yeah, except we accidentally killed the other one." Knorpe also chucked the skull he was holding into the trash, before climbing atop the bar and pissing down into the bin.

"Poor Knappe…" Knippe and Knorpe stared reminiscently into the distance.

"Who the fuck are the three stooges?" asked Kit Mingers, furrowing his whiskers.

"Hey dad," said The Wizard, "I just thought of something. Why exactly did you hire Gary to watch over me, and not ask Aldaerh or someone else I knew?"

"Who?" Ziro looked genuinely bemused. "I'm going to be honest with you, I've never met anyone named Gary in my entire life."

"Huh… that's odd...." The Wizard was too drunk to pursue the issue any further. "Hey Chris… uhh... where exactly are you taking Fabulon, buddy?"

Chris grinned sheepishly. "I just thought I'd give him a surprise tour of my office."

"He's totally passed out." The Wizard raised an eyebrow.

Chapter Twenty-Two

"Yeah, that's what makes it a surprise!" Chris continued to drag Fabulon away. "I can't wait to see his face when he wakes up!"

Deciding not to think about whatever unspeakable acts Chris was about to commit, he turned his focus back to his third *Wizard's Cauldron*. Not long after that, he was feeling right proper as fuck, and decided he wanted to share some personal feelings with Jeff. He walked up to his nephew and placed his hand on his shoulder.

"Listen, Jeff," he said, a glob of boozy drool dripping from the corner of his mouth. "I'm sorry I dragged you into this."

"Oh, wow…" said Jeff, raising his eyebrows in surprise. "I certainly never expected that. I gave up on hinting that you owed me an apology ages ago."

The Wizard burst into tears, forcing a hug on Jeff. To say he was proper would be the understatement of the page. "Come on, my sweet nephew, sit on my lap and let me explain something to you."

Jeff shook his head with a smirk. "I'm fine with just sitting in this chair."

"Suit yourself, this is some real shit I'm about to lay down."

Samantha scoffed, getting up and walking away from the table.

"Okay," said Jeff, rolling his eyes and chuckling, "lay it on me."

"I've always respected the shit out of you, Jeff," said The Wizard, smiling at Jeff, eyes alight with shimmering tears. "I love you. This is the one time you'll hear me say it, but it's true. I never had children, but I see you as a son, and I just want to help you live a life that makes you happy."

"And you think that's something I can learn from *you*?" Jeff shook his head slowly, laughing derisively and not breaking eye contact with The Wizard. "No offense, but when have *you* ever been happy?."

The Wizard frowned. "Maybe as a child? Maybe not, I don't know… I think happiness is just letting time pass and not wanting it back."

"Are you trying to say *you* don't want your time back?"

"Of course I do! Time is kind of like cocaine: after it's gone, you always want it back!" The Wizard leaned forward and did a line.

"Well, I'm not a cokehead, so I should be fine."

"You're a good kid, Jeff…" The Wizard smiled paternally.

A few drinks later, The Wizard was trying to encourage Jeff to make a move on Anasthasia. Jeff kept insisting that he had no interest in her, but The Wizard simply continued to assert that it would be okay because Jeff had his

Crack Open a Cauldron

blessing. Eventually he dropped the issue, and started focusing on getting Jeff laid in other ways.

"You know what, Jeff?" said The Wizard. "Now that we're heroes, it's only a matter of time before the ladies start coming out of the woodwork and trying to work our wood!"

He was interrupted before he could start his plans, however, when a shitfaced Anasthasia got up on a table to make an announcement.

"Hey, everyone!" she shouted, banging a knife on her glass. "Who wants to hear my brother's name?!"

The Wizard's heart froze. His neck snapped in the direction of his sister, with a vicious glare on his face. "Anasthasia, don't you dare!"

She laughed hysterically, almost falling off the table. "He doesn't want me to tell anyone, but I honestly don't know why he hides it."

The Wizard got out of his seat and hurried towards her.

"I mean, it's not so bad. Tell me what you guys think! His name is —"

"*Noooo*!!!" Holding out his hands, The Wizard dove at her.

However, he was too late...

"*Harron Voldedore.*"

A stunned silence fell over the room. The only sound was Anasthasia's drunken laughter. The Wizard looked absolutely mortified as he stared speechlessly at his sister. Knippe and Knorpe looked as though it was a bonus birthday. Suddenly, everyone aside from The Wizard started laughing hilariously.

His face flushed bright red, The Wizard ran into Chris's office. A moment later, however, he ran out and vomited on the floor. "You do not want to know what's going on in there..."

It took awhile for The Wizard to adjust to his shame. Jeff kept giving him shit about his name, and even his dad was laughing at him. He had always wondered why his dad gave him such a horrible name, only to ridicule him for it so mercilessly as a child that he felt compelled to hide it his entire adult life. Fortunately, he had a massive surplus of cocaine, and it did not take him long to have completely forgotten about what had upset him.

By the end of the night, only The Wizard and Ziro were still awake in the bar. Anasthasia was also awake, but after she drank the majority of the drugged punch, she had run out into the night, screaming about getting some

Chapter Twenty-Two

dinner. The Wizard and his father sat at the bar, passing a long wooden pipe back and forth. They were totally toasted at this point.

"You know, if you think about it..." said The Wizard, "we're basically just zombies walking around possessed by ghosts..."

"That's deep." Ziro took a long toke, blowing out a series of smoke rings. "Do you think unicorns ever sixty-nine with their horns?"

"Woah... I just remembered... I forgot...."

"Yeah... I think you should get some sleep," said Ziro, patting his son on the back. "I'm going to wake your sister up and walk her home. You can make it back, right? If you would like, you could come stay at my manor."

The Wizard waved his hand dismissively. "Nah... My tower is like a block away..." He staggered to the coat rack, grabbing his robes. "What's the worst that could happen?"

Ziro shrugged. "If you insist."

The Wizard stumbled out of the bar and onto the dark street. He began walking in the wrong direction, and did not realize that until he had traveled a few blocks. On the way back, he fell asleep standing up a few times. During the few moments he was aware of how lost he was, he regretted washing down that cocaine with two more *Wizard's Cauldrons*. Eventually, he found his way home, leaving his front door wide open as he staggered upstairs to his bedroom.

That night, The Wizard lay on his couch, the cusps of himself at his grasp; in the wake of his own drunken fantasies, what followed was more than you need to know.

Chapter Twenty-Three
The Magic of Malice

t had been just over a week since the strife at the Circle. Ziro Xuntasi was once again the Archmage, and his beard once again well manicured; Circle Tower was nearly restored to its previous condition; and The Wizard was back to riding his father's coattails. Ziro had taken possession of the *Arcane Tomes*, knowing The Wizard would not take proper care of them; The Wizard was fine with this, as long as he once again got to mooch his dad's money. It seemed that everything was once again as it should be.

However, Ziro was still afflicted with a heavy fog of fatigue. Much of his life essence had been drained by those machines, and he had used most of his remaining magical power to defeat Quan. His strength felt like it was slowly returning, but the severity of his condition was such that casting spells still drained him. He knew he would have to take it easy for quite some time before he once again felt like himself.

Late one night, he sat alone in his office, filling out some papers. Since the incident, basically all he had been doing was filling out an absurd amount of paperwork. His office was mostly empty; after having a crew of wizards haul off Quan's enormous furniture, he had yet to fill the area. As he filled out countless forms, he daydreamed about turning the empty space into a cocaine lounge.

Ziro heard the sound of faint footsteps coming from the staircase. The faint odor of tobacco seemed to be wafting from somewhere below. He looked up from his paperwork, but he could not see anyone. As he was extremely tired, he figured it must be his imagination, and returned to his paperwork.

Suddenly, a chill came over him. He did not understand why terror gripped his heart, but he knew that a very powerful presence had entered the room.

Looking up, he saw a man standing before him. The man had a sallow, sunken face and shadowy eyes with irises like fresh blood. He was tall, with a long mane of gray hair and a short goatee, and he wore a set of pitch black robes with sanguine trim. Ziro immediately recognized him.

"Malthas…" said Ziro, his eyes widening in surprise. "I never thought I'd see you again…."

Malthas laughed, stepping up to Ziro's desk and placing his hands on the wood. He leaned in, with a wicked smile on his face. "Is it really such a surprise that I survived that day? I've always taken pleasure in watching how reckless you are, Ziro; that's why you were my best friend when we were boys, and that's why I'm your worst enemy now. I will always outwit you."

"I take it that you're who's responsible for taking the *Arcane Encyclopedia*."

"Naturally; Quan was just a marionette I made dance for my enjoyment while I bided my time in the shadows, waiting for your idiot son to find me the *Dictionary*." Malthas narrowed his eyes in a spiteful sneer. "Although, no one else will ever find that out."

"You're not going to get the *Dictionary*; I'll never tell you where it's hidden." Tensing his jaw, Ziro attempted to hide his fear. He knew he was no match for Malthas in his present state. "If you kill me now, you won't get away with it. If you think that's how you're going to seize control of the Circle, you're madder than I thought!"

"Oh, no, I'm not going to kill you, Ziro." Malthas smiled wickedly. "I could have done that anytime I wanted. No, no, I have much better plans for you." He stepped aside and gestured behind him. "Or, rather, they do…"

An invisibility spell lifted, revealing three figures. One of them was a tiny, round imp, with boils all over its pitch-black, leathery skin; it carried a heavy looking rucksack on its back, and glared with its contemptuous yellow eyes. There was a woman, who was attractive from the waist up, with light blue skin and deep purple hair; however, from the waist down, she slithered upon a scaly serpentine tail. The final figure looked like a regular man; not just any man, however: standing in the middle was none other than Gary.

"Wait…" said Ziro, squinting at Gary. "Aren't you that guy in all the pictures on that timeline in my son's weird conspiracy room? Is it possible my son knew something he wasn't telling me?"

Gary laughed. "No, that's something completely different. At this point, he has no idea of my true identity, and he never will."

Ziro furrowed his brow. "And what exactly is your true identity?"

"It's best if I show you." Gary held up his index finger, before stepping forward a few feet. His neck snapped back, so he faced the ceiling. His jaw seemed to dislocate as his mouth opened unnaturally wide. A cloud of twisting, black energy swirled out of his mouth, forming into a dark plume above his head. Suddenly, Gary's body went limp, falling to the ground beneath the cloud of black haze. A pair of glowing red eyes appeared in the cloud of darkness. The voice that spoke was no longer Gary's, but instead was a rumbling demonic growl. "I am Qatalyst, the last demon prince to still walk free."

"You see, Ziro," said Malthas, walking behind Ziro's chair and placing his hand on his shoulder, "you are going to be Qatalyst's new host. Now that all three *Arcane Tomes* are together, our plans can finally come to fruition. I've been waiting for this day to come since the day we put you in that tube."

Ziro felt as though he were paralyzed with fear. *No… this is different…* He realized he had been afflicted with a paralyzation curse. His heart sank, as he knew he did not have the strength to fight off Malthas's magic. He could not even speak. All he could do was watch, as the dark entity floated towards him. *This can't be happening…*

In one fluid motion, Qatalyst swirled into Ziro's mouth like a maelstrom of darkness. Ziro's body slumped forward as Malthas released his paralyzation spell. For a moment, he just lay motionless. Then, Ziro slowly raised his head up. His eyes glowed with demonic red light for a moment, before returning to their normal green.

"Was the soul transfusion successful?" asked Malthas, leaning down and looking into Ziro's face.

Chapter Twenty-Three

When Ziro first spoke, it was with Qatalyst's demonic voice. Gradually, it returned to its normal tone. "Yes, I've finally taken control of his body. I can't tell you how impatient I've been for this day. I almost killed his idiot son a few times when I thought he was never going to lead us to the *Dictionary*."

"Perhaps that was my mistake," said Malthas. "I should have appointed a better Archmage than Mia Quan. I valued subservience over competence."

"It's okay. What's a few more years when my brethren have been sealed in the Writhing Dark for hundreds? It's not *you* that needs to pay for this. Besides, I always value subservience over competence; why do you think Plompkiss is my right hand man?" He gestured to the bulbous, little imp next to the snake woman. "No offense, Smoiche."

The serpentine woman turned her head in a huff.

Malthas nodded solemnly. "Thank you, master."

Qatalyst had stood up, and was flexing Ziro's muscles, undressing his new body with his eyes. "Hmm... this body feels a lot better than the last. I can feel his power coursing through me. I look forward to being able to harness arcane magic. That has always been the weakness of my kind, but no more; I will be the first demon to tame the Arcanes, and use that power to free demonkind from that accursed seal. Soon, I will surpass my father, and take my rightful place as the demon king!"

"If you don't mind me saying, please don't strain yourself, master," said Malthas. "We mustn't be rash. His magic may be strong, but his essence had been depleted. It will be some time before you have access to his full power. If you make an attempt at spellcasting so early, you could sever the connection to his soul, and possibly even kill him."

"True, I cannot risk it quite yet, but soon I will be able to tap into his deep reservoir of arcane power." Approaching the corpse that had been his vessel, Qatalyst rooted around in the chest pocket. Withdrawing his inscribed mithril lighter and several packs of smokes, he put a cigarette to his lips and took a drag. "Now, it's time to move forward with our plans. Smoiche, would you mind kindly taking this man's form? I don't think Gary's job is done quite yet. I know how to get our dear Archmage's idiot son to play right into our hands."

The Magic of Malice

Smoiche slithered up to Gary's body. Leaning down, she sank her teeth into his neck. The body shriveled like a raisin as she quickly drained it of blood; at the same time, her form slowly shifted to resemble him. Her skin changed color as the scales sank into the surface; her breasts flattened, and her chest bulked up with muscle; the hair on her head changed color and shortened while her beard grew in; the most disgusting part was when her tail split into two legs, strands of sinew briefly hanging between.

Qatalyst averted his eyes. "Eww… you shapeshifters are so gross."

"Look who's talking," said Smoiche, standing up and placing her hands on her now masculine hips. "You just moved from one body to another!"

"That's not the same," said Qatalyst. "Possession is instantaneous. You don't have to watch any revolting transformation."

"Whatever..." Smoiche turned away and walked towards the staircase, staggering a little as she did so; it seemed she was not used to standing on two legs. She stood at the head of the stairs with her arms crossed, watching them with a scowl from across the room.

Grinning eagerly, Plomkiss waddled up to Qatalyst. "Well, what's my job, Lord Qatalyst?"

"Oh, well, you're going to have the most important job of all!" Flicking his cigarette aside, Qatalyst smirked superciliously. "You're gonna follow me around all the time, carry my gear, do my laundry, bring me coffee, and all kinds of neat stuff!"

"Oh, boy! Oh, boy!" Plompkiss jumped for joy, jiggling like a leather sack of lard. "Oh… wait…."

His face fell as he seemed to realize that he always has the same job.

"Your first job is going to be to get rid of that body." Qatalyst gestured to Gary's drained, shriveled corpse. "Make sure it's somewhere it won't be found. We can't risk anyone in the Circle hearing about this, or it might get back to The Wizard and blow Smoiche's cover." He leaned down, frowning sternly at Plompkiss. "Do you understand? I don't want to find out you threw it in a dumpster or something like that."

"Yes, sir!" Grabbing the body, Plompkiss hurried away. As he dragged the corpse down the stairs, the sound of the head could be heard thudding against the steps.

"What is my next task, master?" asked Malthas.

Chapter Twenty-Three

Holding up a finger, Qatalyst lit another cigarette and took a long drag. Reaching into Ziro's pocket, he pulled out a large baggie of his cocaine. "*Our* next task is to christen my new body!"

Malthas grinned enthusiastically. "Sounds like a proper good idea!"

And so, with the people of the kingdom none the wiser, the Archmage was taken by the last remaining prince of the demon race. The demon and the evil sorcerer partied late into the night, getting right proper as fuck to celebrate their treacherous victory.

All the while, The Wizard lay asleep on his couch, dreaming he was skiing down Cocaine Mountain….

FINISHED

Made in the USA
Middletown, DE
14 June 2020